ANGER

'Thrilling, complex and intense. Swedish crime fiction at its best.'

IAN SANSOM, *author of The Mobile Library series*

'This book is really thrilling'

YUKIKO DUKE, *Swedish National Television (SVT)*

'[...] this action-packed debut thriller is, without the slightest hesitation, my pick as one of the BEST BOOKS OF THE YEAR'

IWAN MORELIUS, *member of the Swedish Crime Fiction Academy*

'Tegenfalk has created a sophisticated plot in which the inter-action between the characters feels genuine. Highly recom-mended reading!'

TORKEL LINDQUIST, *National Library Service*

'Sometimes you can catch a glimpse of Donald Westlake as an inspiration, especially in the descriptions of the villains. The story is both witty and exciting.'

DAST Magazine

'Anger Mode is well crafted and an impressive debut by Tegenfalk'

The daily newspaper, Smålänningen

This novel is the first title in the Walter Gröhn trilogy, which includes:

Anger Mode
Project Nirvana
The Weakest Link

STEFAN TEGENFALK

ANGER MODE

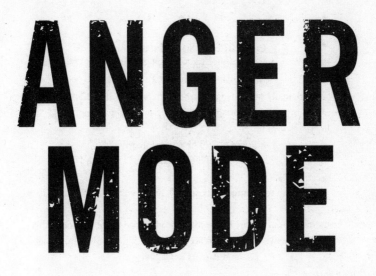

TRANSLATED FROM THE SWEDISH
BY DAVID EVANS

NORDIC
NOIR
BOOKS

First published in Great Britain in 2011 by Nordic Noir Books,
an imprint of Massolit Publishing Ltd, London
www.nordicnoirbooks.com

Distributed in the UK by Turnaround Ltd

2 4 6 8 10 9 7 5 3 1

Cover artwork: Stevali Production
Layout and design: Stevali Production

Originally published in Sweden as *Vredens Tid* in 2009
by Massolit Förlag, Stockholm (www.massolit.se)

Copyright © 2009 by Stefan Tegenfalk
www.stefantegenfalk.com

English translation copyright © 2011 by David Evans

A CIP catalogue record for this book is available from the British Library.

ISBN 978-1-908233-00-4

Typeset by Stevali Production, Sweden
Printed and bound in July 2011 by Nørhaven, Denmark

A fully developed human brain is considered to be the most complex of Nature's creations. The brain is made up of more than one hundred billion nerve cells, and it uses electrical impulses and chemical hormone triggers to control and coordinate bodily functions like blood pressure, fluid balances, and body temperature. In addition, it handles our mental functions such as intellect, emotion, memory and learning.

*"The more mankind researches the brain,
the less is known about it."*

David H. Ingvar (1924–2000), Professor of Clinical
Neurophysiology, University of Lund, 1983–1990

Author's note

Lay juror. In Swedish criminal and civil cases, the jury consists of a judge, who is also the court president, three lay jurors and a court secretary. Lay jurors are appointed by political assemblies and do not have to be qualified lawyers.

"Law Speaker" is an honorary title given to a senior judge.

Prosecutors work for an independent authority within the Justice Department and are the only public officials who can initiate criminal investigations.

Prime Minister Olof Palme was shot down on the streets of Stockholm on 28 February 1986. The murder investigation remains open.

Anna Lindh was a Swedish Foreign Minister who was stabbed to death on 11 September 2003 in Stockholm. After three trials, Mijailo Mijailović, of Serbian parentage, was convicted of her murder.

Stig Bergling was an employee of SÄPO who was convicted of treason for leaking secrets to the Soviet military intelligence service, GRU.

Sunday, 14 September 2004

THE WRISTWATCH GLASS was cracked and the watch hands had stopped at eleven minutes past five. The red Winnie-the-Pooh rucksack, which she had thought herself too old for, lay not far from her body. From a rip in the battered back pack, a small, soft toy pony could be seen. It was light brown and had a small, white star between its dark eyes, just like the pony she used to ride every Sunday.

It was cold. She was lying face down in the muddy earth, eyes covered in mud, legs and arms lifelessly extended in all directions. She saw nothing. Felt nothing. Her heart had long since stopped beating.

A BATTLE SCENE opened up before Hans Jonasson of the Uppsala County Traffic Police when, during a routine drive along Route 72, he made an emergency stop on his police motorbike next to what was left of the car. As one of the most experienced police motorcyclists in the area, he had seen a great deal of death on the roads and the sight of the car crash on the road was all he needed to detect the presence of Death once again at this spot. The kinetic energy from both cars had transformed them into unrecognizable piles of twisted metal.

One of the cars had catapulted into the field and had ploughed a large welt in the muddy topsoil. The other car, still on the road, was sliced into two parts. Bits of glass and metal were spread around the pieces of wreckage like fragments of a falling star. Hans quickly confirmed the absence of skid marks on the tarmac. The collision must have occurred with a brutal impact. Considering the appearance of the vehicles, it would have taken a miracle for anyone to have survived.

He made the call to the county communications centre while he was running to what looked like the front part of the car in the road. He took off his gloves and touched the mangled metal with his hand. It was still warm and what was left of the engine's cooling system was hissing. A human body was wedged inside the demolished steel. The head was hanging forwards and the face was shredded to pieces. Hans squeezed inside and put his fingers against the neck, searching for a pulse. His fingertips registered a weak beat, and the lungs emitted a shallow wheeze. His first impulse was to try to bend up the metal to get the person out, to put the body in the prone position until help arrived. But the casualty could not be moved until the ambulance crew arrived – especially not the head and neck. The only thing he could do was to stop the bleeding and ensure that the airways were more or less open. After staunching the worst wounds using rudimentary bandages made from bits of clothing from the victim, he ran to what was left of the back part of the car. It was empty.

A car approached from the east. From this direction, visibility was better because of a long straight, leading to the tight curve of the road. Hans raised his hand in a stop signal and ordered the passengers to remain in the car. He then swore silently to himself because he had forgotten an obvious, routine precaution and ran back to his motorbike. He lit an emergency flare and placed it just ahead of the curve in the road, where he had been forced to brake, before continuing into the muddy field and towards the second car wreck.

The dark SUV had somersaulted and landed back on its wheels. The roof was partially caved in and the side windows were shattered. The front of the car had been folded back into the roof supports and the laminated windscreen had been partially ripped out of its frame. A youngish woman with long, wheat-blonde hair was sitting clamped between the seat and the steering wheel. Her head was resting lifelessly against the now oval shape of the wheel. From her nose and half-open mouth, blood had flowed and congealed. Hans tore open what was left of the car door and carefully leaned inside to search for a pulse on the woman's neck. An unpleasant chill met his fingertips as they touched her skin. He shifted his fingers slightly, but was still unable to find a pulse. He carefully lifted her head and looked into her lifeless eyes.

More vehicles had arrived at the accident site up on the road. Curious onlookers were shocked at the mangled body that lay in the crashed car on the road. Someone was groaning and retching at the side of the road. An elderly woman held her hands to her face and wept. The sound of approaching emergency vehicles echoed from the edges of the forest while Hans was searching through the remains of the SUV. Suddenly, he stopped by the floor on the passenger side. Something resembling a child's car-seat cushion was wedged between the seat and the floor. The seat belt was not secured, so it was unlikely that a child had been sitting there. Still, he instinctively looked around. The field was bare and the muddy ground was easily visible around the car. He turned towards the road where the first emergency vehicle had arrived. Next to the side of the road and a few metres from the tyre tracks of the SUV, there were some bushes. He made a quick mental reconstruction of the series of events – and immediately turned ice-cold.

She had blonde hair braided in two pigtails and was lying like a discarded rag doll in the bushes close to the road. Hans felt his pulse quicken yet another notch. He yelled to the ambulance crew making their way towards the SUV and an out-of-breath junior doctor with a red emergency kit broke away.

Hans summoned the doctor. With his mouth open and gasping for breath, the doctor threw himself to his knees by the side of the girl, who was lying with her face down in the mud. He pulled his stethoscope from his bag with one hand while putting his finger on the girl's throat to find a pulse.

"Well?" Hans impatiently inquired.

The young doctor did not answer. Instead, he changed the position of his fingers while hanging his stethoscope around his neck.

"Can you find a pulse?" Hans continued.

After a few more attempts, the young doctor shook his head. He carefully turned over the girl's body. The face was covered with blood that had dried with the topsoil from the ground into a red-brown mud mask. The doctor wiped the mud from the girl's face, and her light-blue eyes stared emptily at the clear autumn sky. According to procedure, he still tried to revive the heart with a small, portable defibrillator but, as he feared, it was way too late. The doctor explained that she was probably dead even before she hit the ground. Her neck had presumably been broken at the moment she was catapulted from the car.

Hans nodded at the doctor, who had become pale.

"Bloody shame," muttered the young doctor and slowly stood up with stethoscope in hand. He stroked his chin, as if he was feeling for beard stubble. Hans could see he was having a hard time holding back his emotions. He was not alone in that.

Not far from the dead girl's rucksack, there was a diary. Small pink ponies adorned the cover. The little padlock had been torn off and, on the front, in the pretty, framed name-plate, someone had written "Cecilia" in ornate handwriting.

Hans picked the book up from the ground and opened it. It was written in straggling handwriting, with many spelling mistakes. He started browsing the diary at random and after a while arrived at the last entry. At the top of the page, he read today's date and the time. It had been written less than an hour earlier. Something cut through the wall of indifference that he had built up during his years of police service. Sensitivity was not an advantage in his occupation and those who succumbed to their emotions never lasted long – this he knew.

He took a deep breath and tried to shake off these feelings. Where was his professional detachment when he needed it?

Less than an hour ago, she had been breathing. Living the trouble-free life only a child can. Unaware of all the dangers that are a part of life. Loved and full of dreams.

She was ten years old.

Autumn 2009

1 THE INTERCITY X2000 train from Gothenburg to Stockholm was heavily delayed. Bror Lantz, who had been looking forward to a relaxing trip in first class, was starting to feel disturbed and irritated by the chaos that reigned on the delayed express train. The coffee he drank directly after leaving Gothenburg was a foul-tasting budget brand. Several toilets were out of order, and matters did not improve when even more toilets broke down during the trip to Stockholm. The new vacuum-based sewage disposal system was clearly substandard. Irritated at having to stand at the back of a line of nearly ten metres to queue for one of the few remaining toilets, he recalled yesterday's seminar on the criminal justice system.

He had started to resent his adversaries within the profession, something he had never done before. Mostly, he shrugged his shoulders at their cacophony and instead argued for his own causes, but during the train journey he had a growing feeling that certain forces within the Justice Department were running a conspiracy against him. The day before the seminar in Gothenburg, the Chief Magistrate of the Stockholm District Court had voiced his intention, "off the record", to relieve Bror of his position as a judge in the court. And had this process not *de facto* been in motion ever since the rumours had started? The more he thought about it, the more convinced he became that it was actually what was happening to him.

That Bror was unconventional was no news to him or to anyone else. Through the years, he had been in stormy seas many times because of his liberal point of view. In particular, because of his interpretation of the court sentencing guidelines, which he believed were excessively conservative and counter-productive. But for someone to start slanderous witchhunts against him was something new. His irritation grew at the same pace as this realization.

His mobile phone rang several times, but he did not answer – except for one time, when it was Elsa, his wife. She was disturbed about something, but Bror ended the call abruptly by saying that the train was delayed and that she could eat dinner without him. Unless there was a death in the family, she could wait until he came home. Then he immediately turned off the phone.

As Bror disembarked onto the platform in Stockholm, he felt neither joy nor relief at reaching his destination, just a universal irritation, especially at the people around him. He truly despised mankind and all it stood for at this moment. Everything was one vast, slow torture filled with the smells and voices of people crowding around him.

Bror pushed his way roughly between an elderly couple that he thought was walking too slowly. The old lady fell to the ground, but Bror continued on without apologizing or even turning around. His bad temper transformed into anger as he approached the taxi rank.

OJO MADUEKWE ALWAYS woke up before the alarm clock rang – except for today. From the clock radio, Eva Dahlgren's husky voice sang the hit "I'm Not in Love with You" and Ojo re-gained only sufficient consciousness to press the snooze button as the song was ending. He turned over and burrowed his head in the pillow again. Just as sleep was regaining its hold on him, he pulled himself together and got out of bed. He stayed sitting on the edge of the bed, staring at yesterday's pile of clothes on the floor, and he yawned. His mouth tasted like used cat litter, and his head throbbed to the sound of the traffic outside the window.

He stood up and stumbled towards the window, pulling up the blinds and squinting out at the afternoon dusk. Everything seemed normal and the taxi was still parked outside. Three months without a break-in attempt. Even the bedroom was as it should be. The only thing that testified to yesterday was a glass of water on the night table.

He tried to retrieve any memory about how or when he got back home. After spending a short while searching his memory, he gave up. The only thing he recollected from the office party was that he had danced and drunk more in one evening than he normally did in one year.

Ojo retrieved a newly ironed shirt from the wardrobe. The socks and trousers from yesterday, however, would be good enough for today. He put on his jacket and the black ordinary shoes, turned off the hall light, and locked the door behind him.

The throbbing in his head had quietened slightly and he no longer felt quite as hung over. However, he was very hungry. He stopped at the pizzeria on Finn Malmgren Square. The Turks who owned it gave taxi drivers a thirty per cent discount.

After finishing his meal, he went back to the taxi. Only a few minutes passed before he received his first fare. On the data display, he read:

Pickup: Wahlbergsgatan 12, Segervall
Drop off: City Terminal

He turned the taxi meter on so that the minimum fare was added. The couple that climbed into the taxi was in their twenties. Ojo asked if they were going to the City Terminal, even though he already knew the answer. The man confirmed it with an indifferent mumble.

After dropping off the couple, Ojo parked at the Terminal's taxi rank. The electronic taxi system was as dead as the desert outside his home village and he was far back in the cyber-queue. Few ordered a taxi at this hour, so he put his hope in taxi rank pick-ups instead.

An independent from Kurdistan was in front of him in the rank. He knew who that guy was – a hustler who would charge two thousand crowns to Arlanda airport from the city. Rip-offs gave the taxi industry a bad reputation, especially with the tourists who were often treated badly by some of the independents. A rape also contributed to their bad reputation – even though the police had caught the guilty taxi driver. Unfortunately, anyone could drive a taxi. It did not matter if they were con artists or rapists, as long as they were taxpayers.

It was six-twenty and Ojo had still not got any fares at the taxi rank. Impatience – but, most of all, stress from not getting any cash – crept over him. At this rank, he was not going to get rich. Perhaps it was worth taking a chance that there were customers down by the nearby taxi rank on Vasagatan.

Ojo swung into that taxi rank and had only two taxis in front of him in the queue. The first car disappeared with a woman in high leather boots. The next car moved forwards. There was a short pause in the stream of customers and the driver in front of Ojo took the opportunity to get out of his car. He leaned against the car's front wing and was just about to light a cigarette when a man came up to him. Some words were exchanged and Ojo saw the taxi driver point out Ojo's taxi. The tall man took some quick steps in Ojo's direction. He opened the passenger door, threw in a flight bag, and then sat down behind Ojo.

"I assume you're free," began the man in an unfriendly tone.

"Yes, I am," Ojo answered cordially as he looked for the owner of the unpleasant voice in his rearview mirror.

"Drive to Täby," ordered the man.

Ojo shifted into gear and started to roll slowly away from the train-station forecourt.

"What's the address?" inquired Ojo and tried to catch the eye of the man in the rearview mirror. As he got only evasive glances, he started to punch "Täby" into the sat-nav.

"You don't have to bother with the address in that sat-nav," said the man in a hard voice. "Our little street seems to have been overlooked by the map company. I will give you directions when we get close."

"Okay, it's your money and your decision," said Ojo, while turning onto Vasagatan.

The afternoon rush hour had subsided and Ojo could safely zigzag between cars in the sparse Stockholm traffic. The light dusk spatter had turned into a rainy shower, and umbrella-less people were hurrying along the pavement. The car's wipers were sweeping with increasing frequency. The squeak from the rubber blades relentlessly scraping against the windshield cut through the car cabin.

The man in the back seat was pressing his hands over his ears and the shirt under his jacket was soaked with sweat. He ripped open the top buttons in an attempt to dispel the heat from his body.

"Drive up Sveavägen and into Roslagstull," he hissed impatiently. His breathing became heavier as he rocked backwards and forwards.

Ojo caught a glimpse of the man's face in the rearview mirror. He felt the car rock in sync with the passenger's movements in the rear seat.

"Aren't you feeling well?" asked Ojo, with all the courtesy he could muster.

"Don't bother yourself about that. Just do as I say!" roared the man.

Ojo flinched. Despite the man's unpleasant behaviour, Ojo stood his ground. He could be sick. Ojo had made emergency detours to the hospital too many times and knew when someone was genuinely unwell. Involuntary anger can come from suppressed pain. Ojo had driven all sorts: from screaming, pregnant mothers halfway to childbirth to stocky, two-metre giants whining and rolling around like small kids from the pain of a gallstone. This looked as if it would develop into another emergency trip to one of the hospitals. He wondered what sort of pain the man was in. Hardly gallstones and definitely not childbirth. Perhaps it was a panic attack – or that mental fatigue everyone is talking about and that only seems to exist in Western society. They did not have these problems in Nigeria – only HIV and malnutrition unless, of course, corruption is also classed as a health problem.

"Shall we go to the A&E at Karolinska instead?" asked Ojo in a steady, calm voice. "You don't sound or look especially healthy."

"No, you will drive to Täby. Can you manage that?" The man shouted his answer.

Ojo made eye contact with the man in the rearview mirror and saw how his facial muscles had tensed. It was as if he had an aura of rage cloaking him. Pierced by the man's coal-black eyes, Ojo began to feel a creeping uneasiness. The steering wheel was sticky from his sweating hand and his heart beat like a bongo drum.

"Either we're going to the Karolinska A&E or I'm stopping the car and you can get out," he explained with as much authority as he was able to muster.

The ultimatum was given.

Ojo pulled over and parked, with the engine still running. He turned around to confront the man in the back seat and saw with some surprise that he was pulling his leather belt out of his suit trousers.

"Shut up and drive!" roared the man as he suddenly grabbed Ojo's neck rest with one hand.

Ojo backed down. He instinctively wanted to throw himself out of the car, but then his fear instantly changed to anger. He should not be the one running away. It was his car and his livelihood. He removed his seat belt and was just about to open the car door when he felt the man's belt around his neck. Before he could get a hand between his neck and the belt, the man had pulled it tight.

Ojo could not get any air. He desperately tried to reach the man in the back seat, but he was trapped, locked in his own seat. He lashed out with his arms and finally managed to grasp one of the man's hands. Ojo twisted towards the man's wrist and tried to pull the hand away, but it seemed to be riveted to the leather belt. He stretched for the door handle again, but could not move out of the seat. Alarm turned into panic as the lack of air quickly weakened Ojo. An enormous pressure was growing in his ribcage. It felt as if it was going to explode.

BROR LANTZ PUSHED his knees against the back of the driving seat to get a firm grip. He did not know why he had taken off his trouser belt, nor why he wanted to strangle the driver with such a deadly passion. Quite simply, it felt good and, in some way, like a rebirth. As if a safety valve had been opened at the same moment as the pain in his head went away. Each muscle was tensed to breaking point now, a paradox that he normally would have pondered over – but not now. The harder he pulled, the less the knives cut in his head.

Ojo was ready to let go. The pressure in his chest had disappeared and, instead, he was filled with calm. It was a safe and overwhelming feeling. But then, for a short instant, he regained his senses and was back in the cold darkness. His body screamed with the pain, but he was not ready to die yet.

With a final, all-out effort, he got his arm to the gear stick. His hand shook with nerve spasms as he pushed the button lock and pressed the gear stick backwards. It was as heavy as lead. At the same time, he tried to reach the accelerator with his foot. Even though his leg was shaking, he managed to push the pedal to the floor with his last ounce of strength. The engine raced and the taxi shot with reckless speed across the road into the oncoming traffic.

Bror lost his balance and fell against his flight bag. He tried to regain his balance while fumbling for the belt. He had not yet silenced the driver.

Ojo's final exertion had drained him of any strength. He collapsed over the steering wheel.

As Bror managed to sit up in the back seat, he saw that the taxi he was sitting in was driving headlong into an oncoming vehicle. The airbag exploded in Ojo's face and his head was thrown backwards with lethal force.

Dazed, Bror got himself out of the demolished taxi. The engine had stopped running and a deep, ghostly silence reigned over the car. The front of the taxi was bent inwards all the way to the wheel arches. Oil and radiator coolant was spreading over the ground.

Bror curled up on the ground next to what was left of the taxi and gazed bewilderedly about him. The rage he recently had felt within himself had disappeared. It was as if it had never existed. Suddenly, his stomach muscles cramped, in a vomit reflex. He threw himself on his side and coughed up the contents of his stomach while the tears welled up inside him. He did not want this. He had done nothing wrong. It was not his fault that this had happened. The driver would not be silent, he ...

People started to gather around the scene of the accident. What were they staring at? What did they want from him? One of them approached Bror. Bror pulled his knees up to his chest and hid his face behind them.

More onlookers rushed quickly to the scene of the accident. Some had called the emergency services on their mobile phones. Others used their mobiles as cameras and documented the accident. The newspapers would pay well for a hot MMS picture.

A young man with long sideburns asked Bror if he was injured. The man explained that an ambulance was on the way. He put a reassuring hand on Bror's shoulder and said that everything would be all right.

What did he know of that? What was it that would be all right?

Bror did not care to listen. Sounds merged like a symphony orchestra in which everyone played different instruments. He could not separate what he was hearing, whether it was footsteps coming or going, the rain hitting the tarmac or car doors slamming. He pulled up his knees a bit more and took a deep breath.

Suddenly, it ended and the world around him ceased to exist. One tenth of a second on the wrong side of the road and a life had been torn into thousands upon thousands of pieces. Death had irrevocably arrived.

First, there was the shock. Then, denial came – this only happened to other people. But death was a reality he could not avoid, no matter how much he wanted to. It was eternal and brutally final.

Afterwards, grief flooded him, sweeping every emotion in its path. All that remained was the loss after the love. He hovered between life and death, a rope and a footstool. Soon it would all be over. The suffering would be gone forever and the memories would die with him.

Self-pity stopped him. He wanted the pain. He wanted the loss. Perhaps he was weak, a pathetic little being. The emptiness followed him like a shadow. He thought of her room and her possessions. The smell of her that was still left in her clothes, in her pillows. The soft, tender scent of life and happiness. The cuddly toys that patiently waited in line on the bed.

Sometimes he could feel her presence. He spoke to her, screamed in despair how much he missed her, all the things they should have done and how much he loved her.

Then decay set in – the booze and the sedation. The collapse, but also the recuperation. A new time, a new era.

The rage grew slowly within him. The love transformed itself to hatred for the guilty, hate against the system. They should be punished.

An eye for an eye, a tooth for a tooth. The foundation to the temple of wrath was already in place – in the laboratory, in all the things he and his colleagues had accomplished. They were the best of the best. And what they had discovered was a vital link in a chain that would change the world, astonish everyone, and destroy the religions for which so many had given their lives. A new god would be created: the God of Science.

And now, his vengeance too was within reach. There were some small adjustments still and, for this, he was required to work by himself. He had lied and cheated in order to succeed, betrayed those who had dedicated their lives to help him. Thousands of hours. Nights that passed into days. Months and years. It was a fire that would not go out. Step by step, he had got closer and closer to his goal.

Then the breakthrough came. In the fifth year, he was finally ready.

And yet still he had failed.

But there were others in line, unwittingly queuing to enter the graveyard of his grief.

2 "WALTER!" YELLED CHIEF Inspector David Lilja from his office. He heard Walter's characteristic walk in the corridor – heavy on his heels, yet unusually brisk in his pace for someone soon to be sixty years old. Detective Inspector Walter Gröhn was as capable of making a discreet entrance as a herd of runaway rhinos. Lilja knew that Walter was always incommunicado in the first hour of the morning shift and that he would try to slip into his office unnoticed, just to be able to drink his morning coffee in his office with no interruption. Normally, this was none of his concern. He had a great deal of patience with Walter's idiosyncrasies and whims, as long as they were within reasonable limits and did not expose Lilja to anything that could damage his own reputation. Today, however, Lilja was forced to break with this practice.

Walter had, as usual, envisioned a calm morning break with a mug of coffee and the sandwich he had bought at the café on Flemingsgatan. Under normal circumstances, he would have paid no attention to Lilja's request. It was not even eight o'clock yet. If Lilja wanted something, he would have to come to Walter, and not vice versa.

David Lilja was indeed Walter's superior officer, but this was a more academic than practical rank. For Walter, Lilja's superior rank implied a shitload of irrelevant questions and bureaucratic red tape that had to be observed, despite the occasions he needed Lilja to back him up. Walter had a habit of getting into conflicts with both colleagues and the Prosecutor's

Office, which all too often required the intervention of Lilja. When it came to the art of internal politics, Lilja was like a duck to water.

Walter's lack of social skills did not, however, prevent him from having the highest total of solved murders in his thirty-five-year-long career. With the aid of long experience and an unorthodox mindset that often set aside legal conventions, he was able to sustain a high percentage rate of closed cases. This was unfortunately at a cost to his own career, which had stalled at the rank of detective inspector. He was not considered to be "potty trained" and sufficiently diplomatic for the position of chief inspector.

Over the years, a string of high-profile murder investigations had contributed to Walter's reputation as brilliant yet impossible to work with. One of his most well-known cases involved the murder of the Hungarian twins, which, after a long and prolonged investigation, proved to be the work of a third, and completely unknown, triplet brother. Walter saved the two foster parents from being unjustly convicted for the double murder. This achievement was rewarded with a two-month suspension from duty because of insubordination, since it had entailed ignoring several explicit orders from the Chief Prosecutor.

Walter had not been able to be of any assistance in the investigation into the murder of Prime Minister Olof Palme. This was partly because of his late involvement in the investigation, after the most relevant leads had either been missed or lost due to incompetence. True to his modus operandi, he immediately made himself unpopular with the investigation leaders, whom he accused of incompetence and of having the mental vision of a mole digging a tunnel. Nor was the Chief Prosecutor exempt from his criticism. Walter did not stay long on that investigation.

With a cheese roll in his hand, but without the cup of black Java, he turned on his heel and went into Lilja's office. He found the head of the Stockholm County CID, with his glasses high up on his forehead, behind piles of paperwork. His uniform was impeccably pressed and the knot of his tie folded with military precision.

"Good morning," Walter greeted him, even though he knew that this morning was going to be anything but good. His day could hardly have had a worse start.

"Close the door behind you," Lilja admonished, gesturing at Walter.

Walter shut the door and sank into the familiar visitor's chair in front of Lilja's desk. "I shall get straight down to it," Lilja began in a serious voice, leaning forwards between the paper heaps on the desk.

Walter gazed uninterestedly at Lilja and tried to recall if he had forgotten to fill in some form, or if he had said something indiscreet during the past week. Possibly, it could be about the stuck-up, pinstriped lawyer last week who had persistently repeated her client's innocence like a photocopier. Walter had felt obliged to exchange some less than flattering words with her.

"We've been given a real hot potato," said Lilja and paused theatrically.

Not so much as a nerve twitched in Walter's face. He continued to watch Lilja while thinking about whether he had time to fetch a coffee before Lilja got to the point.

"We have a judge at the Stockholm District Court whom we think is responsible for manslaughter – or even murder," said Lilja.

Walter raised an eyebrow as he removed the clingfilm from the cheese roll. This was not because of what Lilja had just said, but because the cheese roll was so excessively shrink-wrapped.

"So what has this Stockholm District Court judge done then?"

"A taxi driver was killed in a car accident. The judge was the passenger in the taxi," explained Lilja.

"I see," said Walter, thrusting his lower lip forwards. "So, driving judges around is a dangerous business."

"As I said, we have reason to believe so."

"And who's 'we', in this case?"

"Forensics and the Traffic Police."

Walter stared at Lilja for a few seconds. "Since when did the Traffic Police start conducting murder investigations?"

"They don't."

"Yet they seem to think that he has committed murder or manslaughter?"

"This is pure speculation based on witness testimony and the medical examiner's preliminary report," Lilja brushed it aside.

"I see," said Walter, unconvinced.

"It's nonetheless never a good thing when high-level bureaucrats within the judicial system commit serious crimes," continued Lilja. "Especially if there are fatalities involved. That's the reason this is a hot potato and that is why it has landed in my lap."

What makes bureaucrats from the judiciary different from the rest of us? wondered Walter as he took a big bite from his cheese roll.

"It's not good for society's sense of right and wrong if judges are walking around bumping off citizens. They are supposed to sentence people, not be the ones being sentenced. That just doesn't make any sense."

"That it's not good for the public sense of right and wrong, I can accept," said Walter, getting ready for another bite. "But they are only mere mortals like you and me. And if they commit a crime, they will have to face the music and pay the penalty

– regardless of whether they are judges or not. All people in positions of authority are supposed to set a good example."

"Under all circumstances, this must be handled cleanly and with meticulous sensitivity," Lilja insisted. "No bulls in a china shop, please. You'll have to drop whatever you are doing. Under no circumstances is the judge to be prejudged, if you see what I mean."

"You'll have to explain," said Walter.

"I mean, what possible motive could he have unless it was pure self-defence, which is what I personally think seems to be the most reasonable explanation?"

Walter looked inquiringly at Lilja. "In other words, I'm not to get to the bottom of this investigation. Is that what you're saying?"

"I didn't say that," sniped Lilja. "I just want you to remember that this is a judge with an impeccable background who has landed in the middle of, you could say, a disadvantageous situation. And, that self-defence seems to be the obvious conclusion. I believe that you will also reach the same conclusion."

"So you haven't got orders from high up to, shall we say, sugar-coat the investigation a little bit?" asked Walter.

"Absolutely not."

"Besides, I'm not finished with the prostitute's shooting yet," Walter protested, with his mouth full of bread. "The pimp has an alibi, but I'm on the way to untying that knot as well. Laid awake all night thinking it over and …"

Lilja stopped him. "Excellent, but Jonsson and Cederberg will handle the investigation on the female prostitute from now on. I've already spoken to them about that. You are, from this moment on, formally in charge of this office's investigation for the Prosecutor's Office."

Walter had no problems with jumping into a new murder investigation, with or without interventions, divine included.

Just as long as he got to finish what he had started. And Jonsson and Cederberg were unfortunately not among the most talented in the County CID. To be sure, they were his nutters and part of the group that he unilaterally bossed over. But they were a very mediocre pair of murder detectives, who would try to tie up any loose ends by pinning it all on the prostitute. Cederberg was a semi-alcoholic from Värmland, who had problems with multitasking. He was all too easily side-tracked by small details.

Jonsson was his alter ego. He was rigid in his way of thinking and about as creative as an inspector from the tax office. Without Walter driving this two-man engine, the train would definitely go off the rails. They would never be able to break the pimp's alibi.

"And who's going to be on my new team then?" wondered Walter. "I'm assuming that this is not going to be a solo act?"

"Yes, there was one other thing," Lilja added, ignoring Walter. "Your team, if you can call it that, will consist of one other person."

"One person?"

"Yes, a colleague from the Special Investigation Unit. You can meet her later today. The only thing I know is her name, Jonna de Brugge."

"The RSU," muttered Walter. "My team is a single investigator from that new, pedantic, elitist unit, whose only achievement is to hire misfits and academics."

"It wasn't my decision that newly recruited RSU analysts and investigators should serve on active police duty," interrupted Lilja abruptly as he got up from his chair. "However, even though they were picked for their high intelligence, they still need on-the-job experience."

"The Security Service probably doesn't want them tripping over their feet. Otherwise, they'd suit each other well, since both services are as equally unfamiliar with real-life police work," retorted Walter.

"You know very well that RSU was created to support both the Security Service and the regular police, according to "

"According to the American model of the FBI special analysis units," Walter filled in the blanks.

"Whatever. The case file for the judge is lying on your desk," Lilja finished and turned to take a file from one of his piles of paper.

Just as Walter was on his way out of the door, Lilja called him back.

"By the way," he said, while reading something in his file, "how's your progress in that social interaction training that we agreed you would attend?"

"Thanks for asking," replied Walter. "The course trainer and I couldn't interact. She should have taken the course herself first."

"You know what the deal is if you don't complete this training," Lilja insisted, looking up from behind the document.

"I'm giving it another shot," lied Walter. He would rather eat a tin of rusty nails than subject himself to something as meaningless as yet another course in social interaction.

3 KARIN SJÖSTRAND STUCK her head inside Malin's room for the second time that morning.

"It's seven-thirty. You'll be late again."

"I've already said that I'm fucking awake!" screamed Malin under the duvet.

"Okay, I can hear you," sighed Karin as she closed the bedroom door.

It was always the same ritual every morning – nagging and scolding to get the kid off to school. Karin tried in vain to recall if she had been as much hard work and as defiant when she was fifteen. She had always been on time for school and had obtained good grades. But there were more rules and regulations at school in the seventies. Nowadays, it seemed as if school was one big youth centre where all the kids were left in charge of the teachers.

Janne had left Karin when she got pregnant with Malin. He had found a new woman, one who was not expecting. Perhaps it was just as well that he had abandoned them. He would not have been a good father figure anyway. On a few occasions, Malin had asked after Janne, but she did not seem very interested in meeting him when Karin had asked her outright.

It could hardly be Karin's genes that were at fault. More likely then Janne, Malin's long-lost father. There was a lot to be desired when it came to his DNA. It was pretty hard to imagine anything closer to a two-legged pig. He was lazy and incapable of doing anything other than gambling away his wages.

Karin was stressed because she was due to be at the district court by nine o'clock, as a lay juror, for closing statements. She browsed quickly through the case notes to be sure she had not forgotten anything, just in case the court judge quizzed her. A male football player from one of the lower divisions had been shot in broad daylight during a match. The media interest in the incident was huge and it increased the pressure on the court.

Eight forty-five. The door to Malin's room opened and a tired teenager dressed in an oversized T-shirt saw the light of day. Her long, ruffled hair hung over one shoulder and she announced her entrance with a loud, drawn-out yawn. After that, she moved slowly into the kitchen.

"Hello, are you still here?" she yelled, while getting the milk from the fridge.

No reply.

She topped up with cornflakes and some slices of bread from the pantry and sat down at the breakfast table.

"I think it's really bad of you not to get up on time," said Karin, entering the kitchen in her outdoor clothes. "Now you're going to be late for school again," she continued, upset.

Malin casually flicked through a magazine while the cornflakes slowly found their way into her mouth.

"Chill, Mum. I've got it under control," she mumbled, without lifting her eyes from the magazine. "I've got PE this morning, so it's not as if I'm missing anything important."

Since Karin did not have the time for a drawn-out discussion, nor for repeating the same old series of entreaties, she decided to nag Malin only moderately this morning.

"It doesn't matter," she retorted. "You should be on time even if it is only PE. Besides, I don't want you being with that Sanna and what's-his-name …"

"Musse," Malin reminded her.

"Exactly, Mustafa and his friends," Karin said. "Saga's mother has definitely told me that this Mustafa is into drugs."

Malin looked up from her magazine with an irritated expression. "Just drop it, okay! What drugs? Saga's mum is talking bullshit."

"I don't believe that she is," Karin responded firmly.

"Saga is a fucking martyr and her mum's a weirdo. Do you really believe them?"

Karin felt her patience running out, but checked herself. She had an appointment, and this could go on for the rest of the morning if she persisted.

"I don't have time to discuss this with you right now," she said. "But this evening you and I are going to have a serious talk." This last phrase she had uttered many times previously, without having brought about any improvement. But this time, she was determined really to follow through on her word. The only question was what she would use to threaten her with. A move away from the city, perhaps.

Karin shut the front door with a sigh.

After breakfast, Malin went back to her room. She threw herself on her bed, picked up her mobile phone from the bedside table, and flipped to her best friend's number.

"Uuuuh … Sanna," replied Sanna, just awake.

"Are you going today?" Malin asked, while nonchalantly turning her bedside lamp on and off.

"Noooo … I don't think so. Are you?" Sanna answered after a moment's thought.

"PE sucks; shall we check what Musse's doing instead?"

"I know already," Sanna retorted, much more awake. "He's skiving off and hanging with those guys from Rinkeby. He called me yesterday evening and wanted to see us today. 'Take Malin with you,' he said."

"He did?" Malin sat up.

"I think they have something going on. Are you up for it?"

"I dunno," Malin hesitated. "Are you?"

"I am if you are. No fucking way am I going there by myself, and Musse knows that. That's why he wants you to come along."

Malin thought for a brief moment. She thought about what Karin had said, but dismissed it as quickly as her maths homework.

"Okay, it's cool," she said finally.

"I just have to call Musse and grab a bite to eat," yawned Sanna. "Shall we meet at eleven outside the 7–11 by the tube station?"

"Okay," Malin agreed and folded shut her mobile phone.

Anticipation suddenly overtook Malin and she found herself in a good mood. A few minutes ago, everything had felt like shit. Sanna was really the best of best friends and this day had got off to a great start. No schoolwork on her horizon – not today at any rate. Even her mum had been unusually subdued and had not nagged until she was blue in the face like she usually did. That was probably because something at work was taking up her time. As far as Malin was concerned, she was welcome to work around the clock.

4 FROM A CRACK in the cloudbank, the sun found its way through the dirty window in Walter's office. A welcoming warmth met him as he stepped over the threshold. He had not seen the sun for some time. Nor had anybody in mid-Sweden over the past few weeks, and he stood with eyes closed, feeling embraced by the heat. Memories from the summer floated up, and he thought about when he had anchored at a secluded beach and had spent a whole weekend lying on the foredeck with a Patricia Highsmith in his arms and a Bell's whisky. Life had been carefree and he had been far away from the stress of the everyday world. The gentle slapping of the Baltic as it hit the hull of his small sailboat had had a healing effect. It soothed him, even though he knew that he would never heal completely. Not a day went by when he didn't think of Martine.

The sun went behind a cloud and he was back in the doorway. He saw the blue folder tossed onto the keyboard and had just picked it up when he heard a woman's voice behind him.

"Excuse me."

Walter turned around.

"Are you Walter Gröhn?" asked a young lady with inquisitive brown eyes.

"That's correct," Walter hesitated, as if he first needed to recall his name.

"Jonna de Brugge, RSU." the woman smiled and stretched out a hand. "It seems that we'll be working together."

"That's correct," Walter answered, wondering if he should try to vary his replies.

She was young. Young in a way that made Walter feel like an old, dead battery. Probably around twenty-five. She had a soft face with high cheekbones that were framed by shoulder-length, chestnut-coloured hair. Unlike Cederberg and Jonsson, her eyes revealed intensity and focus. Whether they reveal her true character is still to be proven, Walter thought, and shook her hand. She had a firm handshake.

"So, when do we start?" she asked eagerly, eyeing the folder that Walter was holding in his hand.

To Walter, his new partner's boldness came as a surprise. He was used to a calm, sensible pace among hardened veterans, in late middle age, who were more concerned about promoting their own personal wellbeing than operational efficiency. Neither Jonsson nor Cederberg ran the risk of a heart attack, at least not during office hours. That probably applied to the rest of the police staff as well.

"Actually, we can start right away," Walter said and handed over the file. "While you read through this, I'll go and get us some coffee and cake."

"I've already read it," Jonna replied, taking the file anyway. "Perhaps we should go and interview him instead. He's been admitted to the psychiatric emergency unit at Karolinska."

"All right, so now we have saved some time and I always welcome time-saving," said Walter. "We shall go and interview him, but not right now. Instead, maybe you can tell me what is in the file while we walk to the canteen. They've got insanely good pickled herring sandwiches there."

Jonna hesitated at first. She would rather have left for the hospital than go and eat herring sandwiches, which, incidentally, she detested. But now Detective Inspector Walter Gröhn was her superior, albeit temporarily, and it would not look good if the first thing she did was to question his judgment.

"Absolutely," Jonna said and put the file down. "His name is Bror Gustaf Lantz, and he's been a judge at Stockholm District Court for the past eleven years. He's been an employee of the Justice Department for thirty-two years. He's fifty-six, has been married to Elsa Lantz for twenty years, and resides in Täby. No children are registered. He has no criminal record – speeding a few times, but not enough to lose his driving licence. He's had fourteen parking tickets in the last three years."

"A regular Snow White," said Walter, "which, in itself, is not so unusual, considering his profession. They're supposed to set a good example, or whatever you call it."

Jonna continued to recite from memory as they walked down the corridor. "He was found sitting by the side of a crashed taxi on Sveavägen on Friday evening. The taxi had driven head-on into an oncoming car after swerving over to the wrong side of the road. Lantz was apparently the passenger in the taxi, and one witness saw what he thought was some kind of a struggle inside the car while it stood parked at the kerb. It was unfortunately too dark for the witness to be able to describe in detail what was actually going on in the car. The victim was the taxi driver; his name was Ojo Maduekwe. He is, or rather was," Jonna corrected herself, "married to Britt-Marie Maduekwe for three years and had worked as a taxi driver for five months. As far as we know, there are no previous connections between Bror Lantz and Ojo Maduekwe."

"I think we shall rename our Snow White the Evil Queen, or whatever her name was," Walter said and clicked his fingers.

"The Evil Stepmother, perhaps?"

"Yes, that's the one," said Walter.

The forensic technicians found what they think is Lantz's trouser belt in the back seat of the car," Jonna continued.

"The buckle has the Justice Department's symbol etched into it. Apparently, this is an emblem of long and faithful service. Maduekwe also had the symbol on his neck and Forensics believe it can be linked to the belt. Therefore, one might deduce, with a little bit of imagination, that Lantz tried to strangle Maduekwe, probably from the back seat. Maduekwe had burst vessels in his eyes and lungs, which are normally the result of asphyxiation. But the actual cause of death was almost certainly a broken second vertebra in the neck, which probably happened because the steering-wheel airbag detonated too close to Maduekwe's head during the collision. Why his head would be so close to the wheel is not known, just that there were powder burns from the airbag's explosive charge on Maduekwe's face."

"The judge perhaps was pissed off about the cost of the taxi and tried to choke Ojo What's-his-name and avoid the bill," Walter said. In a gentlemanly fashion, he held the staircase door open.

"Hardly believable," Jonna answered dryly.

"Whether Ojo What's-his-name died of strangulation or because of the airbag significantly affects the charges brought," Walter said. "If he died from being strangled, the charge is murder for the Evil Stepmother; if he died because of the airbag, the charge will probably be manslaughter. The difference is a few years' jail time for the judge. If he ever gets charged, that is."

"Why wouldn't he be charged?" Jonna asked, surprised.

"Some among us can unfortunately dodge the long arm of the law," Walter said, and held open the door to the canteen.

Jonna looked at Walter suspiciously.

Welcome to the real world, little girl, Walter thought to himself.

As the herring sandwiches had run out, much to Jonna's relief, there was no coffee break in the police station's large canteen. Walter decided, after a brief lecture to the serving staff in which he deplored the lack of herring sandwiches, to sign out an unmarked vehicle and go to see Bror Lantz at the Karolinska University Hospital.

When they came to the police garage reception, it turned out that the only unmarked car that was available was an old model of a Volkswagen minibus, probably a vehicle that the Drug Squad used. They had a fondness for older minibuses. A stench of ingrained nicotine and something that reminded him of ancient vomit hit Walter when he opened the minibus door.

"Do you have a car?" he asked and closed the door.

Jonna frowned. "If you mean my private car, the answer is yes."

"Good," said Walter. "Do you have it here?"

"Coincidentally, I did drive my car in today because ..."

"Then I think we should take it," Walter interrupted. "I'll see that you get reimbursed."

"Reimbursed?" Jonna cursed the fact that she had taken the car this morning. She had intended to run some errands after work, buy some plants at Weibulls garden centre, among other things. Using her private car for work was something she avoided as much as possible, due in part to the Swedish tall-poppy syndrome, and a stubborn grandfather as well. He was wealthy and used to having things his own way. Jonna had defied him as much as she was able to do without hurting his feelings. But if you belonged to a shipowning family with roots going back to the seventeenth century, it was a simple matter to take away the silver spoon from a pretty mouth when the family fortune was to be shared between heirs. And she could not sell the car without inflicting major bruising to her grandfather's car-obsessed ego. Why did she decide to pick up those plants today?

Still, she knew it was just a question of time before her background would become common knowledge at the police station.

There would be whispering and gossiping behind her back no matter what she did, and parking a million-Swedish-crowns car in the police garage would not make the situation any less difficult.

Walter stared tentatively at Jonna's car, which was parked in a corner of the second floor of the police garage.

"A Porsche 911 Carrera convertible," he declared in disbelief.

"4S Cabriolet," Jonna added. "It's a four-wheel drive. It also has a sequential transmission." No point in being modest now that the cat was out of the bag.

"Looks like a new car," said Walter. "At least, if the licence plate is authentic."

"Almost one year old," Jonna said and unlocked the doors with the remote.

Walter said nothing and instead made himself comfortable in this premier icon of capitalism, a symbol of the industrialized nations' wanton luxury. Probably cost at least three years' wages, Walter thought, and closed the door. The scent of new leather enveloped him.

"But I didn't win the lottery," Jonna began and turned the ignition key. It was better to pre-empt the tide of questions that would inevitably follow. The six-cylinder Boxer engine roared into life and then faded to a muffled growl.

Walter put his seat belt on and tried to raise the seat. It felt as if he was sitting directly on the ground.

"It's an advance on the family inheritance," Jonna explained, and swung out of the car park.

"Since you brought it up," said Walter with a thoughtful look, "where have I heard the name Brugge before?"

"Perhaps as in Brugge Line," suggested Jonna. Now it starts, she thought.

"Exactly," said Walter. "The shipping family Brugge. I knew I'd heard your surname before."

"de Brugge," corrected Jonna. "We have Dutch roots."

Walter looked at her thoughtfully. "Haven't you chosen the wrong profession? Ships should be more suitable for you."

Jonna stopped at a red light. "What was your father's profession?"

"He was a lumberjack for the first half of his life. The second half he spent researching all the different brands of booze."

"I see," said Jonna, immediately regretting the question.

"He became an alcoholic after we moved to Stockholm," Walter continued. "The sawmill in Övik was shut down, and there were no timber stocks in Stock-holm, despite the implication in the name."

Jonna's mouth smiled a little at Walter's irony. "I should have applied to the river police with my background."

"And spend each and every day giving breathalyzer tests to the hobnobbers as they cruise by in their million-dollar yachts? I don't think there's any upside to that job, unless you're looking for a year-round suntan of course," said Walter, looking at Jonna's lightly tanned skin. She definitely had something southern European about her, maybe also a bit of Belgian Wallonia in her ancestry. He had done some genealogy research on himself and had ended up among farmers and peasants north of the Dalälven river.

Jonna did not know what to say. "Not everyone has million-dollar yachts," she blurted out.

"No, true enough," Walter agreed. "I myself have a boat in the same price range as one of the wheels on your car."

Jonna felt the situation becoming even more uncomfortable. This was exactly what she had wanted to avoid. She had not asked for such an expensive sports car. She had escaped from the family's traditionalist claws and made her own way in the world. Made it by herself without their money or connections, and sought a life far away from the demands and expectations that the name de Brugge placed upon a person. Yet still she was sitting here, forced to defend herself. Damn this car and damn my grandfather, she swore silently to herself. There would be a hell of a to-do over this tomorrow. Glib comments and gossip about her money and her family would spread like the plague throughout the department.

But then Walter smiled. "You can relax. I won't say a word about your car or your family, even though it will come out sooner or later. Many here will find it difficult to handle the news about your, shall we say, class membership. Not only are you a woman, you have a background that will provoke many of your testosterone-charged colleagues with muscular arms and wagging tongues – especially the ones who drive around in old Saabs and have second mortgages on their terraced houses."

"I know," said Jonna, pressing her lips together into a thin line. She would not sound embittered. Instead, she was quietly grateful to Walter for the integrity he had shown despite his shabby appearance.

"How long will you be training with the CID?" Walter asked, offering a box of cough drops that he had pulled out.

"Two months, to start with," Jonna answered, declining the cough drops. "But it depends. I don't want to finish in the middle of an investigation; that pretty much defeats the point of the training."

"How many are there at RSU?"

"About fifteen analysts and investigators."

"And the average age is what? About twenty-five or so?" said Walter, with a hint of sarcasm in his voice.

"Most of us are young, yes," answered Jonna.

"And the average IQ is what?"

Walter observed her as she turned onto Torsgatan. She looked relaxed and experienced as she drove and could, unlike David Lilja, conduct a meaningful conversation while simultaneously handling a motor vehicle in a safe manner.

"No idea," she answered after a while.

"But you're supposed to be part of a talented elite," Walter continued.

"And I've also heard a lot of good things about you," Jonna said, changing the topic. "For example, you're apparently a living legend."

Walter cleared his throat. "You shouldn't believe everything you're told," he said. "The police station is one big rumour central. I call it Sweden's biggest sewing circle."

Jonna laughed. "That may very well be true – at least when it comes to real-life operational departments."

If only you knew what it was really like, Walter thought, and then he too laughed.

KARIN COULD NOT get Malin out of her head during the entire journey to the district court. She would have to do something drastic to make Malin take school more seriously.

Outside Alvik tube station, Karin took out her mobile phone. Malin was answering neither the home phone nor her mobile. She hoped that Malin had gone to school, but felt deep down that she had not. Malin would definitely miss PE, as she had already been late. As usual, the school did not help as much as Karin thought they should. They would not even ring and inform her when Malin did not turn up at school. Lack of resources was the usual excuse but, more often than not, the reply was that "It is the parents' responsibility to ensure that the student comes to school."

Karin's anxiety started to grow. The problem was that there was little she could do about it. She needed to concentrate on her work and the deferred football proceedings. Karin shook off her thoughts of Malin and got off the train. In twenty-five minutes, she would be sitting in a courtroom full of lawyers, spectators and a posse of journalists.

THE RED-BROWN FACADE of Karolinska University Hospital towered upwards as Walter Gröhn and Jonna de Brugge passed over Solna bridge. They exited onto Berzeliusvägen and drove towards the psychiatric clinic, which was wedged between two wings. Inside the clinic, they identified themselves and asked to be shown to Bror Lantz's room. A nurse told them to wait by the reception while she fetched the physician who was responsible for Bror Lantz. After they had waited a few moments, an elderly man rushed down the corridor, with his white coat flapping behind him.

"Are you from the police?" he asked, harassed.

"That's correct," answered Jonna politely. She shook hands with the doctor and presented herself and Walter.

"You wish to meet Bror Lantz," the doctor said.

"Bingo," cried Walter.

"You can see him," the doctor answered. "He's been sedated for his anxiety and, under the circumstances, is feeling well. Even so, I anticipate having him here for at least another week."

"Has he had any visitors?" Walter asked.

"His wife," replied the doctor. "May I ask what this is all about?"

"You may ask, but you won't get an answer," Walter informed him, stuffing a cough drop into his mouth.

The doctor pulled in his chin, insulted. "If it affects the patient's health, then I'm afraid that it's very much a concern of mine."

"We are only going to ask some simple questions," Walter reassured him. "No one has ever died from that."

The doctor looked at him suspiciously.

"Has he sustained any head injuries that could affect his memory?" Walter asked.

"Nothing that indicates it; it's just a minor concussion," the doctor answered dispassionately.

"Is his room in this direction?" Jonna queried and started to go down the corridor. She did not have the patience to wait for Walter and the doctor to decide whether Lantz was in a condition to answer questions or not. The doctor did have the right to block police questioning if the patient's wellbeing was at risk. Walter knew this, so she could not understand why he was being so confrontational.

"Yes, he's in ward fifty-five, room twelve," the doctor answered, taken a little off-guard by her direct question. He quickly followed Jonna.

Walter was also upstaged by Jonna's forwardness and was left a few steps behind. He had to dash to catch up. After passing a few wards and making a right turn into a new corridor, they arrived at room twelve.

In one of the corners, there was a wardrobe with one door slightly open. A metal stool and bedside table stood by the bed. Apart from that, there was no furniture in the room. A man with thin hair and closed eyes was lying in the bed. He had a pale, elongated face that was wreathed with a few days' stubble.

Jonna carefully pushed past the doctor and approached the bedridden man. She felt her pulse quickening. This was her second real investigation and her third interview.

"Is your name Bror Lantz?" she began, for the sake of formality, while sitting down on the stool.

The man did not react.

Jonna carefully brushed Bror's arm.

"I think he's sleeping," the doctor said. "The sedative is making him tired. You'll have to come back a little later."

"Thank you, we're fine," Walter said and showed the doctor the door. "We'll call you if we need any more help."

The doctor started to protest, but Walter closed the door after him.

"Can you hear me?" Jonna asked and bent over Bror. "We're from the police."

The man wheezed.

"He's waking up now," Walter said and positioned himself on the other side of the bed.

The man struggled to open his eyes.

"Could I have a little water?" he coughed and looked at Walter. He made an effort to lift his upper body, but sank back into the bed.

"Of course you can have some water," Walter answered. "But not from us, since we don't work here. You know what the union thinks about that. We're from the police and have some questions for you. That is, assuming you are Bror Lantz?"

The man nodded. "Yes, that's correct," he said.

"My name is Jonna de Brugge and I'm with the RSU, and with me I have Walter Gröhn, a detective inspector from the County CID," Jonna introduced them both.

And with me ... Walter thought, and did not know if he should laugh or be pissed off. I will have to pull a bit on the handbrake if she continues like this.

Jonna ran some tap water into a disposable cup and handed it to Bror. He took some sips and put the cup on the bedside table. Walter rolled his eyes. "Right then," he began, "you know very well why we are here."

Bror nodded.

"Let's talk about what happened in the taxi on Sveavägen. Or do you want to drink some more?"

"I don't remember much about what happened," he said, wrinkling his bushy eyebrows.

"No? But you must remember something?" Walter said. "It's not a total blank inside your head?"

Bror said nothing; instead, he turned stiffly towards Jonna. "RSU?" he said, questioning her.

"Now, judge, this is the way it works," Walter clarified. "We ask the questions and you give the answers. We're not playing "Jeopardy" or some other quiz game here. Are we clear about that?"

Silence.

"Let me rephrase the question," Walter continued. "A witness saw you in some kind of a struggle with the taxi driver. According to the same witness's statement, this occurred inside the taxi and immediately before the accident. Why were you fighting?"

"I don't know what you're talking about," Bror answered. "To be honest, that sounds totally out of character for me." He slowly shook his head. "In addition, I find your tone and manner to be very unpleasant."

"What was the struggle about and why?" repeated Walter.

"I don't know," Bror answered, resignedly.

"Don't know!" exclaimed Walter, exaggerating his dismay. "Surely you must know what you were arguing about!"

Bror looked at Walter without saying a word.

Walter bent slowly over the bedridden man. "Was he trying to rob you or did you lose your temper because he was cheating you out of your money?" he whispered.

"I'm really sorry, but I really don't know," Bror apologized and switched his gaze to the ceiling.

"Come on, Mr Lantz," Walter said, exasperated. "We have your trouser belt, which happened to be lying in the car, and the marks on the driver's neck that Forensics can tie in to the belt. You were not intending to strip in the car?"

Bror continued to stare at the ceiling.

"Why don't you just confess?" Walter said, throwing his arms up in exasperation.

"Confess to what?"

"That you strangled the driver with the belt!" Walter yelled.

Bror did not move a muscle.

"What's the last thing you actually remember?" Jonna asked and took Bror's hand to comfort him.

He turned stiffly towards Jonna again and looked thoughtfully at her for a short while.

"I was already angry on the train from Gothenburg," he said. "After I got into the taxi at the Central Station, everything became hot. It was like a furnace inside my body. I heard voices and sounds. After that, I can't remember anything."

Jonna looked at Walter.

"Are you taking any drugs?" Walter asked.

"Why would I do that?"

"Do you have mental problems of any kind?"

"No, that's not it either," Bror replied, irritated.

"You consider yourself to be completely lucid, in other words," concluded Walter. "Yet still, you remember nothing."

"As you may be aware, I'm entitled to legal representation," Bror pointed out in a stern voice.

Walter nodded in confirmation. "Of course, you are. If you feel you need a lawyer to vouch for your absent-mindedness, then of course, you shall have one. But we are only here to collect information at the moment. You're not formally charged with anything yet."

"That's not how you're behaving," Bror answered dryly.

Walter shrugged his shoulders. "Then you're misreading me."

Bror's eyes narrowed. He started to say something, but stopped himself.

"Have you suffered from memory loss previously?" Jonna asked.

"No, no more than any of us who binged during our student years," Bror smiled painfully.

"The circumstances and the witnesses are more than enough to convict you. And that's without the film from the taxi's security camera."

The last statement was a lie. It had not been possible to retrieve any information from the taxi's camera. Some bright spark had installed the camera recorder under the car bonnet, which resulted in its total destruction in the collision. The only thing that Forensics was able to see on their monitor was a snowstorm.

"In your case, that's enough for manslaughter," Walter continued. "You of all people should know what that means."

Bror looked at Walter for a few long seconds.

"Give me a few days and maybe I'll have a better memory."

Walter shrugged, frustrated. "I don't think we'll get much further right now."

"No, you're probably right," Jonna agreed and got off the stool.

Bror watched as the two police officers left the room. Before Jonna closed the door, she turned around. Bror met her eyes without saying a word. Jonna was just about to ask a question when he closed his eyes. She checked herself and closed the door.

"Did you test Bror Lantz for drugs?" Jonna asked the doctor, who was standing behind the reception desk, making case notes.

He hesitated for a few seconds, trying to think.

"No, why should we do that?" He lifted his eyes from the file.

"He heard voices inside his head," Jonna explained.

"I don't know anything about any voices," he answered.

"Keep us informed if you move this patient to another ward," Walter said and gave the doctor his business card.

"We're not planning to move him, but if that happens, you will be the first to know," the doctor replied, dryly.

JONNA LOOKED THOUGHTFULLY at Walter as they came out of the hospital. "I believe he's telling the truth," she said.

"Believing is not the same as knowing," Walter said, seating himself in the Porsche.

"But he doesn't know anything. Rather, he doesn't remember anything," Jonna said and started the car.

"Memory loss is an excuse used by many," Walter said. "His motive, on the other hand, is not as easy to fathom."

"And what could the motive be, then?"

"Well, you tell me," Walter said with a sigh. "He was hardly after the taxi driver's cash."

"It just seems so unlikely," Jonna said, shaking her head in disbelief.

"Yes. What the hell really happened in that car?" Walter said as he put his seat belt on. "The guy must have totally lost his mind."

5 AT ELEVEN SHARP, Sanna appeared, walking around the corner of the hot-dog stand that stood right next to Vällingby tube station. Her baggy camouflage trousers, grey gangster jacket and big smile made Malin cheer up.

"Wossup?" Sanna greeted Malin and gave her a hug.

"Hey, you smell really nice," Malin reciprocated.

"*Escada*; it's my mum's."

"Does she let you use her perfume?" Malin asked, surprised.

"Whatever," Sanna shrugged. "She won't notice anything. She was sleeping like a pig when I left. Guess who was totally pissed yesterday?"

"No, who?" Malin asked even though she knew the answer.

"Mum," Sanna said, on edge.

"Not again," Malin said, faking surprise. She felt sorry for Sanna.

"Check this out," Sanna exclaimed and took out two five-hundred-crown notes that she proceeded to wave in front of Malin's face.

Malin said nothing and stared intensely at the two notes.

"I got them off Mum last night," Sanna grinned. "She was so drunk that she didn't know what she was doing."

"Wow!" Malin said, astonished.

"Jompa won fifty grand on the horses at Solvalla. He came over to our house, totally smashed, with a few bottles of booze. Mum took the bait immediately. They boozed all night like there was no tomorrow. Can you believe it?" Sanna fixed her eyes on Malin and grinned at the same time.

"But Jompa has beaten up your mum before?" Malin said, in utter confusion. "It was over between them?"

"Yes, but jeez," Sanna groaned. "A few bottles of booze and fifty grand. Don't you get it?"

"Sure," Malin lied, not able to figure it out. How could she take back a person who hits her all the time? That Sanna's mum was a drunk, she knew already, but she could not really understand why she kept getting back together with that Jompa character.

"Fuck, we're missing the train," Sanna yelled and set off towards the tube-station turnstiles. Sanna waited for Malin to catch up and, on an agreed signal, they jumped over the turnstiles without paying. They ran down the stairs to the platform and, with the smallest of margins, pushed inside the train carriage just as the doors closed behind them.

"Are there any others coming?" Malin asked as they moved farther into the carriage and sat down in some unoccupied seats.

"Umm ... I think so."

"Who's that then?" Malin asked.

"Habib and the gang, sort of," Sanna said.

She took out her mobile phone to send a text.

"Has he got weed, then?"

"Mmm ... yeah," Sanna replied.

Malin silently observed Sanna.

"It's going to be bloody fun, trust me," Sanna said, looking up from the phone as she finished texting. "Musse's mum and old man are in the Lebanon. It will be totally fucking ace."

"Christ, really sweet," Malin laughed. She put her feet on the seat and looked at the ceiling. She thought about the last time she had tried real cannabis, how fantastic it was, how beautiful it was to disappear into the fog and away from all the fucking must-dos that were everywhere. Sanna was the best friend she could imagine. Today was going to be a great day.

"JONNA DE BRUGGE," Jonna announced and shook hands.

"I don't seem to have had the pleasure of meeting you before," Chief Inspector David Lilja answered, with a blindingly white smile. "But it appears that you're already up to speed."

"Yes, one could say that," Jonna smiled back and turned around to see where Walter had disappeared to.

"You seem very young," said Chief Prosecutor Åsa Julén in a sceptical voice.

"Twenty-six," answered Jonna quickly, at the same time realizing that Åsa Julén must be twice her own age.

"Yes, RSU seems to have a preference for young candidates," Julén said and she looked to Lilja for agreement. He nodded in a non-committal manner that could be interpreted in many different ways.

Jonna glanced at the door and silently swore at herself because she had not noticed that Walter had disappeared behind her. Now she had to stand with those four inquisitive eyes upon her and make small talk to pass the time.

CHIEF PROSECUTOR ÅSA JULÉN fidgeted with discomfort when Walter eventually came into the meeting room. He had been standing with Cederberg in the corridor, embroiled in a long discussion about the pimp's alibi. Walter sat himself down at the small conference table without saying a word. A chill spread throughout the room, and Jonna could detect the frostiness in the eyes of both Walter and the Chief Prosecutor.

Lilja cleared his throat as if he was about to apologize. "Chief Prosecutor Åsa Julén will be leading the preliminary investigation into Bror Lantz," he started and looked authoritatively at Walter.

Walter did not move a muscle. The sight of Julén automatically put him in a bad mood. No amount of coffee in the world could change that.

Lilja started to gather some papers on the table. "Shall we go through the situation on Bror Lantz?" he started.

It was quiet in the room. Lilja looked expectantly at Walter.

"Yes, let's do that," interjected Jonna, when Walter did not answer. "We have initially questioned Lantz," she began, and she felt her hands beginning to sweat. "And what we can say thus far is that he doesn't seem to remember very much of the actual incident. He gives the impression that he wasn't mentally aware during the greater part of the taxi journey. He doesn't know how or why the taxi collided. He has no recollection whatsoever of the collision or of what happened before the collision – other than that he was hot and heard voices in his head. There's no sign of memory loss caused by physical factors such as a blow to the head. According to the doctors, he could be suffering from temporary amnesia due to trauma. In other words, we have nothing to go on at this point, with the exception of the belt and the marks on the driver's neck. You already have the preliminary forensic report, as well as the witness statements taken by the Traffic Police. It wasn't possible to retrieve the camera footage from the taxi, so there's nothing for us there. Additionally, there's no clear motive," Jonna finished, and felt her pulse rate was now at an all-time high. She reached for a glass of water and wondered why Walter had not answered. Maybe he was testing her ability. He probably wanted to see her mess up.

Walter nodded in agreement as both Lilja and Julén looked at him to confirm the validity of his trainee's report.

"Has he said anything of significance at all?" Julén asked, still sceptical.

"Nothing – because he can't recall anything," answered Jonna, encouraged by Walter's silent approval. "And the obvious question is whether he ever will remember anything. In any event, it will be nothing that will be to his disadvantage." Jonna glanced at Walter, who did not move a muscle. He slouched in his chair like a sullen teenager.

The Chief Prosecutor carefully examined some papers she held in her hands. It was obviously the preliminary report from Forensics.

"I can't possibly make a case the way things are now," Julén began. "We're talking about circumstantial evidence such as the marks on the taxi driver's neck and a witness who thinks he saw something. That's not sufficient – with, or without, the belt found on the back seat. In addition, there's no credible motive, and a psychiatric examination just because he says he heard voices is out of the question." Julén looked at Lilja, who nodded in agreement.

Walter straightened up and rested his elbows on the table. "And that's just what you wanted," he said.

"And what is it that I wanted?" answered Julén dryly.

"To shut down the investigation so you don't have to prosecute a judge. It wouldn't look good for a judge to go around strangling people, would it? Or are there personal reasons for your agenda?"

Cover-ups in the police and prosecution authorities made Walter see red. That they existed was common knowledge within the organizations. The degree of whitewashing depended on where a person worked and which position they held, but, in most cases, everyone was always watching each other's back.

"I'm not going to listen to any more of your insults," Julén answered and stood up. "Your mere presence is ample offence, if I may speak freely."

"You can speak as freely as you like, as long as it's valid and constructive criticism," replied Walter.

Lilja glared at Walter while cursing silently under his breath.

"As I said, I will most certainly not raise charges against Lantz. The Traffic Police will finish this investigation, as a road traffic accident in which the taxi driver made a fatal turn without a seat belt. We cannot, of course, charge the deceased for criminal negligence," said Julén, looking at Lilja, who had become even more red-faced than he usually was.

It was silent in the room. Jonna felt her cheeks flush. The whole situation was embarrassing, not for her, but for Julén and Walter. Two adults fighting like kids.

"You'll have my final decision tomorrow," Julén finished and left the room.

"You really handled that well, Walter," said Lilja, breaking the silence. "I'm aware of the unhealthily chilly relationship between you two, but it cannot affect your work. Am I making myself clear?"

"With all due respect," interrupted Jonna, "I don't think I have anything more to add at this time." She looked apologetically at Walter and Lilja.

"I'll write the final report and you'll have it on your desk before the end of the day," Walter said and quickly got up from his chair.

"I can understand your frustration," Lilja answered, "but it's still the Chief Prosecutor who has the final decision. We can safely assume that the preliminary investigation against Lantz will be shut down."

"One hell of an investigation. It will probably go down in the history books as one of our shortest and most cursory," Walter said ironically, and followed Jonna out of the room.

Walter did not know what else to conclude except that Julén was exceptionally lenient in her judgment of Lantz and that he himself was a dutiful police officer following direct orders. Sitting and protesting would not make a bit of difference. If a cover-up was the reason for Julén's decision, it would not be the first time that Walter had encountered this problem. Normally, it was the police who covered up for each other in various situations, not prosecutors that cleaned up after judges. This was a new phenomenon.

But the more he thought about it, the less likely it seemed that Julén would stick her neck out for some judge in the judiciary system.

She loved her job too much and was a person who played safe.

However, he could not do much more in this matter. More important cases were waiting, like that prostitution scandal – unless the pimp also had a prosecutor watching his back.

"Do you fancy tagging along and shooting holes in a water-tight alibi?" asked Walter, watching Jonna, who had just finished draining a can of *Ramlösa* mineral water.

She nodded eagerly.

"I thought as much," Walter said quietly to himself and chewed on a cough drop.

KARIN CAME TO a standstill outside the entrance to the Stockholm District Court and caught her breath. Her anxiety about Malin refused to leave her, despite the fact that in a few minutes she would be sitting with the other members of the court jury to listen to the closing arguments. She took out her mobile phone and searched for the number for Malin's school. She left a voice-mail for Malin's class teacher, Klas Keiier, and asked him to call her back. Then she set the phone on silent mode and put it back into her handbag. "Damn it, what a bad day this is turning into," she thought and went in through the door.

MALIN AND SANNA walked out onto Köpenhamnsgatan, which was right outside Kista tube station, and turned up towards

Kastrupgatan. Grey, three-storey buildings with rust-red balconies spread out along both sides of the street. On almost every balcony, there was a satellite dish, sometimes so big that it hid the whole balcony. Malin felt the cold and damp air find its way through her thin jacket. She began to shiver. Whether this was due to the cold or her excitement, she did not know. Anyway, they would soon be at their destination. They went in through the outer doorway into one of the blocks of flats that lay at the far end of the street and went up to the second floor. Sanna rang the doorbell.

After the chime from the doorbell had subsided, all they heard was a brief silence. Sanna rang the bell once again. Once again, the answer was silence. Sanna put her ear against the door crack to listen for any sound. "Where the fuck is he?" she looked, puzzled, at Malin.

Sanna took out her mobile phone and was just about to punch in the number for Mustafa when she heard steps from inside the flat.

"Fuck, are you deaf?" said Sanna, glaring angrily at Mustafa when he opened the door.

"Chill. I was sleeping, ya know?" answered Mustafa with a yawn.

"Yeah, we noticed," Sanna said sourly. "Shit, I thought you'd pissed off."

"You know how fucking tired I am, right?" answered Mustafa apologetically.

"No, I don't know. You weren't tired this morning when I was talking to you on the mobile," said Sanna and looked at Malin for confirmation.

Malin nodded in agreement, as if she had been there.

"Fuck that," Mustafa said. He turned around and went back into the hallway.

Sanna and Malin followed.

"Habib was here earlier," he continued with his eyes fixed on the floor. "He was shit-pissed at me because I had scored weed for myself and not from him. He wanted to know who the fucking Swede dealer was. I said I didn't know him."

"So?" asked Sanna. "What do we care?"

Mustafa looked up for some sympathy, but neither Sanna nor Malin were interested in listening to Mustafa's whining about Habib. Instead, they went into the living room.

Malin looked around. She had never been to Mustafa's before. It was as if she had come to a foreign country. The décor was oriental, with a large Persian rug covering the best part of the floor. Paintings with motifs from some desert landscape hung on all the walls and, in a corner, there was a hookah filled with ornaments.

Sanna and Malin sat on the sofa. Sanna put her feet up on the coffee table, took out two five-hundred-crown notes, and waved them around.

"Check it out. One thousand," she said to Mustafa with a big smile.

"I told you that you didn't need any cash," Mustafa said and sat down in the armchair facing them. "That Swede dealer is giving away the dope. The only thing I had to do was to make sure you two were here."

Surprised, Malin stared at Sanna, who shrugged her shoulders.

"Who cares?" sighed Sanna. "I don't know this Swedish dealer. Do you?"

Malin shook her head.

"No, we don't know any dealers, and if that guy wants to give away dope just because we're here, then that's cool," said Sanna.

A worried wrinkle appeared on Malin's forehead. "Did you know about this?" she asked Sanna.

"Kind of," answered Sanna, as if it was a trivial detail.

"How does he know who we are? What if it's the cops?" Malin said, worried.

"Are you dumb or what?" interrupted Mustafa. "You remember last week, when we were in town and you guys went home earlier?"

"Yeah, so what?" said Malin.

"This guy came up to me when I was on the square after you'd left. He said he wanted to be my supplier."

"Supplier?" said Malin.

"I told him to go to hell. It could have been the cops." Mustafa shrugged. "The guy said it was cool. He stashed a bag of dope and a note with his mobile number in my pocket. Then he pissed off. Do you think a cop would do that?"

Malin looked at Sanna.

"Fuck, that dope was really good shit," continued Mustafa, excited. "I called him yesterday and was going to buy some. He said that he would give away as much as I wanted if only I took you two along. I asked him how he could know that I know you. He said that I shouldn't ask so many questions, but that it was cool."

"What's cool?" asked Malin. She looked at Sanna, but Sanna had lost interest in the subject.

"How the fuck should I know?" exclaimed Mustafa. "He just said it was cool."

"What did he look like?" asked Malin. For a brief moment, she thought that it could be her dad. But it was impossible that he could be a dealer. She could not think of any other adult that she knew, other than one of her teachers or someone her mother knew. But she could not believe it would be any of them.

"A regular geezer," Mustafa described him. "Maybe thirty, forty years old, with a beard."

Malin did not understand. She looked at Sanna, who looked away. Would a dealer offer free dope just so Sanna and I would be here?

"He's not a perv, is he?" Malin asked anxiously.

"He's okay, I said. Maybe he's seen you some place. It could be a neighbour of yours or something. I don't fucking know."

Malin decided not to be alone with the dealer, regardless of who he was. Obviously, it was someone who knew her and Sanna, but someone they didn't know – unless Sanna was lying. But she never did. She would never lie to Malin.

If the dealer was that dumb, then that was his problem, Malin reasoned; instead she became curious as to who it could be. Maybe a modelling agent or a talent scout. Malin was not a total disaster face-wise, even though there were those who were cuter. Maybe he had seen her on Facebook.

"Wossup? Don't you have any stash at home now?" asked Sanna sourly when she realized that Mustafa was out of marijuana.

"Well … I was supposed to call him when you guys got here," explained Mustafa.

"Well, make the fucking call then. We're here now," cried Sanna.

Mustafa called the dealer, who promised to arrive within half an hour. Malin had abandoned any thoughts about the man and had started to make herself at home in Mustafa's flat. Just the knowledge that she soon would experience the blissful feeling that the marijuana gave her made her almost euphoric. The last time she had smoked marijuana was at Sanna's house. Malin had lied to Karin and said that she was watching rented films with Sanna. Sanna's mother had been at a fiftieth birth-day party in Norrtälje and was not coming home until the next day. Mustafa and Habib had come over to Sanna's early on Saturday evening. Habib had offered free marijuana. It was the first time Malin had tried dope. It was completely fucking fantastic and now she would experience it again. She sank down into the sofa, closed her eyes, and waited for paradise.

6 CLOSING ARGUMENTS WERE finally over and Karin could breathe easily. The press swarmed like flies around dung, because the victim of the shooting was a football player and brother to a high-level CEO of one of the nation's largest industrial consortiums. The pressure on the jury was as great as the pressure on the prosecutor and barristers. For a moment, Karin felt the urge to flee the courtroom and throw herself into a taxi to Malin, away from this circus and back home to her own problems.

She went into the coffee room together with the other court officials and sat down at one of the tables, where she pumped coffee from a thermos. Just as she put her coffee cup on the table, her mobile phone vibrated. She saw from the display that it was Malin's school.

"Hello, this is Karin," she answered eagerly, while hurrying into a nearby conference room.

"It's Klas Keiier," replied a man's voice. "I got your message."

"Yes?" said Karin impatiently.

"Malin hasn't been at school today," he stated, in a careless tone.

Karin suddenly felt a knot in her stomach. Malin had not only played truant from PE. She had not gone to school at all. Thoughts started to spin in her head.

"Are you still there?" asked the teacher.

"Has Sanna Setterberg been in school today?" she asked, with an almost desperate voice.

"No, she hasn't been in either."

Damn it, thought Karin. Then Malin is with Sanna.

"If Malin or Sanna turn up, could you call me?" asked Karin.

"Of course," finished the teacher, indifferently.

Karin called home, but no one answered. Then she called Malin's mobile phone. She got no answer there either. She punched up Sanna's mobile number, but got only the voice-mail. Karin felt increasing irritation that Malin was not only destroying her own life but was also in the process of tearing her life down too. How long should she put up with Malin's behaviour? What was her limit and what would she do when it was reached? Or should she allow her daughter to disappear into the abyss and then pick up the pieces when it was already too late?

No, she would not let that happen. She would take the rest of the day off. The rock in her gut would not go away and she would not get anything done at work anyway. She had never felt such anxiety before. It was as if her maternal instincts were trying to tell her something.

She would go home and search for Malin. And when she got hold of her, she would not scold her, nor reproach or threaten her. She would instead suggest that they go out and eat at a restaurant, maybe go to the cinema first. She would try to win back her daughter, the daughter she had been a few years ago, before she had fallen into the company of Sanna and that Mustafa character.

MUSTAFA LOOKED NONCHALANTLY at Sanna and Malin when the doorbell rang.

"Open the fucking door. Are you deaf?" Sanna hissed and glared at Mustafa.

"It's cool," Mustafa replied as he went out into the hall.

Malin felt her pulse quicken. She hooked her arm around Sanna's.

Sanna looked at Malin with false confidence. "Are you nervous?" she asked.

"Dunno," answered Malin. Yet she was. Nervous as hell.

Mustafa came into the living room. He went right to the other side of the room, and stood with his back against the window. "It's cool," he explained and looked at Sanna and Malin. "He's just fixing his stuff."

In the hallway, there was a rustling sound and heavy boot-steps slowly approached the living room.

Malin pulled on Sanna's arm.

"Stop it!" hissed Sanna as she stared sternly at Malin. Malin trembled when she saw the figure in the doorway. He did not look like a normal dealer. Not like Habib or those she had seen at T-Centralen tube station or the city square. There was something strange about the man. Not just the shabby beard and the emaciated face. Even the clothes he was wearing were strange. He wore a long, dark raincoat that fell all the way to a pair of heavy boots. No normal adult went around in those clothes – not at his age anyway. What Mustafa had said was true though. Definitely not a cop. But what was he then? A do-gooder?

The man went up to Mustafa and took out a small package from his coat pocket. It was carefully wrapped in dark brown tape.

"Smoke as much as you want," he said in a cold voice.

Mustafa studied the package for a few seconds as if he was thinking about something.

"Are you kidding?" he said after turning it over. "Hell, that's awesome. I'll roll a few right away." Mustafa disappeared into the kitchen.

The man sat in the armchair and gazed at Malin and Sanna in silence.

Sanna could not be quiet any longer. "Why did you need me and Malin to be here?" she asked and looked at Malin.

The man said nothing. All that could be heard in the room was Mustafa rolling joints in the kitchen.

"Hello, can't you talk?" asked Sanna.

Malin pulled Sanna's arm discreetly and told her to calm down.

"What is it?" Sanna said and looked at Malin, irritated.

Malin did not know what she should do or say.

Suddenly, the man leaned forwards. "You could say that I have a certain relationship with Malin's mother," he said and looked at Malin with his deadened eyes.

Sanna turned to a terrified Malin. "Is that your old man, Janne, or whatever his name is?"

"Dunno," whispered Malin in a shaky voice.

"Is your name Janne?" asked Sanna boldly. "Are you her old man?"

The man looked at Malin. "No, I'm not her father."

"But you're buddies with her old lady?" Sanna continued.

"You could say that we have some points of contact," the man replied.

"Are you her boyfriend or what?"

The man did not reply. Instead, he stood up and went to the window.

"Whatever," said Sanna petulantly. "Just as long as we get high, you can be friends with whoever the fuck you want to."

The room fell silent once more.

Mustafa came into the living room with some marijuana joints that he had finished rolling. He put them on the coffee table and sat down beside Sanna on the sofa.

"Let's fucking do it," he said and took a spliff. He lit it expertly, sucked in a long drag, and lay back on the sofa.

Sanna snatched the lighter from Mustafa's hand and lit

herself a joint. She drew a deep breath and then gave the joint to Malin. Malin hesitated at first. She could not pull her eyes away from the man who was standing in the window and quietly observing them. Finally, she took a deep drag from the spliff. That was the reason she was here. She closed her eyes and held her breath for an instant. Soon, I will be out of here, she thought. Soon, I will be high and then this won't mean shit. She took a fresh drag and felt the buzz slowly hit.

"Aren't you going to smoke too?" Sanna asked, looking at the man.

The man did not answer. Instead, he opened a window slightly.

"Fuck, you are one shit-cool Swede," Mustafa drawled after a short while.

"Yeah, shit," continued Sanna, "you're fucking awesome."

Malin felt her tension disappear. The man whom she first thought was unpleasant was no longer so threatening. He looked a little weird, but no more than that.

With blurry eyes, she saw Mustafa take Sanna by the hand and stagger into the bedroom. The door slammed with a bang. She tried to say something to them, but her mouth would not obey her. It was as if it no longer belonged to her. After a while, she could no longer sit upright on the sofa. Instead, she lay down. The spliff slipped out of her hand and landed on the floor. She was on her way towards the ultimate nirvana.

He observed the girl who lay on the sofa, filled with her urgent hunger to flee reality. So young, yet still willing to descend into degradation and pawn her future.

She would now have been roughly the same age as the girl on the sofa. Maybe she would have been at school, immersed in study as he himself had once been. Ambitious and with a scholastic mind and talent that lit up each day. She would have spent a lot of time in the stable, training for some competition and grooming her horse down to the smallest detail. She would have been a reflection of himself: a perfectionist with a will as strong as steel.

For a brief moment, he doubted whether what he was doing was really the right thing. But then came the despair and, after that, the hate slowly returned. It was the girl's mother he wanted to hurt. Now she would know the true meaning of loss. The girl lying on the sofa was simply a tool, an instrument he was forced to sacrifice for his mission.

This was a balancing act that required a lot of patience. So many factors could go wrong: the timing, the strength of the dose, the confrontation.

But he had patience. A deadly amount of patience.

He looked at his watch. The time had come.

KARIN WENT STRAIGHT from the courthouse to Sanna's home address in Vällingby. She was taking a chance that Sanna's mother was at home. Even better, she hoped to find her own daughter, but neither Malin nor Sanna were there, and Sanna's mother was as uninterested in her own daughter as Karin was in listening to Sanna's mother gossiping. Just because the woman was an alcoholic and unemployed did not mean that she should let her daughter fend for herself, thought Karin angrily, when Sanna's mother closed the door in her face.

She had not found a single clue that took her closer to finding Malin. She called both Malin and Sanna's mobile phones several times, only to get their voicemail messages.

She had no telephone number for Mustafa. She only knew of him by name. She blamed herself for not having asked Malin for it earlier. Now she knew nothing. She had searched through Malin's room not knowing what she was searching for, and she had called parents and classmates from the school register. That didn't give her anything either. If Malin was not back home by ten o'clock this evening, she would contact the police. She knew that the police would not file a missing persons' report until twenty-four hours had passed, but she persuaded herself that they could at least keep their eyes open. Her throbbing anxiety had developed into stomach pains. Cinema and restaurant visits with Malin now seemed as distant as her good humour.

KARIN TRIED TO eat that afternoon. The food did not taste good. After a few bites of yesterday's leftovers, she threw the food in the rubbish bin. She tried a sandwich, but that was not edible either. Even the wine that she hoped would take the edge off her anxiety was unpalatable. Everything tasted metallic, nauseating – everything except the tap water.

The anxiety within her gradually turned into a rage that grew in proportion to the time that passed without any communication from Malin. After a while, Karin started to talk to herself. At first, it was more of a mutter, with some swear words directed at Sanna and her drunk of a mother. Later, it progressed to soliloquies, in which she loudly and clearly either berated or entreated Malin for one thing or another. It was comforting to talk loudly to herself, to drown out the voices in her head, which all the while were growing stronger. But finally, not even that helped. An unbearable pain cut through Karin's head. Something was happening to her. What it was, she did not know, but she felt like a pressure cooker that was slowly overheating, and the only way out was to …

She could not think like that. It was unacceptable to have these thoughts, but still she did and she became confused, terrified by them.

Then a sudden, stabbing pain, and she spun around with a scream. The spice rack flew to the floor and glass from the little spice bottles shattered all over the kitchen floor.

"Damn it!" she screamed and grabbed her head. The voices became louder and louder. If only she had the kid in front of her now. God knows what she would do to her.

7

MALIN SLOWLY OPENED her eyes. She was freezing, so much so that her teeth chattered. One knee was sore, and she lay on cold, damp grass surrounded by thick bushes. Her trousers and jacket were muddy and she found it difficult to get her bearings. The bushes were dense and stretched high above her. Even if she stood on tiptoe, she could not see over, much less through, the bushes. She could not for the life of her understand how she had ended up here.

The only thing she remembered was that Sanna and Mustafa had disappeared into the bedroom. And, of course, that bearded dealer, the guy who was so unpleasant. He was also there when they sat in Mustafa's living room. Everything after that was obscured by darkness.

Malin became angry. She felt betrayed and abandoned by Sanna and Mustafa.

Because they had done … what? Why was she really angry? Because she had ended up here. How had she, in fact, come to this place? She suddenly realized that she perhaps had been raped. An icy feeling seized her. What if that dealer had done something to her? Laid over her, drooling and panting like some fucking animal? She checked. Her jeans were properly buttoned and she felt no pain in her crotch at least. Probably a good sign. She had to get home and shower. Everything was so fucked up.

Malin fumbled for her mobile phone and found it in her jacket pocket. She did not usually keep it there. She was going to call Sanna, but the display was as blank as her head was right now. Presumably, the battery was dead. Despite that, she tried to restart it by repeatedly pressing the button. The phone remained dead.

"Fucking hell!" she swore angrily and threw away the phone. Now everything was against her. She stood up carefully and limped out between two bushes without picking up her mobile phone. It was dark and she had difficulty seeing.

A two-storey block of flats towered in front of her, and a lamp was alight over the basement door to the building. By the side of the door, a bike stood chained fast. It looked familiar. The bike was hers.

Limping and swearing, Malin made her way around the building and in through the door at the front. There were seven steps up to the flat. She would be able to manage those, in spite of the terrible pain from her damned knee.

Mrs Ekblom's little chihuahua barked as soon as she came into the stairwell. The dog that Malin normally loved was no longer cute. The barking and whining behind the door became an intolerable noise in Malin's ear. She hated the disgusting little hairball that just drooled and whined. Malin spat on Mrs Ekblom's door and swore at the dog to shut the fuck up.

At last, she was standing on the last step and reaching for the door handle, but she stopped herself when she suddenly started hearing vague voices inside her own head. Only faint whispers, but they spoke to her.

What the fuck was going on?

Suddenly, a pain started to grow deep inside her head. The whispers changed to distinct voices that talked over each other. She tried to fight it, but she was filled with an enormous rage. The angrier she became, the more the pain subsided.

Sanna is a fucking loser and Mum is a bloody whore who should leave me the fuck alone.

She tore open the flat door.

IT WAS TEN past nine in the evening when Karin heard the sound of the front door opening. She jumped up from the sofa and went out to the hallway where she met Malin, who was muddied and limping, when she stepped through the door.

Karin advanced with her hands firmly on her hips.

"Where have you been?" she began in a shrill voice.

Malin did not answer and ignored Karin's glare. She slowly slinked towards her room, limping along the hallway wall. Her eyes were as black as coal.

"Are we having difficulty finding an answer?" Karin shouted and grabbed Malin's shoulder. She felt the rage spread to every muscle.

"Get off me!" yelled Malin, trying to get free from Karin's grip.

"You're going to tell me where you've been," Karin repeated as she grabbed both of Malin's shoulders with her hands. She wanted to throw the kid against the wall.

Malin exploded and slapped Karin's hands away. "Get off me, you fucking whore!" she screamed. "Leave me alone."

"I'm not going to. That's over with now!" Karin screamed back and took fresh hold of Malin, who hit her hands away.

"Don't touch me," Malin said and stared hard at Karin with her coal-black eyes.

"Don't you understand what I said, you fucking bitch? You're nothing to do with me!"

Karin shook with rage. Tears welled up as she grappled with her daughter's arms.

"Bloody brat. You're not going to destroy anything anymore," she yelled, as her rage mixed with despair and fear. Her tears blinded her.

Suddenly, Karin received a hard blow to her chin and she staggered backwards. Malin turned around and limped back towards the front door. She had now hit her mother. Some part of her registered how sick this was, but she could not quite get her head round the thought. She had not had any choice. The bitch had tried to restrain her, to imprison her with her bloody nagging. She had to get out and away from the nagging bitch and her shitty life. If only she were dead. Malin tried to think, but the pain in her head cut like a knife. She stopped and pressed her hands against her forehead.

"Can't you just shut your mouth?" screamed Malin. "Leave me alone!"

Malin threw open the front door and was just about to start descending the stairs when Karin grabbed her jacket.

"You're not going anywhere!" roared Karin, so that it echoed around the stairwell. She had to get the damned kid inside, to put an end to all of this now.

The echo of Karin's voice mingled with the barking from Mrs Ekblom's chihuahua. She tried to drag Malin through the flat door, but Malin resisted. She had a grip on the handrail and held on with all the strength she could muster.

Karin grabbed hold of Malin's hair. She pulled so hard that a big hank of hair came loose. Malin screamed with the pain. She quickly spun around to break free from her mother's hold on her jacket and briefly lost her grip on the handrail. In her determination to prevent Malin's escape, Karin then hit Malin full in the face with the flat of her hand.

The blow came as a complete surprise. Instinctively, Malin covered her face, and lost her balance, falling uncontrollably backwards while desperately reaching for the handrail. A dull thud sounded when her head met the rock-hard edge of the step.

It was suddenly quiet in the stairwell. The echoes quickly died away.

The dog stopped barking behind the door.

A weak gasp escaped from the girl. Her body twitched a few times before lying completely still.

WALTER WAS JUST leaving for the evening when David Lilja came into the office. He sat down in Walter's shabby visitor's chair and placed his hands behind his neck. Walter looked at Lilja with some surprise, as he normally never stayed after five o'clock. Lilja was probably the person in the police station who was most eager to go home and who strictly adhered to office hours. On the other hand, he had no objections when Walter worked until midnight.

"I heard that it went well with the pimp's alibi," Lilja began, "and that the rookie from RSU also handled herself well."

"Yes, she's at home getting her beauty sleep so that she can come and play tomorrow as well."

"Do you two get along? From what I've seen, she's quite determined and very forward. That's not exactly the perfect match for you."

"She has perhaps a little too much confidence for her own good. But a few cold showers should bring her feet back down to earth," Walter said.

"And naturally you will see that it happens," said Lilja. "The first thing a person loses in your company is self-confidence."

Walter smiled a crooked grin.

"I don't want to get any complaints from Hildebrandt at RSU," Lilja clarified. "We'll have a lot of use for RSU in the future."

"Why would you get complaints?" asked Walter.

Lilja looked at Walter in disbelief. "In any case, it seems as if you two managed to run circles around the girlfriend. The prosecutor is very satisfied with your work."

"There'll be no problems there," answered Walter. "She was just as brainless as one would expect of an addict with that habit – no more, no less. If the court accepts her as a credible witness, then we might as well scrap the entire justice system."

Lilja nodded approvingly and watched Walter as he stood up from his chair.

"Anything else?" Walter asked as he reached for his jacket.

"What do you mean?" asked Lilja.

"Well, you didn't come here just to ask about the alibi and to gossip about the rookie. It's almost eleven," said Walter, checking the clock above the office door.

Lilja's face hardened. "We have a fifteen-year-old girl who has been in an accident," he began and then paused for effect.

"I see," said Walter, disinterested, as he put on his jacket.

"It's the same situation as always," sighed Lilja. "Lack of resources, lack of manpower, lack of everything." He shrugged.

"Well, that sounds familiar," conceded Walter. "Are we talking overtime now?"

"As you know, Cederberg and Jonsson are assisting our colleagues from the Skåne district for a few weeks," Lilja continued, pretending not to hear Walter's last question. "It's a terrible mess down there in Landskrona. Many believe that it's becoming a lawless region. They're taking part in a murder investigation with connections to Stockholm, but the investigation is being led by officers on the scene. Forensics is not formally involved yet, but may be. If that happens, I'll pull Cederberg and Jonsson back home immediately."

"Let them stay down there permanently," Walter suggested and went towards the door. "You could never have made me go down to that Skåne dung heap. Not even if you asked me nicely."

Lilja remained sitting in the chair.

"Forensics is already en route to the scene of the accident," he said, switching back to the original subject. "You can call Swedberg and get the address from him. The duty shift is already busy with other tasks, so I would appreciate it if you could see your way to at least start the crime scene investigation in order that the shift can take over, once they are finished with the knife victim in Fittja."

"Do I have a choice?" asked Walter.

"One always has a choice," answered Lilja, standing up from his chair. "Or were you planning to take a hot bath with candlelight when you get home?"

"Better than that," lied Walter. "In fact, I have a new bed and a date waiting for me in it."

Lilja raised an eyebrow.

WHEN WALTER ARRIVED, the forensic technicians had already started the technical part of the crime scene investigation. He left the car on the pavement a short distance from the building, because the street was full of parked cars. There were no parking spaces nowadays, not even in the suburbs. He swore because there was little room when he opened the car door and happened to hit a lamppost that someone had coincidentally placed at that exact spot. He noticed a small dent on the taxpayer's Volvo V70 and then continued at a slow pace towards the entrance, where ambulance crew and uniformed police officers were standing around. Only now did his thoughts begin to focus on what was waiting for him. His years as a detective had made him callous and accustomed to most things that had to do with death. Only morticians and forensic technicians were truly comfortable with it. Walter had been obliged to learn how the sweet smell from a corpse whose "best-before" date had expired could attack the nostrils. And how to scoop the remains of a human body with a soup ladle from a grinder at the coffee factory. Such things no longer bothered him. There was, however, something he could never get used to – the occasions when humanity revealed its worst and most primitive behaviour. And this was when children got hurt. Every time this happened, he questioned his choice of profession.

That a rational adult could take the life of a defenceless child never ceased to horrify him. That children died as a result of accidents on almost a daily basis was understandable. That was part of the risk of living, one could say. But that a child could be murdered in cold blood, he could not understand. Every time, he hoped to avoid having to see the corpse of a child when he came to a crime scene, but this time he had the misfortune of knowing what was going to happen.

A small group of curious bystanders had gathered at a distance and was trying to get a glimpse of what was going on in the stairwell. The police tape effectively cordoned off the area around the entrance. The technicians had also managed to erect tent walls inside the door entrance so that they could work undisturbed.

Walter showed his police badge to a uniformed police officer. The officer nodded and held up the plastic tape so that Walter could bend stiffly under it.

"What have we got here, then?" said Walter to no one in particular, as he entered the stairwell and donned the mandatory blue overalls and face mask. He searched for some of the cough drops that he had in his chest pocket while looking around him.

Swedberg, who was standing in conversation with some colleagues who were all wearing blue plastic overalls, turned around. He gave Walter a glance that then moved to the body on the stairs. The body was of medium height and was wrapped in a yellow ambulance blanket. Blood had coagulated on the floor under the body and someone had left a footprint in the red stain.

Walter squatted beside the body and pulled on the latex gloves that he always had with him. He carefully lifted the blanket to confirm what he already knew. A girl of around fifteen, sixteen years, just as Lilja had warned him.

She was pale and lifeless. Her eyes were closed and she looked peaceful, lying there. She was, however, just an empty shell, an object as lifeless as the clothes on her body. This morning, she had awoken to the last day of her all-too-short life, and Walter wondered what she had been thinking in the last minutes before Death took her. For a brief second, he wished he could trade places with her. He felt a pain in his chest and took a deep breath. Always the same powerless feeling, always the same bloody spasm in his lower chest.

He began by examining the girl's head, lifting it up gently so that he could see the fracture at the back of the skull.

Swedberg crouched beside Walter. "Too damned tragic, eh?" he said in a quiet voice, scrutinizing the girl.

"What have you found out?" asked Walter flatly.

"For starters, this is what she had on her," said Swedberg and held up a transparent forensic sample bag.

Walter scanned the contents of the bag: a small plaster figure in the shape of a winged skeleton.

"Mobile phone?" asked Walter.

"Not on her, in any case," answered Swedberg.

"Anything else?"

"Malin Sjöstrand, fifteen years old," answered Swedberg. "Cause of death: blunt-force trauma to the back of the head, probably from the fall on the stairs. We are taking her in for a post-mortem, if you have no objections."

Walter nodded. He stood up and went up the stairs to the uniformed police officers.

"Who's in the flat?" he asked a police officer.

"Ambulance crew and a female officer," answered the police officer tersely.

Walter entered the flat and went through a narrow hallway into a living room. A middle-aged woman sat curled up with her knees against her chin in one corner of the sofa. Her face was almost as pale as the girl on the stairway. Her gaze was blank and her mascara had left black streaks down her cheeks. Beside her sat a woman police officer. Two male paramedics were crouched over the woman and attempting to get a reaction from her. Walter summoned the police officer with a wave. "Is that the mother?" he whispered.

"Yes," replied the police officer. "Karin Sjöstrand, mother to Malin Sjöstrand; she's the one who …"

"Have you discovered anything else?" he interrupted.

"No, nothing. She's currently in a state of shock, according to the paramedics. They want to take her in, but she refuses to leave the sofa."

"I see," nodded Walter. He sat down beside the curled-up woman, who didn't take any notice of his presence.

"My name is Walter Gröhn and I'm a detective from the County CID," he said, in as gentle a voice as he could muster. Tenderness was not his strongest suit.

The ambulancemen noted with interest how Walter tried to connect with the woman.

"Are you the girl's mother?" continued Walter.

No reaction from the woman.

One of the ambulancemen, an older man with a fretful face, explained why she was not answering.

"She's paralyzed with shock," he said, almost whispering. "We want to get her to A&E as quickly as possible." The second paramedic nodded in agreement.

Walter stood up from the sofa and went out into the stairwell. He wanted to be sure that the girl was on the way to the post-mortem and not still lying on the stairs.

"Get some rags and wipe the blood off the stairs, if you please," he ordered the policeman who had been standing by the door earlier.

The policeman turned around, confused.

"Rags?" he said as he stared at Walter.

"Rags, you know, also known as floor rags," explained Walter.

"We don't have any rags with us," the policeman said, apologetically.

"Then you'll have to improvise," suggested Walter. "Go and buy some at the nearest petrol station."

The policeman continued to look confused.

An elderly woman with weepy, bloodshot eyes and a wrinkled face suddenly opened the next door. In one hand, she held a floor mop. Beside her, on the hallway floor, there stood an empty plastic bucket.

"You can take water from my bathroom," she began, in a shaky voice. "I don't have the strength to do it myself, you see. My legs don't carry me so well nowadays." She held out the floor mop with a shaking hand.

Walter scrutinized the hunchbacked old lady, who must have been at least eighty years old. Her blue-silver hair was flattened at the back. It looked as if she had just got out of bed.

"That's very kind of you," thanked Walter. "My colleague in the uniform down there will take care of it. And in return, maybe he can offer to clean your flat since he is already cleaning up." Walter grinned at the lady who smiled back, somewhat uncomfortably.

"Thank you, but I already have a cleaning lady," she said.

The policeman did not appear to be in the least amused as he took a firm grip of the floor mop and bucket and went into the lady's flat.

Walter re-entered the flat. The paramedics had, as gently as possible, tried to get the shocked woman to lie down on the stretcher. They had failed and instead were discussing other options when Walter came in.

He crouched down in front of the woman and stretched out his hand.

"Come on, Karin. We're going to see Malin," he said and smiled sympathetically at her. Karin lowered her eyes from the wall and looked at Walter. An antique Mora grandfather clock struck with slow, sleepy chimes.

"Are we?" she asked, with the bewilderment of a child.

"Yes, we are," Walter smiled. "She's lying at the hospital waiting for you. It's best that we hurry up."

Walter took Karin's hand while he nodded to the ambulance crew to prepare the stretcher. She hesitated for a moment. Then she stood up slowly with Walter's hand firmly in hers. He led her to the stretcher and felt her grip his hand even harder.

"Promise that I'll get to see her?" Her voice was fragile, and she looked into Walter's eyes with a tired, feverish gaze.

"I promise," Walter answered and freed his hand from her grip.

The younger of the paramedics approached Walter after they had loaded Karin into the ambulance.

"I don't understand why you lied," he said, and stared at Walter questioningly.

Walter raised his eyes to the clear, starry night sky. Condensation steamed out of his mouth as he breathed. The pain in his chest had subsided and he could breathe freely again.

"She'll see her again," he said, without taking his eye from the Big Dipper. "I never said under what circumstances."

The paramedic scrutinized Walter thoughtfully for a few seconds. Then he got into the ambulance, shaking his head.

SOME JOURNALISTS HAD merged with the group of bystanders outside the barriers. Walter stiffly crept under the plastic tape that separated the tragedy from the everyday world. When he straightened up, he found himself standing in front of the worst news jackal of them all.

"Jörgen Blad, from the newspaper *Kvällspressen*," said the short, corpulent reporter, while thrusting a minivoice recorder under Walter's nose. Small, chipolata-like fingers gripped the voice recorder, in which he hoped he would win an exlusive from Walter. He held the voice recorder so close that Walter could smell the taco spices on the reporter's hand. Presumably, he had been sitting in some Tex-Mex bar, stuffing himself with a load of greasy enchiladas. Walter hated Mexican food. It was always over-spiced and as greasy as the hair of a high-priced lawyer from the Östermalm district. Since he had a previously unfinished bone to pick with Blad, he decided to keep the process as short as possible.

"Oh, I can always recognize you," Walter began and pushed the voice recorder to one side. "My eyesight is not that bad yet."

"What can you say about the deceased?" insisted Jörgen and thrust the voice recorder forwards again.

"That she's dead," Walter said and started to go towards his car.

"Who's the person in question and how did she die?" Jörgen continued and followed Walter.

"Too early to make a statement," Walter answered abruptly.

"About what?" Jörgen asked. "About who she is or how she died?"

"That, you will have to guess," Walter said and opened the door. "You people at *Kvällspressen* are usually quite adept at making up a story." He slammed the car door shut.

And so the time for the first retribution had arrived.

Finally, he was being rewarded for his relentless work. It had been a difficult task, and he had been obliged to use accomplices, but they were everywhere, the unscrupulous who would sell themselves for a fistful of cash with no qualms. Everything had been carefully planned: the burglary, the planted evidence, and then the girl who became his instrument. She would be the first step on his road to recovery. Another failure was not an option. This war had no victors. All were doomed to defeat. All that remained was to ease his suffering.

The woman would suffer as he had suffered. She had kindly allowed herself to be touched by his vengeance and she would now have to live with the agony of having killed her own child. She would be made accountable and tortured by her own uncertainty, where the questions would eat away at her like maggots on a corpse.

But his victory was mixed with ambiguity. Who was to blame? Who was truly deserving of his fury? He was drowning in his yearning for her. His grief and hate got the better of him again.

WALTER LEANT OVER the girl's peaceful face. Her eyes were closed and her mouth sealed with stitches. He observed her in silence. She somehow appeared alive despite being dead, like a young actress with make-up to mimic the dead in some staged scene.

Her eyelids twitched slightly. Curious, he leaned closer. Suddenly, her eyelids opened. Two black holes grinned back at Walter and he fell backwards, horrified.

He awoke soaked in sweat. The alarm clock showed five minutes past four. The image of her empty eye sockets stayed on his retina, despite the fact he was wide awake. This had been happening more often over the years, these dreams about the children and how death always shrouded them.

He had never been able to confront the pain of Martine's death. He had convinced himself that she was just out of town and would soon be coming back, standing there on the doorstep and greeting him with the warm smile that she had inherited from her mother.

Still, deep down, he knew that this was a dishonest, pathetic self-indulgence. He knew that she had been cremated and that the ashes had been scattered in the wind on that weekday eleven years ago. Anything else was just an illusion to keep him going.

His back felt sore as he got out of bed. He sat himself at the kitchen table, holding his back and massaging it even though he knew it would not help.

He had three injured vertebrae in his lower back, which would never fully heal. He was now paying for his carelessness with his back in his younger years. According to the doctors, there was no point in surgery. Regular exercise would help, but a single session with an over-zealous instructor at the gym had been more than enough for Walter. Walter and endorphins quite simply were not compatible. He had to roll with the punches, as it were.

He laid down again and not only went back to sleep – which was definitely not a common occurrence, especially after a nightmare – but also accomplished the feat of oversleeping. The mobilephone ringtone that played Neil Young's "Heart of Gold" abruptly shattered his slumber.

Newly awake, he grasped his mobile phone and searched for the green button.

"Do you know what time it is?" Lilja began.

Walter had no idea what time it was. He turned around awkwardly and saw that it was nine-thirty.

"It feels like seven?" Walter suggested.

"Hardly," Lilja muttered. "We've picked up Karin Sjöstrand from the psychiatric ward. You were supposed to head up the interview with her at nine-thirty. Or were you thinking of working from home today?"

"Give me half an hour," Walter groaned and got out of bed.

Despite the lack of parking and constant traffic jams, there are some advantages to living in Vasastan if one works at Kungsholmen, Walter thought, as he left the lift on the fifth floor of the police station precisely thirty-eight minutes after Lilja's call.

The interrogation room on the fifth floor was one of the detention centre's smallest. Twelve square metres with no window, one table and four chairs was pretty much all there was. In the centre of the table, there was a microphone from which the cable disappeared down through a hole in the dark oak. Two robust fluorescent strip lights projected a high-contrast glare in the room that highlighted the smallest of facial details with an eerie intensity. A person looked at least twenty years older in here.

Before Walter entered the interrogation room, he pulled Jonna to one side.

"Now, I want you to listen to me."

"I'm listening," Jonna answered, focused. She had sat and waited impatiently for her temporary boss to grace the investigation with his presence. All that talk about Walter being an early riser was obviously an exaggeration.

"It is I who will be asking the questions and you will be observing. This is crunch time, so I want you to stay in the background."

Jonna frowned. "Can't I say anything at all?"

"Preferably not," Walter explained. "This interrogation is not like the pimp and his alibi. It's different this time."

"In which way is it different?"

"The woman in there is not a strung-out crackhead with her brains under her arm. She's in shock and has been given sedatives. This requires a slightly different technique. And I'd prefer to handle this operation myself. You're welcome to watch, but try not to show any facial expressions or to betray your emotions and how you feel with body language. Try to look expressionless."

Jonna nodded her understanding. In accordance with Walter's request, she would do her best to remain expressionless. The only thing she did not understand was the type of interrogation technique Walter was using. This situation was unlike anything that she had learned at RSU. Good cop/bad cop was a classic technique, which she and Walter had successfully used for the alibi witness. Jonna had found her role without being coached by Walter. With three barbed-wire-chewing policemen, the female witness for the alibi could hardly have done anything else than confide in the sympathetic young woman in the police quartet. Jonna was very satisfied with her performance. Jonsson and Cederberg's mediocre contribution, on the other hand, puzzled her. She now understood what the instructors at the police academy had meant by "desensitized and professionally fatigued" officers. Time and circumstance erodes your humanity until one becomes part of the system oneself. And then becomes blind. They quite simply could not see the wood for the trees. But, as usual, there were no rules without exceptions. Walter was the oldest and had the most years in service, but no situation or person seemed to influence him. He was cynical and impervious to pretty much everything. Jonna did not know which was worse. Plague or famine, take your pick.

Walter and Jonna took their seats facing Karin Sjöstrand, who had the not-so-unfamiliar lawyer Rolf Martensson at her side. She had demanded a lawyer even though she was not suspected of anything yet. She clasped her hands and held them tight against her stomach as if in prayer. Her eyes were fixed on the table and her mouth was tight-lipped. At the short end of the table sat the notary Gunvor Janson, in the role of secretary.

Gunvor Janson smiled at Walter, who nodded briefly back. Walter apologized for his lateness and shook hands with Martensson, who had not stood up when Walter had come in. They knew each other far too well to indulge in such niceties. This was not the first time that Martensson had sat on the opposite side of the table.

8 WALTER SCRUTINIZED Karin Sjöstrand closely. The silence in the room was infused with the anguish of a mother who had just lost her child. Her face was sunken and there were dark circles under her tear-worn eyes. Despite this, she sat with remarkably straight shoulders. Wonder how much medication they have pumped into her, Walter thought. When Malin's death sinks into her consciousness, she will certainly break down.

Walter started the voice recorder, began with the usual formalities about who was present in the room, and declared that this was an informal interrogation. So far, no prosecutor was involved.

"How are you feeling?" Walter began and at the same moment the thought occurred to him that he had forgotten his cough drops at home. He had not had time to drink any coffee either. For a brief moment, he considered asking Jonna to go and get him a cup, but he dismissed it almost immediately because then he would be forced to ask the others as well. Such an exercise would delay the interrogation further and he did not have time for that.

Karin's answer came surprisingly quickly. "Well, how do you think I feel?" she said in a low voice, without lifting her eyes from the table.

"We have questioned your neighbour," Walter continued and opened the interview file on Mrs Ekblom. "According to her statement, there was a disturbing shouting match in the stairway before she opened the door and saw you sitting beside Malin at the bottom of the stairs. How would you explain that?"

"You promised that I would get to see Malin again," Karin interrupted and raised her eyes. She had something hateful in her eyes.

"Well ..." Walter dragged out the word. "I rather thought that it would be easier on you if you went to the psychiatric ward and got help. Back home on the sofa, you would only be feeling poorly, and we did not want to have to use force."

For a few seconds, it looked as if Karin was going to pounce on Walter. Throw herself over the table and tear him to shreds. But then she sank back and gazed down at the table again.

"I have nothing left to live for anymore," she said, and her eyes revealed a void. He needed to get the interrogation moving before she completely collapsed. From the corner of his eye, he saw that Jonna looked tearful.

"Do you know why you are here?" he continued in a calm voice.

Karin did not answer. She looked at the table and knotted her hands until the fingertips paled.

"Will you tell us what happened?" Walter continued.

Karin took a deep breath. First, she looked at the notary who had adopted a stony expression. Then, at Walter.

"I hit Malin so that she fell," she said. "It was my fault."

Martensson convulsed, as if someone had woken him with an electric shock.

"It's not at all certain that it happened that way," he began and put his hand on Karin's arm. "You are still in shock and, in that state of mind, one can say a lot of things one doesn't mean."

Karin looked questioningly at Martensson.

"Did you have an argument?" Walter asked.

"I must have been so angry that I didn't know what I was doing. Everything blacked out and I …" Once again, she lowered her eyes to the table.

"Why were you so angry?"

"Malin hadn't been in touch all day. She had played truant from school and was probably with Sanna and that Mustafa character."

"Did you hit her in self-defence?"

"It hasn't been established that Karin hit her daughter," Martensson sternly interrupted. "You will have to rephrase the question."

"Rephrase?" Walter exclaimed. "For Christ's sake, this is not a trial."

"It's still …" Martensson began, but was interrupted by his client.

"No, I think she wanted to get away from me. I really can't remember exactly," Karin tried to recall.

"Can't remember?" Walter repeated and feigned surprise, putting on his glasses. He opened the folder of the preliminary post-mortem report.

"According to the post-mortem, someone ripped a sizeable piece of hair from Malin's head. Could this have happened in the struggle? Is it possible it was you who ripped the hair from Malin's head?" he asked, and looked up from the folder.

"Wait just a minute," interjected Martensson. "My client doesn't remember what happened. There's no point in you asking questions that she can't answer."

"I'm just trying to help her remember," Walter smiled sweetly. "I hardly think that's something you can assist with."

Martensson glared sourly at Walter.

"As you perhaps are aware, we have a witness who claims to have heard you and Malin arguing on the stairs," Walter continued. "Your neighbour, Märta Ekblom, says she heard you cry out, and I quote, 'What have I done?' End quote."

Walter removed his glasses and leaned back in his chair.

The room was quiet. Not even Rolf Martensson said anything.

Karin stared blankly at the wall behind Walter.

Walter rubbed his eyes in a hopeless attempt to wake them up. He felt strangely drained and unmotivated. He threw a glance at Jonna, who sat and fumbled endlessly with her mobile phone. She seemed to have pulled herself together.

The tears were gone.

Karin switched her gaze from the wall to Walter.

"When I came home from the court, I felt irritated," she began. "I just became more infuriated the longer time went by. I couldn't get hold of Malin. Finally, I got so frustrated that I broke a glass. That's never happened before, at least not in anger. I can't tell you why I was so furious."

"Which court?" Walter asked.

Martensson raised an eyebrow in curiosity.

"The Stockholm District Court," Karin answered. "I usually sit on the jury a few times a week."

Walter's motivation returned as quickly as it had disappeared. He glanced at Jonna, who also seemed to have woken up.

"So you're a lay juror?" he asked and tried to regain his focus.

"You can do what you want. I can't live without my daughter," Karin answered in an apathetic voice.

"But it was you that pulled out your daughter's hair?"

Before Martensson managed to open his mouth, Karin answered "Yes" to the question.

"Will you tell us what happened?" Walter continued, looking at Jonna. She was staring at the woman with great interest.

Causing Martensson considerable discomfort, Karin nod-ded an affirmative. The lawyer looked as if he had swallowed something distasteful.

"We had a fight in the doorway," she began, almost relieved. Tears rolled down her cheeks and her voice became weak. "I wanted to know where she'd been, but Malin was very aggres-sive and didn't want to listen to me. I felt consumed with rage. Then I don't remember so much."

"Malin could have fallen by herself," Martensson suggested quickly. "At the very worst, it's a tragic accident," he continued to elaborate. "It's not even proven that Karin caused Malin's fall on the stairs."

"But what about the hair?" Walter asked and glared angrily at Martensson.

"I had it in my hand," Karin said, with tears running down both cheeks. "I had her hair in my hand."

Jonna steeled herself and tried to hold back the wave of empathy that washed over her. It was the first time she had en-countered real and intense grief and, even if she herself had not lost someone dear to her, she could almost imagine the torment that the woman was suffering right now. She tried to fend off the feeling by reminding herself that Karin was a murderer, that she was not to be pitied, that she should be sentenced. But no matter how she tried, she could not picture the woman in front of her as a woman who had killed her own child.

Walter had heard enough. The murderess had said what she had to say and there was not a lot more to add. He could not, however, prevent himself from feeling some sympathy for her. But there was something that was not quite right. To first claim amnesia and then remember that she had Malin's hair in her hand was a little surprising. Amnesia was usually claimed by less talented villains as soon as they were cornered, but she was apparently in a state of shock – in which the brain could not sort events into a logical order. Statistically speaking, it was an unlikely story. A mother does not kill her child just because she is not home on time. That Karin had suddenly become mentally ill and completely insane did not sound feasible either. Walter's intuition told him that she was not insane. Yet, she had caused her daughter's death.

He called the custody officer on the intercom, and a burly male police officer and even larger woman police officer gently took Karin away. She would certainly receive yet another set of sedatives and some counselling on top of that.

The notary, Gunvor Janson, asked if she should close the door behind her. Walter nodded. He wanted to sit for a while by himself in the empty interrogation room. Listen to the silence and to the noise in his head. He pressed his fingers hard against his temples in an attempt to create order from the confusion within.

Just as Walter was about to leave the room, Lilja appeared in the doorway, accompanied by Jonna who seemed to have recovered from the interview.

"How nice of you to take the time to pay us a visit here at the police station," he began. "By the way, how did the interview go with that Karin Sjö ... what's-her-name? According to Jonna, it went well."

Walter leaned back in his chair, absent-mindedly twisting a pen.

"Sjöstrand, yes," Walter said. "We can close her file. She more or less told us herself that she caused her daughter's death in some sort of struggle. The daughter fell down the stairs and landed on her head. According to Swedberg, she died more or less instantaneously. My guess is that it will be a charge of manslaughter against the mother."

Lilja leaned against the doorpost and put his hands in his uniform-trouser pockets. "Yes, something like that. Damn tragedy, that. How can someone do something like that to their own daughter?"

Walter shrugged his shoulders. "You tell me."

"She was apparently a lay juror," Lilja added.

"Yes, do you want me to drop the case now?" Walter asked.

"No, why?" asked Lilja.

"I thought maybe Julén wanted me to do the same as I did with Bror Lantz."

"Spend your time and energy on this instead," Lilja said with a sudden harshness in his voice, removing his hands from his trouser pockets. "Lantz is history. One can't win every battle. The main thing is to win the war."

Walter sighed at Lilja's old, worn-out clichées, but could not resist joining in.

"How can one win the war if one also has to fight against one's own forces?" he said, challengingly. "Warfare on two fronts has never been very successful, if you read the the history books."

Lilja observed that he had no more time to embroil himself in lengthy discussions on history with Walter. He had a meeting to get to.

He has the common sense to flee rather than to fight badly, Walter silently concluded as he heard Lilja's footsteps disappear down the corridor.

"But surely, there are similarities," Jonna said after Lilja's hasty exit. She offered it more as a statement than a question.

"Between Lantz and Sjöstrand?"

Jonna nodded.

"Maybe, maybe not," Walter said. "We shouldn't jump to conclusions over the similarities. Coincidence occurs more often than one would expect. There are actually statistics on it."

Jonna looked at Walter with a pensive gaze. She did not know what he meant. Was it just coincidence? There were a lot of things that correlated with the Lantz incident.

Walter noticed the doubt in Jonna's eyes. "I know what you're thinking," he said.

"What?"

"That I'm either blind or stupid."

"No, I'm just wondering why you're not taking the similarities more seriously."

"I am," Walter said. "But these things take time. One can't jump on every potential clue as soon as it appears. Eventually, you'll be sitting with a big pile in your lap and get nowhere. Olof Palme's murder is a good example of that."

Jonna took a deep breath. There was something in what Walter was saying. He had, after all, worked a number of years on the force but, even so, it did not mean that he was always right.

"So what do we do now?" Jonna asked.

"Give it a day to let things sink in. Making haste is never a good idea. This job requires reflection and deep thinking."

"Deep?"

"Most people see only two dimensions," Walter explained. "Then you solve problems routinely. But sometimes, routine is not enough. If you try to see things in another way – for example, from a murderer's perspective – and put yourself in his or her situation, then you add an extra dimension to your thinking and make space for significantly more possibilities. Jump into the victim's and murderer's mindset and you'll have a totally different view of things."

"Like a form of role play?"

"Roughly speaking," Walter said and nodded. "You're yourself both the stage and the actors on it. The final scene is usually a life-or-death cliffhanger."

"And it's applicable to this situation, you think?" Jonna looked sceptically at Walter.

"It could be."

"But to do that, you must know all the pre-existing circumstances, a bit like the rules of the game," Jonna said. "And we don't have those yet."

"Exactly," Walter nodded. "You're answering your own questions. That's why we're letting things brew for a while. Think a little about it before you fall asleep tonight. That's when the most inspired thoughts are born."

Jonna was not sure if Walter was playing with her. Such a reflective approach had not been taught at the police academy, not even at RSU.

"And how do you attain this depth then?" she asked, with a cautious smile.

"It's not something that can be taught," Walter said. "It either comes naturally or it doesn't."

AFTER SPENDING SOME time in front of the commercial-free late-night news on TV, Walter picked up his mobile phone and dialled Swedberg's number. An idea still remained untested, and he knew that he would not be able to sleep until he got it out of his head.

"Do you have a few minutes at this late hour?" he began.

"Not really, but, since it's you, what do you want to know?"

"Do you know if Malin Sjöstrand had any form of drugs in her?" Walter asked.

Swedberg's answer came quickly. "Actually, she had a little bit of everything. Among other things, there were traces of marijuana and morphine, as well as a substance we haven't quite been able to identify yet. I put the report on the mess on your desk before I went home. If you lift up some papers, you might find it."

"I see," Walter mumbled and wondered in which pile it could be hiding.

He put on a CD and lay down on the sofa with his hands behind his head. Neil Young played "Fuel Line" while he tallied the books on Karin Sjöstrand. Suddenly, he became dizzy and nauseous. His field of vision narrowed and the room started to sway as if he were at sea. The first thought he had was that his sciatic nerve was pinched, since the sofa was well worn and saggy and his back had no support. But he felt no pain in his back or leg, which was what used to happen when an attack started.

As quickly as it came, the sensation disappeared. Walter stood up and the room was as stationary as he was. His vision was restored and everything was as it should be. Perhaps the blood had rushed to his head when he lay down, or he was about to get sick. Even detectives got the flu.

The flu did not materialize. The first thing Walter did the next morning, after getting his first cup of coffee, was to read through Swedberg's preliminary post-mortem report for Malin Sjöstrand. He found it under the latest edition of the *Law & Crime Journal*. The post-mortem report gave him no more than he already knew. He would get the final report as soon as Forensics had completed the analysis of the unidentified substance. As the clock approached eight, the police station slowly became populated with staff. First to the CID coffee corner was Jonsson. He got a cup of tea as he passed and hurried to his office, next to the coffee machine, with his mobile phone glued to his ear as usual.

Shortly afterwards, Cederberg appeared, panting. His doctor had prescribed a healthier diet and that he use the stairs instead of the lift as he moved around the police station. His bulky body mass had to be reduced at all costs, decreed his doctor.

Cederberg accepted the stairs, but not the rabbit food.

"We managed to pin her down good and proper, didn't we?" gasped Cederberg, leaning on one of the chairs. Beads of sweat broke out on his high forehead.

"Just spoke with the prosecutor," Walter answered and continued reading the morning newspaper. "He's going to raise charges against our pimp buddy. He doesn't think that the girlfriend's fake alibi will hold up in court."

"Yeah, at the end, she barely remembered her own name," Jonsson laughed. "What a loser bimbo. One of the funniest interviews I've taken part in."

"Your rookie," said Cederberg. "That little sidekick. She has a really sharp tongue. And she's not completely empty upstairs. She could really become something too."

"Shall I tell her that?"

"Don't be silly, Walter," Cederberg chuckled and reached for some biscuits on the table. "I just can't understand why they insist on recruiting small, dainty girlies who can barely carry shopping bags from Konsum supermarket, much less cuff a collapsed drunk."

Walter glanced at Cederberg's enormous belly and turkey neck, which wobbled as he munched his way through a buttery Danish. He wondered how many metres Cederberg could carry a shopping bag before his heart throbbed off its arteries, or if he was at all capable of bending down without asking for assistance.

"Could it possibly be because of this?" Walter speculated and put his finger to his forehead.

Cederberg shook his head.

That it was Walter who, with some unexpected help from Jonna, had broken the pimp's alibi was beyond all doubt. True to form, Cederberg and Jonsson had not contributed anything decisive. With nodding heads, they had backed up everything that Walter had said during the interrogation and when they actually said something, it was often clumsy.

Cederberg definitely seemed on the way to losing his grip. It was perhaps time for the bottle again. It had been a while since the last time, and he often had difficulties with day-to-day life during his periods between drinking.

Jonna had not performed badly. Without needing instructions from Walter, she had played the good cop and had won the woman's confidence. Walter was almost impressed. Taking turns, they had managed to get the female witness for the alibi to contradict herself no less than three times in the space of ten minutes.

"I heard that you were going down to Landskrona to take charge of the situation," Walter joked and stood up out of his chair.

"The Skåne Swedes are having a little grief with the immigrant gangs down there," Cederberg said, with a serious tone to his voice. "Our colleagues have found a jungle bunny stuck in a barrel with a nine-millimetre hole in his forehead. They expect reprisals and more killings soon, since the guy with the hole in his skull belonged to one of the more violent gangs down there. There are some connections to satellite gangs in Södertälje as well. It could turn into a full-blown bloodbath in Landskrona. Could even make its way up here." Cederberg wiped his brow and took another biscuit.

"Well, then, it's fortunate that you're backing them up," Walter answered with a restrained smile.

Cederberg nodded thoughtfully. "Yes, but the National Crime Squad will want to stick their noses in soon. But as long as there's a connection to Södertälje and no more crimes are committed, we should be able to handle it ourselves, according to Lilja."

"Good, hold the flag high in the face of the National Crime Squad."

Cederberg grinned appreciatively at Walter. "You can count on it."

9 CHIEF INSPECTOR DAVID Lilja had just sat down behind his desk with a cup of coffee when the telephone rang. He groaned irritably and let the phone ring a few times before picking up. It was Swedberg.

"You have to come down to the Drug Analysis Unit at SKL immediately," he began.

Lilja had never heard Swedberg so agitated and was caught slightly off-guard.

"I see," he managed to respond and put down his coffee cup.

"I know it sounds a little cloak and dagger, but I want you and Walter to come here as fast as you can. We have something that we're anxious to show you, with regard to Karin Sjöstrand's daughter," Swedberg continued.

Lilja was not the slightest bit interested in going to Linköping and the National Laboratory of Forensic Science, known as SKL. This would be a task that would take the whole day to complete and he had booked this Friday for personal errands.

Lilja reluctantly conceded after further entreaties from Swedberg to accompany Walter to SKL. The weekly shopping at the Co-op and the cosy hour with the wife would have to wait until tomorrow, Lilja thought, and drained his coffee cup.

"WHY WAS SWEDBERG so agitated?" Lilja said, after passing the Södertälje southbound lane on the E4 motorway.

"She apparently had something in her body," Walter reminded him. "He mentioned it to me yesterday, but he didn't know a great deal."

"It will become clear what has made that man so excited for the first time," Walter continued and looked in the side mirror at Jonna sitting in the back seat. She sat thinking hard about something and had not said much since the interview with Karin Sjöstrand. Slowly but surely, she had begun to realize that reality was a little different outside her glass bubble.

Jonna had had difficulty shaking off her feelings after the interview with Karin. Her head had been full of questions after she had gone to bed the previous evening, and the advice to think things over before she fell asleep felt superfluous, to say the least.

After twisting and turning until three in the morning, she gave up. She got up, made tea, and did not return to her bed again that morning.

One thing was at least certain. She would do all she could to see that all the circumstances around Malin Sjöstrand's death were uncovered. Even if the odds were microscopic, there was actually a possibility that Karin had confessed to the murder for someone else. Why Karin would do something like that, Jonna did not know. But such things did happen.

Or else it was simply a straightforward accident, despite the hair in her hand. Even if Jonna lacked the instincts that Walter had after thirty years on the force, which had made him declare Karin as guilty as a fox in a chicken house, she knew that she was not completely misguided – deep thinking or not.

Lilja swung into the site of the old garrison, where the SKL lab complex was located, and parked the car.

The Drug Analysis Unit was situated in the middle building that was nicknamed The Ship. After spending fifteen minutes waiting in the reception, Lilja's patience ran out.

"Where the hell is he?" he exclaimed and looked over angrily at Walter, who had reclined his head backwards in the comfortable visitor's chair. Jonna stood and browsed through an information folder from the medical institute.

"Maybe he's forgotten about us," Walter answered, with his eyes closed.

"It's been at least a quarter of an hour since the girl called him," Lilja exclaimed and pointed at the young receptionist behind the counter. Before Lilja could continue, Swedberg came out through the security doors with hurried steps.

"Sorry to keep you waiting," he announced. "Just got some updated information – hence the wait."

"What's really going on?" Lilja asked and got up from his chair. "First we have to come here urgently and then we have to sit here and wait."

"Come this way," Swedberg said curtly.

After they each had received their visitor's badges, they walked through the security doors and then a smallish office floor, with Swedberg in the lead. Sparsely scattered white coats sat beside desks in the otherwise empty room. They passed some fortified doors with yellow warning symbols and, through small, round windows, could glimpse different types of lab, but they were immediately told by a tense Swedberg to hurry up. After having gone up a mini-stairway and through a glass door, they arrived at a large meeting room. The room had no windows, but had large, square screens fitted into the walls, which emitted a dimmed, almost convincing sunlight. In the centre, there was a big oval table and, above it, an enormous projector hung from the ceiling.

A woman and two older men sat on the other side of the table, involved in a serious discussion as Swedberg came in and introduced his newly arrived guests.

Swedberg opened the meeting by turning down the artificial sunlight and starting the projector. After a few seconds, an image appeared on the big screen. It resembled bubbles of different sizes, encased in a larger bubble that looked like a transparent melon. Around the melon, there were lots of objects that looked like small seeds. Walter, who thought the image looked comical, wondered if they were looking at genetically modified fruit. Judging by the looks of the others, he decided that this was not the case.

A small, elderly and thin-haired man with a beard, who introduced himself as a professor of genetics, stood up and went up to the screen. He bent nimbly down and picked up a wooden pointer that stood resting against the wall.

"This is a brain cell, also called a neuron," he began, and pointed at one of the smaller bubbles. "A mature human brain is composed of approximately one hundred billion neurons. This specific brain cell is from a dead fifteen-year-old girl called Malin Sjöstrand."

Walter bit his cheek, regretting his premature amusement. Jonna looked at Walter and nodded in agreement, as if she had heard what he had thought. The professor continued. "As you can see, the neuron has been encased by a large nerve cell, known as a carrier. The carrier is, in this case, a synthesis – that is, a fake version of a normal nerve cell. What is remarkable about this synthesis is that it seems to control the real neuron's synapse – in other words, the area where two nerve cells meet to exchange signals. As we understand it, the synthesis is derived from a very advanced component of an agent. The agent is, in this case, part of a compound that we found traces of in the girl's body." He paused.

"If we can isolate the carrier and figure out which mechanisms it is controlled by, we will know how and why they react in the brain and especially which functions they control, even though we're pretty certain which ones they are. Are we clear so far?" He turned towards his visitors.

Walter mumbled an acknowledgment even if Lilja looked as if he had not understood a single word.

The professor continued. "If this is a new illegal substance that we have found in Malin Sjöstrand's body, it would be the most sophisticated to date. Its form greatly resembles adaptive medicines. But we can eliminate that since they are not on the market yet."

"Adaptive medicines?" Walter asked.

"Have you heard about adaptive medicines?"

Jonna nodded while Walter and Lilja shook their heads.

"Let me explain," the professor said. "You could compare it to an intelligent or, if you like, smart medicine. It adapts to the specific scale of damage or infection in the body of each patient and acts with the necessary strength to eliminate the disease in the patient." He paused for breath. "You could say that the adaptive substance first finds out what the body needs and then responds by making the body produce its own, shall we say, counter-measures, in the correct dose and in the correct form."

"However," he said, holding up a warning finger, "it will be five to ten years from today before the first substances are available on the market in the form of pharmaceuticals."

"Obviously not," Walter interrupted the professor.

"It would have required vast resources to have developed this compound," the professor continued as if he had not heard Walter. "The technology behind this can only come from one of the biggest pharmaceutical corporations or from a governmental organization. We suspect that it stimulates one function and inhibits another function in the brain."

"Which functions?" Jonna asked curiously.

The professor looked at the young woman for a brief moment. "One function stops the production of the transmitter substance GABA in an area of the brain called the amygdala.

The amygdala is the brain's centre of fear and rage. GABA simply blocks aggression in human beings. The second function of the substance may even damage the amygdala; we can see a type of scar in certain areas that indicates that. We don't think the girl had these scars before she had the compound in her body. Low or no levels of GABA, together with a damaged amygdala, would lead to the brain being overrun with aggression."

"Why don't you think that she had the injury earlier?" Jonna asked.

"Such a scar in the tissue would have been noticeable much earlier," the professor said.

"In what way?" Jonna continued to question and noticed that both Walter and Lilja had fixed their eyes on her.

"She would have been a very aggressive person even without the compound's effect. However, nowhere near as much as she must have been under the influence of this combination."

"How do we know she wasn't that? Aggressive, I mean," Jonna said and looked from Walter to Lilja and back again.

"We don't know," Walter answered. "But we should be able to find that out by examining Malin's life history."

He sank back into his chair with a worried frown.

Jonna would have given a lot to find out what thoughts were circling in Walter's head right now.

"In any case," the professor said, "it looks as if the compound had been injected into the girl's left upper arm, which is where we have identified two needle holes. We believe the second comes from a small morphine injection."

"We even found traces of marijuana that was inhaled into the lungs," the professor finished, and got a reassuring nod from Swedberg and the other two.

The room fell silent and Walter looked at Jonna and Lilja, who stared, fascinated, at the image of the bubbles.

"How long can traces of the compound remain in the body?" he asked.

"We don't know that," answered the female researcher who had been sitting silently until now.

The professor fidgeted a little. "We will need to seek outside assistance to continue. This is beyond what we can research here at SKL with forensic science."

"How the hell does a fifteen-year-old girl get hold of this advanced drug and for what purpose?" Walter exclaimed and looked at Swedberg on the other side of the table. "This is no ordinary speed dope, if you know what I mean. It appears to turn a person into a walking battletank."

Swedberg shrugged his shoulders resignedly, without saying anything.

"We have to investigate the girl to see how she got hold of the drug," Lilja said.

"You said it, yes," Walter muttered.

"Her relatives and family. In short, her entire life," Jonna enthusiastically added.

Walter groaned at the statement of the obvious.

Lilja looked troubled and had a hard time taking his eyes off the projector screen. After getting some more details about the compound, which left Walter and Lilja none the wiser because of their limited knowledge of chemistry, they agreed to start the investigation into Malin Sjöstrand as quickly as possible.

Just as they were getting up and leaving the room, Walter started having difficulty breathing. He gasped for air. It was as if his lungs suddenly refused to absorb oxygen from the air. The room became suffocating and plunged into a fuzzy fog. He heard voices calling while everything in his head started spinning. Suddenly, his vision went black.

"Hello! How are you feeling?" Lilja asked, bending over Walter.

Walter opened his eyes and looked around. Jonna crouched by him with a worried expression and held his head clear of the floor.

"How did I get here?" Walter moaned.

"Well, I don't know that," Lilja said. "But you fell from the chair. Did you trip when standing up?"

"Not a clue," Walter answered and struggled up from the floor with Jonna's help. "Some sort of blackout," Walter muttered to himself.

"You need to work on your suntan," Swedberg commented.

Walter sat down and caught his breath. He took a cough drop from his pocket and wiped the sweat from his brow.

"We must go to the hospital with you," Jonna said. "You look as if you are very ill."

"Yes, you can't sit here pale-faced," Lilja said. He took Walter's arm.

"Hold your horses," Walter protested. "Nobody here's going to any hospital. I've just not been eating very well recently. Just need to get some food in me, that's all." Walter freed himself from Lilja's grip.

Lilja and Jonna looked anxiously at Walter, who swayed like a newborn foal as he stood up.

"Shall we go?" Walter suggested and went towards the door. He still felt slightly dizzy, but it would probably pass if only he could get some food down.

Swedberg shook his head. "The Superman speaks," he remarked, gloomily.

JÖRGEN BLAD HAD managed to get hold of most of the residents on the staircase. Märta Ekblom was the one who had been most voluble, despite the fact that she was still shocked. Jörgen had been told everything that was worth knowing about the Sjöstrand family. But the most important information had come from another source. He had wanted to publicize the murder of Malin Sjöstrand on the front page. There was a lot of newsworthiness in the girl who had died, most probably by the hand of her mother. That the mother was also a lay juror in the district court and a public official was of such interest that Jörgen thought it would make a huge story. This was no simple murder in the estates between rival immigrant gangs. This was a brutal family killing in the heart of a typical Swedish suburb, a suburb that had got out of control. He estimated that he had about five hours' head start over the other newspapers.

He had been given access to read the interrogation file, as well as the comments that the leading interrogator had made. He had twenty minutes face to face with his informant, who was nervously looking about him. Jörgen also noted smugly that it was Walter Gröhn who was leading the investigation and the interview. If only he knew what I am holding in my hands now, Jörgen thought to himself. This was not just a great exclusive. It would even be payback to Walter for their previous dispute, which had caused Jörgen a great deal of trouble and almost lost him his job.

Jörgen gave the documents back to his invaluable informant and left the café.

THE NEWS EDITOR and his future father-in-law, Sven-Erik Dahlin, refused to allow Jörgen's article to go to print. It described the mother as a cold-blooded murderer. Sven-Erik could not publish it because of certain ethical principles. This decision made Jörgen furious. Sven-Erik actually doubted the probability that the girl had been murdered and that it was at the hands of her mother. That the mother was also a lay juror at the district court, as well as a special adviser for the county council administration, did not help the argument. Sven-Erik demanded confirmation from two independent sources, which Jörgen was unable to produce in a trustworthy way.

Now that he finally had a really good story in the making, he was being totally sandbagged. Even though he asked his boyfriend Sebastian to try, by any and all means, to persuade his father, it was like trying to teach an elephant to ballet-dance. Jörgen's copy was edited down to a news item in which no mention of the cause of death or the mother's background was included. After a stormy discussion with Sven-Erik, who reiterated his position for the last time, Jörgen decided to take the rest of the day off. They would eventually see that he was right. When the information from the police and the Prosecutor's Office became public knowledge, Jörgen would emerge as the victor, even though it would be too late.

For the first time, he had felt remorse. In some strange way, the girl had etched herself in his memory. She had spoken to him and said that he was no better than those he was punishing. So many innocents had to be sacrificed to satisfy his grief. But it was not he who had lit the fire. A blind system with an excessive tolerance towards the guilty had forced him to retaliate – not just to mitigate his own loss, but also to prevent more of the same madness. What he did was just and it was not only his obligation, but also his right, to finish what he had started. Never again would history repeat itself.

He blocked out the girl's voice.

Cecilia was back with him now. Her soft scent filled him with resolve.

IT WAS NINE-THIRTY on Saturday morning when District Prosecutor Lennart Ekwall called the police. He sat listlessly in the wicker chair in front of the open fireplace, with the bent golf club resting between his knees. The massive head of the iron club was discoloured with blood.

His wife lay on the large sheepskin rug in the adjacent room. Her face was colourless and her light-blue eyes stared emptily at the ceiling. Her long, dark-red hair was loose and one of her arms was folded under her body. A broken glass lay a small distance from her unmoving body and the smell of sweet wine dominated the room. From a split in her forehead, blood had mixed with greyish brain matter. The rug, which had been white, was now a reddish-grey.

Ekwall got up from the chair and, dragging his feet, went up to the first floor. Tiredly, he removed his jeans and polo shirt in order to dress more appropriately. From the wardrobe, he selected light beige, smart trousers, a tweed jacket and a dark polo sweater, which he laid out on the bed. It would match the khaki yacht shoes that he had never used. He got dressed and inspected himself in the large wardrobe mirror before he went down to the hall to await the police.

WALTER AWOKE IN a bad mood. A big meeting with the National Security Service, known as SÄPO, was not a common occurrence on a Saturday morning. Presumably, it had something to do with the discovery at SKL. Lilja had woken him up with a telephone call. It was getting to be a bad habit. He informed Walter that SÄPO wanted to get in on the act regarding Karin Sjöstrand. It was anything but good news, Walter thought, as he walked along Sankt Eriksgatan towards the police station. Someone at SÄPO obviously had a light workload.

The National Security Service had the top floor on the east wing, so Walter chose the east entrance instead of the one he usually used. After the customary procedures at SÄPO involving visitor badges, security clearance and security escorts, he was led to the designated room. The guard knocked on the door while moving to one side for Walter to enter. To his surprise, Walter saw the room was full of people. It was as packed as a Bruce Springsteen concert. At least fifteen people sat around a large conference table, and more stood lining the walls. At a whiteboard, County Police Commissioner Folke Uddestad stood and brandished a pointer.

All eyes turned towards Walter as he apologized for being slightly late. To his side stood a suited man who was either a model for some clothing brand or an agent from SÄPO. The difference was minimal. Walter greeted the suit with a nod and the man returned the greeting with a wink.

"Don't overdo it," Walter muttered.

On the whiteboard, someone had drawn squares that were linked to each other with lines. In each square, there were two letters that probably were acronyms for different names. Walter's eyes wandered over the gathering and he concluded that most of the faces were unknown to him. He noticed Lilja looking at him with a morose expression and that his trainee Jonna was sitting at Lilja's side and was also anxious to get Walter's attention. Unlike Lilja, she was at least smiling slightly at Walter.

Walter did not return the smile. Instead, he gently winked, not knowing if that was any better.

"Right then, the last person has finally arrived," Folke Uddestad said, looking at the big clock above Walter's head.

"My apologies for being five minutes late," Walter reiterated. "There was wind resistance on the way here."

A low chuckle broke out in the room.

Uddestad cleared his throat. "The reason we are all here is that the Prosecutor's Office and SÄPO have decided to take over the investigation into the presumed new drug. We can, for simplicity's sake, call it Drug-X. The reason that SÄPO is taking over the investigation from County CID is that there is a possibility that a foreign power is in some way involved. It could also be the case that certain terrorist groups in the country, either with backing or of their own volition, have gained access to this sophisticated compound. Why a fifteen-year-old had Drug-X in her body is, as we know, unclear. But SÄPO has concluded that the ulterior motive is more complex than is apparent from an initial analysis. According to SKL, they need a number of weeks with their finest experts, as well as outside help, to create a clear profile of the substance. Any questions so far?" Uddestad asked and looked around the room.

It was deathly quiet in the room.

The Commissioner continued. "Until we have an answer from SKL, we are shooting in the dark with regards to Drug-X. In any event, SÄPO has divided the investigation team as follows." Uddestad pointed to a suit, who appeared to be a boss at SÄPO. "The team at SÄPO will shake down potential terrorist cells to extract some form of information. The Drug Squad will work in their area to find a probable supply chain for Drug-X. They'll focus their search on the dealers and addicts. The Drug Squad will also be working with the Customs Intelligence section. RSU will support SÄPO with a handful of analysts, who will scan the internet for information."

Uddestad finished by asking if anyone had questions about the briefing. Nobody had any further questions. The Commissioner was just about to close the meeting when Walter coughed.

"Well, how shall we handle the media?" he asked. "This is going to start to leak as soon as we leave the room."

Walter was met by a lot of surprised faces. Uddestad nodded in agreement and explained that the official press spokesman from SÄPO would from now on handle all contacts with the media, in conjunction with Chief Prosecutor Åsa Julén. As a result of SÄPO taking over the investigation, the risk of leaks would also decrease. This applied even to people from the regular police forces currently working on the investigation, because they would be subject to SÄPO's security restrictions and lose the immunity from prosecution given to them by the Free Press legislation. It would therefore be possible to pursue any police informers, which should make any potential whistleblowers stay as quiet as mice.

"A LENNART EKWALL has called in and confessed to beating his wife to death," Lilja said, walking into Walter's office. "He's sitting in the holding cells and, since you're on call this weekend, I suggest you take your trainee to Djursholm and the murder scene before you interrogate him."

Walter looked puzzledly at Lilja. "But she's surely going to go and play with SÄPO and Drug-Y, or was it Z?"

"Yes, she will do. But since Jonsson and Cederberg are on loan, I've borrowed her for the team. In any case, she was the only one available who could come at such short notice," Lilja said.

"I don't need a part-timer as an assistant," Walter explained. "Either ..."

"She is working with you from now on," Lilja declared. "Make sure she is coming with you to Djursholm. Forensics is already there."

AS SOON AS Lilja left the room, Walter reluctantly picked up the telephone.

"Lennart Ekwall apparently finished off his significant other at home in Djursholm and, since I'm stuck with you again, it would be appropriate for you to accompany me there," Walter began as soon as Jonna answered her mobile phone.

"Yes, that's right," Jonna said. "I'll be working with you, but it's Saturday and I was on my way home after our meeting ..."

"You're on stand-by from now on, so you can forget whatever plans you've made," Walter interrupted. "Are you still in the building?"

"Yes."

"Do you have the crotch rocket with you?"

"What's a crotch rocket?"

"The Porsche."

"No, I left it at home."

"You did the right thing. Sign out a vehicle, and I'll meet you at the east entrance," Walter said and hung up the phone.

Just at that moment, Walter felt all the energy run out of him. He was tired of this environment and all these people. Maybe Lilja was right, at least when he had said that it was possibly time for Walter to throw in the towel. Three decades perhaps was enough. For each murder that Walter investigated, he felt an increasing indifference. So why not take an early retirement? He could take the boat out during the summer. But the rest of the time? Work, in fact, constituted the largest part of his miserable, workaholic life – a life with no other real purpose than putting the dregs of humanity behind bars.

He could perhaps become a consultant. Work as little as he pleased. Some discarded investigators could occasionally be called in after retirement as experts in certain activities, and bill a thousand crowns an hour just to state the obvious to up-and-coming bright sparks in police headquarters. That did not appeal to him at all. Walter tried to shake off his mood. As usual, it was pointless to bury himself in thoughts about the future. Jonna looked at Walter with a faint smile as he got into the car.

"Is everything okay?" she asked, almost as if she meant it. At the same time, she let out the clutch of the unmarked police car.

Walter returned her smile. "No, not really. But one has to make it through the day. The best way to succeed in life is to always keep on your toes. Preferably on other people's toes. And I consider myself to be quite good at that."

Jonna laughed and Walter noticed for the first time that she had dimples – like Martine.

"Or to strike while the corpse is still warm," she retorted and turned onto Fleminggatan.

Walter chuckled. She almost had a sense of humour.

"You have reached your destination," the car's sat-nav proclaimed as Jonna drove towards the address from which Lennart Ekwall had called the police. The white-rendered, minimalist, detached house stood in one of Stockholm's most affluent suburbs, with a view over the Stora Värtan river estuary. Large glass panels and straight lines characterized the three-hundred-square-metre, two-storey house. An over-sized balcony framed the house from corner to corner. Jonna parked the car on the gravelled driveway directly outside the entrance. Walter found it amusing that she positioned the car so that it obstructed both incoming and outgoing access for bulky equipment. If nothing else, she was making a reputation with Forensics.

A uniformed officer stood outside the front door and Jonna showed her ID. After completing the routine procedure of donning nylon overalls and face masks, Jonna was ready to enter the house. She waited impatiently for Walter and watched with annoyance as he searched for his cough drops, which seemed to have hidden themselves in some pocket under his overalls.

The first sight that met them as they entered the house was a big hall with a cathedral-like ceiling. Different types of decoration adorned the edges of the ceiling. Some of the hall furniture was in Rococo style, which did not fit in well with the functional design of the house façade.

Looks as if a nouveau-riche Russian oligarch or a blind person lives here, Walter thought as he looked around the hall.

Jonna stopped by a golf club that lay by the side of a wicker chair a bit farther down the hallway. On the side of the golf club, there was a small label with the number "2", which Forensics had placed there. Jonna crouched down and studied the golf club without touching it.

"This one is quite bent," she said and looked up at Walter, who was standing by her side.

Walter said nothing, just nodded, and went farther into what looked like the living room. A big, dark green, U-shaped, English-style leather sofa surrounded a solid-oak table. On the walls hung modern surrealist art in loud colours by artists he had never heard of. His eyes wandered over the objects in the room. Suddenly, he saw something familiar. Troubled, he approached a shelf on the far side of the room and picked up the object. There was no mistaking it. He gazed at the winged skeleton and then took out his mobile phone and dialled a number from memory.

After completing a brief telephone conversation, he continued towards what resembled a dining room. A long, pinewood, dining-room table dominated the cold, white-painted room.

Forensics had rigged up lighting around a body that lay on the floor by the side of the table.

"And here we have Mrs Ekwall," Walter deduced, standing next to the dead woman with his hands in his trouser pockets.

Stig Jonsered from Forensics stood up. He had been sitting on his knees by the body with a UV scanner, searching the floor for traces of blood.

"See here, Walter," Jonsered began, "a woman, fifty plus. Cause of death: a blow to the temple. Murder weapon: probably the golf club that's placed in the hallway. She's been dead for about six hours."

Walter bent over the dead woman and looked at her cracked skull.

"That's a hole in one for Lennart Ekwall," Walter said, at the same time Jonna came into the room.

"A hole in what?" Jonna asked, interested, and then looked at the dead woman. Her lightly tanned face changed suddenly when she became aware of the mess that had leaked from the head. Walter was also kind enough to explain in detail what she was looking at. Suddenly, Jonna rushed out of the room. Through the window, both Walter and Jonsered could see Jonna stand with her hands against the outside wall and violently throw up the contents of her stomach.

They looked at each other and smiled with pure *Schadenfreude*.

Walter proceeded to the top floor where he systematically went through table drawers and cupboards, hunting for objects or clues that could be of interest to the investigation. He noticed an extreme level of tidiness associated with all of the man's things. In particular, the menswear and toiletries were precisely sorted according to method of use. The men's clothes were immaculately ironed and placed on hangers, whereas the shirts were sorted by colour. The suits were also colour-coded, starting with light suits to the left and dark suits to the right. Even the underwear was folded and neatly sorted according to the colour system.

Ties were hung according to width and shoes according to season, with winter shoes farthest in.

There were two bathroom cabinets. One was neat and clean, like a laboratory. After-shave, deodorant and toothbrushes were lined up with military precision. In the other, there was make-up and perfume, all in disarray, and Walter noticed smears of mascara on the cabinet shelves and traces of sticky fingerprints.

Walter heard steps on the stairs and saw Jonna on her way up the beautiful pinewood staircase. She had pulled herself together and most of the colour had returned to her face.

"You must be hungry after turning your stomach inside out," Walter said.

"Have you found anything?" she answered tersely and looked around.

Walter could not help but be amused by Jonna's self-confident demeanour. She obviously had thick skin and there was something about the rock-hard exterior she adopted that appealed to him. And it was not because he felt sorry for her coming from an upper-class family. She needed to prove something. Whether it was to herself or to others was of little importance.

"Messy wife and pedantic husband, to summarize the impressions so far," Walter said and opened a wardrobe door.

"The odds must be one in ten thousand," Jonna replied.

"That the wife is messy?"

"Yes."

"Maybe so. But does it tell us anything?"

"What do you mean?"

"It suggests that he was very neat."

"Well," Jonna said, looking at Walter suspiciously, "either he must be a perfectionist or his wife tidied up for him."

"Maybe so," Walter said. "But if it was the dead woman down there who took care of his possessions, then she would have taken as much care of her own."

Walter showed Jonna the unironed women's clothes.

"Maybe he forced her to," Jonna suggested.

"Very possibly," Walter said. "But wouldn't she also have arranged her own personal things in a similar fashion?"

Jonna pondered for a few seconds. "Maybe that's why he killed her," she said and continued, "perhaps she finally refused."

"Carry on," Walter said, interested.

"Let's assume she was messy by nature," Jonna said. "Finally, she got fed up of taking care of his things. She defied him and Lennart Ekwall lost his temper. He beat her to death because she quite simply refused to continue to clean his clothes. What contradicts such a theory is that he was most definitely not a moron – at least, not if one looks at where he lives and what this house must cost."

"Wife-beaters can be found in all social classes," Walter pointed out.

Jonna looked at Walter pensively. There was somewhat of a discrepancy between his questions and the answers she was giving. He was testing her.

"There could be another explanation too," she suggested.

"Let's hear it."

"Suppose that his wife had some sort of problem. Maybe mental illness or even a drinking problem, considering the wine glass that lay by the body and the time of the murder. It's not quite normal to start the morning off with wine, unless there was a party that lasted all night, which there were no signs of downstairs."

"Intriguing. Tell me more," Walter said.

Jonna bit her lip. "He was a perfectionist. She was an alcoholic. There's the connection."

Walter gestured for her to continue.

"He couldn't tolerate her drinking and making a mess because it disturbed his existence. Many perfectionists have a problem with that."

"I would also be disturbed," Walter objected. "And I'm definitely not a perfectionist. But let's assume a perfectionist has a lower tolerance level."

"In any case, finally, he could take no more and killed her," Jonna said.

"Why hadn't he done it earlier?" Walter wondered. "They have certainly been together for a while."

"Maybe she gradually became an alcoholic at the same rate that he became more pedantic. Eventually, everything culminated in some form of shouting match that ended in death – a vicious circle."

"Do you really believe that yourself?" Walter asked sceptically.

Jonna hesitated at first. Did she believe it? Did it sound like a possible and plausible explanation of why Ekwall had murdered his own wife?

"I really do think that it could have happened like that," Jonna answered in a confident voice. "But we will be finding that out during the interrogation."

"Yes, we will," Walter said and bent down under the bed. It was clean except for a pair of slippers – not even a ball of dust. For his own part, he had stopped looking under his own bed. The number of dust balls that constantly multiplied there made him depressed. It was about time to fix the vacuum cleaner before he suffocated from all the bed mites.

Walter stood up quickly, but suddenly lost his balance. The room started to rock and he was forced to steady himself against the bed. He sat down heavily on the edge of the bed and felt overcome by a cold sweat. His sense of hearing disappeared and the room became blurred.

"Why are you lying on the bed?" he heard Jonna say from the doorway.

Walter opened his eyes. For a brief moment, he did not know where he was or how long he had lain on the bed. The house, Djursholm, Jonna, the floor upstairs. …

He sat up on the edge of the bed. The dizziness had ceased and he could see clearly again.

"I don't know," he answered curtly.

Jonna looked at Walter disbelievingly. "Doesn't this remind you of what happened when we were at SKL …"

"Have you found anything else?" Walter cut her off.

Jonna gave up and shook her head. "I have to show you something."

Walter mumbled something in reply and forced himself to stand up. He swayed, but regained his balance while trying to appear unaffected. Jonna looked at Walter apprehensively as he walked across the room. Now it was his turn to be pale-faced. Again.

"What did you want to show me?" Walter asked.

"In here," she answered and gestured for him to follow her into a small office. She pulled out a desk drawer and showed him a wallet with business cards. Walter opened the zipper of his nylon overalls and fumbled for his glasses from the inner pocket of his well-worn leather jacket.

With his improved vision, he noted the text on the business card. He flipped eagerly through more cards in the holder. They were all identical. Walter put the wallet down and sat down heavily in the office chair that stood next to the desk.

"Well, I'll be damned," he said and looked at Jonna.

Walter took out his mobile phone and punched in Lilja's number.

"Do you have a moment?" Walter asked as soon as Lilja picked it up.

Lilja was on his way home from the police station and had answered in the car.

"No, not unless it is important."

"How about a golfing district prosecutor who has bashed in his wife's skull?" Walter started.

It was quiet at the other end.

"What the hell are you talking about? Are you at Djursholm now?" Lilja asked, irritated, after a few seconds. He was not in the mood for twenty questions with Walter now.

"Yes, we have a district prosecutor who took a swing at his wife's head," Walter repeated.

Once again, there was silence on the phone line.

"Damn it, not again," Lilja groaned. He would be forced to make his way back to the police station to do the paperwork and to inform SÄPO, the County Police Commissioner and God knows who else. No weekly shopping at Co-op or evening cuddles on the sofa today either. It was going to be a long Saturday.

"What shall we do now?" Walter asked, excessively sympathetic when he heard Lilja's exasperation on the other end.

"Finish off the initial crime scene investigation and then come in and interrogate him as we agreed," Lilja muttered. "I will contact SÄPO."

Jonna went down to the kitchen and looked around. She entered a world full of state-of-the-art kitchen appliances: built-in espresso machine; soda stream and ice-maker; heavy, supersized fridge and freezer with built-in LCD screens in the doors. Despite all this, the kitchen looked almost unused. She did not really know what she was looking for, but she systematically went through every space and object. Even the gift packaging for a wine bottle was of the highest quality. "To Lisbeth Ekwall from an admirer," she read, in stamped aluminium, on the beautiful, cylindrical gift container. It was not only the container that was exclusive. The wine bottle that stood beside it and that had been emptied was no less than a Montrachet 2004.

A French wine at about ten thousand crowns per bottle. That's not bad at all, Jonna thought. Lisbeth obviously had an admirer who was both a wine connoisseur and wealthy. It must be the wine that she had been drinking before she received the lethal blow. Forensics would surely be able to confirm that.

Just as Walter came into the kitchen, his mobile phone rang.

"Is she absolutely certain?" Walter asked.

Jonna heard a voice confirm Walter's question.

"What was that about?" Jonna asked curiously, as Walter finished the short and unintelligible conversation.

Walter clumsily extricated a cough drop from the inner pocket of his leather jacket.

"Follow me and I'll show you something," he said and went into the living room. "Do you see anything in here that seems out of the ordinary?"

"Everything," Jonna replied straightaway. "But especially the artwork if I have to choose something specific."

"Aside from that."

Jonna looked at the room from the floor to the ceiling. "No, what would that be?" she said.

"A trained eye can spot it," Walter said. "Just a small detail."

Jonna walked around the room and studied the ornaments in detail. When she got to the bookshelf, she stopped.

"This one," she said and pointed to the small plaster figure. "It really looks out of place here. A little distasteful, actually."

Walter nodded, satisfied. "That's not the only reason," he said. "A similar angel was also found in Malin Sjöstrand's jacket pocket."

Jonna raised an eyebrow in surprise.

"In addition, I just got confirmation that Bror Lantz's wife found a similar figure in her kitchen on the same day that the incident with the taxi occurred."

Jonna looked at Walter, astonished. "In her kitchen? What does that mean?"

"Since she didn't buy it herself, and it didn't fly into her kitchen on its own wings, we can assume that it came to be there by some other means," Walter answered and gazed out of one of the windows.

"Bror," Jonna said.

"No, he didn't recognize the skeleton."

"Then it's someone trying to make a statement," Jonna deduced.

"Yes, unless it's a new trend to leave small angels of death at people's homes."

"Hardly. Of course, it was fashionable to have death skulls for a while, but I find it difficult to see …"

"I thought as much," Walter cut in, who was as trend-conscious as a monk in a monastery.

"The question is why did Malin Sjöstrand have one in her pocket?" Walter asked himself out loud. "She must have bought it or received it from someone or someone planted it on her. She was drugged; anyone could have easily placed it in her pocket without her knowing about it."

"But why? What are they trying to say?" Jonna threw up her hands in despair.

"Maybe nothing," Walter said. "Serial killers have a predilection for rituals of various types; they don't necessarily have a meaning in themselves. To leave this figure as a calling card could be a similar behaviour."

Jonna felt a cold shiver. "Serial killer? Do you mean that someone has drugged them all with Drug-X?"

"Anything is possible," Walter said, "but finding a motive is significantly more difficult."

"It doesn't take much to see that there's an obvious connection between these three deaths," Jonna smiled slightly.

"Yes, but I'm afraid that there will be more chapters to this story," Walter sighed.

SVEN-ERIK WAS FORCED to apologize to his future son-in-law even though it was difficult for him. Jörgen had been right about Karin Sjöstrand. The informant had been accurate and Sjöstrand was now officially charged with the manslaughter of her fifteen-year-old daughter. That she was an expert adviser and politically active in the county council administration as well as being a lay juror in Stockholm District Court made the whole story even more interesting, which contradicted Sven-Erik's earlier view of the issue. He had made a bad judgment call. The tabloids were dominated by the murder of the fifteen-year-old girl, and the mother went under the alias "lay jurywoman". The story in the daily newspapers took up several pages. Psychologists, ex-jurors and politicians now vied to surpass each other with the most outlandish analyses about the underlying factors behind the incident.

First out was *Aftonposten* in their online edition. It was five-thirty in the evening when the news bombshell exploded. The duty news editor at *Kvällspressen* called Sven-Erik at his home and informed him that he had been tipped off about a really hot news item. Sven-Erik literally coughed up his evening cocktail when he heard what *Aftonposten* had gone to print with. He immediately called Jörgen and ordered him in to the news desk so that the duty editor could go through the material that Sven-Erik had just turned down. He definitely did not want to miss anything that could trump the official version. Jörgen's source probably had more details than were included in the official press release and that would give *Kvällspressen* a small but important edge over the competition. Jörgen was asked to contact his source again.

To Jörgen's great disappointment, the informant was not contactable and could not therefore provide him with anything significantly different from the information that the other media now possessed. But he had now received his long-awaited retribution.

Finally, Jörgen would get the recognition he so well deserved at the newspaper. Now he could work like a genuine star reporter without having his cap in hand because of lack of respect. People would listen to him with entirely fresh ears from now on.

10

LILJA HAD JUST returned from his disrupted homewards journey and sat slouched behind a pile of paper when Walter and Jonna came into the office. He asked them to wait while he finished annotating one of the documents.

"I have contacted the Chief Prosecutor, Uddestad and SÄPO," Lilja began, and stood up from his chair, agitated. He went to the window and put his hands behind his back.

"Julén wants to be sure that Lennart Ekwall was not in a state of shock and therefore confessed to the murder of his wife by mistake. This is to be handled in the same fashion as the Bror Lantz case," he said and turned to face Walter.

Walter flushed.

"Explain that to me," he said.

"Not right now," Lilja answered. "By the way, did you find anything of interest at the crime scene?" He looked at Jonna.

Jonna was just about to answer yes to the question when she was interrupted by Walter's abrupt reply.

"No, we didn't find anything".

Jonna corrected herself and looked, surprised, at Walter.

Lilja stared suspiciously at the odd couple on the other side of the desk.

"Shall we interview Ekwall straightaway?" Jonna asked and felt her pulse quicken.

"Yes, it's just as well. You know the procedure," Lilja answered as he sat down heavily in the chair again. He had wanted to avoid all the messy internal politics and instead be at home with a cold beer in his hand in front of the TV. Weekend jobs were the worst he could think of, with the exception of visiting his decrepit mother-in-law, who always complained about how poorly the police protected senior citizens against today's unshaven riff-raff.

"Why didn't you want me to mention that angel of death?" Jonna asked as they walked down to the detention cells.

"Let's save that for another time," Walter answered.

"Yes, but ..."

"I thought you were assisting SÄPO with the Sjöstrand investigation full-time?" Walter cut her off harshly.

"That's what I'm doing now, more or less," Jonna said and reluctantly dropped the angel of death discussion. Walter seemed to be in a bad mood. She did not know why. "But I'm not the only one from RSU working with SÄPO, if that's what you're asking."

"How many investigations are you actually participating in?"

"Right now, it's enough with these two." Jonna laughed nervously.

"That's one too many, in my opinion," Walter declared.

"One could say that I'm not exactly setting the pace in either of them, so I do have enough time for both of them, if that's what you mean."

"No matter, this investigation will more or less be concluded after this interview," Walter said. "If Prosecutor Ekwall sticks to his confession, then the duty prosecutor either has to put together charges or look the other way and kill the investigation, as Lilja was implying. I won't swallow the latter option one more time. I'm definitely an obedient cop, but not blindly obedient."

"I wouldn't follow that order either," Jonna agreed. "The number of investigations being dropped due to lack of evidence is starting to become an epidemic – first Lantz and now maybe Ekwall."

"Bloody banana republic," Walter muttered.

"But Julén did nothing for Sjöstrand. She was charged."

"She was just an ordinary lay juror of the court and definitely not a member of their mutual appreciation society. Or maybe she has the wrong party politics," Walter smirked.

LENNART EKWALL SAT behind a table in one of the slightly larger interview rooms in the detention cell block. Jonna was first in, closely followed by Walter, who was breathing heavily after their fast pace through the corridors of police headquarters. He was quick to sit in one of the chairs and tried to catch his breath without revealing how unfit he was.

Beads of sweat broke out on his forehead and large sweat patches spread under his armpits.

Jonna looked at Walter, rather amused.

He tossed the folder labelled with a file number and the name Lennart Ekwall on the table and let it rest under his right hand so that Jonna could not take it. As he expected, she went quickly to the voice recorder and started the interview with the routine declaration of why the interview was taking place and who was present.

This time, Walter had not given her any rules of conduct for the interview, which was why the ever-ambitious Ms de Brugge was eager to start. Ekwall had already admitted to the murder of his wife so, no matter what Jonna did, she could not ruin the investigation with some rookie mistake.

Jonna glanced at the folder, which, unfortunately, was out of her reach. Walter saw in her eyes that she was about to reach for it. He quickly picked it up and started browsing through the pages slowly, humming to himself. Discreetly, she leaned in a little to get a glimpse of the contents, but Walter closed the folder.

"So, Lennart Ekwall, you don't want a lawyer," began Walter as he observed the dapper man opposite him. Walter had the folder at a safe distance from a now slightly irritated Jonna.

The man was sitting motionless and did not acknowledge with a single movement that he had heard what Walter said. He had a stylish haircut and his face emanated dignity, but it was as stiff as if it were hewn out of stone. Not even the eyelids over his steel-grey eyes seemed to move.

The man looks like a mannequin, thought Walter and looked at Jonna, who was seething with irritation. She probably wanted to tear the file from Walter's hand. He drummed his fingers lightly on the folder before he opened it again.

"From what I can read in the police officer's report, you have admitted to the police officers who were first on the spot that you took the life of your wife, Lisbeth Ekwall, by hitting her head with a blunt instrument." Walter took a break while he pulled out his reading glasses from his breast pocket. "The instrument in question was an iron golf club, which has been placed in the hall. Is that statement correct?" Walter looked up from the folder.

"That statement is correct," confirmed Ekwall dryly, his lips barely moving.

Walter now thought that he resembled a ventriloquist's dummy or a bronze statue more than a mannequin.

"Excellent, then we can move on," continued Walter. "You're apparently a district prosecutor by profession. It's not stated in the preliminary data I have in this file, but is it accurate?"

"Yes, the detective has got that fact right as well," said Ekwall.

Jonna could not be quiet anymore. She fidgeted as she listened to Walter leisurely continuing the interview. They would be sitting here for hours at this rate. She jumped in before Walter could ask the next question.

"Why did you kill your wife?"

Walter turned to Jonna. "We'll get to that later," he said in a calm voice and was about to continue the interview when the bronze statue cleared his throat.

"I will relate the sequence of events to the Detective Inspector and his assistant, if it's of any interest," he suggested and looked from Jonna to Walter.

"Please do," said Jonna before Walter had time to react. He shot Jonna an annoyed glance.

"I usually get up early in the morning, as I did this morning," began the District Prosecutor. "To be more precise, six-thirty. I found my wife lying on the sofa, passed out due to alcohol. The previous evening, she had drunk herself into a stupor, as usual. She is, in fact, an alcoholic."

Walter nodded in agreement, as if he too had an alcoholic wife with all the problems that implied.

"I tried to eat breakfast at seven o'clock before I went out for my usual jog. It takes about thirty minutes and I run along the beach promenade below the house."

"Tried to eat breakfast?" Walter cut him off curiously.

"Yes, it had a bad taste. It was as if all the food had been spoiled."

Walter looked thoughtfully at the bronze statue.

"Carry on," he said, with a wave of his hand.

"When I came home, Lisbeth had woken up and was about to have a breakfast of wine. As usual, I didn't take any notice of her when she was in that mood and, instead, I went upstairs and took a short sauna and then a shower. After I went downstairs to make some coffee, I found an opened wine bottle standing on the kitchen counter next to a parcel from an unnamed sender."

"An admirer perhaps?" suggested Jonna.

Walter motioned to Ekwall to continue.

"In less than one hour, my wife had made herself drunk again by draining the entire bottle. A strange feeling of anger came over me. Usually, I would have just shrugged my shoulders, but this time I felt a real rage within me."

"Anger against your wife?" Walter wondered.

"Yes and no."

"How so?" Jonna asked.

"Well, I was really angry at everything around me – but especially at Lisbeth. I was seething with rage and I'd had enough of her drinking." Ekwall paused and shifted his body for the first time.

"Carry on," Walter said impatiently.

Ekwall drank some water from the glass in front of him. "Suddenly, it was as if I didn't have control over myself anymore. I had a terrible pain in my head that only seemed to dissipate as I yielded to the rage."

"Did you hear voices as well?" Jonna interrupted.

Ekwall looked at Jonna for a moment. "The pain in my head was so excruciating that I must have been hallucinating the voices. But to answer your question, yes."

Jonna nodded and asked him to continue.

"In a furious rage, I went out to the hall and took out a club from my golf bag. I had always intended to use a golf club in self-defence if any burglar got the idea to break in when we were at home."

"The 4-iron was apparently good for the job," said Walter.

"Yes, precisely, the 4-club," continued Ekwall. "With it in my hands and, may I say, in a blind rage, I went into the dining room where I found my wife standing with her back to me. She seemed to be drinking the last of the wine she'd been given as a gift from an unknown admirer."

"Admirer?" Walter said curiously.

"Yes," said Jonna. "And the wine was not just any everyday wine."

"No?" Walter looked even more bemused.

"It was a vintage Montrachet 2004," she said.

"I've never heard of it," Walter replied casually.

"Maybe that's because it's not available as a bag-in-a-box wine," suggested Jonna, equally casually.

Walter glared irritably at his trainee.

"In fact, that wine costs ten thousand crowns a bottle," Jonna informed him.

"Please continue," asked Walter, casting a sour look at Jonna.

"I gripped the golf club with both hands and took aim at her head," Ekwall continued and demonstrated with his hands. "I swung my hips a little more so that the swing would be powerful."

"Yes, you certainly succeeded quite well with both hips and swing," said Walter dryly.

"The club hit her head on the first swing. The rest is history," Ekwall concluded.

There was silence in the interview room.

Walter glanced over at Jonna who was sitting, seemingly absorbed in thought. Maybe she was thinking of some more witticisms.

"It would seem to have happened that way," Ekwall finally added and leaned back in his chair. He fixed his eyes on the floor.

"What do you mean by that?" Walter asked.

"For the simple reason that I remember nothing."

"What do you mean, don't remember?" Walter said in a stern voice. "You've just told us what happened."

Ekwall shook his head in rebuttal. "After breakfast, I took a jog as I just described. During the time I ran, I began to feel contempt towards Lisbeth and her drinking, something I had never felt before. I have always been understanding and I felt sorry for her. I tried in every possible way to get her to stop the behaviour that was destructive to herself and those around her, but she always fell back into drinking. I don't remember much more except that I had thought about who had sent the exclusive wine to Lisbeth and if she really had some secret admirer, which I strongly doubted, given the condition she was in. At the end of the jog, it was as if I was in a daze. The anger that had grown within me must have peaked after the shower. I felt that headache and just needed to get the rage out of my body. After that, it all went hazy. When I came to my senses again, I found Lisbeth lifeless on the floor at my feet in the dining room. With the golf club in my hand and the blood coming out of her head, I realized what must have happened. At first, it struck me that it was a bad dream. But the more I recovered my senses, the more clearly I realized that it wasn't a nightmare. I called the police and told them what had happened."

"You didn't have any other option, right?" Walter said sharply.

"I can't for the life of me understand how I could do something so unforgivable and why I have no recollection of the event." He gazed down at the floor again.

"Could be due to the shock," Jonna suggested.

Walter scratched his neck and put the folder on the table so that Jonna could reach it. She seemed to have lost interest in it.

"If you think you can get away with murder by not remembering anything, then you're wrong," explained Jonna.

Walter winced and stared at Jonna, who had fixed her eyes on the prosecutor.

"Constable," Ekwall began, almost bantering. "I'm a district prosecutor and I know how the wheels turn. I don't intend to get away with anything, if that's what you think. But I can't explain my behaviour because I remember nothing of the incident itself."

"Not remembering anything seems to be this year's new trend," Walter said out loud to himself.

"Listen carefully," Ekwall demanded and fixed his dull eyes on Jonna. "I strongly recommend that you get a basic psychiatric evaluation of me to shed some light perhaps on why I was so irrational and brutal."

"We can do the full loony test too," Walter suggested.

"During my fifty years, I have never so much as touched a hair of any living creature," Ekwall continued. "My service record with the Prosecutor's Office, ever since I took a degree in law in my youth, is spotless. I'm putting myself fully and unconditionally at your disposal, and ..."

He broke off and closed his eyes.

Jonna looked at Walter, who was flicking aimlessly through the file. Further questions did not seem necessary at this time, she thought.

Walter, who seemed to have reached the same conclusion, closed the folder and gripped it firmly. "I think that may be enough for today," he finished. "This will enable Ekwall's colleagues at the Prosecutor's Office to take over from now on."

Jonna nodded in agreement.

"By the way," Walter said, as an afterthought, "where did you buy this?" He took out a photograph showing the angel of death and held it up in front of Ekwall.

"What's that?" Ekwall asked.

"Yes, we wondered that too," said Walter.

"I've never seen it before."

"Are you sure?" Walter asked.

"Completely." Ekwall said nothing more, but just stared at the image before him.

Jonna was just about to turn off the voice recorder when she stopped herself.

"One last question," she said. "Do you have any enemies? Or rather, to rephrase the question, do you know of one or more people, in or outside your profession, who would like to harm you physically or mentally?"

Walter turned to Jonna.

"What kind of a question is that?" the District Prosecutor asked.

"Yes, it may seem a strange question," Walter agreed. "But nonetheless, it requires an answer."

"It's not only police officers who are subject to threats, if that's what you believe," said Ekwall. "Even prosecutors are threatened. But if the question is whether I had any specific threat against me, the answer is no. The last time I received a threat was about two years ago. It was hurled at me by an offender who was being deported and exiled for life. As for whether I get threats outside my profession, the answer is also no. Furthermore, I don't really see where you are going with this. I'm the lawbreaker here and not the victim."

"Obviously," Jonna said.

Walter got up from his chair and put the folder under his arm. "We're finished here, I think," he said and opened the door.

Jonna nodded and turned off the voice recorder. She thanked the District Prosecutor for his willingness to co-operate and left the police officer in charge of the interview room.

"Is it still coincidence?" Jonna said, with a hint of irony in her voice, when they came out into the corridor.

"You could say that the possibility of that is decreasing rapidly," Walter said, concerned. "I wonder if there have been similar acts of violence outside the county?"

"I can find that out," said Jonna eagerly.

"Yes, do that. The question is what the link to Drug-X is in this case," Walter said.

"Yes, all the indications are that it is involved," said Jonna. "I mean, the uncontrolled anger, the inner voices and so on."

Walter nodded.

"But the motive then?" Jonna asked. "What could it be?"

"The motive, yes," repeated Walter. "Either random selection or careful planning by someone with great resources."

"So SÄPO's going to take over this case now?"

"Inevitably," said Walter. "But so far, Ekwall is still our man."

"Why did you withhold the personal file?" Jonna said, changing the subject.

"Improvisation," Walter replied cryptically.

Jonna looked at him, puzzled.

"It was to teach you something you were not taught at the police academy or by the theoreticians at RSU," Walter said.

"You mean you wanted to see how I handled myself without having the information in my hand?"

Walter smiled and nodded.

Jonna looked less than amused.

11 DAVID LILJA WAS glued to the telephone when Walter and Jonna entered his office. He waved them towards the chairs around the conference table, indicating that they should be seated. From the speakerphone, a woman's voice could be heard. Lilja explained that Walter Gröhn and Jonna de Brugge had sat down at the table. He wanted them to participate in the teleconference.

"Let's hear what they have to say," Chief Prosecutor Åsa Julén's voice rang out.

Walter nodded at Jonna to take over. As usual, he had little time for Julén.

"We've just questioned District Prosecutor Lennart Ekwall from the Stockholm Prosecutor's Office, who's therefore a colleague of yours," Jonna began.

"I know who he is," Julén pointed out. "Carry on."

"He has confessed to killing his wife. We already have a signed statement and everything we need. He has also requested that we perform a basic psychiatric evaluation, since he has no idea why he became violent."

"Good God!" Julén exclaimed.

"He beat his wife to death with a golf club," Jonna added.

The telephone line fell silent.

Lilja stared down at the table resignedly.

"The modus operandi seems to indicate that Drug-X is involved," Jonna continued. "So Ekwall should be tested for the drug as quickly as possible."

They heard a sharp intake of breath down the phone line. "Transfer Ekwall to SÄPO immediately," Julén ordered. "We will have to include Lantz, Sjöstrand and Ekwall in the same investigation."

"Absolutely," Lilja said. "I'll take care of it straightaway."

"From now on, this is to be kept under wraps," Julén clarified. "I don't want to see so much as a syllable about this in the media. Is that understood?"

"There'll be no leaks from those of us at the CID at any rate," Lilja promised. Chief Prosecutor Julén did not sound completely convinced as she ended the conference call.

"I would like to know if there are any more concrete connections between Bror Lantz, Karin Sjöstrand and Lennart Ekwall other than that plaster figure," Walter said, pressing the lift button. "Something more than the fact that they moved in the same judicial circles and therefore ought to have known each other quite well. We also need to find out where the death angels can be purchased. They're hardly off-the-shelf items from the corner gift shop."

"Definitely not. But who drugged them and for what purpose?" Jonna interjected.

"Quite right," Walter smiled. "Motive. Can you see any other lead that might be of interest?"

Jonna looked pensively at Walter for a brief moment.

"Apart from the angel of death, there's the food."

"What about it?"

"If all these people were drugged, it had to have been administered in some way."

"Carry on," Walter said.

"Both Ekwall and Sjöstrand complained that what they ate and drank the day they committed the crimes tasted bad."

"Precisely," Walter said. "The only thing that did not taste strange, according to Sjöstrand, was the tap water."

"Then it follows that Forensics should find traces of Drug-X in the food from the homes of Ekwall and Sjöstrand," Jonna said.

"Very probably," Walter said.

"But what about Lantz?" Jonna wondered.

"Whoever drugged Bror Lantz must have been on the train from Gothenburg. And it seems likely that it happened on the train. If we ask Judge Lantz nicely, maybe he can tell us if something on the train had an odd taste."

Jonna nodded. "There should be traces of the drug in both Ekwall and Sjöstrand, similar to the traces in Lantz," she said. "But why was the drug found in Malin Sjöstrand?"

Walter nodded. "That's where the chain of logic is a bit weak. If it's found in Lisbeth Ekwall and the taxi driver, it becomes more consistent," Walter said. "I can't see the link to the last person."

"No, because the taxi driver and Lantz didn't know each other," Jonna said.

Walter scratched his head thoughtfully. "Wasn't the train from Gothenburg to Stockholm late?"

"Yes, I believe that it was," Jonna hesitated.

"How late was it?"

"A little over an hour, if I remember correctly," she said.

"It probably takes a certain amount of time for the drug to take effect from the time it enters the body," Walter said. "The question is how much time."

"You mean that the taxi driver was an unfortunate by-stander. That Lantz was drugged, but that the train got delayed and therefore he didn't make it home to his wife?"

"Exactly," Walter said. "The objective was that he would kill his wife, but he didn't get home on time. Instead, he strangled the taxi driver."

Jonna suddenly looked horrified. "What type of sick drug

is this anyway and who's behind it? Imagine if they poisoned the water supply."

"That thought also occurred to me," Walter said. "But there's another possibility, which I think is the most plausible. I need to confirm a few things first."

"And what is your theory?" Jonna asked curiously.

"I need to run some personal errands for the rest of the day. Perhaps we can meet tomorrow and discuss the matter further. As you know, we're on call this weekend."

"But now SÄPO is taking over the case," Jonna objected despondently.

"Good advice is always welcome," Walter said. "I'll write them a memo later today."

Jonna felt her pulse quicken as things started to fall into place. This was better than the ending of a John le Carré novel.

JÖRGEN BLAD WAS, for the moment, wing-clipped.

Not at the news desk, where he now enjoyed the fullest confidence from the head of the news desk. It was the flow of information from his mole within the police that troubled him most right now. Without any explanation, the police mole had stopped using the method of delivering information that Jörgen had meticulously devised. For a long time before that, he had determinedly looked for a contact and informant within the police who could continually leak information to him. His technique had already been decided. He used the same approach that the Soviet intelligence agency, the KGB, used against foreign diplomats during the cold war.

Within the KGB, there was a unit consisting of female agents called the Swallows. These young volunteers were selected for their loyalty to the Soviet system as well as for their good looks. They were schooled in lovemaking and the technique was as infallible as the sexual urges of their victims. The victim was brought into contact with a Swallow at an embassy function or another appropriate engagement. The Swallow initiated a campaign of seduction against the diplomat, who usually ended up between the sheets. The love nest was, however, rigged with cameras and tape recorders as well as watched by KGB operatives. Before the sexual rendezvous was over, the KGB officers stormed in on the unsuspecting victim. They explained that the newly recorded film was of excellent quality and that the photographs would be sent to the victim's family, his country's news correspondents and his Foreign Office section if he refused to co-operate on certain issues, which was another way of asking him to become a spy.

The diplomat would have to supply the KGB with classified information in return for non-publication of the photographs and, as a bonus, he would also receive money. In most cases, the diplomat accepted the KGB's demands and became a traitor. Jörgen had made himself into a Swallow in the pursuit of information. He lacked the beauty of his predecessors, but had compensated for this with flattering conversation. At the gay club "PinkyTinky", rumours had long since been circulating about a policeman who was a closet transvestite. Jörgen realized immediately that this was the man he had been looking for. After some research, which had forced him to jump in and out of several beds to gather sufficient information, he finally made contact with his victim.

Initially, the operation seemed to fail. Despite an unrivalled charm offensive, he was unable to get his target to bite.

The closet transvestite was hopelessly enamoured with a student from Uppsala and had no plans whatsoever to break up that relationship. Jörgen was therefore forced to split up the lovesick victim and the student. By starting a gossip campaign in Stockholm's gay community, he was able to make the victim's partner look like a notorious nymphomaniac. One month later, the relationship was in ruins and the transvestite was falling to pieces. Jörgen seized the opportunity. With a broken heart, the man was fragile and vulnerable to manipulation and Jörgen's new method of attack was to comfort and confide in him. After a week, the trap was sprung. With a video of the policeman in full leather gear and matching dildo accessories, it was impossible to resist Jörgen's stranglehold. The transvestite had not only lost his partner, but was also exposed to Jörgen's unscrupulous blackmail, and he could find no other way out other than to submit to the manipulative journalist. If the video should ever reach his colleagues, his days on the force would be numbered, to put it mildly. And on top of that, he had to think about what his wife and adult children would say.

If the flow of information had dried up, Jörgen would have a tough time reproducing the Karin Sjöstrand exclusive. He would not be able to shine by using information to which he alone, outside the police headquarters, was privy. But why the sudden radio silence? Was his informant after the video?

The evidence that gave Jörgen his hold over the man was, for the time being, safely stashed. He had decided that the best place to store the video was in a safety deposit box at the bank. The police source probably had not realized that the video would certainly destroy Jörgen's career, let alone how it would affect his relationship with Sebastian. It was therefore just as much in Jörgen's best interest that the images never became public.

Jörgen was worried that his "partner in crime" had realized how high the stakes were for him if he were exposed. Was he now testing Jörgen's resolve, to see if he had the nerve to publish the images?

Jörgen was not sure why he could not get hold of the man. The first place the policeman would instinctively search would be his home and the safety deposit box. But with bent cops, one could never be sure.

His informant was hardly going to ask for a warrant to do a search at Jörgen's place. Even Jörgen's safety deposit box would be subject to the search warrant. His informant would probably hire a thug, perhaps even to use physical violence in the hunt for the video. Jörgen had therefore done something he thought was exceptionally innovative and clever. He had let his mother hire the safety deposit box in which he kept the video. Jörgen then kept the key to that box in another deposit box in his own name. An anonymous key is impossible to trace, he thought. The key to his own deposit box, which was no larger than a bicycle key, was kept in a heart-shaped locket around his neck.

Jörgen was in desperate need of insider information. He understood that something big was brewing. A juicy scandal inside the Swedish court system was, without doubt, a major story that could take him all the way to the prestigious "Journalist of the Year" award. He would confront the informant and force him to deliver information on Karin Sjöstrand no matter what his excuses were. Jörgen sat at his computer and logged into his email account. He typed an email, despite the fact that they had agreed never to communicate over the internet and only to meet at various cafés to hand over information.

From: vagabond_en@yahoo.se
To: mylittlepony972@gmail.com
Subject: What's going on?
Please stick to our deal.
Need info on Sjöstrand ASAP
//J

To Jörgen's great surprise, he got a reply after only five minutes.

From: mylittlepony972@gmail.com
To: vagabond_en@yahoo.se
Subject: RE: What's going on?
Do not know who you are nor what you are talking about.
Please check that your email address is correct.
Mrs Maud

Maud? What a poor imagination, Jörgen thought. He was not sure whether he had been rejected or if his informant was trying to protect himself by claiming it was the wrong address. He decided to send a new email.

From: vagabond_en@yahoo.se
To: mylittlepony972@gmail.com
Subject: re: RE: What's going on?
Come to the last meeting place tonight at 7 pm.
//J

After half an hour, he logged out and shut down the computer. There were no more emails, which could mean one of two things. Either the deal was off and his informant had decided not to follow their "contract" or his informant would come to the meeting place this evening but, for obvious reasons, could not put this into writing. The secrecy surrounding their meetings was the top priority and his informant was most insistent on that point. Electronic fingerprints, in the shape of emails or telephone conversations that could be traced and then link them together, were not allowed.

Jörgen had therefore started a public website, which he named "StockholmInsight", under an assumed name. He hoped it was totally meaningless and uninteresting for anybody who accidentally surfed to the page. The site comprised a few photographs of Stockholm and a description of a few points of interest. In one corner of the page, there was a header that read, "Café of the week". Under it, Jörgen posted the name of the café where the meeting with his informant would take place. The time and date were posted on the left-hand side of the page, in the form of fabricated events that were supposedly happening during the week.

Accordingly, the coded message was "Café of the week: Vete-Katten, Kungsgatan 55" and "Event of the week: Poetry reading with Michael Rhenberg in ABF Building, Sveavägen 41, 18 November at 8:30 pm." The meeting place would therefore be Vete-Katten at eight-thirty tonight. Jörgen considered the system foolproof and was satisfied with the way it worked.

He wondered if his informant would show up tonight. The Swallow tactic had been ingenious and he had felt confident that it would last for many years. For the first time, he felt disheartened.

12 AT SEVEN-THIRTY ON Monday morning, Chief Prosecutor Åsa Julén first got hold of the Director-General of the National Courts Administration, Margareta Fors.

Margareta Fors had landed at Arlanda airport after a long and tiring flight from Los Angeles. One week at a conference that she just as easily could have done without and her mood was at an all-time low. On top of that had been a shock that remained in the body like a stubborn cold. They had hit severe turbulence over Greenland, and the ninety-tonne jet had flown like a paper plane at ten thousand metres. After one hour, the sporadic shaking had stopped. She herself was not particularly afraid of flying, but it was only when the cabin crew became pale-faced that she had felt anxiety creep over her. She never usually panicked, but she was seriously preoccupied by the prospect of not landing in one piece.

After that incident, it had been quite impossible for her to sleep during the remainder of the trip, even though she was behind on her sleep. She knew very well that she could not influence the situation in which she found herself, with a useless seat belt around her stomach. She was at high altitude and completely in the hands of others. Yet she had been so damn scared.

Margareta first turned on her mobile phone when she sat in the taxi driving home to Östermalmsgatan. Before she could finish punching in her home number, the phone rang. She looked at the display, which showed an ex-directory number. In a weary voice, she answered.

Earlier that morning, Åsa Julén had spoken with the Minister for Justice and the National Chief of Police, who had already been updated with the details of the Lantz and Ekwall cases on Sunday evening. The Sjöstrand case was being tossed around by the press already, so they knew about her. Åsa was anxious to get hold of the Director-General to give her the latest news. Both woman bureaucrats had known each other since their university days, but saw each other more seldom nowadays. Work and family took up most of their time.

"I apologize for the early telephone call," Åsa began. "But I need to inform you about a few things."

Margareta answered hesitantly. "I see."

"The Minister for Justice and the National Chief of Police have already been informed," Åsa continued.

The manner in which Julén started the conversation and the tone of her voice did not bode well. Neither did the fact that she called so early in the morning. If the Minister and the National Chief of Police had already been informed by the Prosecutor's Office, it had to be something serious.

The first thing that occurred to Margareta was another Anna Lindh type of murder – that a cabinet minister had been murdered by a random loony. The mental health reform that allowed severely sick psychiatric patients to self-medicate had infuriated many within the judicial system. The number of maniacs walking the streets was steadily increasing. This was all attributable to weak and inconsistent legislation from the politicians, as well as the constant cutbacks. Those ticking time-bombs were walking among ordinary people, just to provide treatment that was more humane and less costly to society. Who would pay the price for its failure? The sick, who needed psychiatric care, or somebody who just happened to get in their way and paid with a life? Margareta felt anger building within her as she speculated.

"Carry on," she said in a cold voice.

District Prosecutor Lennart Ekwall has confessed to murdering his wife," Åsa said.

At first, Margareta did not believe what she had heard. "Can you repeat that?" she asked.

"He has admitted during a police interview that he killed his wife with a golf club in their home. But that's not all," Åsa said.

That a district prosecutor had killed his wife was a catastrophe for the reputation of the justice system in the country. This much, Margareta understood. But how did this involve the National Courts Administration? This was really a problem for the Prosecutor's Office.

"As you know, Judge Bror Lantz of Stockholm District Court was involved in a car accident with a fatal outcome," Åsa continued.

"Yes, I'm aware of that," Margareta answered. "But that was an accident."

"There's reason to believe that he is guilty of manslaughter by strangulation of the taxi driver. In actual fact, most of the evidence indicates that this is the case. We just can't prove it. And there's no motive."

Margareta felt an icy chill spread through her body. "What's going on?" she exclaimed. "Are people going crazy? Isn't it enough that Karin Sjöstrand killed her own daughter?"

"We have a credibility crisis brewing and there's a risk of panic spreading among staff in the courts system," Åsa explained. "For the time being, the media don't know about Ekwall and Lantz. They're content with Sjöstrand right now; I couldn't cover that up. It was just a matter of time before it leaked out because there was an eyewitness in the stairwell, which the media had managed to uncover. For Lantz and Ekwall, it looks better. The Lantz case is still classified as an accident and will stay that way. Ekwall has no witnesses."

"Cover up," Margareta Fors repeated. She did not understand what Åsa meant – or if she wanted to understand.

"The Security Service have taken over the investigation, since it may involve sabotage by poisoning or drugging officials within the justice system," Åsa said.

Margareta took a deep breath and looked listlessly through the car window. The closer they got to the city limits, the thicker the traffic became. She did not have the energy to analyse the consequences of these events just now. The trip had been quite exhausting and she needed sleep, a lot of sleep, before she could focus. If she could just rest, she would be able to tackle the problems the next day.

She wrapped up the conversation with Åsa so that she could call her husband. She felt the knot in her stomach turn into something uncontrollable. For the first time in a long while, she started to cry.

THERE WAS NO weekend overtime or on-call duty for Walter. After writing his memo, he went to Karolinska University Hospital for a consultation with a specialist about his increasingly frequent dizzy spells. After only three questions, the doctor arranged for Walter to be admitted and sent to radiology.

Once his cranium had been x-rayed and the doctor had studied the x-rays, Walter sent two text messages, one to Jonna, in which he briefly informed her that the next day's meeting was postponed, and one to David Lilja, in which he described in more detail the reason why he would not be able to work for a while. Walter turned his mobile phone off and lay down in the hospital bed. If the worst should happen, his life had been quite pleasant until now.

Or was life really that pleasant? After Martine's death, his life had mostly been about moving on.

COUNTY POLICE COMMISSIONER Folke Uddestad was the last to enter the conference room. It was nine minutes past nine on Monday morning by the time Chief Prosecutor Åsa Julén addressed those attending.

"Can we have an update on the situation?" she opened the meeting impatiently.

"Before we start, I just want to inform you that Walter Gröhn can't be here," interrupted David Lilja, apologizing. "He has recently been admitted to hospital."

There was a brief pause.

"That's unfortunate news," Uddestad said, without seeming very interested. He cleared his throat. "Yesterday some surveillance and investigative work was done by the duty officers at the Drug Squad and SÄPO," he began. "So far, none of the dealers or suppliers has heard anything about a new type of drug on the market. However, today is the first day that significant operations will take place, so it's too early to draw any conclusions. The Drug Squad will shortly mobilize large numbers of staff. With such a massive operation being launched, we'll most probably be able to establish where Drug-X is coming from. SÄPO also has a lead that's probably the most solid one at present. It concerns, among other things, a suspected terrorist cell, based in Sweden, which doesn't have a huge respect for our country. What makes them particularly interesting is that they specifically denounce Swedish laws and courts."

Uddestad handed the audience over to Martin Borg, a team leader in the Security Service's Counter-Terrorism Unit. He had a muscular build and penetrating, steel-grey eyes. His hair was crew cut and he wore a dark suit, which hung well on his frame.

"At the Counter-Terrorism Unit, we have, for some time, been following an Islamic group, known as Wahhabists, whose goal is to turn Sweden into an Islamic state and to introduce Sharia law," he started stiffly. "For those of you not familiar with Wahhabism and Sharia, Saudi Arabia is an example of a country where these strict religious laws are implemented and also where the majority of Wahhabi followers are. And I think we're all familiar with conditions in Saudi Arabia." Everybody nodded in agreement.

Martin gave a wry smile when he saw how his colleagues from the local police pretended to be well informed on the subject.

"Women are dressed in sheets like ghosts and are severely oppressed by men," Martin continued and watched both of the women in the room. Neither Åsa Julén nor Jonna de Brugge raised an eyebrow. So naive. Without people like me around, they would soon be forced to wear the burka, he thought.

"We estimate that there are about twenty people in total in this group, of which there is a fanatical hardcore of ten beard-ed men in nightshirts, who have their base in a flat in central Stockholm," Martin said.

Jonna grinned when the word nightshirt was used, but she got an admonishing stare from Julén.

"The group also has a motley bunch of followers, who are a few hundred in number, mostly young, unemployed men from immigrant housing estates with roots in the Middle East. They have very strong financial links with high-level contacts in Saudi Arabia. That's also where you find most of the followers of Wahhabism, which is a fundamentalist movement within Islam. We believe that we have enough evidence to justify a raid on the group. If the Prosecutor's Office gives us the green light, then we can hit them as early as tomorrow. The National SWAT team is ready to go."

A tense silence filled the room. Martin adjusted his tie and sat in the chair to the side of the whiteboard. He looked over the company in the room. They were a sorry bunch. He had, however, not expected better. They were like the general population: naive and simple-minded, completely oblivious to the battle that was going to involve them all. The entire Western civilization would fall into an Islamic dark age if nothing was done. In medieval times, Muslims had tried to subvert European culture, but Europeans had a short memory. Now Muslims were flooding the refugee centres, cheered on by idealists who wanted to consign the continent to the abyss. The sight of the sheepish faces around the table only strengthened his conviction that he was doing the right thing.

All eyes were now on Chief Prosecutor Åsa Julén.

"You say that they reject our laws and courts," she deliberated. "Can you explain that further?"

"Of course," Martin answered without standing up. "The group has the aim of turning Sweden into an Islamic state. They're financed by Prince Hatim al-Amri, one of several thousand princes in Saudi Arabia, who has considerable resources at his disposal. The prince finances resistance groups in Iraq and Afghanistan and is known as a loyal Wahhabist and opponent to the West. As we understand it, the Swedish group's strategy is to lay a carpet of mosques all over the country. They have over twenty planning permissions, from Malmö in the south to Luleå in the north. In this way, they can set up a base to begin actually recruiting."

"What recruiting?" Julén asked.

"By controlling the mosques, they will pressure the Muslim communities, in particular the Sunnis and their imams, to move in their direction."

"The direction of Wahhabism and Sharia law," Julén concluded.

"Exactly," Martin said. "With four hundred thousand Muslims in the country, there's great potential. And their voices would definitely be heard. Each year, Sweden takes in about fifty thousand refugees with Islamic religious beliefs and, if we compare the Swedish reluctance to have children against the Muslim preference for breeding, Sweden will soon have changed its population. This is the process that this group is trying to accelerate. In twenty to thirty years, there will be as many Muslims as there are ethnic Swedes in this country. Then it will be too late to stop the transition to an Islamic state."

"But what does this have to do with Drug-X?" Julén interrupted sceptically. "Building mosques and preaching about an Islamic state doesn't mean they have access to Drug-X. What would be the purpose?"

Martin gave a slight smile. Her naivety obviously had no bounds.

"Our terrorist Prince Hatim al-Amri actually owns a pharmaceuticals plant that develops and manufactures pharmaceuticals mainly for Muslim countries in the third world. There's also one of the world's most advanced centres for genetic research in the desert about three hundred kilometres from the capital Riyadh. Muslim scientists from all over the world work there. The USA would have normally bombed the centre to bits, if not for the fact that Saudi Arabia is one of their most reliable allies in the region. They look the other way as long as the oil keeps on flowing and the Saudis keep on buying American weapons for billions of dollars each year."

Julén looked cautiously at Martin. "So you mean that Drug-X is coming from a terrorist prince in Saudi Arabia?"

"In all probability, yes."

"And the motive?" Jonna asked, unconvinced.

Martin looked cynically at Jonna. "That should be obvious," he said, wondering if RSU had lowered their recruiting standards. "They create chaos and insecurity in the Swedish justice system. The Muslims can then, with good reason, demand to have their own laws and courts, since the Swedish courts cannot be trusted. And in the longer term, they can impose their justice system on the rest of the population when the time is ripe."

"That's certainly not a possibility," Julén objected and looked around the room.

"Who could have thought that a handful of lunatics armed with Stanley knives could bring down the Twin Towers in New York?" Martin said. "Or take out parts of the Pentagon itself, the brain of the American military?"

Julén felt herself begin to sweat. This could have major ramifications internationally and, as the head of the investigation, she would be making all the critical decisions. She had no one else to turn to, apart from her formal superior the Prosecutor-General.

Luckily, all that was being asked for now was a search warrant for one house. The other matters would be handled later. Showing the ability to act was most important right now, especially with the Security Service. They normally knew what they were doing. This would be her second terrorist case after the Libyan citizens that she deported last year.

"I will see to it that you get your search warrant directly after the meeting," Julén said.

"The Prosecutor's Office is now taking over the investigation along with SÄPO as the acting police authority, since this case now falls under the anti-terrorist legislation."

The room fell silent.

Jonna could not stomach the speed of the changeover and was unable to stay quiet.

"So the motive for using the drug is political?" she asked.

"Yes, definitely political," Martin answered dryly. It seemed as if he had a little pike on the hook. A wannabe policewoman from RSU was definitely not going to stand in his way right now.

Jonna frowned.

Martin sighed out loud. "Let me explain it in another way for you," he slowly explained as if Jonna was mentally challenged. "The courts are the main pillar of any judicial system. If they are infiltrated by outside forces that can, in one way or another, influence the court verdicts, or if the courts are simply neutralized by physically stopping them from functioning, then the credibility of the system and the state disappears. Eventually of the whole constitution. This can bring about the end of democracy in a society. What usually happens after the system breaks down is that someone intervenes and, with drastic action, tries to get society functioning correctly again. Sometimes, it returns to a democracy, but more often it becomes a totalitarian regime. Sometimes an Islamic state."

"So Drug-X is a threat to national security and therefore even the constitution because traces of the drug were found in the daughter of a lay juror?" Jonna asked and saw that Folke Uddestad was avoiding eye contact with her. He looked almost uncomfortable.

"Yes, you could put it like that," Martin answered, but felt his patience with the pike beginning to fade. He forced back his mounting irritation with a smile. "But not only that. We have two further reasons to believe it – to be precise, Lantz and Ekwall. We suspect that even they are victims of Drug-X."

Jonna frowned extravagantly to show that she did not quite understand the logic of his reply. "Why not just kill all the judges and magistrates in all our courtrooms or just blast the buildings into rubble? Why go the long way round and drug the daughter of a court official? They could just as easily have used a more readily available drug if they wanted to put a particular person under pressure, or whatever they were after ..." She did not bother to finish the sentence. Nobody was listening to her. A combination of anger and resignation overcame her. She had a good mind to mention the angels of death, as well as Walter and her theory, but decided not to do so. Walter had said he was going to write a memo; he probably knew what he was doing.

The theory that the Security Service had suggested was so utterly nonsensical that she no longer wanted to discuss it. What she knew about Islam and Muslims, be they terrorists or not, was sufficient for her to realize that this was a dream scenario for SÄPO, rather than a genuine threat assessment. The Muslims provided a feeble excuse to create a tangible enemy. With those deduction techniques, you could always come up with an enemy.

It surprised her that the others kept as quiet as dummies. Not even her colleague from RSU, Fredrik Regnell, had opened his mouth. He normally had the gift of the gab and offered a sound analysis on almost anything. Now he sat silently in his chair and watched Jonna's futile attempts to shoot holes in the Security Service's theory.

Jonna did not have much experience of investigations. This was her second since she had accepted the position as analyst with the rank of special agent within RSU. But despite her meagre experience, she felt that the investigation that was being taken away from her was going off the rails even before it had properly started. Now it would be under the umbrella of SÄPO, and Julén and the Security Service were actively searching for a motive that presented people as a threat to the Swedish constitution and democracy. The motive was so far-fetched that, by comparison, the conspiracy theory about Elvis Presley's alien abduction seemed feasible.

MARTIN BORG KNEW that he had won a double victory when he left the meeting. He now had the Chief Prosecutor Åsa Julén eating out of his hand and he had deflected the little pike's attack. Normally, it was Folke Uddestad who, for personal reasons, was slow to take the Security Service to his bosom, but this time he had probably realized the futility of discrediting his analysis of the facts. Unlike the RSU bimbo. Martin knew the type. She was one of those who would always challenge her colleagues. Always sticking her nose in and never realizing the consequences of her actions. But he had the facts on his side and had presented them well. The rest would be a walk in the park.

DAVID LILJA ASKED Jonna to stay behind in the room after the meeting was over. He closed the door after the last person had left and sat down opposite her. He appeared to be under a little stress.

"I've just been informed that Walter is suspended indefinitely," he said.

"An internal investigation against him will be started as soon as he is discharged from the hospital."

Jonna stared at Lilja, shocked.

"Whatever for?"

"I can't go into that," Lilja replied. "It's a matter for Internal Affairs only. But the shit has hit the fan for the last time, you might say."

"That's really disappointing news," Jonna said, suddenly feeling very awkward.

"Well, it may seem a bit harsh, but he only has himself to blame for it," Lilja replied dejectedly. "He always has to do things his own way and that ultimately gets punished."

"What happens now then?" Jonna wondered.

"Yes, that's why I wanted you to stay behind," Lilja said.

"Walter's suspension, together with his hospital stay, means that we no longer have a place for you at County CID. I will inform your superior Johan Hildebrandt at RSU."

"That's disappointing," Jonna said.

"What's disappointing about that?" Lilja asked.

"That Walter is suspended. But, most of all, that SÄPO's suspicions about the Islamic activists are so far-fetched."

"Really? And what do you base that on?" Lilja asked, while gathering up the documents he had taken with him to the meeting.

Jonna bit her lip and looked at the whiteboard. "Do you have a moment?"

Lilja shook his head. "I'm sorry. Take it up with Julén or SÄPO, if you must. This case is no longer on my agenda. And in the not too distant future, neither is Walter."

Lilja stuffed the documents in his briefcase and thanked Jonna for her efforts at the CID. Then he left the room.

Jonna watched Lilja with a blank expression. Then she laid her forehead on the table, defeated. She had not even asked why Walter was lying in hospital.

13 IT WAS AS he had feared. Despite everything, he still hung onto the last shred of hope. He had been sitting at the café for over three hours, waiting. Three hours of tense waiting that added up to six cups of coffee and two Danish pastries with cloudberry jam. Jörgen was shaking from a mix of irritation and high-caffeine intake when he left the meeting place. The informant had now definitively demonstrated that the deal was off. The bastard had thrown a spanner into the works of Jörgen's advancing career. On his way back to his flat, Jörgen's brain was on overdrive. Should he threaten to publish the video? That was a high-stakes threat that could jeopardize his own journalistic career if he was forced to follow through. But if he airbrushed some of the stills so that it was not possible to identify him as his informant's partner, he could perhaps find a way out of the dilemma.

He had walked for fifteen minutes before he got home to the flat at Odengatan. He had promised himself that he would make a decision before he arrived. If only Sebastian had not gone to South America. He still could not ask him for advice, except by disguising the problem and talking about a third party. Sebastian always had an opinion on all manner of things. Suddenly, Jörgen felt how much he missed him.

Jörgen opened the door to his ninety-six square-metre, four-room flat and immediately saw that something was not right. The hallway felt strangely empty. The coat rack with its outdoor coats was missing from the wall, as was the black-stained chest of drawers that he and Sebastian had bought at Stalands furniture store. As he entered the living room, he first thought that he was in the wrong flat. His eyebrows shot upwards in surprise as he discovered the debris on the floor. What had once been a bookshelf, armchairs and a kitchen table with handmade, Finnish beech chairs was now lying destroyed on the floor. Jörgen carefully lifted the table top of the kitchen table. Underneath were the remains of what had been an Italian bedside table in solid oak, now as flat as an IKEA pack. Not even his bed had survived the devastation. Who had done this? Who could get into his flat unnoticed and why? He froze when he heard the parquet flooring creak behind him.

JONNA WAS SUPPOSED to report to the head of the RSU, Johan Hildebrandt, for debriefing, but decided instead to clock out and take the rest of the day off. Her frustration from the meeting had gradually turned into indifference and she felt fed up.

She slammed the car door and remained sitting behind the wheel with the car keys in her hand. With her gaze fixed on nothing in particular, her thoughts ran in circles in her head, in exactly the same fashion as when her relationship with Peter had irrevocably come to an end. After trying to find the appropriate emotions, with an obsessive's compulsion, to redress the situation, she had found herself stuck in an emotional no-man's-land. On closer analysis, she realized she had never really loved Peter. At least, not in the way he had expected. He had demanded a form of unconditional, submissive passion. Love with a capital "L" was an illusion. She had compensated for her lack of suitable emotions with something else. Something more contemporary, like sharing the washing up and the bills, or even just having a healthy sex life or somebody to come home to or to go to parties with. The flat had felt abandoned during the first weeks after the break-up and it would take a long time before she would be able to bare her soul to somebody else again.

She put the key in the ignition and took out her mobile phone. It had been on silent mode since the meeting and the display showed five missed calls and three messages. A few years ago, there would have been significantly more. After she had started at the police academy, her contact with old friends became more sporadic. They quite simply had nothing in common anymore and just rehashed old memories or stuck to stilted and superficial chitchat. Most had already started families and bought houses, which dominated the topic of conversation. By breaking up with Peter, she had gone from square one in the social monopoly game to the margins of the game board.

Sandra Kalefors was one of her few girlfriends who still had not locked herself in with a family and thrown away the key. A boyfriend that she occasionally dated was the closest she had got to a committed relationship. Sandra had called three times and left two text messages. It was probably a date for dinner at one of their favourite bistros or for cruising the bars to hunt for young studs in baggy jeans.

Now was not the time for Sandra or RSU.

Instead, she set a course for the Karolinska University Hospital and Walter, to keep him up to date with the latest developments in the investigation or, rather, the lack of investigation as far as they were concerned. She also wanted to know how he was feeling. She had no idea what had happened, other than he obviously had been suddenly admitted to the hospital.

Jonna was obliged to show her police ID in order to visit Walter, who lay in a room in ward twelve, close to the ward where Bror Lantz had lain a week earlier. An argumentative and self-opinionated intern was of the opinion that Walter would not be up to having any visitors and therefore asked her to come back later.

TEFAN TEGENFALK

Considering how the day had progressed, she was not in the mood to humour the sanctimonious student doctor. So, against regulations, she flashed her ID and hoped he would not make a telephone call to complain. After some grumbling, the intern asked one of the nurses to show Jonna to room thirteen. She was allowed fifteen minutes, not a second more.

Jonna looked at Walter silently as he explained.

"In the brain?" she blurted out. He described it as if it was only a broken finger. There were actually benign tumours too; she knew that. Not even a cynic like Walter could have hidden something as monumental as the beginning of his own demise.

"So that's why you had dizzy spells," she added. "Because the tumour has been pressing on a nerve that controls your sense of balance."

"Clever girl," Walter said.

"When are they going to operate?"

"Apparently, a specialist surgeon, Täljkvist, has shown an interest in digging into my skull," Walter explained, moderately enthusiastic. "He's a specialist in something called neuro-navigation. Also, he thinks I'm a challenge because the tumour has spread between the cerebellum and the brain stem. At any rate, he wants to take it out as soon as possible. So tomorrow, it's party time."

"Getting a specialist to operate sounds really good," Jonna said, trying to sound encouraging.

"Sure," Walter agreed, "just as long as he's under sixty and without a hangover."

Jonna laughed and fidgeted a little. She did not know if she should tell him that he had been suspended from duty pending the result of an internal investigation. He would, of course, be informed about it in due course. But should she break the bad news to him? She was unsure if she was even authorized to do so. That kind of information was probably subject to a confidentiality regulation. Jonna decided to start with the news of the investigation itself.

"The Ekwall and Sjöstrand investigations have been cancelled and a new one has been started under SÄPO and Åsa Julén," she started, rambling on. "SÄPO is of the opinion that an Islamic terrorist cell is behind Drug-X, and they believe there are links to Ekwall and Lantz as well. According to SÄPO, the objective of the terrorist cell is to neutralize our courts and, by so doing, the whole infrastructure of a functional society, with the aim of preparing the way for their own laws. SÄPO are also looking for traces of the drug in the taxi driver and in Ekwall's wife."

Walter's face turned dark red. He was just about to say something when the door was opened by the intern. The thin-haired man went up to Walter and asked if everything was okay, but frowned when he saw Walter's troubled face. He turned to Jonna and made it clear that her fifteen minutes were now up.

Jonna got ready to leave the room, but Walter ordered her to stay. "Sit down," he said and gestured at Jonna.

"No, you should rest now," the intern explained and gave Walter a stern look.

"No, thank you," Walter refused, in a firm voice. "I know when I need to rest."

"But ..." the doctor began.

"You leave and you stay," interrupted Walter, pointing first at the intern and then at Jonna.

"I don't think ..."

Walter stopped the doctor, saying he shouldn't think excessively. The doctor sighed morosely and then left the room. Before he closed the door, he said he would be back in another fifteen minutes. If Walter did not accept his advice, he would be forced to relinquish responsibility for his health.

Walter asked the doctor to close the door behind him.

Jonna continued to relate in detail what had transpired during the morning meeting. Walter had calmed himself down and nodded patiently as Jonna described how the meeting had progressed.

"That didn't sound good at all," he concluded, after she had finished her report. "It sounds very far-fetched to me."

"I agree completely and I have a few thoughts," she replied and pensively bit her bottom lip.

"I see."

"Yes, if we ignore Drug-X to start with …" Jonna slowly began.

"Carry on," Walter abruptly replied.

"To date, we have three murderers if we include Bror Lantz. But we have absolutely no motive for the murders. At least, no motive that is so far credible."

"Nothing new about that," Walter rudely retorted.

"The problem is that none of them know why they did what they did. Why did they become overwhelmed with a rage that disappeared when they took a life? Also, everyone except Lantz has confessed."

Jonna suddenly paused.

"Carry on," Walter said. "You said that you had been thinking. Not that you were going to start thinking."

Jonna sat quietly in the chair and looked as if she had forgotten her name.

"Who would want to punish a prosecutor and a judge?" she finally said.

"Apparently, an Islamic terrorist cell that wants to throw the Swedish justice system into chaos by poisoning its practitioners," Walter answered ironically.

"Yes, but, apart from them, who else?"

"There's no shortage of loonies out there," Walter chuckled. "According to SÄPO's own reports, there are about one thousand mentally ill people who could potentially bury an axe in anybody's head. Then we have all the opponents of the legal system, anarchists, left- and right-wing hooligans and, of course, those that have personal reasons for revenge."

"It's precisely the latter that I've been thinking about," Jonna said.

"Revenge?"

"Exactly. Somebody who's been wrongly convicted or, in some other way, feels violated or damaged and wants to wreak vengeance on the court system."

"By drugging people with a compound that only national governments and the largest pharmaceutical corporations can in theory produce?" Walter asked dubiously.

"Something like that," Jonna suggested, without sounding completely convinced. Maybe this was as far-fetched as SÄPO's theory after all. The more she thought about it, the more difficult it became to believe it.

"Funny you should mention it," Walter said. "I was thinking along the same lines myself. But I couldn't join up all the dots. Why go to all the bother of such an advanced drug? Why not simply kill the relevant judge or prosecutor?"

"You're right," Jonna said. "Why make everything so complicated?"

"How did you progress with the plaster figures, by the way?" he asked and closed his eyes.

"I sat up most of the evening and surfed the net," Jonna said. "I finally managed to find the manufacturer."

"And?"

"They're manufactured in the USA by a small company that sells exclusively over the internet. According to their home page, they only have these figures. All on the death theme. I almost got the feeling that they were Satanists or something else cult-like."

"Taking into account the time difference, I assume you were able to call them?" Walter said.

"Naturally," Jonna said. "But I got nothing."

"What do you mean, nothing?"

"I said I was from the Swedish police and wanted to know if they had any customers in Sweden and, if that was the case, the names of the people they had sold the little angels of death to. But they were not so eager to please."

"Why not?"

"Translated literally, they told me that I could take my baton and stick it up …"

"I get the picture," Walter said. "We will have to see if SÄPO reacts to the death angels in the memo I wrote. They could contact the FBI and obtain some assistance to get the list of Swedish buyers."

"Presumably," Jonna said.

"Is there any reason to discount SÄPO's terrorist theory?"

"Absolutely," Jonna replied resolutely. "I don't believe that stuff about the terrorist prince. In that situation, he would have poisoned almost all the water supplies in the Western world – or spread panic and chaos in some other way."

"Good," Walter said and opened his eyes. "It so happens that I have a proposition."

"Well, there was something else," Jonna said cautiously, before Walter could continue.

THE FIST CAME from nowhere and he fell heavily to the floor. A burning pain spread across his face as he drifted in and out of consciousness. Distant voices echoed in the confusion into which he had so suddenly been thrown. Jörgen had turned around when he heard the parquet flooring creak behind him, but did not register what happened after that. One second, he was standing and looking at the pile of furniture on the living room floor; the next second, he was lying on the floor in a sea of pain.

"Noooo, Chri-ist, you hit too bloody hard. His fucking lights went out!" Jerry Salminen roared in Finnish Swedish and punched the wall with his fist. A fist-sized hole appeared in the plasterboard wall.

Tor Hedman went towards the rotund man on the floor. He approached carefully and nudged the man's head with his size thirteens. At first glance, the man did not seem to present much of a threat. Even so, Tor was on his guard when he bent over him to see how hard he had taken the blow. He had read the Lisbeth Salander novels and knew not to judge a book by its cover. If a thin anorexic could floor a blond giant, then this little fatso could take Tor, despite the fact that he was over two metres tall and had been a hardened criminal for thirty-five years.

"What the hell are you doing?" Jerry exclaimed.

"You can never know for sure," Tor said and pointed at the man with one of his skinny, tubular arms.

"Know what?"

"He could jump up and nail us both," Tor answered and looked at Jerry with a serious face.

Jerry was just about to ask Tor if he was a complete idiot, but stopped himself, because he already knew the answer. If there was one thing Tor detested, it was being called an idiot. Jerry knew this after eight years in his company.

Despite his one metre and seventy-five centimetres of height, Jerry looked like one of the seven dwarfs next to Tor. Not widthwise, however. Jerry pumped iron seven days a week and had been regularly taking steroids for the last four years. He had a natural aptitude for bodybuilding. Jerry's forearms were as big as Tor's thighs and, on the beach, he received envious stares from men without muscles and from women of all ages and shapes. He could thank his mother for his genetic pedigree; she was built like a Finnish sauna.

Jerry looked around anxiously. They had gone through the entire flat without finding what they were looking for. Was it a CD or a DVD? Was it a file on a PC or a videotape? Or was it one of those fucking USB memory sticks that were so small that they could be hidden inside an arsehole?

Jerry didn't have a clue. "Nix, he must have fucking hidden it somewhere else," he swore and started to pace around the room. "We've bloody well torn the whole fucking floor to bits and still not found any fucking multimedia evidence."

"But we don't know what to look for," Tor said, waving his inner-tube arms about. "The bloke said that the sucker would know what we needed to find." Tor looked up from the man on the floor and gazed inquiringly at Jerry.

"I know that, but Christ," exclaimed Jerry, unable to control himself any longer. "No fucking way are we going to find that out if you nail the fucker before he's spilled his guts." He kicked the heap of wreckage on the floor.

A muffled groan came from the floor as Jörgen recovered consciousness. He squinted with one eye, not able to make out anything. The pain from the eye that had swollen shut after the blow rushed through his nerves. His head was about to explode from the pain. It felt as if his brain was at least three sizes too big.

"Water, quickly. He's waking up!" Tor screamed and took hold of Jörgen's hair. He was going to drag him into the bathroom, but did not have the strength.

Jerry shoved Tor out of the way and instead lifted up Jörgen by his arms. Jerry only worked out for the body mass. Strength was incidental. It was therefore with some difficulty that he dragged the paunchy journalist by the arms into the bathroom.

Jerry heaved Jörgen's upper body over the toilet rim and pushed his head into the bottom of the bowl.

"Flush it," he shouted at Tor.

Tor flushed the toilet and a gurgling sound was heard deep down in the toilet.

"Good, he's coming to," Jerry said and gritted his teeth as his arms began to shake from the exertion. The fatso was hardly a featherweight.

"Flush again, fuck it," Jerry ordered and forced Jörgen downwards against the porcelain as hard as he could. Jörgen moaned from the pain and the water was coloured red with blood, as his nose had been broken. He flailed wildly with his arms while choking violently.

Jerry pulled Jörgen's head out of the toilet bowl and let him drop to the bathroom floor. Jörgen coughed up toilet water while blood spurted out of his nose.

"Now tell me, what the fuck have you done with the multi-media evidence?" Jerry screamed and squatted down beside Jörgen.

At first, Jörgen did not understand. It felt as if he had been run over by a truck. He fumbled with his hand, over his fore-head, down towards his swollen eye and then his nose. His eye had swelled to the size of a tennis ball and his nose was as broken as a bad engagement.

He pressed the tennis ball and an excruciating pain shot through his body. Jörgen could not contain the pain and howled uncontrollably.

"So far, so good. Now he's talking at least," Tor concluded.

Jörgen started to hyperventilate in an attempt to lessen the pain. It felt as if he had a thousand needles in his eyeball.

"So answer me!" Jerry yelled. "What have you done with the evidence?"

"Who are you?" Jörgen blurted out between deep gasps.

Jerry was really fed up with everything. Everything had gone wrong from the very beginning.

Zlatan, the locksmith, had made a fuss and wanted more cash to pick the door lock. Then they had been forced to wait until the sucker came home, since they could not find the evidence despite having slashed the furnishings to shreds. And anyway, it was Jerry who should be asking the questions, not that fucking loser on the floor.

Jerry twisted Jörgen's wet hair. Jörgen screamed and flailed his arms in defence.

"What have you done with the evidence?" Jerry shouted in Jörgen's ear.

"What evidence?" Jörgen asked in despair. He felt the tears pour out of him.

Jerry thrust his face so close Jörgen could feel his bad breath.

"Shit, why is it so fucking difficult to get you to talk?" Jerry hissed, with saliva bubbling at the corners of his mouth. He pressed one finger on Jörgen's swollen eye, but quickly removed it when a heart-rending screech bounced off the bathroom walls.

Tor found a rag on the drying rack above the bathtub, which he pushed into Jörgen's mouth. The screech was muffled to a faint groan. Then he took hold of Jörgen's wrists and bent his arms behind his back, while pressing his knee into Jörgen's back. With a nylon band he had in his back pocket, he tied Jörgen's wrists together.

"Fucking shit. We're going to have to take the bastard with us," Jerry swore and stood up dejectedly.

"Now listen, you fucking pile of shit," Tor shouted and glared at Jörgen. "Because you're finding it so bloody hard to talk, we're going to have to take you with us. Perhaps your memory will improve when we start softening you up on our home patch."

The pain around Jörgen's eye was fading slightly. It was his nose that was the worst. Since Jörgen could not talk with the gag in his mouth, he nodded his understanding instead. Things were beginning to fall into place. This was no random flat break-in by some drug-crazed heroin junkies. These guys were pros, and they were not looking for valuables like money or jewellery. The police informer must have sent these thugs to repossess the video. What the thugs called "the evidence" was, in actual fact, the video. The informer had obviously been very reticent about any details concerning what he wanted to be taken back, which indicated that, despite everything, he was still very worried about what it contained. Even if his informant had decided to break their contract, he was also not going to leave any loose ends. Jörgen was now forced to think of something fast.

The first thing he needed to do was to get the gag out of his mouth. If he could get just a few minutes with these guys, he was sure he could bring them round and get out of his current predicament. He could offer them cash for his release. Twice the sum that his informant had paid them for the job. But what guarantees did Jörgen have that they would not kill him even if he gave them the video?

To even have a productive conversation with these two hooligans, the rag had to be removed from his mouth. Jörgen started to mumble and shake his head, but had to stop as the pain shot through his head like a lightning bolt.

He took a few deep breaths through his nose, which had started to swell up again, and tried again. He emitted short bursts of sound without moving his head. His head still felt as if it would explode with the pain.

"What?" Jerry asked, pulling Jörgen to his feet.

Jörgen had a hard time keeping his balance as the blood rushed to his head. He sat down heavily on the toilet and looked pleadingly at Jerry as he continued to mumble.

"Do you want to say something?" Jerry asked.

Jörgen nodded his head cautiously. He was forcing back the tears.

"If I remove the rag from your cakehole, then you'd better not start bloody yelling," Jerry ordered.

"One more scream and I will start pressing that bump again. Understood?" Jerry fixed his eyes on Jörgen and held his index finger in front of the swollen eye. Jörgen carefully nodded.

Jerry pulled the cloth from Jörgen's mouth so hard that he thought his teeth would follow.

"Are you going to talk to us now?" Tor asked, and sat on the edge of the bathtub. Jörgen tasted the bleach-like aftertaste of the cloth that Sebastian normally used to clean the toilet. He wanted to throw up his lunch, but managed to keep his gag reflex in check.

"Can I have a little water?" Jörgen asked, but was rudely interrupted.

"Right then, talk, you fucker," Jerry yelled impatiently. He wanted to hear Jörgen say where he had hidden the evidence. No fucking shit about fucking water.

Jörgen realized he had to choose each word as if it were a gold nugget. In particular, the muscle mountain shouting with a Finnish accent seemed to have a very short fuse.

"I was a bit dizzy at the beginning of our meeting," Jörgen began to talk. "But there were obvious reasons for that, you see," he said and grinned feebly in an attempt to lighten the mood. It was like telling a joke to a deaf mute.

The tall one impatiently signalled to Jörgen to continue.

"It's the video you're after. Am I right?" Jörgen said matter-of-factly and watched the two hooligans.

"Video? I don't fucking know. It's some type of multimedia evidence," the tall one answered, waving his arms in frustration.

"Yes, but video is a form of multimedia," Jörgen explained pedantically. "Multi means many; media means different forms of information like photos, video, music, games, data files, etcetera. And multimedia is the combination of those two things. So, that's what's meant by the term multimedia evidence."

It fell silent in the bathroom. Jörgen looked first at the hulk and then at the tall one, who was apparently showing a "Service not available" sign – he looked as if someone had pulled out the plug during a live programme.

"Jee-sus Christ!" Jerry swore loudly in Finnish after he had thought for a moment. "You know what we want, so all you need to do is to get it for us. No more fucking bullshit. You talk like you swallowed a bloody dictionary. And we also want any copies, if you have made any. Understood?"

Jörgen nodded. "I understand," he said. "The problem is that I don't actually have the physical video with me. And it's quite a complicated procedure to get hold of it."

"Why's that?" Jerry asked impatiently.

"The banks have to be open for me to get to it."

"You have it in a safety deposit box?" Tor asked.

Jörgen nodded.

Jerry's face darkened. His jaw muscles danced as he snarled through his teeth. "If you're lying, I'll put this mop handle through your skull." He glanced at a floor mop that was standing by the side of the washbasin.

"I have no doubt about that," Jörgen answered. "But it's the honest truth."

Jerry kicked the bathroom wall and said something x-rated in Finnish. A bit of grout from between the tiles fell on the floor. If it was correct that the video, or whatever the hell it was, lay stored in a deposit box, this meant trouble. Neither Tor nor Jerry could get to the deposit box without being forced to identify themselves. Neither of them had fake IDs in the name of Jörgen Blad. Letting the bastard walk into the bank himself

– even if accompanied by Tor and Jerry – was like walking into the lion's den and hoping that nobody was home.

The banks were bristling with CCTV and had one in every bloody corner. Neither Tor nor Jerry wanted to be caught on film with a soon-to-be John Doe or on a missing persons bulletin on the Channel 3 crimewatch series "Most Wanted". Then they might just as well walk into the nearest police station and turn themselves in. So that tactic had a load of unnecessary risks. Therefore, there were two options left. One was to take a chance, let Jörgen fetch the video himself and risk him alerting the police via the bank staff. Alternatively, they could arrange a false ID, which would cost about twenty thousand and take about a week to fix. There was still a risk that Jörgen Blad would be known by someone at the bank, which would lead to the whistle being blown if one of them tried to impersonate Jörgen. Even if nobody knew Jörgen, they would be captured on CCTV and the police would trace back the slob's last days if he disappeared or ended up as a stiff on a rubbish tip somewhere. They could disguise themselves with wigs and fake beards. But some of those bank staff had eagle eyes, or even a sixth sense, for disguises and unusual behaviour.

Jerry scratched his head thoughtfully. This was beginning to get too complicated, even for him. Personally, he wanted to put a bullet in the forehead of the sucker and then go home and train. But he couldn't. They had promised to retrieve the evidence – at least the fucking lanky git had promised – and a reputation for breaking contracts would mean a bad start for their future business. It would in fact kill their newly launched enterprise. Tor and Jerry would be shunned like the plague and branded as unreliable. Nobody would want to have any contact with them, not even with a barge pole and protective gloves, except for Haxhi Osmanaj who was dying to get his hands on them. Preferably around their necks. Why the fuck had they taken this job?

"There is another alternative," Jörgen suggested and stood up from the toilet on shaking legs.

"Yes, that we liquidate you," Jerry answered and glared at Jörgen with coal-black eyes.

"That's also an option," Jörgen agreed. "However, it doesn't sound so appealing to me."

Both criminals stared blankly at Jörgen.

"What I wanted to say was this," Jörgen continued and contrived a weak smile. "I will double whatever you're being paid for this job."

A brief silence in the bathroom.

"Do you think we're completely daft in the head?" Jerry exclaimed, while glancing instinctively at Tor.

"Absolutely not," Jörgen insisted in a hesitant voice. "But what alternative do you have?" He made a silent prayer to avoid getting the mop handle speared through his head. Jerry's brow wrinkled in thought. He needed to think, but his brain seized up. It was impossible to concentrate in this company. No matter how much he tried to analyse the situation, his train of thought ended up somewhere else. Right now, he was thinking of his and Tor's previous employer, Haxhi Osmanaj. To have the Albanian mafia after your head was not exactly without its difficulties. They were between a rock and a hard place. Whatever they did, they would get really burned if they could not successfully deliver that video to the buyer, according to their deal. They could hardly return their advance and say that they had failed, or screw the original client by letting themselves be bought by the mark. Their newly formed crew, called the Original Fuckers, currently with only themselves as members, would be as popular as an electric eel in your swimming trunks. Jerry needed to sleep on the problem and clear his head of the day's confusion. But before that, he would do a late leg-development routine at the gym. He had neglected his thighs lately.

"OK, this is what we do," Jerry suggested when he had finished thinking. "I need to get some shuteye. We'll tidy up the bastard and take him to the garage. Then we'll figure out what to do with him tomorrow."

Jerry grabbed Jörgen and shoved him towards the wash-basin. "Wash the blood off your face," he ordered and cut the restraining bands with pliers. Jörgen rinsed the blood from his face and dried himself on Sebastian's hand towel. He needed to feel the scent of Sebastian. Right now, he missed him immeasurably. He pulled the comb through his curly hair a few times and felt that he was beginning to get control of the situation. These two were not the sharpest criminal minds he had encountered and that could be his salvation.

Tor had become surly. Jerry had not consulted him about how they were going to handle the situation at all, but had instead taken the decision himself, just like that, out of thin air. It was high time to show Jerry what he thought about it.

"Stop," Tor said in a cold voice.

Jerry, who was on his way out of the bathroom, stopped short and turned around, surprised.

"To get into the safety deposit box, we need a key. Or what?" Tor began.

Jerry looked impatiently at Tor, who had sat back down on the edge of the bathtub.

"Of course," Jerry answered irritatedly, although he had actually forgotten about the key.

"But where's the key?" Tor asked, looking from Jerry to Jörgen.

"How the fuck should I know?" Jerry answered, glaring at Jörgen.

"Give us the key to the deposit box, you fucking pile of shit," Tor said and moved towards Jörgen.

"I have it on me, actually," Jörgen answered politely.

"You have it?" Tor repeated, surprised.

"Here it is," Jörgen said and held up a small, heart-shaped locket that hung around his neck. "The key is inside."

Tor examined the locket that Jörgen was holding.

"There is just a small problem," Jörgen informed him.

"What's that?" Tor grunted.

"The key is for a safety deposit box, where I keep the key to another deposit box where the video is stashed. And that deposit box is in another bank."

At first, Tor looked as if Jörgen was speaking another language. Then, he exploded. "You're making everything so fucking messed up. I'm going to fucking beat you to death!" he screamed and made as if to punch Jörgen, who crouched down.

"We're going to do as I said," Jerry intervened. Tor's lower lip was trembling with rage.

Jerry pushed Jörgen out of the bathroom while also keeping an eye on Tor's fist. He could not be fully trusted.

"If you try anything, I will cut your throat. Understand?" Jerry glared long and hard at Jörgen.

Jörgen nodded to indicate that the message was understood.

They left the demolished flat and took the lift down to the foyer. As they emerged onto Odengatan, they saw that darkness had fallen and there were few people out in the chilly autumn evening. The street was almost deserted.

They started to walk towards the car that Jerry had illegally parked on the corner of Birger Jarlsgatan and Odengatan. A parked car suddenly switched on its headlights and drove slowly behind them. Tor saw that it was a newly registered, dark blue BMW 5 Series, but because of the dark he could not see the driver in the blacked-out interior. From force of habit, he kept watching the car from the corner of his eye. Not because he was suspicious about anything; it was just a paranoid habit that he could not control. Nobody knew his and Jerry's whereabouts, except for the go-between who had given them Jörgen's address.

They had only a few metres left before they reached the stolen Volvo V70, which was today's means of transport, when the BMW quickly began to accelerate. The dark-tinted rear window slid down and, at the same instant, Tor saw a weapon inside the gloom of the interior. "Get down!" Tor roared and threw himself at Jerry and Jörgen, who were a step ahead of him. All three of them fell in a heap on the pavement behind a parked Opel. A muffled automatic thudding could be heard from inside the BMW as someone emptied a magazine from an Uzi with a silencer. The bullets smashed through the car windows and hit the house wall behind them, ricocheting loudly.

The sound of the Uzi stopped abruptly and a car door opened. Footsteps sounded on the street.

Jerry was the first to recover from the shock. "Chri-ist! Son of a bitch!" he roared and rolled over onto his back. From the trouser lining of his light-grey jogging pants, he tore out a Kel-Tec P-3AT pistol. It was small enough to fit into the palm of a normal-sized hand. He stretched out his arm and shot blindly five times in rapid succession through the Opel's shattered side windows, in what he thought was the direction of the BMW. They sounded more like small firecrackers than pistol shots.

Jörgen covered his ears and pressed himself against the ground as hard as he could. He was not sure if what he was experiencing was real or if he was still unconscious and in the middle of a bad dream. In all probability, he was awake, because his trousers were now wet and warm. He had wet himself.

Suddenly, he heard a rapid stream of loud explosions. It was Tor, who was kneeling on one knee and emptying his automatic Desert Eagle Mark XIX at the BMW. The lack of strength in Tor's arms made him unable to control the weapon, which was soon pointing straight up in the air. But it was more than enough. The BMW made its getaway, its tyres screeching.

Tor shook from the strain of the Desert Eagle's powerful recoil. Basically, he had only sinews to rely on and had the stamina of an eighty year old. He stared at the house wall, where the bullets had hit, and decided that he had missed the BMW with every shot. The car had stopped about six metres away from them and he had still missed it by a large margin. Actually, it looked as if he had been aiming at something else.

Jerry at least seemed to have been successful in hitting the BMW.

Tor scratched his chin, thinking. His newly acquired automatic pistol was a difficult piece to master, especially in automatic mode. He would have to practise more.

"Hell, we have to get out of here before the cops show up," Jerry yelled. He was pale and his voice was shaking.

Tor stumbled over to the stolen car. It seemed to have survived the rain of bullets. He tore open the driver's door and sat behind the wheel, racing the engine.

Jerry cast a quick glance at Jörgen, who was laying face down on the pavement, trembling in a pool of his own urine. He heard the fat bastard let out a whimpering sound. After giving it some quick thought, he decided not to try to drag Jörgen with him into the car. The way it looked now, he would be more of a liability than anything else. Everything had changed with this shootout. Something was just not right.

"We'll be back!" Jerry hissed as he ran to the getaway car.

14 THERE ARE OCCASIONS in life when one wishes one was never born. This was exactly how Jörgen felt as he stood up on trembling legs after the gunfight. The saying "from the frying pan into the fire" could not more aptly describe what he thought of recent events. His head was exploding and his body shook from the shock of the gunfight. It actually lasted only a few seconds, but had seemed to last an eternity. What had just happened? An internal dispute in the crime world? Had the madmen in the car been after him or was it the two thugs that they wanted to kill?

Right now, Jörgen wished that he had never tried to blackmail the police mole. He gazed around, aimlessly. Strangely, there were no people on the street except for an old lady who, completely oblivious to the gang shootout, was walking her dachshund farther down the street. Surely, somebody must have heard the shots echo between the walls. He looked up at the windows facing the street. Some were lit, but most were dark. A middle-aged man in a white Saab 9-5 passed by Jörgen as if nothing had happened. Then a young couple emerged from a doorway. The man held his arm around the woman as they walked towards Sveavägen. She was laughing and seemed happy. Jörgen felt the tears well up inside him. He limped back to the entrance to his block of flats while fighting back the tears. He had injured his knee when the skinny one had roughly wrestled him to the pavement. He had probably saved the lives of both Jörgen and his Finnish partner with that tackle. A strange thought, but that was exactly what had happened. His life had been saved by his own assassin.

Just as he was about to open the entrance door, he paused. He carefully touched the swelling around his eye. It felt like red-hot pins and needles. He did not dare to touch his nose. He only had to look at his reflection in the door's glass panel to relive the pain. There was little doubt that his nose was broken. It was swollen, mainly on one side, he noticed. He looked terrible. Borderline grotesque – that was how Sebastian would have described him. He slowly started to come out of the initial shock.

Why was he standing here at the entrance and what was he going home for?

For a start, he had practically no home left to return to and besides, he needed medical attention – A&E, at that. His face burned and was so painful that he did not know if he could keep himself from fainting. The longer he examined himself in the door pane, the weaker he felt.

Jörgen heard the sirens drawing nearer from different directions. Soon, the police would be here. Apparently, somebody had either seen or heard the gunfight. That was only to be expected. He considered his situation and decided that it would be best to visit a hospital as soon as possible. Perhaps someone was standing in a window, watching Jörgen right now with telephone in hand and talking directly to the police. If he went inside the entrance, the police would soon be swarming up the stairway. They would be going door to door, and those who did not open up would get a visit anyway. That was the procedure when dealing with serious villains. Talking to the police was the last thing he wanted to do now. He was in deep shit, as they say.

He had been punished just like the other two. Lennart Ekwall, the arrogant prosecutor who had refused to listen to any entreaties, now stood himself as the accused before the tribunal. A powerful emotion overwhelmed him as he saw the evil-doers escorted from their homes in handcuffs. He felt no remorse, nothing that deterred him. This was how vengeance felt and he knew that his was righteous. The hatred burned within him with an ever-stronger flame.

She was speaking to him again.

WALTER SEEMED ALMOST apathetic after Jonna had dispensed with official channels and told him he was suspended from duty, pending an internal investigation that would start as soon as he was discharged from the hospital.

"It's not the first time this has happened, you know," Walter said and tried to downplay the gravity of the situation.

"No, I can see that," Jonna said and smiled awkwardly. "But it could be the most serious infringement."

Walter looked inquiringly at Jonna. "What do you base that on?"

Jonna squirmed. "Lilja said that this is one time too many. You have used up your favours and so on."

"Really? Is that what he said?" Walter remarked dryly. "Anyway, I haven't received an official notification yet. Which *de facto* means that I'm still a detective with the CID. And before I have the notification in my hand, I can initiate a new investigation. Which is what I intend to do. With or without Lilja and definitely without the phony detectives at SÄPO." He reached determinedly for his mobile phone, which lay on the bedside table.

"What are you doing?" Jonna asked.

"I'm going to become a pain," Walter said. "A chronic pain."

"You're calling …"

"Julén." Walter filled in the blank.

Walter, however, never got the chance to use his phone. Without knocking, an older man man strode through the door to the hospital room. He was wearing a long, black wool coat, well-pressed trousers, and shoes polished to a mirror shine. The man observed Walter dispassionately for a few seconds before breaking out in a smile.

"Walter, Walter," he admonished and moved to the centre of the room. "So this is where you've been hiding."

"This is just what I don't need right now," Walter muttered and put his phone down.

"You know why I'm here," the man greeted him and walked over to the bed.

"Straight to business like a tart's punter and with the charm of an iceberg," Walter stated.

"Let me guess," the man said.

"Please do," Walter answered.

"Could you possibly be referring to me?" the man said.

"You've always been very self-aware," Walter laughed sarcastically.

Both men sized each other up for a few seconds. Jonna watched, surprised by the icy chill that was obvious between them. Finally, the visitor backed down.

"Do I need to explain the grounds for the decision?" he asked in a tense voice. His smile gave way to a stern expression.

Walter nodded. "I'm all ears," he said.

"In the first place, you have performed illegal searches of both the national identity and the criminal records databases."

"Who hasn't done that?" Walter countered. "That became common practice back in the days of the Olof Palme investigation. Go on."

"Then we have the complaint from the Drug Squad, who maintain that you sabotaged two years of undercover operations by not consulting them before you shook down all known associates to the pimp Kenneth Haglund, now on trial for murder."

"For God's sake, he had beaten a tart to death. What should I have done? Waited until the Drug Squad gave us permission to investigate a murder? They just lost a few drug dealers in the operation. I pointed that out when they came complaining to Lilja. Two small-fry dealers against one murderer. What other choice did I have?"

"Don't look at me," the man said and shrugged apologetically. "I'm just the messenger."

"As a former murder detective, you would do exactly the same," Walter said with some bitterness.

The man just shook his head. "Do you keep them there?" he asked and looked at the cupboard standing in the corner of the room.

Walter nodded.

The man served Walter some papers, went over to the cupboard and started to poke around in his clothes.

"Perhaps I should introduce myself," Jonna said and went towards the person she assumed was from Internal Affairs. She had felt invisible ever since this comedian had marched into the room.

"Not necessary," he said curtly. "I already know who you are."

Jonna looked at the man, as surprised as she was irritated.

"But I don't actually know who you are," she replied and took a step towards to the man.

"Lindström, Internal Affairs," muttered the man as he searched through Walter's clothes.

"Stay away from him," Walter said from his bed. "Above all, don't shake his hand. He's as friendly as an electric fence."

Jonna said nothing and instead sat in the visitor's chair. Internal Affairs was not exactly known for having the most convivial personalities on the police force. Investigating colleagues obviously required a certain type of mindset. There was, perhaps, a method in their madness. A trait that was needed to prevent them from empathizing with colleagues whom they were charged with investigating. The pressure on them was not insignificant. Still, that alone did not excuse his behaviour.

The man picked out the shoulder holster with Walter's service weapon, a Sig Sauer, and removed the magazine. In a practised manner, he pulled back the slide to ensure that the chamber was clear of any rounds. For safety's sake, he double-checked Walter's pockets for any extra magazines or rounds that he might have. From the wallet, which he found hidden deep down in one of Walter's Ecco loafers, he removed the police ID and the badge. He put everything in a transparent evidence bag and sealed it.

"Right then," he said and approached Walter. He quickly examined the notification papers and Walter's scribbled signature. Then he signed a receipt confirming that Walter's weapon and police ID had been taken into his custody. Finally, he wished them a good day and left the room as quickly as he had entered.

"I've known that man for many years," Walter exclaimed as soon as the door had closed behind Lindström. "We've worked together more than once. We actually worked together during the Södermalm riots many years ago. A really smug bastard."

"But now he's at IA," Jonna interrupted.

"Yes, but this doesn't change anything really," Walter explained. "I'll make sure that there will be a new investigation, based on the memo I wrote. Even with this small hiccup, I can start working on Lilja and Julén, and Lilja at least eventually does what he's told," Walter concluded.

Jonna started to protest, but checked herself. That Walter no longer was on the force was really his problem. That he also believed that he could get a new investigation started sounded more like fantasy than reality. How could a detective at the CID possibly convince SÄPO and the Chief Prosecutor to open yet another investigation on Drug-X?

At any rate, Jonna would do what she could to persuade her supervisor to forward a memo to SÄPO, about why the terrorist theory could not be a feasible one. She would instead suggest that someone convicted in the courts was seeking revenge on the District Prosecutor and the court jury. Even if that theory was not completely plausible, it was the most probable of the two. Even Walter agreed on that.

IT WAS PAST two in the morning when Jonna, for the seventh time, gave up any hope of sleeping. With her eyes fixed on a spider on the ceiling and brooding about how she was going to phrase the report to her supervisor at RSU, she was once again trapped in a mental loop. The report should not sound too far-fetched. It had to be a balanced mix of facts and qualified assumptions that led to a final conclusion, which pointed to one or several perpetrators, who could be traced through the court cases handled by the relevant jurors and the District Prosecutor. Certainly, there were gaps in her theory about the perpetrator's method, but those questions would be answered by an investigation, if it were given adequate resources. The problem Jonna faced was SÄPO, which was now leading the ongoing operation with Åsa Julén in charge of the preliminary investigation. Jonna bit her lower lip, thinking it over.

THE MEMO THAT Jonna proposed to her supervisor was forwarded, registered and archived at SÄPO without any further action. Johan Hildebrandt was so alarmed by the total radio silence that he had to check whether his memo had been received by the addressees, which it had. However, nobody paid it any attention. Not even the Prosecutor's Office had bothered to send a reply. Julén deferred to SÄPO, where the memo seemed to have disappeared into a black hole.

TOR HEDMAN TURNED into the parking space by Danderyd's hospital and parked the car. He was shaking from the after-shock of the gunfight.

"Fucking hell. That was so bloody close," he said, shaken, and lit a *Prince* cigarette. His hand trembling, he took a deep drag and exhaled the smoke through his nose. Jerry glared con-temptuously at Tor. Smokers were not only daft in the head, they smelled like fucking ashtrays too. And the passive smoker was just as much at risk as the idiot sitting with a coffin nail stuck in his cakehole. Jerry grabbed the cigarette from Tor's mouth and tossed it out of the car window. "Oy! I told you to bloody lay off smoking in the car," Jerry growled.

"But I ..."

"No fucking buts," Jerry interrupted. "We bloody nearly got our skulls filled with lead. We have to think now. Don't you get it?"

Tor silently swore to himself: he was being denied a smoke in the car even after they had barely avoided being smoked themselves.

"Just listen," Jerry went on. "What happened on Odengatan was a good thing. So bloody good that I could even kiss ..." Jerry dug deep into his memory to find someone to swap spit with, but came up empty.

Tor looked in amazement at Jerry, who apparently was rapt in intense thought.

"This is too fucking good to be true," Jerry finally said, and slammed his fist into the glove compartment so that the door flew open.

Tor raised an eyebrow and looked dubiously at Jerry. Had he lost it? Was he in shock? Less than fifteen minutes ago, they had been in the middle of a shootout that could have cost them their lives. Now Jerry was sitting there and saying it was a good thing. Tor did not understand anything.

"What's so good?" Tor asked sceptically.

"Who knew that we would be on Odengatan today and at exactly this time?" Jerry cried out.

"Nobody knew about it," Tor answered. "I haven't talked to anybody, unless you have?"

"One person knew," Jerry concluded.

"Who then?" Tor wondered and immediately thought of the go-between.

"The bloke who gave us the job, of course. It was the bastard who told us to visit that bloody loser and to strong-arm that evidence from him. He was also the one who told us which day and what time to do the job."

"So what?"

"Don't 'so what?' me," Jerry said. "He screwed us. So now, we can screw him good and proper. Are you up for it?"

"Dunno," Tor hesitated, trying unsuccessfully to follow his logic.

"Or we can just walk away from this job now without getting a bad reputation. And toss this key on the rubbish tip," Jerry said, holding up Jörgen's key to the safety deposit box.

"But why did he try to set us up? What would he stand to gain?" Tor asked and groped after the cigarette pack in his inside pocket. He was dying for a ciggie now.

"I have no fucking idea. But we'll find out," Jerry said, with eyes like red-hot coals.

"It could have been a trap set by Haxhi," Tor suggested and stuck a new *Prince* in his mouth. Just as he was about to light it, he stopped himself. Jerry was angrily watching the cigarette hanging from the corner of Tor's mouth. Tor sighed and instead got out and sat on the wing of the car, where he concentrated on blowing smoke rings while he thought.

Jerry's brow was deeply furrowed. Certainly, he and Tor could still clean up this mess with their reputation intact. First, their go-between Omar would have to vouch for the evidence before they could send the journalist to swim with the fishes. Tor and Jerry had been given a free hand to handle the job in their own way. The important thing was that they succeeded. One hundred thousand up front had not been a problem. Jerry would have to talk with Omar, who had given them the job. He needed to get directly in touch with the client. Without Omar's involvement.

AFTER HAVING BEEN x-rayed and wheeled in on a bed to a room on one of the wards, Jörgen quickly began to take stock of his situation. The first things he was sure of were a broken nose, an agonizing headache and an eye that was blocked up tighter than an Egyptian pharoah's tomb – perhaps permanently, if the radiologist's reaction was anything to go on. Furthermore, the police mole and God-knows-who-else were after his scalp. It seemed as if the whole human race had turned against him. He had finally incurred the wrath of God for his sins. The only positive thing he could put in the equation was that his skull seemed to have stayed intact. Dr André had cheerfully informed him of that fact before he finished his rounds.

THREE UNITS OF the National SWAT team, the NI, were deployed around the rented property on Atlasgatan. Team Alpha, which was the main force, would be performing the flat search itself. To avoid destroying any evidence, and as this was classed as a high-risk operation, it was decided to strike hard and without warning. Team Bravo would cut off any escape routes and had therefore sealed the building perimeter as tight as a drum. The third team, Delta, would provide backup for the other two teams. The assault would take place at 03.30 hours exactly. It had taken less than three minutes to deploy the teams and Martin Borg waited impatiently. Two minutes to go. Clouds of condensation rose from his mouth in the chilly morning air. He was content with all the preparations that his group at the Counter-Terrorism Unit had made. First, snatching the investigation from the amateurs at County CID, then planning and leading the operation with NI and, finally, being on the brink of an operation that would probably turn the tide in his favour. The fire smouldering inside him flared up when he thought of how these dirty animals poisoned the Free World with their twisted ideology. The Taliban were the worst of them all. Directly after 9/11, an American Air Force general had said that he would bomb Afghanistan back to the Stone Age.

Obviously, he was unaware that the Taliban had already taken the country back to that era.

The walkie-talkie crackled into life.

"Alpha, breach." Two short words came from the task-force leader.

Martin was jolted back to reality. The time had come and the leader of the NI task force had given the signal to enter the building. Now we will show them how a democracy works at its best, he thought, and squeezed the charm that he wore around his neck.

"Affirmative, breach," the Alpha-team leader answered.

Police officers in black uniforms and ski masks were standing pressed up against the wall by the stairwell. Three of them ran towards the flat door with a battering ram. In less than six seconds, they had forced the door open. Two more police officers rushed to the doorway and fired in tear gas and stun grenades, which exploded with loud bangs. With MP5 submachine guns drawn, the rest of the team stormed into the block of flats, shouting over each other that they were from the police, in case anybody came to another conclusion.

Alpha-team leader Anton Edvinsson was the first to enter the flat. The smoke from the tear gas had spread out like a fog, which made it impossible to see more than an arm's length in front. He slowly swept the air in front of him with his MP5. The light from the torch attached to his submachine gun cut through the smoke like a laser beam. Out of the corner of his eye, he could see his colleagues following behind him and flanking him at the side of the hallway. He signalled to his wingman to cover the door that was ahead of them. He was going to open a glass door that seemed to lead into the living room. His colleague moved quickly forwards and positioned himself to the left of the glass door. Edvinsson tested the handle, which was unlocked. He took a deep breath and threw open the door, shouting "Police!" so loudly that his voice almost cracked. Sweeping the room ahead of him with the MP5, he rushed in, together with the officer who had been covering him. Two policemen quickly moved up behind them. When the room was secured, Edvinsson positioned himself in front of yet another door, again backed up by a colleague. It was like ballet. Their pattern of movements was well rehearsed and each advance had a purpose. Nothing was left to chance. Even though the element of surprise was important, safety was always first.

Edvinsson tore open the unlocked door and suddenly found himself facing a bearded man in a nightshirt.

WHAT IS TAKING such a long time? Martin Borg thought impatiently and watched the backs of the NI task-force controllers sitting by their monitors. He drummed his fingers against his thigh and threw a glance at his colleague Ove Jernberg, who seemed to be completely oblivious to the gravity of the situation. That did not surprise him. Ove was an idealist; he had drifted through life and had never known which side of the fence he should stand on. He changed principles like a teenager swaps clothes. Martin wanted to believe that he had been successful in converting him to his reality. But he was not completely sure that he had succeeded.

Even more men, most of them with beards, stood lined up along the wall. They all had their hands in the air.

"Down!" Edvinsson roared and pointed with military precision at the floor as adrenaline pumped through his body. He kept the MP5 aimed at the man standing closest. Only when some officers crossed his firing line did he lower his weapon. The men were getting down onto the floor, but apparently not quickly enough – they were thrown on their stomachs by the charging police. Their hands were handcuffed behind their backs.

"All five subjects secured," the police radio finally reported.

Martin immediately felt a hundred kilos lighter. The few minutes of radio silence had been infinitely long. He had felt a knot growing in his gut. Not out of fear of one of his men being injured or even killed. That did not concern him. He had been afraid that there would be no one in the flat. The Surveillance Unit had a habit of not being able to keep track of the location of those they were monitoring, even when they had beards and were wearing nightshirts. Lack of resources was the usual, tired excuse. So he was relieved that the subjects had been secured. He was looking forward to the subsequent interrogations, when he would break them one by one. He could not wait to get started.

Members of SÄPO's forensics team had just arrived when Martin marched in through the demolished front door. The door frame had been ripped off its hinges by the force of the battering ram. They have taken off the kid gloves, he thought, and smiled contentedly. The team leader, Anton Edvinsson, stood in the hallway with his helmet under his arm and the ski mask pulled upwards into a woolly hat.

"Did they offer any resistance?" Martin asked.

"No, they just looked surprised," Edvinsson answered and took a swig from his water bottle. "So would I, if someone broke in and rammed a machine gun in my face at three-thirty in the morning."

"Anything else of significance?" Martin asked dryly.

"Check out their study," Edvinsson suggested.

"Study?" Martin said, surprised.

After entering the flat, Martin understood what he meant. The room Edvinsson called a study was crammed full, with bookshelves, desks and different types of containers. Drawings illustrating buildings lay rolled out on long desks lined up along the walls.

"Blueprints!" one of SÄPO's technicians concluded, bending over one of the desks. He wore blue nylon overalls with a hood and a white mask that not only effectively blocked bacteria but also turned his voice into static.

After teasing his way into overalls and putting on his face mask, Martin went into the room.

"Alf?" he asked and approached the technician.

"Not quite," the man answered. "Peter Danielsson. Alf and I are like identical twins in these suits."

"What am I looking at?" Martin asked and stared at a drawing.

"Detailed blueprints of buildings," Danielsson answered. "The majority seem to be mosques."

"Which mosques then?"

"Not a clue," Danielsson answered, shaking his head. "But the drawings are in Swedish. If you look at the dates in the headers, most of them are no more than a few years old. Perhaps these are ongoing construction projects."

"Nothing else?" Martin asked, disappointed.

"No, not so far," Danielsson answered.

Martin looked troubled. Mere drawings of mosques would not sit well with the prosecutor. Whatever their purpose, this case would never hold up in court. It was, after all, not illegal to build mosques if one had building permission. He could still claim that the group had received terrorist funds. But until the terrorist prince was on the US blacklist, this would also be a dead end. The most he could do would be to freeze the group's assets for a while, but there would be hell to pay when the prince found out. The royal family in Saudi Arabia would send the yanks to read the riot act to the primitive Vikings in the north. If there were no traces of Drug-X in the flat, there was only one way forwards.

"ABDULLAH KHALIL: THIRTY-EIGHT years old and born in Sudan. Came to Sweden as a refugee eight years ago. Is that correct?" Martin Borg asked and looked at the bearded man facing him. It was six-thirty in the morning and Martin felt euphoric. He was not the slightest bit tired despite the fact that a full day had passed since he last slept. He took a large sip of coffee and grimaced when he realized that the coffee had gone cold.

"So you don't want a lawyer to represent you because you don't accept our democratic form of government and all that it represents in terms of rights and obligations. Is that correct?" he continued his interrogation. He already knew what the answer would be.

The man was silent. He did not move a muscle, instead looking down at the table as if he was praying.

"What are you using the blueprints for?"

The man looked up and laughed contemptuously.

"Well?" Martin asked impatiently.

"If we have done anything that displeases the great Allah, we shall be punished," the man began slowly and with a heavy accent. "And only then, not by you unbelievers. Who are you to forbid us to build mosques, God's houses?"

"We will ask the questions and you will answer. This is how interrogations are usually done, if you didn't already know that. What were you using the drawings for?" Martin repeated.

"That is between us and Allah," the man answered defiantly. "We are under no obligation to tell you anything."

The man fell silent.

"Who owns the drawings you had in the flat?" Martin continued.

"Allah does," the man continued his defiance.

"Most likely, he does, but who got hold of them? Surely not a task for Allah," Martin joked, trying to start a conversation with the man.

"Allah creates everything in this world. Everything you see around you is created by the Almighty."

Martin sighed and rubbed his face. He was getting tired of this.

"It's late and I'm getting fed up with listening to your mindless ranting about Allah. We can easily find out how you came into possession of the drawings and which buildings they represent. I hardly think that God or Allah is the owner of the blueprints. Once again, what were you going to use the drawings for?"

The man slowly shook his head. "The material world you live in is so empty," he said. "You cannot see the light because you are blinded by your own arrogance and filled with a self-righteousness that will be your downfall."

"I see," Martin said and leaned back in his chair. He surveyed the man and irritation began to build within him. It was as if he were mocking Martin – in fact, the entire SÄPO organization. Yet he could not avoid feeling a grudging admiration at the self-assurance and calm that these fanatics radiated. They were perhaps at peace with themselves and their faith, which was what made the scumbags the difficult and fearsome adversaries they were. Fanatics were always difficult to break down. Especially the ones that submitted to a higher power in the form of something as abstract as a god or a dead prophet. The Americans had had little success on the Guantanamo base, despite better resources and fewer restrictions. As a colleague in the CIA had expressed it, "It's ten times easier to turn a communist than a brainwashed, Islamic terrorist."

The communists' loathing of the West during the Cold War had been deep and entrenched, yet the Islamic radicals' hatred was of such magnitude that it could be subdued only with death. Few communists would give their lives as readily for their cause as an Islamist suicide bomber would. The enemy was no longer nations like the Soviet Union and its satellite regimes. The enemy was now among us. It could be your neighbour or a co-worker. And they struck indiscriminately at both military and civilian targets – hard and soft. Women, children and old men in wheelchairs were of no significance. They were all unbelievers and were to be wiped out for the Holy Cause.

"Let's skip all that stuff about God owning the drawings for a while and change the subject completely," Martin suggested and looked at his papers. "Is the name Karin Sjöstrand familiar?"

The man looked at Martin as if he had suddenly started to speak in a foreign language.

"Why would I know her?" he asked and shook his head in denial.

"Lennart Ekwall, then?" Martin continued. "District Prosecutor Lennart Ekwall."

The man did not reply.

"Perhaps the name Bror Lantz then?" Martin leaned towards him. "He's a judge at Stockholm District Court, if that rings a bell."

The man remained expressionless.

Martin needed to do something. The towelhead had shut down completely.

"I myself have a problem with some of the laws and courts that we have in this country," Martin resumed, changing tactic. By showing understanding of matters close to the interview subject's core beliefs, one could, in the best of cases, build up an empathetic relationship, which enabled information to be gleaned by reading between the lines.

The man said nothing and just stared condescendingly at Martin.

"I have nothing against Islam or its practitioners. We need diversity to survive as a civilization," Martin tried. In fact, I'm rather fascinated by Islam and would like to learn more."

No reaction.

"Wouldn't you like to see children playing side by side wherever they are in the world and regardless of their religion?" he asked, with a touch of desperation in his voice. He has to take the bait now, Martin thought. At the very least, he would start to vent his righteous anger at US politics in the Middle East.

Not a single muscle twitched in the man's face.

15

MARTIN BORG CLOSED the file and asked his colleague to take over the interrogation, if one could even call it an interrogation. He walked down the corridor after progress with the interview had stalled. It was still early in the morning and he needed space to think. Martin's contempt towards those who were appointed to defend democracy increased with each day that passed. The majority of his colleagues were blinded by naivety and preoccupied with political correctness. That would plunge them into the abyss. He leaned back against the wall and popped a piece of nicotine gum in his mouth, while tracing the contours of the charm with his thumb. It was worn down after protecting him for twenty years.

A feeling of impotence enveloped him. It was like trying to dam a waterfall with his bare hands. Did no one understand the kind of threat posed by the Islamization of Europe? Why were everybody's eyes closed? Probably because they were not aware of the truth. They were not as informed as he was himself and never would be because of the censoring of the press, as well as the politicians competing with each other to demonstrate their tolerance. All that he could do was to convince the general population before it was too late.

Martin walked into interrogation room "C", where he found his colleague Ove Jernberg in the middle of questioning another of the Holy Prophet's lackeys.

Martin waved Ove towards the doorway.

"How's it going?" Martin whispered.

"He's as silent as the grave," Ove replied.

"Has he said anything at all?"

"Not really, just that it's Allah who decides and dictates what he and his brothers are doing."

"Nothing about the drug? Not even a hint?"

"Not so much as a syllable," Ove answered, shaking his head.

"We have three more left to question, but it's hardly likely that any of them will say anything that will help the investigation. On the other hand, one bonus is that we are spared any legal eagles spouting off about the law. We'll just have to keep chipping away at them and try to wear them down. Besides, we should get a shot at other members of the Allah fan club. It seems, however, that they are out of the country."

"When will the Chief Prosecutor be put in the picture?" Ove asked.

"In a few hours. We have a meeting with Åsa Julén at eight-thirty."

Ove nodded and returned to the interrogation.

CHIEF PROSECUTOR ÅSA Julén was fifteen minutes late for the meeting on the investigation of which she was in charge. Stressed out, she sat down, complaining that the traffic remained busy, despite the congestion tax, an economic recession and increased petrol prices.

Martin Borg gave Ove Jernberg and the head of the County Drug Squad, Michael Stjerna, a meaningful look. All three smiled a little at Julén's harassed entrance.

The County Police Commissioner, Folke Uddestad, was the one who opened the meeting, which irritated Martin. Lack of sleep did not improve his mood. It was, in fact, SÄPO that now led the operational part of the investigation and he was the most senior officer from SÄPO in the room. Commissioner Uddestad contributed nothing to the investigation. He was probably more of a hindrance, with his bureaucratic rigmarole and concern about motives. Martin knew that the Commissioner would actively meddle in the investigation now. He had probably prepared many counter-arguments.

"Well, as you all know, we have taken in five people for preliminary questioning. And as we feared, we haven't managed to get anything out of them," Uddestad began, taking a bite of a gingerbread biscuit, which then broke into pieces and ended up in his mug of coffee. For a moment, he lost track.

Martin saw an opening.

"It's correct that we haven't got anything out of the initial questioning," he began. "All five have also waived their rights to legal aid, which perhaps says more about their antagonistic position to Swedish society than their religious beliefs."

The room fell silent as all eyes were directed towards Uddestad. Martin watched the Commissioner as he fished with his spoon in the coffee mug. A clown in a uniform, Martin thought, and felt angry that somebody like Uddestad could become a police commissioner. But if an idiot like Uddestad could make County Police Commissioner, then Martin could very well become a department head eventually. This fact eased Martin's irritation slightly.

"How's it going with the detective work? Has the Drug Squad found any leads on Drug-X?" Åsa Julén asked.

"Very few," Michael Stjerna answered. "And that worries us."

"In what way?" she asked.

"Normally, there's always someone who knows something," Stjerna explained. "We've shaken down every fuck – dealer and supplier," he said, correcting himself. "They all look at us like village idiots when we press them. Which can only mean one thing."

"That the drug originates from a tightly-knit gang," Martin interrupted. "Coincidentally, we have such a group here in the building."

Stjerna nodded in agreement.

"But the interrogations are not making any progress," Julén pointed out.

"No," Martin admitted. "We need more time."

Julén deliberated for a brief moment. That the suspects had not said anything was, in itself, suspicious. When suspects had nothing to hide, they were usually talkative. But she was walking a tightrope; she was aware of that. "Innocent until proven guilty" was playing in the back of her mind. The new laws, however, made her decision considerably easier. She had something to fall back on.

"I will invoke the anti-terrorism laws from now on. I have gained approval from the Prosecutor-General and the Minister for Justice. You will have more time and more room for manoeuvre. The limited period of detention is no longer an obstacle," she informed them.

All signalled their approval, except Uddestad, who raised the question of whether it was unlawful to withhold blueprints of mosques.

"We have examined the technical drawings we found in the flat," said Alf Gunnarson from SÄPO's forensics team. "Most factors suggest that they are building plans for new mosques, as well as of some mosques that are already completed. Some are entire buildings; others are premises in larger properties."

"I see," Julén said, with a worried frown. "What are we really getting out of the drawings? Are there any secret tunnels indicated or storage facilities where they might want to keep something secret? Anything that can be classified as terrorist activity?"

"We have found nothing so far," Gunnarson said.

Julén looked hesitant.

Uddestad shook his head doubtfully. "We still have to identify a link to Drug-X, the two court officials and the district
prosecutor, which is the original reason we are sitting here. Also
if the terrorist prince is indeed supplying them with the drug."

Martin bit his lip hard. That tosser could not keep silent.
If he were allowed to continue, he would make Julén waver.
At heart, Åsa Julén was a coward and disliked taking risks;
everyone who had to deal with her knew that. Martin must
get the County Police Commissioner away from the investigation before he did any damage, but, even for a team leader
of SÄPO, that was easier said than done. The prosecutor in
charge of the investigation made the final decision. She was,
for all intents and purposes, Martin's superior and, to top it all
off, Uddestad was also personally connected with a big player
in the political world. And it was not just any politician. Of
all the bloody zombies in parliament, it had to be the Minister
for Justice. Even if a politician could not directly interfere and
give them instructions, they could whip up public opinion over
individual cases. In any event, the Minister for Justice had a
legitimate reason to be concerned about any investigation involving the judicial system.

"We'll establish the backgrounds of the detainees and turn
over every stone. Sooner or later, I'm convinced that we'll
find a connection," Martin said, reading the mood around the
table. He had to avoid losing his temper.

"Very possibly, but we need to have other options,"
Uddestad replied and threw up his hands. "Personally, I think
this is far-fetched – terrorist princes notwithstanding."

Uddestad was apparently going to question every decision
and suggestion from Martin's direction. He felt his blood boil,
but controlled himself and decided to let Julén deal with the
problem.

"SÄPO's in charge of this investigation from an operational perspective," Martin said respectfully. "And I've been appointed to advise the head of the investigation. I therefore have a mandate – after consultation with my superior, Åsa Julén, of course – to make the necessary decisions regarding activities, strategies and other matters that may move the investigation forwards." He looked at Julén, who fidgeted uneasily.

Julén felt uncomfortable caught in the crossfire between the County Police Commissioner and the investigation team leader from SÄPO. That there was friction in the investigation team was, in itself, nothing unusual. When this happened, it was usually between the prosecutor and the police. It could sometimes be a healthy dynamic that produced new ideas, since the friction usually developed when the investigation was not making any progress. But this situation was more or less unique: a police commissioner and the Security Service more or less in open confrontation. She had known for some time that Commissioner Folke Uddestad did not have a high regard for the Security Service. She knew less about Martin Borg. She had heard some rumours that he possibly had some difficulties working with female colleagues, but he was not alone in that. This dispute could blow up into something messy. She discreetly scratched behind her ear.

"Yes, that is so," she began, with some hesitation in her voice. "But the Minister for Justice himself also made it very clear that the Commissioner should participate in the investigation, and neither the Prosecutor-General nor myself have any objection to that. What role the Commissioner has in this context is perhaps not entirely clear yet and, until that is clarified, SÄPO leads, quite rightly, the operational part of the investigation. But regardless of that, I am, in fact, in my role as Chief Prosecutor, still in charge of the investigation. And as I see things right now, there's no reason to allocate our resources other than on the group of individuals that's currently being detained and their associates. Until someone can convince me of the contrary, we shall continue as SÄPO proposes."

Everyone nodded in agreement, except Folke Uddestad.

Martin added that he would gladly accept ideas and suggestions, especially from the Commissioner who, with his extensive experience in law enforcement, certainly would make a valuable contribution to the investigation.

Uddestad was the first person to leave the room.

Martin assessed his situation directly after the meeting. He was now faced with three different challenges. To begin with, he had an operational problem in the form of the uncommunicative gentlemen with the beards. After the initial interrogations, he realized that it would be difficult to get them to open up. However, he believed that, with some creative thinking and a slightly unorthodox technique, he had a solution to that problem, a solution that he had often used successfully on previous occasions.

The second challenge was more of an internal one and had so far had not been a problem, but it could eventually become one. That problem was Åsa Julén. Martin had two reasons to be concerned about her. To start with, she was a woman and women were, by definition, weak and naive. The second reason was her unwillingness to take risks. She would need persuading before she went ahead with a prosecution. Anything to protect herself in the event of a possible failure. Her record consisted almost exclusively of prosecutions in which the burden of evidence was so much to her advantage that a not-guilty verdict was as likely as a pathological liar telling the truth. Yet no battle could be won without taking risks; any soldier would testify to that fact.

So Martin and his team would have to present a mountain of conclusive evidence that would make it impossible for Julén to lose in court.

The third and final problem was also internal and its name was Folke Uddestad. While Martin believed he had a good understanding of and control over the other two cards in his hand, there was still this joker in the pack. Therefore, he would be forced to take special measures to ensure that Uddestad did not query every move in the investigation. That there was no love lost between the County Police Commissioner and the Security Service was not news. Back in the middle of the 1980s, it was discovered that Uddestad appeared in SÄPO's top-secret list of police-authority personnel who could pose problems, because of so-called "strongly dissenting views on police activities". Consequently, Uddestad regarded SÄPO as a snake in the grass. The top-secret list, however, was not sufficiently secret to prevent it from ending up in the public limelight, just a few months after it had been created. Rumours of a mole deep within the Security Service grew stronger after that happened. In the beginning, many believed that it was a political decision from the government to create the list and to monitor individual officers with the police authorities. This quickly proved to be incorrect. The initiative had been taken by some high-level SÄPO officials, who believed that a certain moral decay prevailed within the police force. Therefore, they felt forced to act and identified individual police officers, to prepare for a "cleansing" of those who represented the decay. These moral guardians still were firmly entrenched within SÄPO, despite a media storm of hurricane proportions.

Martin stroked his chin, deep in thought. Everybody has a weak point, a secret they would not want to see the light of day. He needed only to find Uddestad's weak spot. He was not concerned about getting sponsors for such a project within SÄPO. Together with the head of SÄPO, Anders Holmberg, and the National Police Board, Uddestad was pushing hard for the creation of a Swedish-style FBI, and the establishment of RSU was the first part of the process. This idea was shunned like the bubonic plague among officers within SÄPO. First, he needed to start with his immediate superior Thomas Kokk and his network of contacts higher up in SÄPO's hierarchy. That would also resolve the third and final problem.

A smile found its way onto his troubled face and, all of a sudden, he felt elated. It was as if he had had a small epiphany. Now, he needed only to schedule all the steps in his plan. He took out his personal laptop and started up Microsoft Office Project. He christened the project "Three Crowns" and began to input the variables.

WALTER GRÖHN OPENED his eyes at Karolinska University Hospital one hour after the brain surgeon Täljkvist had completed the operation. Walter had insisted that he was unconscious during the operation. For the life of him, he could not understand why they wanted to operate on his brain under only local anaesthetic and while he was fully awake, although it was routine. The removal of the tumour lying inside Walter's head had gone as planned, despite the complexity of the procedure. The medical profession deserved a certain recognition after all, even if he thought the majority of those practising it consisted of snotty brats who each earned the salaries of twenty nurses. After having tried to use his recently operated-on brain to reconsider the facts of the drug and the murders, he was finally forced to give in to the ensuing fatigue. It was as if someone had slowly dimmed the lights.

The following day, Walter woke up early. The clock stood at five-thirty. With some surprise, he looked around the room. He must have been moved during the night, because he was in the company of three other patients. Faint breathing was the only sound that he could hear. Opposite him was a young girl with red hair, who apparently had a broken leg. It was in plaster from her thigh down to her toes. Across from him and to the right was a foreign woman, about forty, with her mouth half open. Her blanket had fallen off and he noticed she was bandaged around one breast under her nightgown. An amputated breast. Probably cancer. The bed directly to the right, however, Walter could not see. A screen separated the bed from the rest of the room. However, he could hear deep snoring at regular intervals, revealing that he had a man as his closest neighbour. Just before eight, the nurses came in with breakfast. A blonde assistant nurse bade good morning to Walter and placed a tray with sandwiches, orange juice and coffee on the bedside table. Walter took a big bite of a cheese sandwich and drank the glass of orange juice. The nurse went behind the screen and woke up the snoring man. He was lying with his back facing Walter. The man wearily cleared his throat and remained still for a minute before he finally sat up on the edge of the bed and started picking at his breakfast. Walter said hello to the girl and the one-breasted lady, who had also started to wake up. As if on cue, the man turned around. At first, Walter could not see who it was because of his battered face. But then the curly-haired man started talking and Walter choked on his coffee.

"Well, if it isn't the detective!" Jörgen Blad burst out, so loudly that the others in the room could not help hearing. The one-breasted woman and the redhead directed their gazes first at the man with a face like a colour chart and then at the new patient with the bandaged head.

Walter cleared the coffee from his nose and put his coffee cup on the bedside table. "What's happened to you then?" he asked, carelessly. "Have you stuck your nose in one time too many?"

Jörgen's grin remained on his face.

"What about you?" he asked and drew a halo in the air around his head.

"Had some rubbish in my head that needed to be removed," Walter answered.

"A bullet?" Jörgen quickly became serious.

"Hardly that," Walter said dryly. "A tumour."

Jörgen's face looked concerned. "Is it serious?"

Walter shook his head in denial.

"I had a ladder fall on me, myself," Jörgen said, sighing melodramatically.

"Sounds feasible," Walter answered, equally melodramatically, and turned his back. With all the sick people in the country, the odds must have been one in a million that he would end up with Jörgen Blad in the bed next to his. Nonetheless, there he lay. One of them was going to have to change rooms.

Jörgen looked thoughtfully at Walter's back for a long while. An idea had popped out of nowhere and refused to get out of his head. Suddenly, he saw everything clearly. Why hadn't he thought of it earlier? There was actually an alternative and a possible way out despite everything that had happened.

"Are you interested in a win-win deal?" Jörgen asked, after pondering for a moment. Walter did not answer, but became more and more irritated by the reporter's presence.

"If I were you, I would listen," Jörgen continued. Walter did not bother to reply. If he was quiet long enough, the wretch would perhaps tire, at least until one of them switched rooms. But then a twinge of curiosity appeared like a piece of spam email in his inbox. What could a journalist offer that would benefit both himself and the police?

Walter was no stranger to cutting a deal with criminals, as long as the payoff was greater than the cost of the favour. But to bargain with journalists was a completely different business. The crooks were actually a better bet, because they were relatively predictable, but you never knew where you were with journalists and the media. I suppose it couldn't do any harm to listen to what the scumbag has to say, Walter thought.

"Listening never killed anyone," Jörgen grumbled.

Walter turned around. "What is it you want to say?"

"I can give you something if you give me something in return," Jörgen explained.

Walter looked carefully at Jörgen. "Such as?" he replied sarcastically.

"How about a high-ranking policeman who leaks information like a sieve and, on top of that, is consorting with serious villains?"

"Sounds highly unlikely," Walter said sceptically.

"Why do you think I'm lying here?" Jörgen said, getting up from the bed and putting on the hospital slippers.

"Well, perhaps it was a ladder?" Walter suggested.

Jörgen looked at Walter with a smug expression.

16 "I CAN'T DO anything more now," Johan Hildebrandt insisted and shook his head in resignation. "At SÄPO, they're extremely irritated about the memo, and I'm having my head bitten off, since they think we're spreading wild speculation with absolutely no reason or evidence. Apparently, SÄPO's been talking to the CID, where Walter Gröhn has also submitted a similar memo. Gröhn is, of course, also suspended from duty pending an investigation by Internal Affairs. Thomas Kokk was exceedingly upset that we at RSU are undermining SÄPO."

"And Åsa Julén?" Jonna asked.

"She was kind enough to forward her copy of the memo to Martin Borg at SÄPO, who in turn went with it directly to Thomas Kokk, who already had the same memo, which he had received from me," Hildebrandt said and studied Jonna grimly with his sharp eyes.

"I don't understand why they're so upset," Jonna said. "Initially, they ignored the memo and now when you ask them to acknowledge its existence, they're infuriated by its content. What's the real issue here? They only have to confirm its receipt, even if they find it of no interest. As for 'wild speculation', what does that mean?"

"I don't know," Hildebrandt said, morosely. "But this matter lies a long way outside our area of responsibility, a fact that the security service, police and prosecution authorities have explained to me with absolute clarity."

"This is quite ridiculous. What are we going to do?" Jonna asked, throwing her hands up in frustration.

"We?" Hildebrandt exclaimed, disapprovingly. "We should definitely not do anything. To be specific, 'we' means you."

JONNA LOOKED AT the huge building that was the police headquarters through the window at Rut's café. Her latte was tasteless and, for the first time since she had started at RSU, she had doubts about the choice she had made. She began to ponder her situation in life. Instructors at the police academy had warned them. The system shapes each individual police officer. Brutal environment, brutal cops. Corrupt society, corrupt cops. And so on. But the country she was living in was neither brutal nor corrupt. It was however plagued by the envy attributable to a tall-poppy culture, popularly known as Jante's Law; a practice that was probably not pursued so zealously anywhere else in the world. This envy-based egalitarianism was of course reflected even in the police force.

Perhaps she would have been better off never applying to MIT and subsequently to the police academy, and instead doing as her father wished. Getting an education in business and economics and then working in the family's shipowning company. By now, she would have been a middle manager making eighty thousand a month. In another five years, she would have been vice president and, after yet another five years, she would have taken over from her father as CEO.

She could have been financially independent and in charge of over two thousand employees and thousands of tonnes worth of vessels. But she would also probably have died of stress before she had reached thirty-five.

It had taken her father a long time to get over Jonna's decision to pursue another path. Jonna was the first from many family generations not to work within the company that her ancestors had built up. He had turned his back on her and nearly banished her from the family. They had not spoken for years. Eventually, her father had given up and accepted Jonna's decision. He had not argued even when she applied to the police academy, but acknowledged her enrolment with a reserved "how amusing for you".

Jonna's brother, three years younger, was always around for last orders at the bars in the Stureplan entertainment district. With her father's reluctant approval, he had been selected as the person to eventually take over as CEO – despite the fact that he lacked Jonna's intellect and preferred to play with sports cars and speedboats.

Jonna's desire to be a police officer had been born from a sense of fairness she developed as a child. She had no idea where it came from, but she had poured out lemonade with exact precision and shared biscuits equally between her friends. If anyone was bullied at school, she was always the first to berate the bully, which had inevitably resulted in her becoming the target of the abuse. She had an almost compulsive need to be honest, even if this occasionally led to difficulty.

Jonna's thoughts were interrupted by the ringing of her mobile phone. At first, she hesitated, but then saw Walter's number on the phone's display.

"It's time to start the ball rolling," Walter began, as if they were still in the middle of a conversation.

Jonna took a deep breath in order to compose herself when she heard Walter's determined voice. Well, it can't get much worse than it is now, she thought.

"Is the operation already over?" she asked.

"Yeah, sure," Walter said, as if it was a trivial thing. "With today's technology, they can do most things in their coffee breaks."

"What a relief. You must feel really happy that it's over," she said in a cheerful voice.

"Yes, of course."

"When can you go home?"

"In about ten days, according to Darth Vader, the laser expert. He says that I can't move about or leave the bed for at least a week. I'm already beginning to feel as if I'm strapped into a restraint bed."

"Darth who?" Jonna said, puzzled.

"And I'm only allowed to go to the toilet assisted by a nurse and in a wheelchair," he added.

"How inconvenient for you," Jonna said, attempting to sound sympathetic.

"Now let's get to the reason I called you," Walter said, lowering his voice. "It's a well-known fact that private investigators have never been very successful at solving crimes."

"That's probably true," Jonna assented.

"But if it's police officers freelancing for an investigation, then it has a very different outcome."

"Really?" Jonna said, with mounting apprehension in her voice. She saw where he was going with this conversation.

"Favours returned for favours given by former colleagues and so on," Walter said. "You know what I mean."

Jonna murmured that she understood.

"As things stand today, it's not going to be possible to start a new investigation," Walter continued. "I've spoken with Lilja, and nothing of any sense is coming out of that man at the moment. Apparently, I am well and truly tainted by the drug operation that went wrong. And the memo that Lilja forwarded to SÄPO was appreciated about as much as a North Korean propaganda film at the Oscars. Julén is not returning my calls, despite dozens of voicemail messages. She ought to be more appreciative; it's the first time ever that I've left her a voicemail."

Jonna hesitated before responding. "I know where you're going with this talk about freelancers. You want me to use the police databases and start digging up information on court cases, even though I am neither authorized nor involved in the investigation anymore," she replied in a stern voice.

"That's one way of putting it," Walter retorted. "You see, there have been some developments here at the hospital."

"Really, such as?"

Walter lowered his voice to a whisper. "We need to talk, but not on the phone. The problem is that I share a room with a few patients. And, as I said before, I'm stuck in this bed for a week. You need to come here and wave your police badge so that we can talk undisturbed in another room. Say you need to question me, or something like that. My bed has wheels, so they just need to roll me out of here."

"Wait just a minute," Jonna burst out, leaning back in her chair. "I have just been given an unambiguous reprimand from my superior. He apparently got complaints from SÄPO, the police and Åsa Julén about the memo. Not that I understand the reasons, but that's how it is. If I want to end my career in the police force, then I only have to follow your suggestions. How long do you think it will be before Internal Affairs pays me a visit, and asks me to turn in my badge, if I do as you say?"

"A few days, at the most," Walter said.

"Exactly. And what would be the point of that?" Jonna replied, irritated.

"Two days under normal circumstances. But we'll do this a little differently," Walter whispered, barely audible.

Jonna sighed so loudly that it sounded like a gust of wind over the phone line.

"If Mademoiselle would be so kind as to get her well-trained derrière over here, I will explain everything," he said, trying to sound convincing.

Jonna quickly reappraised her situation. Visiting Walter again could hardly do much damage. What she did on her own time was not anyone's business and, as long as she did not break the rules, she had nothing to worry about. She would, however, have to be careful about waving her ID around. If somebody at the hospital called RSU to check up on her, she would be in trouble.

"I'll drop by to see how you're doing. Nothing else," Jonna finally resolved.

Walter accepted her terms and she drank up the last of her latte and paid the bill. She could not help smiling a little in spite of herself. There was something childish and yet mischievous about him. You never knew what to expect with Walter Gröhn.

MARGARETA FORS, DIRECTOR-GENERAL of the National Courts Administration, and the Chief Magistrate of Stockholm District Court and senior judge, Law Speaker Evert Kihlman, looked long and hard at Åsa Julén, who had, in broad terms, explained how the investigation into Bror Lantz and Karin Sjöstrand was progressing. She had informed them that the Security Service had taken over the investigation from the local police. Also that they had, on reasonable grounds, arrested a group of Muslims whom they suspected were not only behind the events surrounding Lantz and Sjöstrand, but had also precipitated District Prosecutor Lennart Ekwall's tragedy. Since the Muslims were not very talkative, there was no news, except that which SÄPO had already reported. How and where the so-called Drug-X had been obtained was still unclear, but everything pointed towards a terrorist prince in Saudi Arabia. The motive behind this was fairly well established.

Evert Kihlman had a troubled frown between his eyes, and he stroked his hand pensively over his three chins.

"Let's rewind the tape a little," he began, both calm and factual. "I must confess that I'm having difficulty understanding the motive. Why should these supposed Islamist terrorists be interested in Stockholm District Court?"

Åsa Julén squirmed a little.

"It may sound rather far-fetched, but the fact is that these individuals have clearly broadcast their contempt for Swedish society. First, they admit to not recognizing our courts or, for that matter, Swedish law. They want to introduce strict Islamic law, in the form of Sharia, and ultimately turn the country into an Islamic state when there are sufficient numbers of Muslims in Sweden. Therefore, SÄPO considers it probable that these individuals are in some way behind recent events. They have resources, money and, very likely, the technology."

Kihlman exchanged a pointed look with Fors.

"Is that all you have to go on at the moment?" Fors asked.

Chief Prosecutor Åsa Julén looked apprehensively at the Director-General. She wished Martin Borg were sitting beside her to explain the operational details, which was where the conversation was now heading.

Julén shrugged unapologetically. "That's all we have so far. There are no other leads today."

"SÄPO contacted me this morning to inform me that there's no longer any threat towards Stockholm District Court," Fors said pointedly. "The plan to place our staff under protection has therefore been withdrawn, which also affects you at the Prosecutor's Office. Are you really sure about this?"

"If SÄPO has made that assessment, then it's probably also correct. I have no opinion on that."

"But what do you believe yourself?" Kihlman countered, leaning forwards on his elbows.

Julén looked unsettled.

"To recap, I don't have any thoughts. Instead I have absolute confidence in what SÄPO says and recommends."

"Do you think that sounds reasonable?" he kept on.

"You will have to expand on that a little," Julén said, her tone changing.

"I'm not sure I can explain my question much more, since it was relatively straightforward and unambiguous," Kihlman replied and looked at her inquiringly.

Julén sighed quietly.

"To respond to your question, the answer is yes. I think that it sounds reasonable. And, as I said earlier, we have no other leads at this point."

Kihlman was not satisfied. "Are you investigating any other possibilities at all or are you completely fixated on these Islamist activists?" he asked.

Julén silently swore to herself. This was Borg's damned field of expertise.

"As far as I know, they are 'fixated' on this group," she replied.

"As far as you know," Kihlman said dryly, "but you should know for certain in this type of case. It's still you, in your role as prosecutor, who's in charge of this investigation."

Margareta Fors quickly realized that the conversation was getting out of control. Åsa Julén looked increasingly uncomfortable.

"It all seems so absurd, with drugs here and terrorists there," Fors interrupted. "As you can appreciate, Åsa, we are just concerned for our colleagues. My staff and I want to be assured that you will do everything in your power to ensure that these tragedies will not repeat themselves."

Åsa Julén nodded, relieved at Margareta's intervention, and said, with a reassuring smile, that she fully understood their concerns.

Evert Kihlman did not look reassured.

WHEN JONNA OPENED the door to room thirteen, the last patient was finishing her evening coffee. She hastily greeted the other patients as she walked over to Walter, who was lying on his back with half-shut eyes and his hands resting on the blanket. The tray of food on his bedside table was untouched.

"Can you help me to the toilet?" Walter began when he saw that Jonna had come.

Jonna stared perplexed at Walter. "I will talk to the nurses."

"No, just fetch a wheelchair so that we can do it ourselves," Walter said. "I can't get any farther than the dayroom before they force me back to bed again. I am not allowed to leave the bed or the room, except to visit the toilet."

"Well, I'm not sure …"

"Do as I say," Walter ordered. "Spare a thought for what my brain has been through."

"Well, that's exactly what I'm doing," she said sternly. Reluctantly, she fetched a wheelchair from the corridor and wheeled Walter into the toilet.

"We have to talk quietly in here," Walter whispered as soon as Jonna locked the door behind her. "It's as soundproof as a cardboard box. The scumbag tested it."

"Who's the scumbag?" Jonna asked, who was not very keen on the situation. Standing and whispering with Walter inside a hospital toilet was not something she found very satisfactory, even if it was a handicapped person's toilet that was as large as her living room.

"The one in the bed next to me. And that's partly why we're here," Walter said, looking up at Jonna from his wheelchair.

"Keep going," she said grimly.

"The scumbag is actually called Jörgen Blad and he is a journalist," began Walter. "But he's also a real shark. He has no scruples. Under normal circumstances, I would keep myself as far away from him as possible. Or give him a good beating. I feel a bit torn between the two alternatives. In any event, he's prepared to trade information about a leak high up in the police force."

"Trade information?" Jonna said suspiciously.

"Yes, he claims that a senior police official is leaking information to criminals. He wants to make a deal where we get the information about the mole if we give him everything on Sjöstrand. You see, a little information has already been leaked, from police headquarters or the Prosecutor's Office, about a dangerous drug that makes people crazy."

Jonna looked at Walter as if she had not properly understood what he had just said. "I don't understand what you're saying," she said. "First fact: you're not on the force anymore. Second fact: we – or, rather, I – am no longer participating in the investigation. And third ..."

"Take it easy," Walter said, interrupting her. "I've already figured out how we're going to do this. And we must do it; it's our goddamned duty. Besides, this will be my ticket back into the force. And if what Blad is saying is correct, it's a very serious situation. The crooks have a mole inside police headquarters itself. Do you understand how much damage this person could do?"

"Yes, I get it," Jonna said. "But why can't this Blad go to someone else? David Lilja, for example?"

"He knows that I'm leading – or, rather, was leading – the investigation," Walter corrected himself. "And from his own experience, he knows that I don't work by the book all the time. He has seen that with his own eyes. I'm the only one he can do this type of deal with."

Walter smiled a wry smile.

"Does he know you're suspended?" Jonna asked.

"No, I haven't told him that yet."

"But he can find that out in a moment if he calls and asks . who's in charge of the investigation," Jonna remarked.

"Very possibly, but that's a minor concern right now," Walter declared. "You'll have to take care of the operational role as my man – or, rather, woman – in the field while I run the investigation from the bed."

"What investigation?" Jonna's eyes narrowed.

"We follow our original theory and act on it. But relax; you'll not be risking your job. There are other ways to run a freelance investigation. But before we talk more about that, I want you to go and fetch the scumbag."

"In here?" Jonna asked.

"Yes, but hurry up. We can't stay in the toilet for too long," Walter said and waved at Jonna to get going.

Jonna closed the door behind her with a bang. She glanced along the corridor and, for a brief moment, thought about leaving Walter to his fate. She had no obligation whatsoever to help him with a freelance investigation. Why care about someone she had only known a few weeks and who was not even her colleague or supervisor anymore?

Some situations force a decision that can change a person for the rest of their life.

This was similar to the situation in which she had decided not to work in the family business. Precisely the same feeling of foreboding hit Jonna now. She found herself at a crossroads and knew her decision could cast a permanent shadow over her future.

But if there was no risk, then it could do no harm to at least tag along and listen. The man that she had briefly greeted earlier was lying down and doing a crossword puzzle.

"Jörgen Blad?" she asked abruptly.

Surprised, the man looked up from his newspaper. "Yes," he answered.

"Please follow me," Jonna asked.

Jörgen thought about saying something first, but changed his mind. Instead, he got out of bed and put his slippers on. The one-breasted woman and the girl looked at Jonna and Jörgen with great interest as they left the room.

Jonna knocked on the toilet door and nodded at Jörgen to enter.

"Well, then," Walter welcomed them.

Jörgen forced a smile. "An unusual place for a rendezvous," he said and looked down at Walter in the wheelchair.

"We don't have time for your bullshit," Walter ordered, in a low, forceful voice. "The only room I can visit is the toilet. And talking in the ward with the other two and their flapping ears is not an option. This, by the way, is my colleague, Jonna de Brugge," he continued, pointing at Jonna, who looked anything but amused.

"Nice to meet you," Jörgen greeted her, his grin widening.

Jonna did not move a muscle.

"You understand why we're here, surely," Walter said and looked inquiringly at Jörgen.

"Do I look as if I fell off the banana boat, perhaps?" Jörgen answered and shrugged.

"More like you were hit by an express train."

"I'll be completely honest about it," Jörgen started cautiously. "But that depends on you being equally as honest with me in return."

Walter's eyes narrowed. "It was you who started talking about a win-win deal and exchanging information. If what we hear sounds interesting, we're open to a discussion on the subject. If it's bullshit and lies, we'll close up your other eye instead."

Jörgen scratched his head. "I want all the information on Karin Sjöstrand," he said. "And I mean everything. Stuff that will give me an exclusive. From what I've heard, there's a drug on the market that drives people crazy. I want to know what the connection with Sjöstrand is, and everything about the Security Service raid against that terrorist cell which also has something to do with the case. There are unconfirmed rumours circulating that suggest a connection. I want to know the truth."

"We'll decide that after you've told us what you have to share with us," Walter said.

"How do I know you won't blow me off?"

"You don't. But unlike you, we still have a code of honour."

Jörgen's expression became suspicious. His grin gave way to his misgivings. He turned around and looked down at his slippers while he slowly traced his foot along a crack in the tiled floor.

Walter watched Jörgen with increasing irritation.

"Do I have your word that you will help me?" Jörgen asked once he had finished thinking and traced his slippers over several tiles.

"Help? What are you talking about? We're just exchanging information, on my terms," Walter said.

"It's a little more complicated than that," Jörgen explained in a miserable voice. He described from beginning to end how he had blackmailed the police mole for information, using a secret movie in which he himself had a role. He described everything in detail up to his beating and the shootout. Finally, Jörgen explained how he had cleverly stashed the video and how the thugs had taken the key from him.

When he thought about it, he had nothing to lose by telling the truth. He could perhaps have gone to someone else in the police, but then he wouldn't get the added bonus of the trade in information, which, after all, was worth a great deal to a journalist. Gröhn was nothing if not pragmatic, something that could not be said about the majority of his colleagues.

"Him, of all the people in the police force!" Walter cried out, disillusioned. "You mean he's a closet transvestite who sells himself like a prostitute to both you and the crooks?"

"I have him on film," Jörgen repeated.

"If what you say is true, then we have a big problem," Walter continued.

"Where do the crooks fit into the picture?" Jonna asked. She had listened to Jörgen's story with mounting interest. "What has the police mole leaked to them?"

"I don't know that, but obviously he has dealings with criminals. Just look at my face. He hired thugs to get hold of the video," Jörgen replied.

"And now you want protection?" Jonna said.

Jörgen nodded. "A new identity and secret address."

"We can assist you with that, but neither I nor Walter is involved in the investigation anymore. SÄPO has taken over." Jonna dropped the bombshell in a dispassionate voice.

Jörgen looked at Jonna uncomprehendingly. Walter gave her a disappointed look and muttered something, but Jonna did not pay any attention to Walter and instead explained why the Security Service had taken over the Sjöstrand investigation and why Jonna and Walter believed that the terrorist theory was a dead end.

She knew that she was breaking a dozen rules and regulations by divulging what she knew to a private citizen, but she did not have to listen very long to what Jörgen had said before she had made up her mind. A senior police leak on top of SÄPO's madness was too much for her to look the other way. Jonna continued to talk about Judge Bror Lantz and District Prosecutor Lennart Ekwall, as well as what was known about Drug-X.

Jörgen stared at Jonna, dumbfounded. What she had delivered exceeded his wildest expectations. This story topped by light years the information that had already been leaked by the police. Drug-X could turn respectable people into walking killing machines. Must be the century's biggest ... what? Threat? Or news exclusive? The latter sounded significantly better. If Walter and this police chick were right, he would be first with the story. He immediately saw the headlines in his mind's eye: "NEW DRUG CREATES KILLERS." Or "BRUTAL SLAYINGS BY COURT OFFICIALS." The headline was not important. The news value was enormous. And if it came out that the Security Service were mistaken about the terrorist plot, then he was a sure thing for the "Journalist of the Year" award.

"You can participate in our parallel investigation in exchange for the video," Walter said in a hard voice. Jonna had started the ball rolling. Now he just had to play along. "You will have first-hand information that nobody else has. You will be an embedded journalist, as you like to call it. But nothing of what we have said here, or what we discover later, can be published until we give you permission. If I see the smallest indication that you are welching on the deal, I'll make sure that the goons who are looking for you find you."

Jörgen nodded that he understood. "When do we begin?"

"We have to start by identifying the court cases the judge, lay juror and district prosecutor worked on together," Walter began. "There must be a common factor."

Jörgen nodded.

"At the same time, you must hand over the video," Walter said.

Jonna was now forced to decide if she was going to be a part of this madness, which was, on so many levels, bizarre. The whole story with Drug-X was so absurd that it was more at home in a Hollywood film. Now, she was forced to be a freelancer just because those idiots at SÄPO did not know

any better, and so that Walter would get a shot at being reinstated, however that was supposed to work. That a senior police chief had become involved with a disreputable journalist
was equally as far-fetched. And that the bisexual county police commissioner had subsequently hired goons to take care
of the journalist was bordering on the limits of what Jonna
could take in.

Walter saw the doubt in Jonna's eyes. "Now listen up," he
whispered, barely audible.

"As you know, every keystroke entered onto the police
database is monitored."

"You don't need to state the obvious to me," Jonna insisted.

"But we need access to the District Court database, even
though a number of documents are in the public domain."

"What's your point?"

"You'll recieve the telephone number of a man, or rather a
freak of nature, who can help you to get access and browse the
databases without being detected."

Jonna looked at Walter suspiciously.

"You have a natural intuition which will enable you to become a really excellent cop," Walter continued, with no trace
of flattery. "You should accept the fact that you have a talent.
There are, in fact, colleagues with over thirty years' experience
who don't even come close to being able to do the things that
I've seen you do so far."

Jonna now looked at Walter uncertainly. She could not tell
if this was an attempt at cheap persuasion or if he really meant
what he said. But it did not matter; she had already decided
anyway. She would definitely not be weak and submissive like
her mother. She had promised herself that a long time ago.
Nowadays, it was all about following her own convictions and
she was actually a little proud of what Walter had said – if he
really meant it.

"What's wrong with a little hacking here or there?" said Jörgen, looking at Jonna. "It's for a good cause and, by the way, quite a few political parties have engaged in it."

"Check on Tor – or Headcase, which is his nickname – and that Finn," Walter said. "If you need to lie, tell them that you need to question them to get information regarding a tip-off. You don't need to give any more details. It's perfectly legal and in accordance with regulations."

"Yes, but you may have forgotten that I'm no longer on loan to the CID," objected Jonna. "At RSU, I can't devote my time to running checks on people as I please. And I don't even know their real names."

"I seem to recall that Headcase's full name is Tor Hedman or something similar. The only thing I know about the Finn is that he's called something like John or Johnny Salminen. They're both in the criminal records database."

"And in the unlikely event that I manage to find them without bending the rules, what details should I question them about?"

"You're just going to scare them a little by telling them that they're being watched by the police. And that if they touch so much as a hair on Jörgen Blad's head, we'll know who's responsible. They'll understand the implications of that message."

Jörgen smiled at Walter's last point.

Until just recently, the detective's attitude towards Jörgen Blad had been chilly, to say the least. Jörgen gradually began to regain his confidence. There was indeed a way out of this miserable mess, as well as a bonus that he could never have dreamed of.

17

OMAR LEANED BACK in his armchair and threw his feet up on the dark oak desk. Jerry Salminen stared with envy at his Italian hand-sewn shoes and wondered how much they cost.

"My time is valuable. Get to the point," Omar said and brushed some imaginary dandruff flecks from his tailored Armani suit.

Jerry cleared his throat. "Well, as I said on the phone, we didn't grab the geezer you wanted. Instead, we got those fucking Albanians shoved up our arseholes. Your contact has royally arse-fucked us by giving the same job to Haxhi."

Omar did not answer. Instead, he began to study his nails. One was about to split. "Yes, you seem to have had your arses fucked, to use your own words," he said, without lifting his gaze.

"He has fucking screwed us over!" Jerry cried out.

"What makes you think that?"

"But I told you on the phone. Me and Headcase were almost eating lead. And he was the only one who knew that we would be at that bloody Jörgen Blad's place at exactly that time."

"But how do you know that it was Haxhi? It could have been anyone."

"I heard them jabbering in Albanian before they drove off with their tails between their legs. They were probably not expecting us to be armed. Your client has ratted on us to Haxhi."

"That's not very nice," Omar declared, totally uninterested.

"We want to talk to the guy and ask him why he screwed us over," Jerry said.

"You see, that's not quite how it works in my line of business," Omar explained.

"What business is that?" Tor asked.

Omar took his feet off his desk and leaned forwards with his hands together as if in prayer. "Now, listen," he said. "I'm just a broker and have nothing to do with the services on offer. A broker handles the connection between a buyer and a seller. It could be services or just plain goods, and I get a small cut so that I can eat every day. If I were to start blabbing the names of my clients, I wouldn't last in this business. No one would risk hiring me. Discretion is a matter of honour."

"Yeah, yeah," Jerry said, shaking his head. "We know that already. But how the fuck could Haxhi find us if that bloke hadn't told him?"

Omar shrugged his shoulders while pretending to be looking for an answer deep in the recesses of his mind. He hummed something to himself while fiddling with a gigantic signet ring. The gold ring was as big as a five-crown coin and embellished with a huge diamond, and it obviously sat too tightly on his finger. Omar's concentration briefly switched from the signet ring.

"I don't have a clue how Haxhi found you, to be honest," he said, and folded his hands. "And you won't get any help from me. You'll have to handle your war with Haxhi yourselves."

"That's exactly what we're trying to do," Jerry explained and started to lose patience. "At least give us the telephone number to your fucking client."

"Don't take that tone with me," Omar warned him, and fixed his eyes on Jerry.

Jerry quickly calmed himself.

"You could always call him and ask if it's okay to talk directly with us on the phone. A question never killed anyone," Jerry suggested in a mild voice.

Omar glanced at his mobile phone by the edge of his desk. Then he shook his head in refusal. "No, I can't do that. Sorry, boys."

"Bloody hell, Omar ..." Jerry pleaded, without success.

The explosion made Jerry fall off his chair. The all too familiar smell of burnt gunpowder stuck in his nose and his ears were ringing. He quickly felt all over his body to see if he had been hit. A quick glance around the room revealed that there were no uninvited guests. Only that Tor and Omar sat paralyzed in their chairs. Omar's eyes were wide open and fixed on the wall behind Jerry. Tor sat expressionless, with his hands under the desk.

A tense, unpleasant silence filled the room. Jerry was rapidly becoming charged with adrenaline and his body started to shake. He slowly stood up and leaned over the desktop towards Omar's ribcage, which was moving with small, convulsive jerks. A faint gurgling came from his mouth. Suddenly, Omar coughed up blood and it hit Jerry in the face. Jerry recoiled, falling back into the chair he had just fallen off. Omar's upper body slowly started to topple forwards and finally fell onto the desk, where it lay motionless. His hands were still entwined as if in prayer.

Jerry dried the blood off his face and then stared at his bloodstained palms. He felt the taste of Omar's blood in his mouth. His stomach began to heave and he threw himself sideways to vomit. The contents of Jerry's stomach mixed with Omar's blood on the floor. The sight of the sludge made Jerry throw up until only bile was left. He retched and sat down heavily in the chair, his forehead soaked with sweat. His pulse was racing as if he had completed a leg workout at the gym.

"I have to clean this shit off me," Jerry gasped and stumbled out of the room without paying any attention to Tor. He had not vomited this much since his upset stomach in Thailand.

When Jerry returned, his face free of blood, he was visibly shaken and was still breathing heavily.

"Why the fuck didn't you wait for my signal before you shot him?" he snarled between breaths.

Tor still sat frozen in his seat. "It ..." he began.

"Nobody heard the shot at least," Jerry angrily cut him off. "This building's as empty as your head."

"It went off too soon," Tor finally blurted the words out.

This was the second time Tor had killed someone. The first time was eight years ago when a neighbour had interfered while they were breaking into a house in Nacka. The bloke was suddenly standing there in the living room with a baseball bat in one hand and a mobile phone in the other, threatening them with both the police and a beating. Tor panicked and shot the man twice in the stomach, and once in the head to put an end to his whimpering. There had been a hell of a fuss in the newspapers after that happened. This time, it was supposed to feel easier. "It's the first time that's the worst," Jerry had said. "You get used to it, just like everything else. Human beings are made like that." Jerry's mum had been a psychologist, so he knew about that sort of stuff.

"So, it went off too soon," Jerry echoed and scrutinized Tor closely. Tor hung his head and he sheepishly fiddled with his Desert Eagle Mark XIX, which still had a hot barrel.

"I fucking swear I'm going to rip your head off one of these days," Jerry growled.

Tor rubbed his neck. "What do we do now?" he wondered.

Jerry thought for a brief moment. "We have to dump Omar somewhere."

"Where then?"

"How the fuck should I know?" Jerry screamed and kicked over the wastepaper bin by the side of the desk. "I have to think." He sat in a worn leather sofa that stood next to the wall and pressed his hands against his head. Fuck, everything always has to be so complicated. Nothing was going their way right now.

Tor nodded, showing that he understood. Jerry had to think and it was best to shut up. All at once, Tor thought of Omar's signet ring. As a John Doe, he had no need for it now. Carefully, he lifted Omar's head and pulled out his clenched fists. He glanced at Jerry, who was lying on the sofa with his eyes fixed on the ceiling.

Tor uncurled Omar's fingers so he could grab the signet ring. He twisted the ring while pulling it. No matter how much he pulled, he could not get it loose. From his jacket pocket, he took out a Hong Kong copy of a Swiss army knife and pressed it against the finger as hard as he could. He leant on the knife, but it could not cut through the bone. Tor looked around and saw a stainless-steel paperweight on the desk. He reached for the paperweight and smashed it onto the knife blade.

The crash snapped Jerry out of his meditation. He looked at Tor, who turned around with a grin and held up something golden in his hand.

"What's that?" he asked, irritated.

"How much do you think this is worth?" Tor asked, staring at the shiny trophy.

Curious, Jerry went over to him and studied the signet ring. He weighed it carefully in his hand.

"Judging from the fat diamond, we ought to get fifty grand for it. At least."

"Fucking sweet." Tor lit up.

At first, Jerry nodded his appreciation, but soon became sullen again. "We don't have time for this shit, so we won't bother taking Omar with us. We'll make it look like an ordinary robbery instead."

"But what about DNA and that shit?" Tor asked hesitantly.

"To hell with it. There's lots of crooked deals done here and every hard ex-con in the country has left DNA in this room. The cops will have a hell of a time trying to sort us from most of the maximum-security villains."

"And the cake mix you dumped on the floor?" Tor persisted.

Jerry looked at Tor. That was a point. The vomit that he had sprayed on the floor was mixed with Omar's blood. That cocktail would be much more difficult to explain away in a police interrogation. It was very probable that the police would identify Jerry's DNA in the mess. And since both he and Tor were in the police's fucking DNA database, all the cops had to do was to collect the first prize. Trying to clean up the traces of DNA was not an alternative either. No amount of mopping and scrubbing could stop a conscientious bastard cop from eventually finding a trace.

"Okay, we'll have to torch the place and burn the DNA and Omar instead," Jerry decided after quickly thinking it over. "Go downstairs and siphon off the stiff's car. Then bring the juice back here. We are going to have a bloody big bonfire."

Tor looked confused. "But I don't have a petrol can," he said.

"Then you'll have to im–pro–vise. Check if he has a spare tank. Use your head," Jerry said, regretting the last sentence. He signalled to Tor to get going. He would meticulously search through Omar's room. If someone came round before he and Tor were finished, they would deal with the problem then. Right now, they had to find the client.

After searching the ramshackle industrial building, Tor had established that there was nothing that could be used to empty the petrol from Omar's car. What Jerry had said was true. The warehouse was stripped clean, down to the last screw. The only thing that could possibly work was an oil barrel that stood outside a wooden hut on the other side of the yard. He stood and rubbed his neck, thinking. What a fucking dump. Why the hell had Omar placed his office in the middle of nowhere? It was five kilometres to the nearest houses and at least fifty to Stockholm. The industrial buildings and adjoining wooden hut looked as if they could collapse at any moment. Bearing in mind Omar's expensive habits and cars, money was not a problem. He could easily have owned an office on Stureplan among the law twisters and stock-market yuppies. That would have made it easier to do business with him. Why he insisted on staying in this rundown shack was beyond Tor's understanding.

Tor was suddenly flooded with remorse. It was only now that he realized that they had cut off the hand that fed them with the jobs that gave them the biggest money. Without Omar, he and Jerry would have a hard time finding work. Like a spider in a net, Omar took care of all the contacts and handed out jobs from different clients as contracts. As Omar's subcontractors, he and Jerry's performance had been exemplary, which in turn had generated new jobs. Now his nervous trigger finger had cut the umbilical cord to the cash cow and their future. Had Jerry really thought about the consequences?

From the boot of the stolen Saab 9-3 that he and Jerry had arrived in, Tor pulled out a hose and his well-worn, grey steel toolbox and walked over to Omar's new Mercedes-Benz GL450. He looked at the five-metre-long monster SUV, which cost about the same as three upmarket houses in Tor's home town, Klockhammar.

After emptying the petrol from Omar's car, there remained only the problem of getting the barrel up to the office. With fifty litres of petrol, the barrel weighed at least eighty kilos. He would have to ask Jerry for help.

With some exertion, Jerry picked up the oil barrel by himself. He was now suffering for those missed workouts, and it took a great deal of groans interspersed with Finnish swearwords before the barrel stood where they wanted.

"I haven't found shit in here except for his mobile and a laptop," Jerry said, breathing hard after he put down the barrel next to Omar's corpse.

"*Nada.* Unless he's hidden them bloody good. But who'd risk stashing stuff here? He has his cash abroad, for sure. His mobile, on the other hand, is full of phone numbers. One number in particular is interesting," Jerry explained.

"Which one?"

"Check it out," he said and held up Omar's mobile phone. "Do you see the letters 'HO'?"

Tor nodded.

"HO must be Haxhi Osmanaj."

"You think so?"

Jerry nodded triumphantly. "When I pushed him to call up the client, he looked at his mobile. I bet he's got all the numbers he uses in this phone."

Tor clapped his hands. "Fucking sweet."

"Yes, but the number for Haxhi is of no use to us, unless you want to call and ask him out on a date."

"Why did you show me the number then?" Tor asked, shrugging.

Jerry gazed at him patronizingly. "Let me explain it to you. If you search through Omar's call history, you can see that Omar has called the same number after almost every incoming and outgoing call from Haxhi. You can see that from the time log. Omar either called, or got a call from, the client every time Haxhi called Omar, or when Omar called Haxhi. This number must be the squealer that screwed us. Got it now?"

Tor nodded that he understood, although he really did not. The logic in what Jerry was saying was as murky to him as a pint of Guiness. Instead, he dwelt on his misgivings about Omar's death and their lack of future income. How were they going to get by without Omar's contracts? Go back to stick-ups? Or breaking into houses and stealing cheap jewellery again? When Omar came into their lives, they had secured a ticket out of the thieves' ghetto. He had slowly and safely taken them up the criminal ladder to the top rung. As things looked now, they would have to creep back into the ghetto again and start doing the kind of jobs that respected villains never dirtied their hands with. Most of all, there would be no big money anymore.

It was time for Jerry to tell him what their future plans were now that Omar was no longer around. Maybe it had not been a smart thing to shoot him after all, even if they suspected that both Omar and the squealer had grassed on them to Haxhi.

"What are we going to do now that Omar's gone?" Tor asked. He tried to sound as if he didn't care – anything to not wind Jerry up.

"It'll be all right," Jerry said. "The important thing is that we take it one step at a time. To start with, we'll shut the mouths of anyone who grasses on us. If we don't do that, we'll get no respect and, without respect, we won't get any jobs. So Omar's client is the next in line."

"How do we get our hands on him?" Tor asked.

"Let's see if we can trace the mobile number. If we're lucky, it's not a pre-paid phone."

"If it's pre-paid, what then?"

"We'll soon find out," Jerry said and picked up the mobile phone. He dialled the missing numbers service.

To their disappointment, the number was indeed for a pre-paid mobile phone. It was not registered in any name and therefore not possible to find out who owned the phone or their address.

Jerry swore and scratched his head, irritated. Everything was so fucking complicated now. He was going to have to choose his words carefully. The slightest hesitation or hint of deception in Jerry's voice would alert the squealer. Jerry would have to lie with the same conviction that he used when the cops questioned him, which was something he had successfully pulled off five or six times already.

After a quick mental rehearsal, he had the scam clear in his mind. Now it was just a case of make or break, betting everything on one card.

"All we have to do is to call the number and see who picks up," Jerry said and punched in the number on Omar's mobile phone. When the squealer saw that it was the dead man's phone number, there would be a reasonable chance that he would answer. Three rings later, and the game was in play.

18

MARTIN BORG WAS stuck. Not one of the fucking bearded Muslims had said anything of substance. The investigation was treading water. The only thing happening was the media gorging on various theories. Finding the leak was SÄPO's highest priority. It was presumably someone from the Prosecutor's Office or the local police who, fortunately for them, were no longer involved. Maybe the flow of information to the media would finally stop.

In the investigation itself, there was nothing that even hinted at a breakthrough. It was therefore time for unconventional methods.

Before he started the project plan for Folke Uddestad, he needed to get the towelheads to talk. He took up his personal laptop, since the police computers were monitored. After logging onto the Telia 3G network with his top-up card, he went through his private mailbox. The only email of interest was from Omar. He had arranged for the goods to be delivered in a bag that was placed in a storage locker at T-Centralen railway station. He loved the symbiosis between the criminal underworld and society's highest guardians. It could not get much better than this.

The only misgiving Martin had about Omar Khayyam was that he was a Muslim. But sometimes ideals had to be compromised to get ahead, even if it hurt deep down. Omar's network of contacts was truly a wonder. There was nothing he could not fix, whether it were services or goods. It seemed that his old contacts within various intelligence agencies were still active, despite the fact that he had long since left the Syrian intelligence service for Sweden where he had, under false pretences, secured a permanent residence visa and, later, Swedish citizenship.

With some difficulty, Omar had even managed to get hold of Diaxtropyl-3S, also called a truth serum by some. Diaxtropyl-3S was developed for the CIA by a US military research unit for biomedicines. It was vastly superior to the Russian's SP-117 and the sodium pentothal used so prolifically by the Chinese. However, there was an export ban on Diaxtropyl-3S in the USA and all use of the drug required advance approval from some bloody committee in the US Congress. This apparently concerned neither Omar nor the CIA.

Martin did not go to the police garage where he usually parked his private car. Instead, he walked out onto Sankt Eriksgatan and went to his silver-grey Volvo V50, which was parked on Fleminggatan. He opened the cover of the fuel cap and removed a storage-locker key. The cover had not been locked so that Omar could put the key inside. He read the numbers on the small note when he was sitting in the driving seat.

MARTIN HAD SELECTED selected Hisham ibn Abd al-Malik, as he seemed to be the weakest of the towelheads mentally. He seemed ripe for an encounter with the unconventional drug. With a little luck, he would be gushing information by breakfast time. Information that could be interesting enough to start the investigation moving forwards.

Martin needed a breakthrough – and soon. Without it, Chief Prosecutor Julén would chicken out and Martin would lose face in front of his superiors. That would be a disaster, not only for his own personal career, but also for that which he and his kind were fighting for. He had gambled everything on this lead and knew that he was right. It was the perfect opportunity. Soon the masses would be made aware of the true face of Islam, and many small trickles would, in time, create the populist tidal wave that was necessary to wash the Muslims away from the ramparts of Europe. Martin read through the personal file of Hisham ibn Abd al-Malik one more time.

Hisham ibn Abd al-Malik was thirty-one years old and originally came from Yemen. He had lived in Sweden for four years and had already married a Swedish woman after two. Naturally, the idiotic female had converted to Islam just as quickly as she had been knocked up. Martin observed Hisham, who looked tired but determined.

"All right then," Martin emphasized the words as he sat on the edge of the table. "Here we are again. How are you feeling?"

The man shrugged, indifferent.

"Do you know what this is?" Martin said and opened a metal case.

The man looked without interest at Martin as he took up two syringes from the case.

He held up one of the syringes to the fluorescent light.

"Our colleagues at the CIA use this," he explained. "Five millilitres of this will make you tell us one or two truths. Ten millilitres, and I will trust you like a brother. With fifteen millilitres in your blood, I will believe every word you say. The drawback with fifteen millilitres is the risk of a sudden heart attack."

The man still said nothing.

Martin looked at Ove Jernberg, who stood with his back against the door, nervously shifting his stance. It was a bad sign. Fucking wimp, Martin thought. Nerves like a rabbit. He should be called Game Over instead.

Martin dropped his gaze from Ove and turned towards Hisham again. He took the other syringe from the case.

"This one has the opposite effect. When I inject this one, you will wake up within thirty minutes and the traces of the sodium will disappear in your piss. No trace and nobody to accuse me of anything. Who's going to believe a story as far-fetched as the police drugging their guests to make them sing?" Martin also held the syringe in the light and studied its light-blue content with a certain fascination.

"You're evil to the core," the man said calmly and looked up at Martin.

Martin laughed. "How nice of you to finally talk to us."

Hisham did not reply and continued to look at Martin.

Martin took out cable ties and pliers from a brown attaché case he had brought with him. "The powers-that-be sometimes have little tolerance for the methods one must use to keep democracy alive." Silence in the room. The only thing that could be heard was Jernberg shifting his feet.

"You may think I'm an evil policeman because you see democracy as your enemy," Martin continued. "But I'm fairly convinced that the majority of the citizens out there support us in this struggle." Martin stretched out his arms like an evangelical preacher at a revival meeting.

Hisham cautiously smiled behind the beard. It couldn't possibly be the case that the Swedish police were so utterly incompetent. At first, he had refused to believe it, but the longer this continued, the more certain he became that it was indeed the case. For some reason he could not really work out, the Swedes actually believed that the Islamic Brotherhood was a group of terrorists planning terror acts in Sweden. Certainly, the Brotherhood had proclaimed its desire to introduce Sharia law in Sweden. But that was an opinion and was, of course, not going to happen unless the Government and Parliament, by the will of the people, accepted the new order. Which, presently, was hardly realistic since there were many more Christians than Muslims living in the country. Time was, however, the Brotherhood's greatest ally and persistence would eventually pay off.

"Why are you grinning?" Martin asked, as he and Jernberg bound the man's hands and feet to the chair.

"I think this is all a misunderstanding," Hisham answered calmly.

"That's what they all say," Martin laughed.

"You can do whatever you want to me and my brethren. All you will get is the truth and that's not what you're looking for."

"We'll soon find that out," Martin informed him. "Try not to think about it; just relax and let us take care of you for the next few hours."

Martin held up the disposable syringe and flicked it with his index finger a few times.

"How much do you think I'll need?" Martin asked, looking first at Ove Jernberg and then at the man in the chair.

"Ten?" Jernberg replied.

"What do you prefer?" Martin asked the man in the chair. Hisham was expressionless.

"Well?" Martin inclined his head to one side. Hisham sat motionless with eyes closed, as if he was praying to himself.

"Since you seem to have lost your tongue, I will have to decide for you," Martin remarked with a sigh.

"Use all you have. Then you won't have to waste any more time. Allah will reveal the truth shortly," Hisham said calmly.

"Now we're talking. Fifteen millilitres it is," Martin decided.

He selected one of the veins in the man's lower arm and carefully emptied the contents of the syringe. Afterwards, he put the empty syringe in the case and looked at Jernberg.

"We've never done fifteen," Jernberg said in a low voice.

"No, but I have a feeling that this one could be tricky, and we're going to tug every shred of truth out of him. Better too much than too little. We don't have a lot of time."

"And if he has a heart attack?"

"Well, then he has one," Martin replied matter-of-factly. "Who's going to suspect we have given him a heart attack? We've just been questioning him, and he got so stressed by all his lying that he collapsed."

Jernberg loosened his tie knot and lowered his eyes to the floor. Martin felt an increasing irritation. Jernberg had become soft lately. Gone was the strong conviction that had made Martin take him on board for this crucial odyssey to hunt down the enemies of democracy. It would, in time, become a problem.

Martin swayed impatiently back and forth while looking at the clock. After a few minutes, Hisham began to feel a heat rising from within him. It was as if Allah had filled him with his presence. He felt happy. His heart thumped and his eyes became blurred. This must be as close to paradise as a person could get.

"Now let's see what the prophet has to tell daddy," Martin said and started up a voice recorder.

First, they started with some simple control questions. This was always done to verify the interview subject's state of mind and that he was not "abnormal", that he really was susceptible. Some interview subjects had demonstrated a certain ability to fight against Diaxtropyl-3S. Why was not known, but it was probably because the subject had a specific chromosome that did not allow the brain to be affected in the correct fashion. Statistically speaking, one in ten thousand had this "abnormality". If excuses and hesitation already were apparent during the preliminary control questions, then there was no point in continuing.

"I want to know your name, your age, and where you come from," Martin began.

Three straight questions in succession, exactly according to the rule book. He observed the irises of the eyes between answers, looking for signs that indicated hesitation.

"My name is Hisham ibn Abd al-Malik. I'm thirty-one and I come from Yemen," Hisham replied, slurring his words.

"Are you married?"

"Yes, to Mona ibn Abd al-Malik."

"Excellent," Martin replied. "Let's get on with the reason why we're sitting here today." Martin flipped through some files.

"We know from reliable sources that you are financed by Prince Hatim Al-Amri of Saudi Arabia to build mosques. Is that correct?"

The man nodded slowly.

"The purpose of building the mosques all over Sweden is to spread Islam and to build bases for your coming war with the infidels. Is that correct?"

The man said nothing.

"Surely, given the facts, isn't that your goal?"

"We are Allah's servants and want to spread the true faith," Hisham slowly answered.

"The true faith," Martin repeated and paused for effect. "With what means do you intend to spread it?"

Hisham closed his eyes. "With God's word and through many mosques."

"No other methods? Like undermining the Swedish court system, for example?"

Hisham opened his eyes and stared confusedly at Martin.

Even if Diaxtropyl-3S was the best truth serum, its dosage was, as with all other serums, not an exact science. Martin knew that. Mostly, one could achieve a ninety per cent degree of truthfulness, but this was not related to the type of lies that could evade detection.

"Is the name Bror Lantz familiar to you?" Martin continued.

The man slowly shook his head.

"Do the names Sjöstrand or Ekwall mean anything to you?" Martin felt his frustration gradually building.

Suddenly, the colour drained from the man's face. Beads of sweat quickly formed on his forehead and he started to breathe heavily.

Martin threw a look at Jernberg, who had also turned pale.

Hisham's eyes rolled back and his body convulsed. A powerful muscle contraction snapped his head backwards. His body tensed and he became as stiff as a shop-window mannequin.

"Shit. Heart attack!" Jernberg screamed.

"He doesn't look well," said Martin coldly.

What was not supposed to have happened just did. Diaxtropyl-3S, while effective, had the disadvantage of affecting the heart muscles. This was the first real set-back for Martin and it came just when he least needed it.

He took out the syringe with the light-blue anti-serum and emptied the contents into the man's convulsing arm. He put the empty syringe back in the case and snipped the restraining bands. Then he put everything in the brown attaché bag and turned towards Jernberg, who had frozen by the door.

"You can raise the alarm while I perform a token resuscitation attempt," Martin ordered. Jernberg was on his way out of the door before he had finished the sentence.

Martin threw Hisham from the chair, turned him over on his back and watched the life run out of him.

After a while, Marin heard footsteps quickly running down the corridor. He kneeled down and pretended to massage the man's chest. A male paramedic was the first to enter the room. He politely, yet firmly, pushed Martin aside to make space for the defibrillator so that he could try to get the heart beating. After a few resuscitation attempts, the paramedic shook his head, then continued to give a heart massage until the ambulance crew arrived. Twelve minutes later, Hisham ibn Abd al-Malik was pronounced dead.

19 THAT SAME NIGHT, Martin Borg had to make an oral statement regarding the events surrounding the sudden death of the detained Hisham ibn Abd al-Malik to the custody officer for SÄPO's Counter-Terrorism Unit. Later on, a more thorough investigation would be carried out, based on what the coroner discovered.

After quickly perjuring his way through the formal interview, he went in to Ove Jernberg. He found a greyish, pale ghost behind the desk.

"Nerves getting the better of you?" Martin asked and settled down in the chair on the other side of the desk.

Ove turned to face Martin. "What do you mean?"

"Well, I'm wondering if you can pull this off."

"Why the fuck did you give him fifteen millilitres?" Ove exploded and glared at Martin.

"Now, let's calm down," Martin replied, popping a piece of nicotine gum in his mouth and massaging the tension in his neck. "There's no reason to panic. He had a heart attack due to stress from putting on a phoney act. It doesn't have to be more complicated than that. That's what I told the custody officer. And that's what you will say now."

Ove stared at Martin with eyes like black coals. The thirty-year-old father of two looked as if he was going to jump across the table at any moment. But then he sank back in the chair and stared at the floor.

"When you are done with the custody officer, come down

to the garage. We're taking a road trip," Martin went on, noticeably disturbed by Jernberg's outburst. It was no longer a question of if, but when, Jernberg would become a liability.

"Get in there now and remember what to say," Martin ordered, waving his hand at him.

Ove reluctantly stood up and went towards the door. As he opened it, he turned around. "What about the traces of the serum and anti-serum in the body? A corpse can hardly piss out the residue."

"True," Martin answered and reached for a magazine on coarse fishing. "But corpses can't talk. Even if the coroner should find traces of the cocktail in the body, they can't connect it back to us. And why would you and I want to drug someone without authority? Any motive would be unconvincing and so far-fetched that not even …" For once, Martin could not come up with a fitting metaphor. He stopped and started reading the magazine. "In any event, they probably won't find anything," he said, but did not sound too confident.

Ove turned without saying a word.

After even Ove had lied his way through the short interview that the custody officer was duty-bound to conduct with all persons involved, he found himself sitting beside Martin in a requisitioned civilian vehicle. At high speed, they made their way out onto the Essingeleden motorway. After passing Botkyrka, Ove first broke the silence and asked where they were going.

"Omar's," answered Martin curtly as the speedometer passed 170 kilometres an hour.

"To that rat hole he has in Gnesta?"

"Yes, we need more chat cocktail," Martin said. "Even if one of the towelheads has kicked the bucket, we have to continue with the others. They're going to sing whether they want to or not. We should probably use a smaller dose next time."

Ove did not know what to believe anymore. Martin seemed to have lost it completely and was about to drag them both over the edge. Ove was responsible for Hisham's death. Perhaps not directly responsible for the killing, since he had not injected him, but he was still so deeply implicated that he could end up with a prison sentence.

He had to find a way out of this madness. After the car ride to Omar's, he would ask for a leave of absence until he could get a transfer. Blowing the whistle on Martin was not an option. Martin would bring him down as well.

"Why are you doing this? You're breaking your own rules," he said, trying to get an idea of what was behind Martin's sudden passion for taking uncalculated risks.

"He's not answering his mobile," Martin said, with a worried frown.

"That's not normal. You can call Omar at four in the morning and the scumbag answers like a walking answering machine. I've been trying to reach him for hours without so much as a single voicemail."

"What makes you think he's at his office?"

"He spends his life in two places: at home and at that shitty warehouse, or whatever he calls that old, derelict industrial building with a desk. If he's not at home, then he must be there."

The answer did not make Jernberg any the wiser. "Wouldn't it be ..."

"We have to get those fucking Muslims to talk," Martin cut him off and floored the accelerator pedal. The Passat's speedometer struggled up to 200. Ove looked at Martin. Ever since they had discovered the group, Martin had changed. His propaganda about the threat from Islam had become increasingly frenzied. Ove had bought a few of Martin's arguments, but far from all of them. The perception of Muslims and Islam as a general threat to Europe was a concept that belonged in the Germany of the 1930s. He kept that to himself, however.

At first, Ove had thought that using Diaxtropyl-3S was pretty harmless under the circumstances. It was no worse than getting someone drunk and then trying to get them to talk – just a needle instead of a bottle of vodka. But the more Ove thought about what he and Martin had done, the more unsure he became. Martin's web of contacts in the underworld was constantly expanding. The righteousness of his cause obviously meant anything goes to Martin. As he understood it, Martin even had a special connection with certain pensioned-off colleagues who, in the eighties, had frequently used contacts within the criminal underworld to achieve success.

Ove was playing a high-risk game and had an inkling of what was really going on behind the scenes. He had finally seen the darkness behind Martin Borg's glossy façade.

Martin slowed down when they got to within a few hundred metres of the warehouse. He parked the car behind a thicket so it would not be seen from the road.

"Why are we stopping here?" Ove asked, when Martin killed the engine.

"Something's not right," Martin said and got out of the car. He took out his Sig Sauer, pushed in a full magazine and then put the pistol back into his shoulder holster.

Ove reluctantly opened the door and got out after he saw what Martin had done.

"What are you doing?"

Martin looked contemptuously at Ove, who had folded his arms like a sullen old landlady. "What does it look like?"

Ove did not reply.

"You can never be too careful," Martin said and started to walk down the gravelled road.

"If we're expecting trouble, then we ought to ask for back-up," Ove shouted at Martin.

Martin pretended not to hear and continued walking towards the warehouse. Swearing, Ove kicked the car door shut and ran after him.

The small industrial site was long since abandoned. Trees, dense bushes and thickets surrounded the industrial buildings and dandelions sprouted through the tarmac, which had long cracks in it. At the top of one of the buildings, there was light shining from some windows. Martin stopped behind one of the buildings. Jernberg stood behind him. In the yard, they saw the outlines of a Saab 9-3 and a Mercedes GL450.

"Omar's car," Martin thought aloud.

"Whose is the second?" Ove asked.

"Don't know, and we can't see the registration number from here, so we can't check. We have to get closer." Martin crept along the wall of the building to the next corner. Jernberg followed closely behind.

They crossed the yard, running softly, and pressed them-selves against the wall by the side of the entrance to the ware-house with the lights upstairs.

"I can see the registration plate on the Saab," Ove said.

"Check out the owner," Martin said, without taking his eyes off the doorway.

Ove took out his mobile phone and made a short call.

"We have a Stig Wikner," Ove whispered. "Born 1965 and living in Täby-Kyrkby. It's clean except for a few parking tick-ets and a speeding offence two years ago. The car is not listed as stolen."

"Call him," Martin said curtly.

"Who?"

"The car owner, of course."

"Why?"

"Just do as I say," Martin retorted, irritated.

Ove took out the phone again. After a while, he got hold of the car owner's mobile number. He made yet another call and talked this time to the owner.

"Stolen without the owner knowing?" Martin said.

"The owner is in the Canary Islands and thought the car was parked at Arlanda airport."

"Not anymore," Martin said, rubbing his tired eyes.

"So we are dealing with pros. Someone who needs a car for a longer period of time without the owner reporting it as stolen," Ove said.

Through a small window in the door, they glimpsed a staircase and the outline of the steps leading up to Omar's office. Martin carefully opened the door, just enough so they could squeeze through. They positioned themselves on either side of the staircase and silently climbed the stairs. Ove went first.

Adrenaline was pumping through Martin's body. Just as he was about to tell Jernberg to draw his weapon, the door to Omar's office opened and a cone of light shone down the steps in front of them. Two men came out of the door and stood in the doorway with the light behind them for a few long seconds. The man who came out first was short and stocky with a crew cut. Behind him was a long and lanky figure. Surprised, the two men saw that they were not alone on the stairs.

The four men stared at each other in a frozen silence.

Ove was the first to move. While he shouted that he was a policeman and fumbled for his police badge, the others pulled out their weapons. The man with the scrubbing-brush haircut shot first. Ove had only just managed to look up when the first shot came, and the bullet pierced his left lung. Then there were three more shots in rapid succession. The last bullet hit his head and he fell down and rolled onto Martin, who had retreated down the stairs.

Martin managed to aim his Sig Sauer and fire a few shots at the man in front before Jernberg's rolling body made him lose his balance. The scrubbing brush collapsed with a whimper and fell down the steep staircase. From the corner of his eye, Martin saw the tall guy aim a pistol at him. As the man screamed something, a deafening chatter was heard from his automatic weapon.

At first, there was no pain. Only after he had succeeded in throwing himself around the corner of the stairwell did Martin see that he was injured. His jacket was torn, and his right arm was bleeding profusely. Probably just a superficial wound. Then he heard heavy footsteps on the stairs coming towards him. Martin switched hands. He was not used to shooting with his left hand. He backed away with his back to the wall. To try to throw himself through the doorway would simply be suicide.

Suddenly, the footsteps stopped. Martin tensed every muscle in his body and held his breath as the shadow of a hand holding a pistol slowly appeared around the corner.

Before Martin could react, the man fired. A bullet hit the wall behind Martin a few millimetres from his neck. The sound of the bullet hitting the wall temporarily deafened him. He quickly wiped the cement dust from his eyes, aimed at the hand and fired off all the rounds he had left in his magazine. It was kill or be killed. His left hand shook from the adrenaline and fear of death. One after another, the bullets hit the wall behind the man.

When the mechanical report of the Sig Sauer's bolt sounded out as his last round left its chamber, a roar reverberated down the stairwell. Martin's last shot had hit the man's hand and his weapon fell to the ground.

After a little fumbling, Martin loaded a new magazine and quickly moved up to the corner of the stairwell. He picked up the weapon that lay at the bottom of the stairs and carefully looked around the corner.

The wounded figure was sitting a little way up the stairs, and Martin could see that his hand was bleeding. He was groaning with pain and rocking his upper body.

If there were any more trigger-happy maniacs, they would have made themselves known by now. Martin dismissed the thought and cautiously climbed the stairs towards the man, his weapon aimed at his head the whole time. The man looked up at Martin just as the gun barrel touched his forehead. He immediately fainted.

Martin frisked the man for weapons, but found none. He was no longer a threat.

After turning over Jernberg's body, he could see that the back of his head was missing. What a bloody fool, Martin thought. Reaching for his police badge instead of his weapon cost him his life. Also, he was not wearing a vest.

Less than five minutes ago, Ove Jernberg had been alive. Now he was dead and, oddly enough, Martin felt nothing. Just one less problem. Martin noticed that the wounded man had woken up. He had ripped off one of his shirt sleeves and was trying to wrap it around his hand while he snarled through his teeth from the pain. Martin was tempted to put a bullet in his back but stopped himself, thinking how it would look after a post-mortem. He would have a hard time explaining why he had shot someone who was already wounded in the back.

A few metres farther up the stairs lay the man with the scrubbing-brush hair. Martin stepped over Jernberg and up to the other body. Scrubbing brush had landed on his back with his eyes staring at the ceiling. His mouth was wide open and Martin could discern a certain surprise in his expression. He had probably not expected to hang up his guns like this. Martin bent down and picked up the gun that lay by the man's hand and stuffed it in his jacket pocket. He observed, quite contentedly, that he had managed to put a bullet just below his throat. The bullet had certainly severed his aorta, a large artery. He must have died instantly.

He went down to the man on the stairs, who was quiet. He had managed to stop the bleeding by tying a knot around his hand.

"Actually, I should just put a bullet in your skull right now," Martin snarled as he pushed the barrel hard against the man's temple. He carefully squeezed his finger against the trigger and looked the man in the eyes, intensely. He was probably not worth the hassle that Martin would face in an ensuing internal investigation.

"Don't shoot," the man stammered. "I know a lot. A whole shitload of stuff."

"Right, you know plenty," Martin replied dryly. "For example, that you're about to become a corpse."

The man said nothing, staring, petrified, at Martin.

Suddenly, the pain in Martin's arm flared up and he was forced to take the gun away from the man's head. He felt his wound with his hand. The arm had swollen and was throbbing fiercely. The bullet must have hit him worse than he had first thought.

"It was you that shot first, motherfucker!" Martin shouted as he took off his jacket.

"Self-defence," the man excused himself and moved back against the wall like a whipped dog.

"Self-defence? Firing shots at the police? Is that self-defence? You must be a complete idiot."

"I don't like being called an idiot," the man said, defiantly.

Martin was so surprised by the man's arrogance that he lost his train of thought. He suddenly felt a surge of rage, aimed his pistol and fired a shot.

The shot echoed around the stairwell. The bullet grazed the wounded man's hand and he screamed and rolled into a ball. More likely from shock than physical pain.

"You fucking idiot!" Martin shouted. "I don't give a shit what you like."

Martin's arm was more shot-up than he had first thought. The bullet had penetrated deep into the muscle, but at least it didn't seem like it was still there. The pain increased with each pulse beat. He needed medical attention.

But first he had to get his story straight. What was he going to say? How should he explain the incident? Why had he and Jernberg made their way to the warehouse outside Gnesta without backup? What was the mission? Who had sanctioned it?

Everything had gone wrong from start to finish. First, the Arab towelheads and now this. He would have to put together a believable story. But how could he do that as long as this shit was still alive? He would surely spill the beans for a shorter sentence. Just as well to silence him for good anyway. Better a dead witness than a live one.

But then he started to think about Omar, the reason that they were here in the first place. Where was Omar and what were these two trigger-happy characters doing here?

Martin had no more time to consider this because an acrid smell forced its way into his nostrils. Under the door to Omar's office, he saw smoke rising. Martin opened the door and looked into the office. He stopped in the doorway. The fire was spreading over the carpet and onto the office furniture. At the other end of the large room, something resembling a human body was in flames. It was an unpleasant sight. At first, he thought about trying to put the fire out with the fire extinguisher that was mounted on the wall, but realized that it was pointless; the room would soon be engulfed in flames.

He moved down the staircase, which was slowly filling with smoke. The man was gone, but had not got very far. Stumbling, he was trying to leave by the entrance door.

"You're in quite a hurry. Are you late for an appointment?" Martin said and shut the door. He shoved the man, who fell to the floor, put his shoe over his injured hand and pressed down. The man screamed and, in desperation, tried to pull Martin down to the floor with his other arm. Martin reacted by kicking him in the stomach, which made him lose his grip. The man moaned and was close to losing consciousness.

Martin took a handkerchief he had in his pocket and put it in front of his face. He watched the man for a few seconds until he appeared to come to again.

"If ... only you knew ... about Omar and his deals. ... Your name ..." the man coughed in the smoke. He tried to get up but could not.

"My name?" Martin coughed back.

"Sure ... Your name ... with the others," the man continued, coughing heavily.

"Which others?" Martin moved towards the door.

"Other ... cops," the man tried to talk.

"Names of other cops?" Martin repeated.

The man tried to nod, but was unable to.

Flames flared out of the burning office. The heat and smoke was so strong that Martin was now forced to make a critical decision if he wanted to make it out alive. It would be best to leave the man to burn here. A more natural cause of death would be hard to arrange. If only the man had not just said what he had said. Omar had names of other cops? In that case, which ones? Was Martin on the list despite using a false name? Why had Omar been killed and what did this man really know? Martin took hold of the door handle, but changed his mind at the last second. There were too many unanswered questions.

Coughing violently, Martin took hold of the man's legs and dragged him through the door, into the fresh air. He dragged him across the tarmac until he had no strength left.

He bent over with his hands on his knees, gulped in some air, closed his eyes, and enjoyed the fresh air filling his lungs.

The pain in his arm was becoming unbearable. It felt as if it was going to explode with each new heartbeat. Dragging the man out had not done it any good, but he hoped that it was worth the suffering. He gritted his teeth from the pain. Now it was time for this chicken to sing like a canary.

"Okay," Martin said and took out his Sig Sauer. "What did you want to tell me?" He pressed the mouth of the gun against the side of the man's chin.

The man stopped coughing. He turned to face Martin and saw the muzzle of the Sig Sauer staring him in the face.

"Well then?" The pain in Martin's arm was taking its toll on his patience.

"My hand doesn't hurt anymore," the man said, examining the bundle around his hand.

"Of course you don't feel anything. You don't have a hand left to feel any pain," Martin said.

"I have a proposal," the man quickly responded.

Martin stared at Ove Jernberg's murderer. Was he losing his grip on the situation? It was as if he no longer made the decisions. He could not lose his temper. Control was his signature and had made him successful. If it had not been for that equal opportunities cunt, he would have been section leader by now. She had fewer years, was less deserving and, to top it all, was half-coon. There was that shit about a multicultural perspective, new gender directives applauded by Agency Director Anders Holmberg and others to look good for the politicians. Martin had to suffer for that. Who knew if he would ever get another fucking chance? Everyone was so fucking afraid of being politically incorrect in every situation. Bloody closet commies.

"If you promise not to top me, then I swear you'll get everything I know about Omar and that fucking trannie cop."

"Trannie cop?" Martin's forehead wrinkled in puzzlement.

"Yeah, the bloke who double-crossed us on the contract to snuff out that fucking journalist."

"Journalist?"

"Yeah, he'd been blackmailing the trannie with photos of them shafting each other in the arse, dressed in latex and leather. You know him; he's a fucking high-roller police commissioner." The man forced a grin.

"Wipe that grin off your face," Martin growled and pushed his pistol harder into the man's face.

"That faggot cop gave the job to Haxhi instead. The Albanians tried to waste me, Jerry and the journalist queer in the middle of town, but we shot our way out," the man rambled on.

Martin took the gun away from the man's face. "That's a little too much bullshit for me."

Martin already knew about the recent gun battle in central Stockholm, but so did anybody who watched the news or read the newspapers.

"What do you mean?" The man looked serious. "What I'm telling you is as fucking true as … as cows are vegetarians!"

"Now shut it!" Martin yelled. "I'll tell you when you can talk. I'm getting tired of your blabbing. Start by telling me your name; why you and the scumbag who shot my partner came here; why there's a fire; and why you were so fucking stupid that you opened fire on two police officers."

The man did not answer.

"Maybe too many questions at once?" Martin said sarcastically while grimacing at the dreadful pain in his arm. "Answer my questions!" he yelled and gingerly rubbed his arm in an attempt to ease the pain.

"My name is Tor Hedman, but they call med Headcase."

"What's your business with Omar?" Martin asked.

"Me and Jerry got jobs from Omar."

"Jerry? Is that the pile of coals on the stairs?" Martin looked at the burning building.

"Yes," Tor answered and shrugged. "We used to steal cars and rob upmarket houses before we met Omar."

"What sorts of job did Omar fix you up with?" Martin repeated, irritated.

"Things like debt collection or eviction of tenants from different properties. Sometimes it could be both collection and eviction at the same time. See, first you take the cash, then …"

"Yeah, I get it. Keep going."

"Me and Jerry formed a gang we called the Original Fuckers. We shortened it to OF."

"No kidding."

"Have you heard of OF?"

"No, can't say I have."

"Whatever, so …" Tor lost his focus. "Fuck, we even tattooed OF on our backs. We were going to expand, Jerry said. OF would be just as big as the Albanians or even the Yugoslavs. But Jerry's dead now. So what am I supposed to do?" Tor lowered his eyes again.

Martin looked at Headcase, mildly amused. "You'll have to rename the gang OL."

"OL?"

"Original Losers," Martin laughed.

"Bloody hell!" Tor suddenly burst out. "Why did you have to come and fuck everything up?"

He flinched, touching his wrapped bundle.

"We put out some feelers and, after a while, Omar contacted

us. Among other things, we got the job to turn that faggot in-side out. At first, we didn't know what we were supposed to grab from him, except that it was some type of multimedia evidence. We went to his flat, but the bastard messed it up and said that he stashed the shit in some fucking safety deposit box. In the end, we were forced to take him with us. When we got to the street, those bloody Albanians jumped us. They were going to cheat us out of the job and snuff out me and Jerry. You know, two birds with one stone. The client grassed us up to Haxhi."

"Why would the client give the job to someone else?" Martin asked, wondering why he was even listening to the man.

"Haxhi had told the client they would do the job for free as long as they were given OF. The Albanians didn't like that we started our own crew and were pinching their clients. They wanted to waste us for good."

"Haxhi, is that Albanian?"

"Yes, he's their boss."

"How do you know that Haxhi made this offer to the client?"

"Omar had made notes about everything in his lap-top. Names of all the clients, how the job went and so on. Everything was on it."

"Did Omar show it to you?"

"Not directly. Jerry found it out after we whacked Omar. He had his laptop in the desk drawer."

"You got into Omar's computer?"

"Yes."

"How could you get into the computer without a password?"

"Jerry searched Omar's mobile first. He had written the password on his speed-dial list. It said 'Mhamuth' and then a load of letters and numbers. People usually store their pass-words and card codes in their contacts list as fake names. Even a bloke like Omar did it."

Martin's mouth tightened. He used the last four numbers of his social security number as the code for his cash card. The complex but foolproof password for his laptop was stored as a fake SMS on his mobile phone. Maybe it's time to change that habit, he thought.

"Omar didn't want to help us get in touch with the client. We just wanted to know how Haxhi knew that we were in the flat. But it was against his policy, he said – although he gave the name to Haxhi who in turn offered to do the job for free. But he wouldn't tell shit to us. So we were forced to take Omar down as payback and to set an example. Well, actually, the gun went off by mistake. Shit happens. To cover our tracks, we torched the whole place."

"But before that, you hacked his computer?" Martin asked, interested now.

"No, first we rang the client. Jerry found the number on Omar's mobile and called the bloke. He said that Omar had given him the number and that he, Haxhi, and that journalist were all sitting in the same room like one big, happy family. Jerry lied that we had all joined forces against him. Jerry pressured him for cash, and he said that he knew where he lived and worked and that Haxhi had changed his mind about working for free. The bloke finally got really pissed off and said that he was a high-ranking police chief and that he was sick of the blackmail and all the bullshit. He was going to send some special task-force characters after us if we didn't stop fucking with him. Jerry told him to go to hell."

"What a genius," Martin sighed.

"But I know his name."

"How do you know that? Did he say his name?"

"Nope, but we found out later because it was in Omar's computer. Omar had everything on that computer, a shitload of contact names. Quite a few dirty cops were on there."

"So, what was his name?" Martin was eager to know.

"Who?"

"The police chief, of course."

"It was Folke Ugglestag, or something like that," Tor answered.

"Uddestad?"

"Yes," Tor replied.

Martin shook his head. "Unbelievable. Totally, fucking unbelievable," he said aloud. "This can't possibly be true!"

"Why not?" Tor asked.

"Who else knows about it?"

"Knows what?"

"That he's a high-ranking county police chief called Folke Uddestad."

"Well ..." Tor said, dragging out the word while he thought. "Omar, me and Jerry. Don't know if Haxhi knows that he's a cop boss. He probably only has the top-up card number, but doesn't know his name. And, of course, the journalist, who was obviously blackmailing the cop about something. Anyhow, he's the one with the photos and the sex video in the safety deposit box. I ..."

"How do you know it's a sex video and photographs?" Martin interrupted.

"Omar had written in the computer that the video and photos showed the journalist and the cop shafting each other in latex gear. Two gay bastards fucking each other. Disgusting!"

Martin pushed out his lower lip, making popping sounds like a fish while he mulled things over. "I think I understand now," he said thoughtfully. Something interesting was beginning to take shape.

"That they're both poofters?" Tor wondered.

"How did Omar know what was in the photos unless Uddestad told him about them?"

"I don't bloody know."

"But why did he tell Omar? The less known about what the photos show, the better for Mister Police Commissioner."

"How am I supposed to know that? Do I look like a fucking fortune teller or something?"

Martin rubbed his chin. "Where's the computer and Omar's phone now?"

"I have the mobile in my pocket," Tor said triumphantly. "But the computer is still in the warehouse."

"Bloody hell," Martin swore. "That computer was worth its weight in gold."

"But I have the hard drive thingy. It's in my other pocket," Tor smirked.

"You do?" Martin looked astonished at the prize idiot, who nodded, confirming that he had the hard drive. How the hell had he missed both the hard drive and the mobile phone when he frisked him for weapons earlier? That oversight could have cost him his life.

"Was it Jerry who removed it?"

"Yes, he was a smart guy," Headcase smiled.

"A regular hero," Martin said, stretching out his hand. "Give me the mobile and the hard drive."

Tor shook his head in refusal. "No, then you'll just finish me off here."

"I could do that right now if I wanted to."

With the gun pushed in his face once again, Tor had no alternative but to give up Omar's mobile phone and hard drive. Martin stuffed the phone and the small hard drive in his jacket pocket.

"What happens now?" Tor asked anxiously. Without the hard drive and mobile phone, he felt naked. He had lost his trump card.

"Well, then," Martin said, wiping sweat from his forehead.

He stood up and felt his arm, which made him groan with pain. "Logic dictates that I should finish you off."

Tor lowered his eyes from Martin and tried to stand up, but was unable to get further than all fours. His muscles quivered and would not carry him.

Martin shook his head and, with his left arm, took hold of Tor's jacket. He pulled him up until he could stand by himself on wobbly legs.

Events and people had come together to suddenly conjure weaknesses and opportunities out of thin air. Martin saw them all clearly. To have the County Police Commissioner, Folke Uddestad, by the balls was almost too good to be true – especially since he had already proven susceptible to blackmail. Hardly surprising, considering what the photographs showed. He wondered what the journalist had been given to keep quiet.

Things would be so much easier with a police commissioner in his pocket. It would improve Martin's career prospects significantly and, of course, simplify his campaign against the enemies of democracy. A winning lottery ticket.

In addition to Martin and Headcase, the only one who had any knowledge of this was that journalist. It was important to steer this ship carefully and avoid any rocks. He was already sailing in dangerous waters.

Martin considered Tor, who had now taken a few stumbling steps. To shoot him here and now would only give him a shitload of problems. Where would he hide the corpse? He couldn't transport it in the car that he and Jernberg had arrived in, since it was a police vehicle and would be the subject of an internal investigation, with Forensics all over it. Besides, he would have to stay and wait for his colleagues, with whom he would soon have to raise the alert. Perhaps it was not that risky to let the fool walk away. He was, after all, party to a cop killing so he would keep his mouth shut until Martin, or someone else, arrested him for that crime. But this was not the time to take risks; he did not know anything about this Headcase. He could not know how trustworthy he would be in the long term.

"Okay, this is what we do," Martin said. "You'll get your deal."

Tor looked disbelievingly at Martin, who had put his gun back in his shoulder holster.

"You're going to start working for me."

"Me working for the cops?" Tor asked, surprised.

"Yes and no," Martin said, trying to find an example that the genius in front of him would understand. "Imagine that I'm running a small shop in a shopping centre. And you're going to start working for me in the shop."

"Doing what?"

"You'll be working for me and not officially for the police. Do you understand?" Mentioning the Security Service was irrelevant right now.

"I will be your personal snitch?"

"Yes, but more than that. You'll be my right-hand man and do what I tell you to do without questioning or moaning about it. But if you play silly games or run your mouth off or work for someone else, then I'll pull the plug on you faster than you can shift into first gear."

Tor looked thoughtful. "Do I have any choice?"

"You can say no and be dead in five minutes. Or take a percentage of what we make. Shall we say twenty?"

"What are we going to make money from?"

"You'll find out later," Martin lied. The idiot really believed that Martin was teaming up with him.

"First things first: we have a few other things to take care of. We both need to get to a hospital. But not the same hospital, for obvious reasons."

Martin wiped more sweat from his brow, feeling his arm. He was starting to get feverish.

"Can you drive a car?" Martin asked.

"I should be able to manage. I have Omar's car keys and it's an automatic."

"Excellent," Martin said. "Omar's car is also not on the stolen car list like your Saab is now. Do you have anything in the Saab that can lead back to you?"

Tor thought for a brief moment, then shook his head. The only thing he had in the car was the toolbox, and that could not be traced to him personally. It had been stolen from a cellar in Sundsvall three years ago.

"Good," Martin said. "Take Omar's Mercedes and drive to the A&E at Stockholm Söder hospital. Tell them that you were working on your summer cabin and that you accidentally shot yourself in the hand with a nail gun. Meanwhile, I'll torch the Saab to destroy your DNA and fingerprints."

"Will they believe me?" Tor asked, stressed. "The hospitals have to report all gunshot wounds immediately to the cops. Everyone knows that."

"As long as there's no bullet, then there's no risk of that. By the way, what was the name of the journalist?"

"Jörgen Blad," Tor said. "A short, dark-haired fatty. Didn't understand much of what he said. He talks faster than fucking Bugs Bunny."

"Never heard the name. It will be interesting getting to know him a little better."

"Do we waste him before or after we have grabbed what he has in the safety deposit box?"

"Don't worry about that now. Give me your mobile number and get going to Casualty. Park Omar's car a few blocks away and don't fucking park illegally. We will have to torch that one too, later on. You know what the score is. No fuck-ups or it's bye bye, Tor. It doesn't matter where you hide, I'll find you regardless. Understood?"

Tor gave Martin his mobile-phone number and staggered off towards Omar's Mercedes-Benz GL450.

Martin watched the car drive off and, for a split second, wondered if he really should let Tor get away. But as an accomplice in a police murder, he would probably not be a problem. A life sentence behind bars was not something to look forward to.

Martin contacted the duty officer at SÄPO who, in turn, alerted the county communications centre, who then requested police, fire engines and ambulances. SÄPO also sent the on-duty unit from Stockholm, consisting of five men, two of whom were forensic technicians. While waiting for the cavalry to arrive, he memorized the story he had invented. Everything had to be airtight. Every detail of the story would be scrutinized by Internal Affairs and they were not easily fooled, especially when it came to a cop killing. The sky was going to fall in on Martin in the coming days. Thus far, however, he felt he had control over the situation.

A small distance into the forest, he hid Tor's and Jerry's guns and Omar's mobile phone and hard drive under a rock. For safety's sake, he sprinkled petrol from the police vehicle's spare tank to disguise the scent from any sniffer dogs. He washed clean the blood trail left by Tor on the tarmac with washer fluid from the Saab, which he then set on fire with the remainder of the petrol from the spare tank. The practical cover-up was ready and the story nicely tied up any loose ends.

Despite the circumstances, he felt elated. Almost euphoric. The knowledge that the hard drive lay waiting for him with all that information gave him hope. A new era was dawning in the life of Martin Borg and it looked very inviting.

He squeezed his charm tightly. This will strengthen our cause, he told himself.

20 THREE HOURS HAD passed since Jonna had left the hospital when she rang the "freak", whose real name was Serge Wolinsky. A tired and grudging voice declared that, no matter who was calling, he had neither the time nor the desire to hold a conversation. Jonna managed to say Walter's name just as he was about to slam the phone down. He fell silent. Then a heavy sigh could be heard on the other end.

"When, where and what?" he said.

Jonna hesitated.

"When, where and what?" Serge repeated.

"When? As soon as possible. Where? Well, why not at your place? But as far as what goes, I was hoping you could tell me; otherwise, I'm talking to the wrong person," she said, and hoped the answer would be good enough for this man of few words. The telephone line was silent.

"Shall we say in one hour? You're in the Stockholm area, right?" Jonna continued. She could hear her own breathing in the telephone and thought for a minute that he had hung up. But then, she heard him. "Ringvägen 96. Second floor. It says Albert von Dy on the door. You can figure out the door code yourself," he said quickly and hung up.

Charming fellow, that one. No wonder he and Walter seem to have hit it off, Jonna thought.

Jonna had managed to drive exactly one hundred and seven metres and shift the 911 into fourth gear when her mobile phone rang.

"I've been discharged," announced a happy Jörgen Blad.

Not another complication! She had assumed that the journalist would be bed-bound for at least a few days longer.

"That's nice," she lied.

"I was able to nag my way out of here. At my own risk, according to the doctor."

"That's very nice. But I'm a little busy right now. Let's meet at your hotel room tomorrow morning. And when the bank opens, we'll tackle the practical task of fetching the stuff you have in the safety deposit box."

"I can hear that you're driving a car."

"Yes. So what?"

"Then you can pick me up at the main entrance."

"Why should I?" Jonna asked.

"Well, partly because there is an imminent risk of something happening to me on the way to the hotel, and partly because I want to accompany you to the place I think you are going. Or have you already forgotten our agreement?"

"But you were supposed to check into a hotel until we had made permanent arrangements for your security. That was the agreement. Besides, nobody knows that you were admitted to the hospital unless you have told them yourself. So what can happen to you on the way to the hotel?"

"Sure, but now I have a clean bill of health and you're on your way to the freak, and I am tagging along. Otherwise, there'll be no security deposit box tomorrow."

Jonna had no other choice but to take Jörgen with her. And it was what they had agreed. She made a U-turn on Torsgatan and drove back towards the hospital.

There was no mistaking the glee in Jörgen's eyes as he got into the car.

"A Porsche Carrera," he smiled.

Jonna did not answer him. She felt a general annoyance,

particularly when it was a task that involved Walter. He was the hockey player who spread chaos all over the ice rink, and she was the goalkeeper who had to catch all the pucks, or missiles, that kept coming from all possible directions. And here was yet another puck, with only one eye and an attitude that made Hollywood divas seem sympathetic.

"Is this your car?"

"Yes," she sighed.

"Police salaries seem to have outrun the cost of living," he continued, squeezing the upholstery.

"Indeed," Jonna answered. "We take home at least a hundred and fifty grand every month plus overtime. After tax, of course."

"Okay, it's no business of mine if you have made the money for the car legally or not."

"Exactly. It's none of your business," she said and turned onto Sankt Göransgatan.

Jörgen shut up.

"Have you then?" he asked after they had driven for a short while.

"Have I what?" Jonna sighed again.

"Bought it legally?"

"You will have to find that out yourself; you're the journalist."

Jörgen shut up again. He said nothing during the rest of the journey, spending his time trying to clean an imaginary spot on the car's leather interior with his index finger, which he repeatedly moistened with his mouth.

Jonna was about to comment several times, but held back since it was better if he stayed quiet. Not until they arrived and were standing outside the entrance to Ringvägen 96 did he open his mouth to speak.

"Is this the place?" he asked, looking up at the façade.

Jonna did not reply. Instead, she keyed in the door code that only postmen and emergency crews used when they needed to access locked foyers of blocks of flats.

They took the stairs to the second floor and buzzed the door with the nameplate for Albert von Dy.

The door was opened by a hollow-eyed, skinny figure with an overgrown beard and straggly hair pulled up in a ponytail. He was wearing an oversized and faded T-shirt that read, "100% AUTONOMOUS".

"Jonna de Brugge," Jonna introduced herself, stretching out a hand.

The man stared suspiciously at Jonna and then Jörgen. His eyes flitted between the one-eyed journalist and the woman police officer. Finally, he threw open the door.

"A real comedian," Jörgen murmured. "He can be the entertainment at my next garden party."

They followed the man to something resembling a living room. In one corner, there was a sofa covered with pilling grey fabric and a table full of old coffee mugs. The remainder of the room was furnished with half a dozen smaller computer desks. On each of the desks, there were at least two screens and one high-end computer. Bundles of electric and data cables lay in a tangle on the well-worn parquet wood floor, along with lots of dust balls. The way in which the equipment blinked and flashed made Jörgen think of Las Vegas. Everywhere, cooling fans whizzed in the warm room. The windows were screwed shut with strong bolts and appeared unopenable.

"You're not much of a cleaner, are you?" Jörgen said after tripping over some cables and knocking over a stack of empty pizza boxes.

The man glared at Jörgen with expressionless eyes.

"You're not a great talker either, right?" Jörgen murmured

and sank into the sofa. Like a housekeeper, he started brushing away crumbs between the lines of coffee mugs.

"Thank you for letting us come," Jonna began. "As I didn't get to introduce myself by the door, let me try again. As I said, my name is Jonna de Brugge and I work with Walter Gröhn in the police. With me, I have Jörgen Blad who is … our expert in certain matters."

She looked pointedly at Jörgen, who grinned at the deception.

Serge looked curiously at Jonna and then at Jörgen. "Expert in which matters?" he asked disbelievingly.

"We can talk about that later," Jonna quickly replied, trying to change the subject. "I assume that you are Serge Wolinsky?"

Serge frowned. He did not like getting a question instead of an answer.

"That might be correct. Be …"

"And I understand that you're a friend of Walter Gröhn," Jonna continued. It was important not to lose pace so that he would not have time to analyse and question.

"I wouldn't say friend," Serge answered formally.

"But you obviously know each other, right?"

"Regrettably, he knows me," he answered, emphasizing the word "me".

"How long has Walter known you then?" asked Jonna, stressing the word "you".

Without answering, he got up and went over to one of the computers. His fingers moved like lightning over the keyboard and he seemed to be searching for something. Finally, he found what he wanted. Jonna looked at Jörgen, who shrugged his shoulders.

"So, a journalist?" Serge said contemptuously and glared at Jörgen.

"And expert," Jonna quickly added but realized that he had probably seen through her lie. It had taken less than thirty seconds. Things went fast around here. If only the police force was as efficient. There would be a shortage of unsolved crimes.

"You journalists are no better than cops," he said and stood up.

"What do you expect me to say to that?" Jörgen asked, feigning insult and winking with his healthy eye like a labrador puppy.

"We're not here to discuss the media's role in society," Jonna explained.

Serge threw up his hands. "What do you want me to do for you then? Fix your broadband connection? Clean your computers of spyware?"

Jonna leaned forwards. "Walter said that you could fix it so that we get access to a certain ..."

"Walter, always Walter," he interrupted Jonna. "You know what? You can tell him this is the last time I do anything for him. I've paid back my debt many times over by now."

"What debt is that?" Jörgen asked, also leaning forwards towards Serge.

"Some other time," Jonna interrupted. "I need help to use the criminal records database without being seen. Can you set that up?"

Serge pulled in his chin. "Aha, now we are getting warm," he said, waving his hand in the air.

"I also need to get into some public and restricted databases at the Stockholm District Court," she added.

Serge looked at Jonna, thinking hard. "That's quite a tall order at such short notice," he said.

"I don't know who you are or what you can do and, to be honest, I don't want to know. But I'll ask you again for the last time. Are you going to help me or not?"

She tried to sound friendly, yet firm. As if he had no choice, even though it was a question.

Serge assumed a troubled expression behind his beard.

"What are you looking for?"

"We're under no obligation to tell you that," Jörgen answered dryly.

"I won't ask you again," Jonna said, in a sharper tone.

"I know," Serge answered. "Now you're going to threaten me with Walter."

"Correct. I'm following his instructions. Your dealings with Walter are none of my business. But if it makes it easier for you, then you can imagine that I am Walter."

"Albeit a little more attractive," Serge said, forcing a smile.

"So what's it going to be?" Jonna started to stand up from the sofa.

"You need a microrouter," Serge answered quickly.

"A what?" She sank back onto the sofa.

"What do you know about computers?"

"Not much more than the average user," she said apologetically.

"Okay," Serge said. "A router is a type of switch that is designed just to sit in a data network and direct traffic between computers so that the right data goes to the right computer. Do you understand?"

Both Jonna and Jörgen nodded.

"The criminal records database is physically separated from the network and computers that use email and the internet at the police station. All the different police stations are connected using what is known as a Virtual Private Network, or VPN, that's impossible to connect to from the internet no matter how smart you are, because it's physically separated. The reason for restricting access to the internet is to prevent attacks on the system that breach the firewall and then fake or clone a computer within the system. If you could do that, then you would just have to hack the passwords and security-level codes, and then you could do anything you wanted within the database whenever you wanted. Also, every key stroke in the system is registered and it sends alarms according to special rules."

"Sounds like a foolproof system," Jonna said.

Serge laughed. "There's no such thing in the world of computers. And certainly not if the breach is carried out from within, which is often the case with companies and the authorities."

"You mean that it's the employees who are responsible for most of the hacking attempts?"

"Yes, that's correct. It can be done intentionally, by the employee, or unintentionally, when a Trojan – a type of virus – finds its way into the employee's computer when they use an innocent website or open an email."

"But then it's impossible to hack into it from the outside," Jörgen concluded.

"As I said, nothing's perfect in the world of computers. Not even the Pentagon has managed to avoid being hacked."

"So how are we to do this?" Jonna asked.

The hollow-eyed beardie lit up. "Coincidentally, I used to be one of the consultants that helped to design the criminal records database for the police. I was a subcontractor for the consultancy company that had the task of developing the whole system. I had full access to the project and the source code just by signing a piece of paper about confidentiality, which didn't mean anything to me. Naturally, the Security Service did a thorough background check on me and all the other consultants."

"And access to the source code means what?" Jonna asked, not at all interested in his career as a consultant.

"It's very simple," he continued in a superior tone. "As the programmers in the consultancy company were birdbrains, I added a few back doors that the idiots never managed to find.

At first, it was mostly for my own amusement and to see if they'd find them during testing of the code before the first release. They never did. In fact, I'd bet that nobody outside the Von Dy group can find those back doors, since they're hidden in some anonymous SET variables."

"How does the back door work and what's the Von Dy group?" Jonna asked, now more interested in Serge's achievements.

"Von Dy is the name of a world in cyberspace that I and a number of hackers created a few years ago. We belong to no state or society; we're completely autonomous. Physically, I sit here in the south of Stockholm. But in reality, I live in Von Dy's cyberworld where I also count for something. I have no use for the society outside these four walls."

"What's the weather like in there?" Jörgen joked, looking at the computers.

Serge pretended not to hear. "A back door is exactly that. One can enter the system without using the main entrance, which, in this case, checks the security levels, passwords and traceability. You can compare it to a secret passage that allows you to creep in and look at as much information as you want without being registered or detected. You can even add or delete information."

"Sweet," Jörgen said, impressed. "I'd love to learn how to use that back door."

"That will never happen," Serge replied dryly.

Jonna was becoming uneasy about Serge's skills. What Serge had just bragged about was a very serious matter. It was not just a question of "borrowing" and using a few colleagues' log-in identities or getting a little help from one of Walter's friends in the police IT department. It was much more than that. If what he was saying was true, then Serge could have full control of the criminal records database and God-knows-what other regulatory systems. How could that be possible? And what kind of leverage did Walter have on this guy that made him so eager to spill details about his criminal activities in the world of information technology? What agreement did Serge have with Walter that enabled him to sit in his sleazy flat with no fear of reprisal for his hacking activities?

She was being sucked deeper into these illegal practices. The very foundation of the justice system was at risk if any single person could walk in and out of a back door in the criminal records database and change records at will. A key stroke could turn innocent people into criminals and criminals could be as clean as whistles. Of course, there were other databases to cross-check the records against – for example, the courts and other law enforcement institutions – but still. This exposed how vulnerable the modern IT society was.

"I don't understand," Jörgen said. "Why are you telling us all this? What we now know could be used against you. For me, as a journalist, this is a huge exclusive. Even sensational. What's to stop me from calling the news desk right now?"

"Well, for one thing, there's me," Jonna said sharply and fixed her golden-brown eyes on him.

Serge smiled slightly and answered as if he had been posed the question before. "You can always try. First of all, nobody, and I mean nobody, is going to find any evidence that can tie me to anything remotely associated to hacking. I never leave a single byte of information. And second, my brothers and sisters in Von Dy would make your life hell for the foreseeable future."

"What type of hell are we talking about?" Jörgen asked, sceptical.

Serge extended his thumb. "One: your credit cards will be unusable and will also be cloned and used elsewhere all over the world for all sorts of dubious transactions. Two: rumours and computer-manipulated images depicting you in compromising situations – let's say, sex orgies with cocaine-powdered noses – will be sent to every inbox at your workplace and to your personal circle of friends. Three: the tax authorities will be chasing you for massive tax evasion, since you will suddenly have an account in an offshore bank with a considerable amount of money that 'coincidentally' can be traced to mafia activities in, let's see, the Baltic states. And if you're really unlucky, you may find yourself linked to something more serious, like a murder or a paedophile ring. I could make this list very long, but I'm sure you get the point."

Jörgen looked unconvinced. "I don't know if I believe all of that. That sort of thing only exists in films."

"The only way to find out for sure is to test him," Jonna said with a wry grin. "Do you have a favourite park bench that I can reserve for you?"

Jörgen clammed up.

"Let's return to the actual procedure to get inside the criminal records database," Serge said and went over to one of the desks. "I have built what I call microrouters. This little device is, as you can see, no larger than a mobile phone, but contains an Octeon microprocessor, RAM, or memory, and a huge flash disk. It also has two ethernet ports that are connected to the local area network, or LAN, that the database is also connected to."

Jonna nodded. "Say no more; I think I understand. Not the technical part, but the purpose of that microrouter. It gets plugged into the network of the criminal records database and can therefore hack the system. In other words, I am going to be a Trojan horse."

Serge smiled. "Not entirely wrong. You will place the microrouter between your office computer and the network wall socket. As the unit has a small GSM module for GPRS, which is the same as mobile surfing, I will call the microrouter using a normal phone and enter a PIN code. The device will then automatically dial up a mobile operator network and log into a server, set up by me and located somewhere on the other side of the world, using the GPRS connection. In that way, I can communicate with the microrouter, using the internet anywhere in the world. All that I need is a SIM card for a pre-paid mobile internet service. Even though GPRS is partially encrypted, you can never be sure what the FRA, the Swedish version of the American NSA, is up to nowadays. They can quite easily eavesdrop on GPRS traffic and have become quite proficient at sticking their noses into everybody's business on the internet.

"Naturally, I borrow IP addresses from hacked PCs all over the world, so it's impossible to trace me."

"Aren't you being a bit paranoid?" Jörgen joked, but quickly stifled a chuckle when he realized that no one was listening.

Jonna examined the microrouter that made it possible to hack the criminal records database with a certain amount of fascination. "But that means that you will also be connected to the network when I access the database?"

"It's not that easy, I'm afraid," Serge answered with a grin. "You can't hack the database from your office computer. It's not used for anything except to provide a clone identity for me. In other words, I copy and borrow your computer's identity. In order to get in via the back door to the database itself, I must first be able to enter the net work of the criminal records database unnoticed. To put it another way, before breaking into a mansion using a small basement window, I have to check that I can drive up to the house without getting stopped by a security guard."

"Have you done this before?"

"A few times," Serge answered.

"With Walter?"

"Maybe."

Jonna stood up and went over to one of the computer desks. She stroked one of the screens with her hand while her thoughts spun in her head. "How great is the risk of getting caught?"

Serge shrugged. "Well, apart from the risk that someone sees the microrouter in your office, it's almost non-existent."

"This is tantamount to espionage," Jonna said quietly to herself.

She went over to one of the grimy windows and looked down at Ringvägen and the sparse traffic below. Her thoughts turned to the police academy and what she had learned there, what the instructors had said about being misled by veteran colleagues. She also thought about what Walter had said and done and, most of all, about his dedication even though he was suspended and risked being brought up on charges. Why would he do that? What was his motivation, other than the slim possibility of being reinstated?

Six months after finishing her training and leaving the police academy, she was now in the process of committing so many serious offences that the prosecutor would need a small print shop to list all the charges. She was really putting her whole career in law enforcement at risk. Not to mention the personal risks she was taking: criminal prosecution and, in the worst scenario, a prison sentence. Why should she expose herself to such things?

Hardly for Walter's sake, nor to prove to herself that she was not as weak and submissive as her mother.

Breaking the law to solve or prevent other crimes was the only logical justification that she could think of – to commit a lesser offence and prevent a greater one. This was exactly the sort of situation you should not get involved in. The instructors at the academy had relentlessly hammered this message home to the bunch of naive cadets who believed that the world was black and white, good and evil. Was it morally acceptable to sacrifice one human life to save a hundred others?

If the answer was yes, then where did one set the limit? Fifty? Thirty? Perhaps two lives, as long as it was more than the original sacrifice?

She could still walk away without getting into trouble. But then that sense of justice got in the way, like an irritating stone in her shoe. And she had never been afraid of taking risks.

"How do we hack into the District Court databases, then?" Jonna asked and sat down facing Serge.

"A little trickier, but not impossible," he said quickly. "Somebody must get the microrouter placed between a computer, used by a judge or some other authorized court employee, and the network socket in the wall. It's important that the computer is connected to the databases so that I can get into the system."

"Using a back door?"

"Nope." Serge shook his head. "I don't know of any back doors in their system and, since I was't involved in the development of their database, I haven't been able to add any of my own. The District Court database is apparently based on some French software that is so messy not even the distributor wants to go in and mess with the code. It's obsolete and based on Unix. Unix has some bugs that are not known about except by a small group. A few have unfortunately surfaced and been fixed by various companies in the Unix business. But there's one bug that hasn't been detected yet and that allows you to access the operating system's core and, using that method, it's possible to hack into the application, which, in this case, is the French database. It's only a matter of time before that hole is also blocked, but for now it might be a viable alternative. Definitely worth a try, if you ask me."

"How do we get inside, literally speaking, I mean?" Jörgen asked.

Jonna pressed her lips into a tight line. "Perhaps Walter has a solution to that problem."

"He has played with the idea before, but has never acted on it. Presumably, there was too much risk involved," Serge said.

"Presumably, yes," Jonna said bitterly. "But now he wants me to do things he wouldn't dare do himself."

"Exactly," Jörgen added. "If he was half the man he thinks he is, then he would do it himself and not send a rookie police chick to do the job."

"Quite possibly," Jonna said. "But right now, we don't have time to wait until Walter is man enough for you, or until he's been discharged from hospital so that he can play secret agent on his currently unlimited leisure time."

"So what do we do then?" Jörgen asked, throwing his hands up in frustration.

"Not *we*," Jonna said, smiling at Jörgen. "You."

"Me? What do you mean?"

"You will have the honour of doing a good deed for once, probably the first unselfish thing you have done in your entire life. Since you've got the gift of gab, you're going to show just how persuasive you can be."

"What are you talking about?"

"You're going to play the part of infiltrator and see to it that a microrouter ends up under the right desk at the District Court. And that's non-negotiable."

"You're telling me to break the law," Jörgen squirmed.

"As if that bothers you!" Jonna exclaimed.

Serge prepared two microrouters. Meanwhile, Jonna sent Jörgen to buy two pre-paid SIM cards in the local shop, which stood fifty metres farther down Ringvägen. The probability that one of the journalist's many enemies would appear there were negligible, she thought. And she did not want to advertize her own face in a shop that most likely had security cameras. If the cards should, for any reason, be discovered, the shop would be registered as the origin of sale when they were traced. The police could get that information from the service operator. And if the customer paid with a credit card, then it was even better. Then, there would be no need to wade through all the mug shots to find a name to identify the face, which was a job that would not take an experienced team more than a few hours to do anyway. If the buyer was stupid enough to pay with a credit card.

Jörgen paid for the SIM cards with his gold American Express card.

21 IT WAS TEN past one at night when Detective Inspector Walter Gröhn woke up with a jolt. He looked around and realized that he was alone in the room. The bed on the other side of the room was still empty. His former room-mates had tired of the constant telephone calls, and he had finally been put in a single room. Walter had not been slow to point out that he was a policeman and needed to use his phone, preferably in privacy, since murderers were not going to take a vacation just because he was in a hospital bed.

He had also managed to convince Jonna to work for him, despite his suspension and the fact that she was no longer on loan to the CID. And that she would be forced to break a few laws.

On the whole, he had been quite successful thus far, considering the circumstances.

In addition, his headaches had subsided and he felt surprisingly energetic. Sure, he could do without the suspension and a potential charge of serious misconduct, but he had been in similar situations before and had managed to come out the other side with both his reputation and his job intact.

The problem this time was Chief Inspector David Lilja. Walter no longer had him on his side. Lilja had not opposed the complaint from the Drug Squad. How many times had Walter helped Lilja break hopelessly stalled cases where colleagues had run into a dead end and made Lilja look bad? Walter had jumped in and taken over murder investigations from other detectives just to save Lilja's reputation and career.

On the other hand, Lilja had backed up his detective when he had fallen from grace or stepped over the line. Walter stopped counting after seven, more or less, serious transgressions during the eight years that Lilja had been his superior. Maybe the well had finally dried up. Lilja had probably been given an ultimatum: get rid of Gröhn – or go down with him.

He wondered if that owl still worked in the police union. The man with the enormous glasses. What was his name again? Right, Håkan Modig. That's the bloke. He owed Walter a favour.

A few years ago, Walter had helped the owl's sister to get rid of an ex-boyfriend who had become a nightly stalker. Perhaps I should make a call to the owl and the union, he thought. And ask how the sister is getting along.

He turned over in his bed and thought about Jonna. Tomorrow, she would have unlimited access to the criminal records database if everything went according to plan. Although with types like Serge Wolinsky, you could never be sure. He was as slippery as seaweed and as trustworthy as a Russian black marketeer. But she had sufficiently thick skin on that freckled nose to handle Wolinsky and she was cool enough to pull it all off. Walter was sure of that.

The District Court database was, however, a long shot and it would be difficult to achieve; that was obvious. It required somebody on the inside, a person who worked on the premises and who could place the microrouter in the right place while avoiding detection.

Two years ago, Walter had needed to get into the District Court's intranet. A senior official at the court was running a paedophile ring and, as usual, there was a lack of hard evidence. Unfortunately, he had failed to find anyone who could plant the device. The plan went down the tubes, and the evidence necessary to start an investigation against the bureaucrat and his supposed accomplice at the court's IT department was never gathered.

Hacking into the District Court's intranet and databases would, without doubt, give the biggest payoff, but it would require Jonna to use all of her talents to have even the smallest chance of success. That Wolinsky would have to burn some brain cells too. Walter had so many favours owed him by that slippery eel that he could continue to use him until he retired.

AFTER DROPPING OFF Jörgen outside the Hotel Gripsholm, Jonna spent the rest of the evening lazing on the sofa, watching TV and eating diet yoghurt with sugar-free muesli. She made a few calls and went to sleep in her oversized bed at 2 am. Before she closed her eyes, she reflected on her lack of company. She missed having someone to share her day with, but most of all to share her bed. It was over a year since she had shared a blanket with someone of the opposite sex. It was time to do something about that. Either she had to get a smaller bed or find someone to occupy the side of the bed facing the bedroom window.

If only she was not so damned demanding. She was as picky with men as she was with her bed. Not too soft, not too hard; not too low, not too high. Just the right width and with a long warranty. All for a reasonable price with home delivery included. And, last but not least, it had to be good-looking too. Mission impossible? She resolved to be more flexible and tolerant of shortcomings.

That was her plan. Time to look at life with new eyes – to stop the search for perfection and let Fate reveal what it had to offer. Within reason, of course. With that perceptive insight, she finally fell asleep.

IT WAS ONLY when Tor Hedman arrived in Stockholm that it dawned on him what had in fact occurred. He gradually came out of what had been a shock-induced, comatose state of mind. The realization of what had happened at Omar's now hit him with full force.

Jerry was dead.

One cop was dead and he was an accomplice in a cop murder.

Omar was dead.

The hard drive and his Desert Eagle were gone.

To top it all, his hand was hurting like hell. Despite the fact that his diabetes dulled his nerve endings, he could feel the pain. It came and went just like his nerves usually did.

But it could have been worse. He could have been just as dead and charred as Jerry. He shuddered at the thought. Now he was sitting in Omar's Mercedes on his way to the hospital and, afterwards, he would be the cop's right-hand man. Right-hand?

He did not have a right hand anymore. That fucking psycho had seen to that. There were no more honest cops anymore. What is this country coming to when the cops are grabbing stuff that rightly belongs to others, like himself, for example?

Tor was filled with righteous rage. He should not be forced to grass on other villains. And now he had to work for a crazy cop. Rage shot through him like a lightning bolt and he yelled out loud. He screamed as much as he could while swerving across the motorway lanes. After a short breather, he screamed again. It actually helped.

After screaming for a time, the pain in his hand died down a little and he felt calmer. Tor was not sure if that cop was for real or just sick in the head. The guy lets him walk away – someone whom he neither knows nor has any background info on. Except his name … and the pre-paid phone number. Someone who had shot his partner and tried to waste him on the stairs. If Tor knew anything, he knew that this guy was a sick, psycho bastard.

Tor groped for Omar's signet ring in his pocket. What had Jerry guessed it was worth? Seventy grand? He held the ring up and rolled it round. It was as big as a toilet seat but still quite classy, he thought, pushing the ring onto his left thumb. Omar's ring finger had been as thick as Tor's thumb.

"Not so daft," he said to himself out loud, holding up his hand. A thumb signet ring – maybe not so practical, but fucking bling-bling. Shame he was going to have to sell such a heavy piece of jewellery.

Maybe he would not have to when he started working for the psycho. He would definitely be free of Haxhi with a cop as a partner. He had promised twenty per cent. Maybe not such a bad deal when all was said and done. But twenty per cent of what? Debt collection for the taxman? Tor had no idea how dirty cops made their money.

The drawback with working for cops was that you became a grass, or confidential informant, a CI, as the cops called it. CIs did not have much worth in the underworld. They were even lower than cops and whores. A career as a CI was not a long one. The majority of CIs ended up as pieces of butchered meat in some suburban park. No matter how he tried to stay hidden, there would always be somebody looking for him.

Then the feelings of guilt came. Tor thought of Jerry – how the psycho had shot him on the stairs and then left him to char on the barbeque. What a fucking exit for the Finn. The OF era was over for them both. All that was left was the tattoo on Tor's back. Their bright future had disappeared with Jerry. When Haxhi was history, he would settle the debt with the psycho. Put a bullet dead centre in the psycho's forehead with best wishes from Jerry. That was how it would end.

Bolstered by his new plan, Tor swung off the Liljeholmen bridge and onto Folkungagatan. He parked the car on Magnus

Ladulåsgatan, a good distance from the Casualty entrance at Söder hospital, in accordance with the cop's instructions. He locked the car and walked towards the entrance. He presented himself with his name and social security number to the nurse at the counter and explained that he had a problem with his hand. Because of his clothes and the fact that he did not have any form of ID, there was some suspicion about his identity, but after ten minutes he was lying on a trolley, with one doctor and two nurses hanging over him.

"What's happened to you?" the doctor asked, carefully unwrapping the bundle.

"I managed to shoot myself in the hand a few times with a nail gun," Tor replied. Just like the cop told him to say.

"You did what?"

The nurses exchanged glances.

"I was working on my summer cabin and then the shooter went off," Tor continued casually, as if he was talking about a broken nail.

"Shooter?"

"Uh ... yes ... the nail gun."

The doctor carefully poked at the hand, a frown appearing on his forehead. Tor turned his head away. It had been traumatic enough wrapping his shirt sleeve around the gunshot wound in his hand. But then he had been in shock and everything had happened as if on autopilot. Like being a trance. Now his head was almost clear and he had absolutely no desire to discover how much was left of his hand.

"You don't feel any pain?" the doctor asked, slightly surprised after examining Tor's hand.

"Nope ... maybe a little. I'm diabetic, so I probably should be feeling more."

"You have a high pain threshold?"

Tor nodded.

The doctor turned to one of the nurses. "I think we'll need some intravenous morphine and a saline drip. Check his blood sugar levels as well."

The nurse nodded and hurried off to another room.

"This one will have to go straight to the duty surgeon," he said to the other nurse. "I'll make the call so that they're ready and prepped for the patient."

"Will I have a hook instead of a hand?" Tor asked the doctor.

The doctor laughed. "We don't know if you'll need a prosthetic yet," he said. "But you don't have to worry about a hook. That might have been the solution way back when. Today, we have a completely different technology and there are fantastic prosthetics if that becomes necessary. But it's not definite that you will even need one. These days, surgeons have a great deal of expertise and instruments that can fix just about any type of injury involving, for instance, broken bones or damaged tissue."

Tor scrutinized the doctor. Either the bastard was lying and telling him a load of bullshit to keep him calm or he was speaking the truth. Fuck, I might walk away from this with just a scar on my right mitt.

It did not take long before he was on the operating table, staring up at a sea of lamps that were turned towards him, and he realized the gravity of the moment. His hand was going under the knife – his right hand, of all things. The one he pissed with. Wiped his arse with. Not to mention what it did in female company. This was the mate that took care of everything in his daily life. To end up with one of those prosthetics, or whatever else they were going to fit him up with, did not appeal to him in the slightest.

If they did not have hooks, what did they use? A gripping claw? Like the one the roadsweepers pick up rubbish with?

What if he pressed too hard? His dick would explode like an overcooked hot dog.

He would have to learn how to use his left hand for everything. From taking a piss to brushing his teeth and tickling the pussy of his favourite slut, Ricky. All the things his right hand did such a good job at, he would have to teach his left hand. That would be a challenge.

Someone who introduced herself as the anaesthetist entered the operating theatre. All he could see was her eyes; the rest was covered by her green scrubs. After a short monologue in which she mechanically and in great detail described what was going to happen, she connected a tube to the drip that Tor had in his arm. Afterwards, the surgeon and a few more green-coats entered, which seemed to complete the surgery team. The anaesthetist put a transparent mask over Tor's mouth and nose and asked him to breathe normally and to count slowly backwards from ten. Tor did as he was told and made it to three before everything became black.

MARTIN BORG HAD been admitted to the Karolinska University Hospital. The doctors quickly established that he had a gunshot wound in his arm, abrasions on his knees and elbows, as well as a mild form of smoke intoxication. He was also suffering from loss of hearing in one ear. The doctors wanted most of all to determine if he had suffered any internal damage from the toxic fumes of the fire. Furthermore, they were concerned about his mental state. The incident in Gnesta had resulted in the death of a colleague as well as his shooting and killing of another human being. Both could be ranked among the most disturbing and traumatic events that a police officer could experience in the profession.

Martin thought himself that he had probably never felt better, despite the media buzz as a result of the incident. With one dead SÄPO agent and another injured to boot, the tabloids now saw a chance to fill their coffers quickly with fresh cash.

The media feeding frenzy had started.

What made the next day start on a flat note was the news that the Internal Affairs investigation would be led by Ante Bäckman. How the hell a person like Bäckman could end up with an Internal Affairs investigation was a complete mystery to Martin. He was a total good-for-nothing. It would consist of a few interviews and the writing of a few reports; then the whole circus would be buried in the archives.

But before it blew over, SÄPO's own shrinks, the psychologists on the fourth floor of the police station, would try to restore Martin's mentally shredded psyche. At least, that is what they seemed to believe their role was.

We'll see who really needs help, Martin thought, after the two women psychologists sat down in chairs next to his bed. One hour later, they left Martin with troubled expressions.

Later that day, Martin also seemed to have taken care of the Bäckman problem. The scumbag had brought an argumentative colleague who had asked one or two sophisticated questions, but not so tricky that Martin wasn't able to answer by sticking to his story. As long as he stuck to his version, everything would be under control. He had filled all the obvious gaps by putting the blame on Jernberg. He simply traded places with him – everything from the contact with Omar to the trip to Gnesta. The only thing he left out was the Diaxtropyl-3S.

Before Bäckman left the room, he asked if Martin had been visited by any police colleagues.

"Nobody except for the shrinks," Martin answered.

"There will also be a special investigation into the man who died during your interrogation," Bäckman remarked before he closed the door.

The ball is rolling, Martin thought to himself. A special investigation for the towelhead. That means that I will be taken off the case completely. That would probably have happened anyway, given my so-called mental distress after Jernberg's death. He smiled slowly as he remembered the hard drive. It was time to change the direction of his mission. He did not have any other options anyway.

22 JONNA FETCHED JÖRGEN at ten past eight in the morning. He had slept badly because his injured eye was playing up.

"I need sleep to function properly," he complained as soon as he sat in the car.

"You can sleep tonight," Jonna promised, offering a packet of chewing gum.

Jörgen shook his head dejectedly.

"I'm not mentally prepared for a visit to the District Court," he said.

"Then you'd better start preparing yourself now. You do have all day," Jonna chuckled.

Jörgen looked as if he had swallowed a fly.

Jonna drove from Mariefred and onto the motorway towards Stockholm. She accelerated the Porsche quickly, until the speedometer showed 160, while she turned on the stereo system. From the speakers, some late-nineties Madonna emerged. Madonna must be over fifty, Jonna said to herself, looking in the rearview mirror. Wasn't that a small wrinkle under her eye?

Tonight, she was going to party hard. It was high time to investigate the street value of Jonna de Brugge and what was on offer on the open market. It was time to pick herself up and stop waiting for Mr Right to come knocking on her door.

"How about a change of clothes?" Jörgen suggested, examining his jacket. To be on the safe side, he also sniffed his armpits. Lately, his clothes had been through the wars and he was long overdue for a change into some clean threads.

"Well, then you had better buy some new ones. We're not going back to your place, for reasons I'm sure you appreciate," Jonna explained.

Jörgen suggested that they go to a galleria to buy some clothes, a suggestion to which Jonna reluctantly agreed.

In less than thirty minutes, Jörgen had purchased a grey blazer, a light-blue shirt that was a little tight in the neck but very chic, and sand-coloured chinos. And light tan, suede shoes that were more comfortable than fashionable. That was about as long as it took Jonna to visit one shop. And even then, the likelihood that she would find something to buy was minimal.

Forty-five minutes later, Jonna parked the car on Norr Mälarstrand.

"Here's the microrouter," she said, holding out one of the two small metal boxes she had been given by Serge.

"You'll position the other one, right?" he answered, stuffing the tiny metal case with its accessories into an inside pocket.

Jonna nodded.

"Easy for you – you only have to bend under your desk at work and hook it up."

"You're so right," Jonna laughed, pointing to the car door. "Being a police officer has some advantages."

Jörgen wrinkled his nose and got out of the car.

It took Jonna over twenty minutes to get from the entrance on Bergsgatan to her office on the third floor. Rumours flourished about the incident involving the murdered SÄPO agent in Gnesta, and every colleague she bumped into had something to add to the flood of speculation. Apart from the stories that the newspapers' online editions were pushing, various "reliable sources" were unofficially adding their own snippets of information on events.

Who the deceased villain was and who the injured fugitive was; why it had happened and who lay behind it. She had heard at least eight names suggested and a number of different accounts of the incident.

Finally, inside her office, it took less than a minute for Jonna to connect the microrouter to the internal police network. The SIM card was already inserted. To be on the safe side, she moved the wastepaper bin so that it obscured the wall socket.

Now it was done. She was sweating with nervousness or perhaps it was unusually hot in the room. She suddenly sensed that someone was standing behind her. She turned around, but the door to her office was still shut. She sank into her chair. Her heart was beating as if she had run a hundred-metre sprint. "This is the first and last time I do something like this," she muttered to herself.

After calming herself with a cup of coffee and some aimless surfing on the internet, she began to think about Jörgen. Wonder how it is going for agent Blad. If my nerves are making me jumpy, then he should be somewhere in the stratosphere, she thought, and bit her lower lip, pensively.

IT BEGAN WELL. Jörgen had presented himself to the security guard in reception as a journalist from Kvällspressen, which he in fact still was. Despite the press credentials, the uniformed bodybuilder was unwilling to be of any assistance. The press officer was not to be disturbed at any time or by anybody. Jörgen protested that he was not just anybody. Jörgen was a reporter at Kvällspressen, and the appointment he was trying to get with the person responsible for talking to the press was not just for small talk. He had started with security at reception. He could hardly be more formal, he said. The guard let his chewing gum rest between his teeth while he thought for a moment. Finally, he picked up the phone.

ULRIKA MELIN HAD had contacts with Jörgen in recent years. She was fairly familiar with the dark, curly-haired crime journalist from Kvällspressen. He was not the most sympathetic soul in the world, but no worse than the other jackels from the media, if you evaluated him from a strictly professional perspective. On a personal level, he was, however, attractive. Not so attractive that he made sparks fly, but enough to get her imagination working, like a sweet-and-sour sauce that tickles the tongue.

She noticed that he did not have a ring. Possibly, he could have a casual girlfriend, but that was not a show-stopper – at least not for her.

Now she would have one more opportunity to meet him in a tête-à-tête.

Not that she was desperate in any way. For her, it was her work at the District Court that gave her life meaning. To be a public servant was a privilege and required a small degree of self-sacrifice. But somewhere in the back of her mind, a small seed had been planted and was growing. Her biological clock was ticking relentlessly. Motherhood was beginning to take up an increasing part of her daily deliberations. Not a day went by that she did not wonder what it would be like to breastfeed a newborn ... or to cut the nails of tiny toes and fingers. This time, she would not chicken out at the last minute. She would go the whole distance and nail her proposition to his forehead if necessary. It would be impossible for him to misinterpret her advances.

She made a quick visit to the ladies' room to check her make-up before she went down to the main entrance.

"What can I do for you?" Ulrika greeted him when she came out of the entrance doorway. Jörgen stood up from the visitor's chair and took her outstretched hand.

She gazed at Jörgen for a few seconds. His swollen, bluish-purple eye piqued her interest.

"That looks painful," she said, wrinkling her nose a little.

"It looks less painful than it is," Jörgen answered, being a little ironic. "Being a journalist has its obvious disadvantages."

Ulrika smiled. Jörgen smiled back.

"So, what has brought *Kvällspressen* here?" she asked and folded her hands girlishly in front of her. God, my hands are so sweaty, she thought.

"I'll get straight to the point," he said, adopting a more serious expression. "Actually, I need to talk to you in private."

"In private?" She gave him a curious look.

"Can we go and talk somewhere?"

"What's it about?"

"I'd rather we discussed this somewhere else – not where there's people," Jörgen said, looking around.

"I see," she said, trying to hide her excitement. "There's a café just down the road on the left. I'll just get my coat."

Café? Jörgen thought. What in God's name was the woman thinking of? You don't go to a café to talk in privacy.

Jörgen put an end to Ulrika's café plans.

"I don't think a café is such a good idea," he made the excuse.

"No? What do you suggest?" she asked, surprised.

"I suggest that we go inside and find a private room," he said, pointing towards the office section.

"Perhaps we should do this after working hours?" she suggested, laughing. Now he has to get the hint, she thought.

"No, it's rather urgent, so I'd like to get this sorted here and now," he answered, slightly confused.

She felt indecisive. What did he really want? It was obviously not a clear-cut attempt at a date.

"Forgive me for asking," she said. "But is it something personal or does it possibly have something to do with Karin Sjöstrand?"

Personal, Jörgen thought. Why personal?

Suddenly, he understood. The woman was coming on to him. That is why she was so eager to go to a café and to meet after work. The more he thought about it, the more sense it made. She had been giving him signals like a traffic light and he had not noticed anything. Why should he? Why would he waste one second trying to read between the lines of a woman court secretary?

Should he play along or tell her the truth: that he was gay and had a boyfriend? She would probably pull up the drawbridge right in his face, which would stop him getting into the building. That would seriously jeopardize the operation, perhaps even make it impossible. If he was not successful, he would have both Walter and that police chick after him. At this point, he already had enough people out to get him; he did not need to be adding any more.

"You could say it is both personal and work-related," Jörgen lied, forcing a smile. "I'd prefer that we talk in your office, if it's really not too inconvenient."

He gently touched her arm.

"No, not all. Sounds like a good idea." Ulrika returned the smile.

Jörgen put on the visitor's badge that the bodybuilder gave him, after signing the visitor's book. He followed Ulrika in through the security doors and towards the lift. They got off on the second floor and she showed him into a small meeting room where she asked him to wait. As soon as she had closed the door, Jörgen took out the microrouter from his inner pocket. He bent down, looking under the big conference table for a suitable network socket. The only sockets in the room were fully visible on the wall of the room and were hidden temporarily by a few chairs.

Damn it! That's not good enough, he thought. The box is going to be seen as soon as someone moves the chairs. He had to find another room. He opened the door and stuck his head out. To the right, he could see the lovesick lady standing in a doorway to another room, discussing something with someone. All the remaining doors in that direction were closed. Five metres away, on the left side, there was a door ajar. That would have to do.

Taking care that Ulrika did not see him, he walked with light steps down the corridor to the open door. He opened the door a little and stuck his head inside. There were three desks there, three desks with piles of papers and files. Nobody was at their desks. Perhaps they were on a break. There'll not be a better opportunity, Jörgen thought. Jörgen was just about to enter the room when he heard Ulrika's voice in the corridor.

"Where are you going?" she called and walked towards him.

He hesitated. Should he pretend not to hear her, quickly enter the room and install the microrouter under one of the desks? He realized that there was not enough time for that.

"I'm looking for the toilet," Jörgen apologized, shrugging his shoulders as if confused.

"Well, it's not in there. That's where I sit, with two other secretaries."

"Really?"

She led Jörgen to the lavatory, which lay a few metres down on the same side.

"I'll wait outside," she said. "We're not allowed to have strangers running around the corridors, even when the office doors are locked."

"I understand. I apologize for my little detour," he replied and went into the lavatory.

A little while later, they were sitting in a small meeting room. Ulrika poured coffee from a thermos and handed the cup to Jörgen. She looked excited.

"Milk or sugar?" she asked, smiling coyly.

Jörgen shook his head. He felt his stomach churn. For the first time in his life, he was having a hard time finding the right words. He had to choose each word carefully – not too intimate, yet not too uninterested. Just enough charm to indicate a natural interest in her. This was worse than physical torture.

He had to get into her room and be there alone for at least a minute – however that was supposed to happen. And to make it more complicated, there were two other people working in the room. It was like a town hall meeting.

He sipped the coffee and put the cup down.

"Well," he started slowly, lowering his eyes to the coffee table, "we've met on a few occasions here at the District Court."

"Yes, that's right," she agreed.

"There are two things I need to ask you," he continued. "The first is personal and the second is work-related."

"Go on," she urged impatiently and leaned forwards over the table.

"Let's start with the work-related thing then. I have some questions concerning Karin Sjöstrand. It's well known that she worked at this court."

Ulrika's face changed. It became hard and sharp-featured, despite the fact that she was just as pudgy as Jörgen.

"I can't comment on our employees. Especially not those being investigated by the police."

"No, of course not," Jörgen quickly replied.

A brief silence settled on the room.

Ulrika stared intensely at Jörgen.

"Then let's move on to the personal question," he said, clearing his throat.

Her expression changed again. She folded her hands on the table and regained her excitement.

"I'm quite interested in you," he managed to blurt out.

It felt as if he had jumped off a cliff.

"Interested?" Ulrika repeated, as if she had misheard.

"Yes, the way a person can be interested in another."

"Which way is that, then?" she said, feigning surprise.

"Well, how you work and how you are as a person."

Once again, it was quiet for a few seconds.

"What do you expect me to say to that?" she said.

"Let me rephrase that. I'd like to get to know you better," Jörgen said.

Ulrika laughed and brushed her ear with her hand. "Did I perhaps just hear a pick-up line?" she said. He's as slow as treacle, she thought, but was still happy that he finally had confessed what she wanted to hear. If he had not made an advance, she would have done it. It was that simple. That question about Karin Sjöstrand was just an excuse to come here. He was here for her sake.

"That's one way of putting it," Jörgen answered and felt his breakfast wanting to check out.

"I don't really know what to say," she said, looking Jörgen in the eye. Nice and easy, Ullis, she thought. Play a little hard to get. Let him do the work.

"Are we talking about dinner?" she finally asked.

"Yes, but only if you want to. I'm being a little too forward, perhaps," he said, with an embarrassed smile.

"Well, a dinner cannot hurt. We've all got to eat," she answered, glowing.

"Excellent," Jörgen said. "When are you free?"

"Tonight, perhaps," she answered quickly.

"Any particular place?" he asked.

"No restaurant, please. I've eaten out way too often lately," she lied. "Home cooking never fails."

Jörgen swallowed. She expects me to invite her back to my

place, he thought. The flat looked like the day after an Ozzy Osbourne party. Sebastian's going to have a fit when he gets back next week.

"It's a bit messy at the moment with builders all over the flat," Jörgen said. "I'd love to invite you to my place, but it's not possible. It's a bit messy, to say the least."

"I see," Ulrika said. "There is, however, no mess at my place. Not yet, anyway," she laughed.

"So you're inviting me to dinner?" Jörgen responded.

"Shall we say seven o'clock?"

"It's a date," Jörgen said and immediately had a stomach ache.

Jörgen and Ulrika exchanged telephone numbers and went out into the corridor. The little metal box was still in Jörgen's pocket. He had only one chance and he had to take it now.

"One other thing," Jörgen said, stopping. "It would be interesting to see your office."

"Whatever for?" she asked.

"Well, mostly out of curiosity. I'm a journalist and we are, by nature, a curious breed." Take the bait for Christ's sake, he prayed silently.

"I'm afraid there's not a lot to see," she laughed and continued towards the exit.

"I'm betting there is," Jörgen insisted.

"Well, I don't know," Ulrika hesitated.

"Just a little peek," Jörgen persisted.

"Well, okay then. It's actually against the rules, but I can say that I know you. You're hardly a complete stranger." And you'll be much less of a stranger soon, sweetie, she thought.

She took Jörgen to the room where she and the two other court secretaries had their workspaces. The room was empty.

"Where are the other two?" Jörgen asked, looking around the empty office.

"They're on a half-day course today."

"I see," he said, sitting in one of the office chairs. Beginner's luck, he thought.

"That's my workspace," she smiled, pointing to the desk next to him.

Jörgen quickly changed desks. He sat in the chair and leaned backwards with his hands behind his head.

"Nice chair," he said, rocking carefully.

"Be my guest," she replied.

Jörgen pushed the chair back and, from the corner of his eye, glanced under the table. He spotted both network and power sockets on the wall under the desk. A network cable seemed to lead from the socket to Ulrika's computer. The spot was good enough. The microrouter would not be discovered unless someone bent down under the desk and knew what to look for.

The only problem was how to get the woman out of the room so that he could connect the box without being detected.

"I have a lot to do," she said. "And since I'm going to make dinner by seven o'clock, I'll have to get back to work to finish on time today."

She clapped her hands.

"Of course," Jörgen said, getting up from the chair.

He followed her to the door.

As soon as she entered the corridor, he locked the door behind her and threw himself under the desk. He tore out the microrouter from his jacket pocket, fumbling with a network cable and the small power adapter. He heard Ulrika knocking on the door and yelling something. Jörgen was so frantic that his whole body was shaking. He fumbled with the network cable in the wall socket, removing it. His hands felt as if they would not work. No matter how he pressed the small tab that held the plug in place, it would not come loose. At last, he jerked out the cable and plugged it into the socket on the microrouter. He heard it become quiet on the other side of the door and guessed that she was looking for her keys. He plugged the power adapter in an electric socket and the power cable into the microrouter. Now he could hear the key turning in the lock.

Just as he plugged the network cable between the wall socket and the microrouter, the door opened. Jörgen dived out from under the table.

He met Ulrika's stare while on all fours beside the desk.

"What are you doing?" she asked, somewhat irritatedly, with the key in her hand.

Jörgen stood up. He pretended to stumble.

"I suddenly became very dizzy," he lied, and clutched his forehead.

Ulrika looked at him thoughtfully. "Dizzy?"

"Yes, I don't know what happened. Suddenly the room started to spin and I had to grab something to avoid losing my balance and fainting. I grabbed the door handle, but I fell backwards and the door must have locked itself shut."

Ulrika raised an eyebrow in disbelief.

"I didn't want to grab you. Then we would have both fallen into the corridor," he persisted, seeing the doubt in her eyes.

"That was very considerate," she said, "but how did you end up at the desk?"

"I must have rolled over here."

"Rolled?"

"I think so. Don't really remember."

"Are you sick?" she wondered. "An illness, perhaps."

Jörgen shook his head. "No, it was just something momentary – perhaps too much excitement taking its toll."

"I see," she said and nodded.

Jörgen interpreted the nod as a sign that the story was swallowed and the incident was now history.

They parted at the entrance and agreed that she would call him one hour before the dinner was ready.

23 WHEN JÖRGEN STEPPED out onto the street in front of the district court, he felt an enormous sense of relief. He had succeeded where Walter Gröhn had failed. He had successfully planted that little metal box inside the very heart of the Stockholm District Court and in a place that would almost certainly avoid detection. He only hoped that he had connected it to the right network. There were no other options available and he assumed that Ulrika Melin, in her role as a court secretary, was connected, and had access, to the correct network.

This was investigative journalism of the highest order. Even Günter Wallraff would be impressed by the precision and skill with which Jörgen Blad had performed. What was a little undercover work among Turkish miners compared to the mental pressure that he had had to endure under Ulrika Melin's desk? He had voluntarily flirted with a straight woman to facilitate the hacking of a Swedish court database. All this to uncover the truth and expose a major scandal. It had required nerves of Swedish steel.

Before he could put this behind him, he needed to get the microrouter back. To leave it sitting under the desk was not a viable option. Sooner or later, it would be discovered and would point the finger at Jörgen as surely as traffic cones to a council roadworker. So he was forced to stay in that woman's good book for a little longer, even though his stomach rebelled at the thought of wine and candlelight. After that, his part would be over.

Jörgen walked down Norr Mälarstrand and sat down in a coffee shop on the corner of Garvar Lundin alley. He turned his mobile phone on and keyed in in the number of Officer Jonna de Brugge.

"It's done," he stated curtly.

Silence on the other end of the phone.

"Then I underestimated you," Jonna replied.

"I'm not a person to be underestimated," Jörgen said, swelling a little with pride. A little flattery and gratitude never went amiss.

"I will try to remember that," she replied.

"So what happens now?" he asked.

"If you have succeeded in planting your box in the right way and in the right place, all that remains is for Serge to do his part of the job. The critical part of the operation is hacking into the court databases," Jonna explained.

"Yes, I know that," Jörgen said. "I meant, where am I to go now?"

"In two hours, I'm going to leave the police station and call in sick. Afterwards, I'll pick you up so that we can visit the bank where you stashed the evidence on Folke Uddestad. Then, we'll go directly to Serge and I'll start to search any police databases that I can get into with a little illegal help from him."

"That sounds like an acceptable plan," Jörgen answered. "There's just one glitch."

"What?" Jonna inquired.

"The key to the security deposit box was stolen from me."

"The key was stolen!" Jonna exclaimed.

"Take it easy; I'll fix it," Jörgen said defensively. "The glitch can be fixed. We just have to fetch the spare key. You see, I stashed a spare key under the sink at my mother's – as a safety measure in case I lost the original key. It's a safe bet that nobody will look there and my mother is blissfully ignorant about it. You will have to keep her busy while I fetch the key from the kitchen."

"In other words, we have to go to your mother's before the bank. For your sake, I hope she lives locally. The clock is ticking and the banks close at 3 pm," Jonna declared.

"Calm down; it'll be fine. She lives in Högdalen. She's a pensioner and is almost never out. It will take no more than thirty minutes."

"There's another detour as well," Jörgen quickly added.

"Okay," Jonna said, resigned.

"We actually have to visit two banks, since I keep the key to the safety deposit box with the evidence on Folke Uddestad in a second bank, and that's the bank we have to go to first."

Jonna was quiet for a few seconds. She felt her blood pressure rise.

"You're a master at making simple matters complicated, both for yourself and others."

"And one final thing while we are making plans," he finished. To be on the safe side, he forced a chuckle.

"There's more?" Jonna cried.

"I have to go on a date tonight."

"A date?"

"Yes, with a woman who works at the District Court," Jörgen explained.

"You're joking."

"If only I was," he sighed.

Jörgen gave a short account of the afternoon's events and why he was forced to stay in court secretary Ulrika Melin's good books.

At first, Jonna was against Jörgen's date. It was hardly the time for any social activities, but she quickly changed her mind when she realized the precariousness of not removing the microrouter. If Jörgen got caught, it could lead to Jonna. That was something she had not considered when she sent him to buy top-up cards. Why had she not let Serge buy the cards instead? However hard she denied it, she knew the adage "no smoke without fire" would linger in an investigator's mind. Jonna had herself been taught that. And even if she were acquitted in a court of law, she would always be guilty in the eyes of her peers.

Jörgen had two hours until Jonna had to pick him up. He felt restless and his fingertips were itching. If only he had his laptop. Headlines for the exclusive were popping up in his head like popcorn. He already had sufficient material to be the kingpin of the news desk. He was embedded. As fucking embedded as a person could be, and in something so big that it could only end with a sure-fire success. A clear case of the right man in the right place.

He reached for a daily newspaper on the table next to him and read the headlines with a smirk. If he did not get the "Journalist of the Year" award after this, he never would.

But first, he had a date to get through. Jörgen checked the time. He was dreading what the evening had in store. What did a woman of her type expect from the evening? Probably a happy ending between the sheets. Jörgen felt a strong impulse to throw himself into a taxi to Arlanda airport and to take the first plane out of the country.

AS SOON AS Jonna finished the call with Jörgen, she rang Walter.

"I'll soon be dead from scurvy," Walter declared after realizing that even the apple pie was not fit for human consumption. If you survive the operation, then the hospital food will finish you instead, he thought.

"Both microrouters are in position now," Jonna briefly informed him. She herself was eating out tonight. A tasty chicken meal at a good restaurant before it was time for the nightclub.

"Both?" Walter replied, surprised. "Have you planted one at the District Court too? How did you manage that?"

"Jörgen Blad managed to plant the microrouter there by befriending a female employee of the District Court chambers."

"Unbelievable." Walter's voice had an approving tone.

"It may well be."

"And what does 'befriending' mean?"

"Not a clue, except that he has a date with her tonight," Jonna replied. "He didn't go into detail and I didn't ask."

"But how the hell did he manage to plant the device there?"

"He managed to put it under the woman's desk during an unsupervized moment – if we are to believe what he says," Jonna said.

"Is there any reason not to?" Walter's tone altered.

"It's difficult for me to say from one phone conversation. Unlike you, perhaps, but then you are better acquainted with him."

Walter muttered something to himself that she could not hear.

"When will you start digging?" he went on.

"As soon as I've gone off duty and after we have fetched the evidence on Folke Uddestad. After this call, I'll go and make up a story for my boss. Tell him that I have a fever and have to get to bed. To be honest, I don't feel very comfortable telling lies."

"If you're forced to lie, then you owe it to the other person to do it with a lot of credibility," Walter said ironically.

"Something you can teach me?"

"Anytime."

"And another thing," Walter said, changing the subject, "I was in touch with a friend at the police union this morning."

"Really?"

"There's a slim chance that I will be reinstated soon."

"How did that happen?" Jonna said curiously.

"David Lilja and company may have made a mistake when they suspended me."

"A mistake?"

"It's a long story. But to keep it short, the Drug Squad didn't have all their facts straight when they filed the complaint. With a bit of luck, that could tip the scales in my favour. Besides, I have some chips that I intend to cash in with certain individuals. If everything works out, it might still be possible to salvage this old wreck after all."

"How fortunate for you," Jonna said. "The old-boy network is just another form of police corruption, you know."

"To be part of the system, I would have to have friends. I don't," Walter pointed out. "I'm talking about favours given and returned; some unfair decisions that need to be corrected."

"It's the same thing," Jonna argued.

"Perhaps a grey area," Walter said. "Like breaking the law to prevent other crimes from being committed."

"But that applies when the laws are not good laws," Jonna said.

"Laws are only theory. The challenge is their practical implementation. A law can prohibit an action that another law depends on to prevent crime."

"A catch-22 situation."

"Exactly," Walter said emphatically. "Some legislators seem to have a distorted view of reality and of the laws that already exist. I could give you dozens of examples …"

Jonna interrupted Walter. They seemed to have become permanently sidetracked. She suggested that they continue the discussion over a glass of wine when Walter was discharged from the hospital.

The grief tore at his heart.

His memories transported him to a place where he was lying on his back with a blue sky above and endless fields that disappeared over the horizon. A warm summer breeze washed over him.

"Daddy?" she asked and lay down beside him. She was out of breath after running up the hill. "Is Grandma in heaven now?"

He looked at his daughter. Her inquisitive eyes.

"That's what the priest said," she added anxiously when he did not answer.

He smiled and put his arm around her. "Grandma is in heaven," he said, even though he knew there was no such thing.

"Can she see us now?" she asked and pointed at the sky.

"I'm sure she can," he lied, taking her hand. Faith was the last hope of mankind. Something that made it possible to endure the fear of death and the final destination.

"Can she hear us too?" Cecilia asked, but suddenly realized that might not be such a good thing. Then Grandma could hear her say bad words.

"Perhaps," he replied, although he knew the truth. It was they, he and his colleagues, who were God. Heaven was on earth and the body kept the soul alive. They had the answers, the truth that would deliver mankind from its ignorance.

He was jolted back into the room with the windows facing the garden. Raindrops from the bluish-grey cloud spattered against the window-ledge. The time had come for the fourth one. Everything was prepared and he felt no remorse.

THE GNESTA INCIDENT caused the highest officers within the Security Service to call an emergency meeting the next morning. The head of the Counter-Terrorism Unit, Thomas Kokk, described in brief terms the events of the night. The head of the Security

Service, Agency Director Anders Holmberg, looked troubled and a little irritated where he sat, hunched in the meeting room together with the others from the organization's executive. He was upset that one of his agents had been killed in action, in what was the first casualty in the history of the Security Service organization. He was also irritated that he had been pulled out of bed at five in the morning and therefore had not been able to sober up from last night's drinking session with the Jägermeister club.

To summon the executive for a matter involving an operational incident was a rare occurrence. It had not happened since the murder of Prime Minister Olof Palme. The executive was responsible, first and foremost, for the administration of the organization, such as the yearly budget expenditure and other such matters, and for ensuring that designated targets were achieved. They were directly accountable to the government, Parliament and the National Police Board. But the incident was of such a nature that even the executive had to be informed of the situation. That had to be done by the Agency Director himself, together with the head of the operational unit involved.

Agency Director Anders Holmberg still felt drunk even though he had drunk three cups of coffee, one after the other, as soon as he had arrived at the police headquarters in Kungsholmen. His stomach was in turmoil and a throbbing headache had enveloped him.

This was not one of his better days.

"This is the first time in the history of the Swedish Security Service that an agent has been killed during a police operation," Holmberg said in a tense voice, after Thomas Kokk had finished his initial briefing. He massaged his temples with his fingers, hoping to ease his growing migraine.

An uneasy silence surrounded the table. All that could be heard was the wheezing from Chief Inspector Sten Gullviksson's chronically obstructed airways.

That it had to happen during my time as Agency Director is so typical, Holmberg thought. He hated being associated with failure – it was one of the reasons that Holmberg's career had been so successful. His previous work as the director of the Fortifications Authority had been an unprecedented success story. He had transformed the old-fashioned, traditional institution into a modern and profitable organization and he intended to reform the Security Service in the same way.

There was no room for failure.

"So, what do we do now?" Holmberg said, waving his arms. The sudden movement made his head flash with pain.

Thomas Kokk raised a finger. "We need a new leader for the Chief Prosecutor's terrorism investigation. Martin Borg is responsible for the investigation, but he's currently receiving medical attention for his injuries and is, according to the preliminary evaluation by our psychologists, not mentally fit to carry out his duties. Effective immediately, he's also removed from active duty until Internal Affairs have finished with their investigation into the Gnesta incident. I have informed Chief Prosecutor Åsa Julén about the change in operational leadership."

"I see," Holmberg replied. "Who's the new operational leader?"

"I'm thinking of taking over myself and taking charge of both surveillance and investigative personnel."

"Sounds like a good idea," Holmberg said. He had great confidence in Thomas Kokk. It was he, using contacts outside the sphere of the agency, who had pushed for the promotion of Kokk from section leader to head of the Counter-Terrorism Unit last year. Kokk was, like himself, an academic with a legal background. And people like him should be promoted within the institution. There were still far too many spy hunters left who seriously believed that there still was a Russian threat and therefore were still trying to take the biggest chunk of the Security Service's funding.

Still, Kokk had, unlike Holmberg, also been to the police academy and had done his time on the streets as a patrolling policeman before he was recruited to special police operations. His background as a real cop had given him some degree of acceptance from the veteran spy hunters, even though he was an academic.

A perfect compromise and a smart first move by the ex-director of Fortifications, Holmberg had reasoned, when he received news that the promotion had finally passed through the needle eye of the promotions board and was approved.

"But," Holmberg continued, drawing out the word after some thought. "What do we really have on that Islamist group other than the financial transactions from that terrorist prince and the probable link to ... was it called Drug-X?"

"To be frank, nothing at this moment," Kokk said, almost apologetically.

"As you know, the house search only resulted in a few construction drawings and an awful media storm. We're currently analyzing the drawings. None of the interrogations have given us anything either."

"And you're sure that the detainee – Hakim, or whatever his name was – died of a heart attack?"

"Before the post-mortem has been done, we assume that is the case."

"We'll have problems over him," Holmberg said. "When people die in Swedish cells, there's usually a hysterical debate in the media – especially since he belongs to an ethnic minority."

Troubled, Kokk agreed.

"You didn't get anything from the informant in Gnesta?" Holmberg continued.

"No," Kokk answered. "We don't know what the hot tip was since the informant is probably dead. We're assuming that he and one of the perpetrators and Ove Jernberg were trapped in the burning building. According to Martin Borg, the CI had information that he wanted to give to Jernberg – but only face to face."

"I see," Holmberg said.

"The identification process is fully under way. We hope to have preliminary results later today."

Holmberg nodded, reflectively. "Have you received any results from the laboratory in England on Drug-X?"

"No, not yet," Kokk answered.

"Can we speed things up?"

"I wouldn't think so, but I'll check with SKL immediately after the meeting."

"Good." Holmberg could hear his head pounding.

"Human Resources will handle Jernberg's family. If that's of interest to anybody," Gullviksson hoarsely interjected. "They and our psychologists are, at this moment, visiting his wife and their two sons."

"A terrible tragedy," Holmberg sighed.

Once again, the room fell silent for a few seconds.

"Well, then," Holmberg concluded and stood up. "If no one has anything further to contribute, then my press secretary and I will go and face the media. I don't want them to try to link the Gnesta incident and the death of the detainee as retaliation from our side. That could be the start of a political crisis and it has to be avoided at all costs."

24 THE VISIT TO Jörgen's mother took more time than anticipated, since the seventy-three-year-old lady insisted on offering coffee and small almond biscuits called Finnish Sticks. Forty minutes after their arrival, Jörgen had managed to retrieve his key from under the sink.

Their visits to the banks went without incident. Before Jörgen handed over the small memory stick with the record of his and Folke Uddestad's intimate rendezvous, he proposed that he should now be allowed to publish parts of what they already knew.

Jonna looked at the journalist as if he was joking. Then her eyes darkened, and she tore the memory stick from Jörgen's hand. It was a lame attempt and he should have known better than to ask her.

At ten minutes to four that afternoon, Jonna and Jörgen rang the doorbell at the flat of Serge Wolinsky.

"Let's rock and roll," Serge said, making space for Jonna in front of one of the computers. He himself sat at another computer and was fully occupied with hacking into the District Court database.

"Am I logged into the criminal records database now?" she asked, sitting in the chair.

Serge nodded.

"Were you already logged into the database before I arrived?" she asked. The microrouter had been connected to the network for about six hours, which raised the suspicion that Serge had already been in and poked around in the police database. She bit her lip and thought, I should have waited until I left the police station before connecting the router. The problem was that she had taken sick leave. It would not have been feasible to wait any longer, given the trips to the bank in that short period of time.

Serge shook his head.

"Are you lying to me?" Jonna asked.

Serge shrugged, not understanding why she asked.

The bastard, she thought irritatedly, and was surprised at her ill temper. She had not had time to eat lunch, which meant that her blood sugar was at an all-time low for this year. If Serge had done any serious tampering in the database, she was responsible. Unofficially, of course, as no one would know that it was she who had made it possible to hack the database, if it was even detected. She was, at any rate, unable to verify if he was telling the truth. She might as well let go of the suspicion.

As Jonna suspected, her searches in the criminal records databases yielded meagre pickings.

That neither Lennart Ekwall, nor Karin Sjöstrand, nor Bror Lantz had a criminal record, she already knew. Also known was that Sjöstrand's daughter and the taxi driver Ojo Maduekwe had clean sheets. The only one that had a conviction was Ekwall's wife. She had been arrested for driving under the influence by a police patrol outside the Museum of Natural History seven months earlier. That information was not much help.

Using the database and Walter's recollections, she was, however, able to identify the two villains who had made the violent home visit to Jörgen: they were Tor Hedman and Jerry Salminen. Both had long criminal records with countless visits to the prison system. Tor Hedman's record was a never-ending story. He had started his criminal career in his early years and had stuck with it. At age fifty, he was still very active.

Salminen was a native of Finland, which, however, had not stopped him causing problems for the Swedish justice system over the last ten years. He had been convicted of an impressive number of crimes given the short period he had been in Sweden. There was no mention in the databases of whether he had a criminal record in Finland.

Jonna concluded that neither of them had a known address. They had been released from Kumla prison ten months earlier. If Walter did not know where to find the two stooges, which was unlikely, it would be impossible for her to find them.

The searches in the police databases were not going to give her any more relevant information.

"How are we doing?" Jonna asked, turning towards Serge.

Serge nodded encouragingly. "The microrouter is at least connected to the correct network."

"How do you know that?"

"Because I'm already inside the Unix kernel and I can see the processer calls to the French database," he answered dryly.

"How much time will it take to hack into the French database?" Jörgen asked, a little sheepishly, stretching sideways to get a better view of the screen. What he saw did not, however, make him any the wiser. Lots of small command windows covered the screen with text and numbers scrolling upwards randomly. The text was totally incomprehensible, as were the numbers.

Serge took no notice of Jörgen. He was focused on what the screen was displaying and his small piano-player fingers danced quickly over the keyboard as he hopped between the different command windows. One of the windows did catch Jörgen's eye. It looked as if Serge was chatting with someone.

Short, cryptic messages were being exchanged all the time. Three different chat names popped up regularly: Typhoon, Alphaville and Beest.

Just as Jörgen was about to point out the chat, Jonna came and stood behind Serge. She watched, fascinated, as Serge's tapping fingertips flew over the keys. She also noticed the small chat window in the bottom left-hand corner of the screen.

"Who are you chatting with?" she asked, pointing at the chat window.

"Some members of the Von Dy group are helping me," Serge answered, distracted.

"What do you mean by 'helping'?"

"To get in," he mumbled.

"To the District Court network?" Jonna said. Her eyes narrowed.

Serge sighed resignedly. "We have split the intrusion into four parts. Each one of us focuses on different processes. Since we are already inside the Unix kernel, which was the easy part of the operation due to the open bug, the most difficult part remains. To figure out how the APIs work so that we can make FAPI function calls to the database."

"FAPI?" Jonna said, puzzled.

"The software interface between two applications. F means fake. So fake calls."

Jonna suddenly realized how little she knew about how the hacker elite worked, despite her years at MIT.

"Nobody gave you permission to involve a bunch of hackers in this."

"I had no choice," Serge defended himself.

"Why not? I was under the impression that you were a real computer genius."

"Yes, but …"

"Understand that accessing the police databases doesn't impress me at all. Considering that you had back doors, all you had to do was walk straight in. And the microrouters are not rocket science. Any proficient hardware engineer could design and build them. They're built with standard components. The District Court database is a completely different challenge and requires a very special kind of competence."

"Agreed, that's exactly what I'm trying to tell you," Serge said and threw up his hands in frustration.

"That you need help from other hackers?"

"Precisely. Even if I'm good, it's a tough nut to crack. Bloody difficult, like I told you."

"But why didn't you inform me first? This is not a hacker convention where anyone's invited to participate just because you can't handle your side of the deal."

"I thought it was more important to get the job done as quickly as possible than to waste time on red tape by calling you."

"Red tape?"

"Yes, and also these individuals are not just anybody," Serge said in a bitter tone. "They're almost as good as me and are all members of Von Dy. Nor do they know anything about the purpose of what I am trying to hack, except that it's a database. They don't have access to the network."

Jonna turned it over in her mind for a while.

"If you're lying, I guarantee that a couple of thugs in leather waistcoats will be standing outside your door within a few hours," she lied, glaring at him intensely.

Serge tried to feign indifference.

Jonna took this as a sign that he was not lying. Serge showed her samples from the chat that seemed to back up his claim. Jonna knew that he could fake the chat log if he wanted to, but chose to believe him. In the circumstances, she did not really have any alternative.

It was five to six in the evening when the first breakthrough came.

Serge yelled so loudly that the half-asleep Jörgen almost fell off his chair.

"We can communicate with some of the APIs now," Serge said, excited.

Jonna went to Serge. "What does that actually mean?"

"That we more or less know how the APIs are built," Serge said, pointing to a program window that once again displayed lots of incomprehensible text. "We have run some automatic programs that continuously test the function calls of the database and, by doing so, learn how the APIs behave. With that information, the programs use a probability algorithm to calculate the probable structure of the APIs. Like the way you attempt to reverse-engineer a binary file to its source code. We've succeeded in getting a really good picture of their structure now."

"What happens next?" Jörgen asked, interested now.

Serge turned to Jonna with a grin, tugging at his beard. "I think we'll break through the wall before the night is over," he said.

Jonna looked at her wristwatch. The evening activities for her and Jörgen were due to start soon. Jörgen had received a telephone call to tell him that dinner would be ready in just under an hour. He had not looked amused.

"That sounds good, but I don't think that Jörgen or I have anything to contribute for the time being," she said, looking pointedly at Jörgen, whose thoughts were elsewhere.

"Quite right," Serge answered, preoccupied. He was already back in the virtual world.

"Call me as soon as the next important barrier is passed. I have my mobile on at all times," Jonna said firmly.

Serge muttered something inaudible from the living room.

Jonna considered going back to the police station to pick up the microrouter. After a little deliberation, she decided it would be unwise. It would need unnecessary explanations the next day, since each entry and exit would be registered.

Because she had taken sick leave earlier that day, it would look strange that she went there later that evening. There were always industrious colleagues burning the midnight oil at the department whom she could run into.

She planned to be on sick leave for a few more days, so the most sensible thing to do was to steer clear of the police station and any of her supervisors.

Always stick to the simple solution, she thought to herself.

"Do you want me to drop you off at that woman's place now?" Jonna asked, excessively helpful. She turned the key to her Porsche and the six-cylinder Boxer engine roared.

Jörgen did not answer, looking as if he was on his way to his own execution. Twenty minutes later, Jörgen stood outside the entrance to Ulrika Melin's building. Jonna's face beamed, and she waved a few colourful gestures at him before she burned rubber and drove off.

Jörgen gazed long and hard as she disappeared. He had a big knot in his stomach. It felt like he had swallowed the troubles of the world, only to become constipated. Without the promise of his exclusive story, he would never have endured this.

His mobile phone beeped just as he was about to open the entrance door. It was an SMS from the news desk. He suddenly developed a guilty conscience about not ringing work for several days and not answering the text messages and calls that regularly popped up on his mobile phone's display. He had tried to call Sebastian, but got only his answering service. He understood of course that there was not much coverage in the mountains of Peru, but he could at least have tried to leave him a message. The country must have some landlines.

From the start, Jörgen had thought the idea of going to Peru to climb mountains was a crazy project. He had had many loud debates with Sebastian as soon as he proposed the idea, that Saturday evening eleven months ago. Especially when he found out that he was travelling together with Filip and André, two half-crazy and, unfortunately, affluent gays who were not only constantly seeking adventure but also very keen to explore the human body. They are probably sleeping in a tent at two thousand metres altitude and in a ménage à trois right now, Jörgen fantasized in the seconds before Ulrika Melin opened the door to her flat.

JONNA OPENED THE door to her flat just before eight that evening. She decided almost immediately not to plug the USB memory stick with Folke Uddestad into her computer, even though her fingers itched with curiosity. It could wait until tomorrow. Instead, she poured an ice-cold beer and took a shower. Fifteen minutes later, she had finished the shower and the beer. She changed into jeans and a white blouse. While opening another beer, she called Walter and informed him that Serge had made a breakthrough with the District Court network and that she did not intend to look through the evidence on Uddestad that she had obtained from Jörgen. She simply did not have the time this evening.

Walter grunted that it could not take much time to open a few photos on the computer, but Jonna replied that it was not negotiable. He switched eagerly to the computer hacking and pointed out that she should stay with the freaky Serge and make sure that he was not up to no good. There was an imminent risk that he would use this opportunity for his own ends.

Jonna rejected his suggestion as unnecessary. It was impossible for her to keep tabs on Serge and monitor everything he did. The skills that he possessed were not ones that you could learn at any university. They were the product of a very keen intellect, experience and an almost manic obsession. The man lived for his computers and networks and sat in front of a computer screen every waking moment. How he made a living, she did not want to know.

JÖRGEN HAD NO no appetite. Even though Ulrika Melin served oven-grilled chicken with homemade potato salad, he could not down more than a few mouthfuls. She followed him constantly with her eyes and smiled as soon as he met her light-blue eyes. She was loaded with expectation, like an atomic bomb.

Jörgen cringed when she asked if there was something wrong with the food.

"You're eating like a bird," she said with a smile.

Jörgen excused himself and went to the toilet where he spat out a mouthful of food and then rinsed out his mouth. He gulped some water and looked at himself in the mirror. He was pale. He looked worn and undernourished, although the scales at the hospital told another story. How could that be?

One hour later, Jörgen and Ulrika ended up on the sofa, each holding their own glass of red wine. She put her legs up in a provocative pose and lit a few candles on the small coffee table. Jörgen sipped the bag-in-a-box wine. It was a young Merlot from South Africa that left a sour, metallic aftertaste.

They made a toast and she welcomed him for the second, or was it the third, time. Jörgen complimented her choice of wine and gazed around the living room. As far as he could see, the majority of the furnishings came from flat-pack stores.

"Do you like my flat?" she asked, delighted. "I've tried to put my personal stamp on the room."

Jörgen nodded in approval. "You have a really original style."

"Do you really think so?"

After fifteen minutes, Ulrika had attended to three errands in the kitchen. After each task, she moved a little closer to Jörgen. Now she was sitting so close that her knee nudged the outside of his thigh. He crossed his legs, gaining a few centimetres, but it did not take long before she, by using the excuse that a candle was not standing straight and then adjusting it, took back the remaining centimetres.

Jörgen felt a cold shiver go through his body when their legs touched again. The moment he dreaded had now come. The success of the evening was now in the balance.

He realized that there were two options. He could firmly refuse her and blame the fact that they did not know each other very well. She would probably feel rejected, and the situation would end on an anticlimax that would mean that he would not get to meet her again, which was very unfortunate in terms of the microrouter.

The other, and presumably better, alternative, from the investigative journalist's perspective, was to empty the bag-in-a-box as quickly as possible and pray that his memory would fail him from now on. Whatever happened that night, he hoped to be blissfully ignorant about it for the rest of his days.

It was ten past two when Jörgen found himself naked in Ulrika's bedroom. The room was spinning, and he had a hard time getting his mouth to work. Clothes lay in a pile on the floor. Presumably, he had had assistance in taking them off. No matter how he tried, his lips would not form any words – just an unintelligible, continuous slurring. He observed Ulrika with blurry eyes as she took off her clothes. When she was wearing only knickers and a bra, he tried to sit up on the edge of the bed. Despite emptying the bag-in-a-box, he still possessed way too much consciousness. She had drunk only three glasses of wine the whole evening. Jörgen must have tossed back almost two litres. Yet he was still fully conscious of what was about to take place. A shudder ran down his spine. He was on the verge of panicking, but calmed himself by taking some deep breaths through his mangled nose.

Then she removed her bra. He turned around and saw two breasts exposed in the glow from the streetlight outside the window. Jörgen had difficulty focusing and Ulrika's naked body blurred into the rest of the room.

She discarded her semi-transparent knickers and an overgrown bush grinned back at Jörgen. With the speed of a ferret, she jumped up on the bed and flipped Jörgen on his back. She straddled him with a serious expression and stared into his eyes.

Then she broke into laughter that sounded like screeching seagulls.

"You turn me on," she said, unabashed.

Jörgen did not have the strength to fight back. With eighty kilos of female flesh on top of him, there was not much he could do. Instead, he closed his eyes and fell into a drunken slumber.

Seconds later, he was brutally awakened by a cold hand on his crotch.

25 JONNA CALLED JÖRGEN's mobile phone at five-thirty in the morning. She had just received a call from an exhilarated Serge Wolinsky, who announced that he was now inside the District Court database. She waited for seven rings on Jörgen's mobile phone. On the eighth ring, a woman's voice answered.

When she described herself as a friend of Jörgen's and asked to speak to him, she was met with silence at the other end. After a few seconds, the woman asked what kind of friend she was. "Just a friend," Jonna answered drolly.

The woman explained that Jörgen was busy sleeping off a hangover and therefore could not be disturbed. She took a message and promised that Jörgen would call his "friend" back when he woke up, which in all probability would not be before the afternoon, given the amount of alcohol he had consumed the previous evening.

Jonna had herself only consumed two drinks the evening before, not counting the two beers she had in the flat before she went to the club and the wine she drank with her meal. One of the two drinks, a San Francisco, she drank together with Sandra at the San Marino restaurant in Blasieholmen.

After an exquisite dinner of chicken breast poached in white wine and a rather expensive Chardonnay, both girlfriends finished the evening at the trendy club Le Cheliff, down on Stureplan. There, she had her second drink, a dry martini. The queue to Le Cheliff was nonexistent, which was unusual.

Perhaps even the brats were feeling the financial recession. After the usual buttering up of the musclebound bouncers on the door, they were both let inside.

As soon as they had hung their coats in the cloakroom, Jonna was approached by a tipsy plumber. He introduced himself as Tomas without the 'H' and was twenty-nine. He had his own business and a brand new van with the logo "TOMBOY AB". He wrote off most of his expenses to the company, except for booze, and had a fifty-inch plasma TV in his living room at Farsta. "Chicks like handymen," he declared, raising his hand as if swearing an oath. Just in case she wondered, he never cleaned his own pipe by himself and if she needed help cleaning her drains, then he was the man for her. He managed to share this information in one single breath. Jonna thanked him politely for his interest, but declined his invitation. She would think of Tomboy next time she had a "blockage".

They continued to mingle farther in towards the half-empty dance floor where the music pulsated at a high volume. A disco gigolo got them in his sights just as they got onto the dance floor. The gigolo fixed his eyes on Jonna and threw his arms out as if he was about to dance 'Zorba the Greek'. Obviously, there was nothing wrong with his confidence. He loosened his tie and started to shake his hips. At a table next to the dance floor, the rest of his seven-man gang sat and clapped in time with his hip gyrations.

Jonna rolled her eyes. Sandra laughed at the spectacle even though she had to limp off the dance floor.

The gigolo adjusted his Beckham faux-hawk haircut, the tip of his tongue appearing through his lips. Spinning, he circled around Jonna, shaking his hips all the while, before ending up behind her.

Before she could turn around, he had grabbed her around the waist, trapping her arms. He pressed against her, resting his chin on her shoulder as his tongue searched for her ear.

That was more than enough now, Jonna sighed in resignation. Perhaps some teenager might have fallen for the dancing hotshot, but definitely not Jonna de Brugge.

Jonna tried to break free, but Don Juan refused to let her go. Instead, he tried to get her to follow his hip moves. She felt his hot breath panting in her ear. The enthusiasm of his gang at the table knew no limits. Their clapping hands were in the air and there was an occasional wolf whistle.

Jonna lost her temper. She took hold of his index finger and bent it backwards until he had to loosen his grip. Then she turned around, still holding the finger, and did a reverse pirouette so that he ended up in front of her in a classic police grip. She pressed his finger carefully upwards until he became co-operative.

She maneouvered him to the party table and parked him, where he sat down, humiliated.

Jonna sat down beside Sandra, who was sitting at a corner table far from the pumping loudspeakers. They laughed at the incident on the dance floor. Sandra shook her head and reminded Jonna that she was always the one who attracted the whackos. Jonna agreed, but had no real explanation for it. It was not as if she did it on purpose. Presumably, it had something to do with her looks. If that was a good or bad thing, she was not sure. Sandra suggested that her good looks might be the problem. Only the overconfident idiots, who had nothing to lose, dared to chat up, in her words, a "top of the line" woman.

Before they left Le Cheliff, Jonna was once again approached. This time, it was a middle-aged lawyer who was as uptight and puffed up as the shirt across his belly.

He bought both Jonna and Sandra dry martinis and got straight to the point. Subtlety was not his thing. He considered Jonna to be the best-looking woman of the night and wanted therefore to make her a proposition that she could not possibly refuse.

Before the plump lawyer could say anything else, Jonna had taken out her police badge. She looked the lawyer straight in the eye and asked him to continue. The proposition never materialized and the lawyer hastily left the club with a bright red face.

"Girl power!" Sandra cried, doing a high five.

"This is about as good as it's going to get," Jonna dismally concluded, checking her watch. For the twentieth time, she checked to see if she had missed a text message or a phone call.

They left the club just after two and ended the night with a hug at the taxi rank on Stureplan. Sandra took a taxi back to Hammarby Sjöstad while Jonna debated with herself whether she should walk home, which would take half an hour, or take a taxi as well.

She was aided in her decision-making by a pushy taxi driver, who wanted to take her for a set fare of one hundred and fifty crowns. She chose to walk.

Jonna fell asleep at five past three in the morning. Alone in her oversized bed.

AT SEVEN O'CLOCK in the morning, Jonna rang the doorbell to Serge Wolinsky's flat. She was met by a pale and red-eyed Serge in only his underpants.

"I was just going to hit the sack," he said apologetically, looking down at his boxer shorts, which were two sizes too big and had a Hawaiian theme with a red sunset.

"Not anymore," Jonna smiled and walked straight in.

"Do you have coffee?" she asked, looking at the kitchen.

"Yes, but you'll have to make it yourself," he said from a wardrobe in the bedroom.

Jonna looked around the messy kitchen. Dirty dishes that must have been at least a week old were piled in the sink, begging to be disinfected. After a while, she managed to locate the coffeemaker behind a pile of empty tins. She made a full pot.

Meanwhile, Serge had put on some clothes and had ended up in front of one of the computer screens.

"Take your pick," he said, pointing to a list of data files.

"Is that the server at the Stockholm District Court?" she asked and took a sip of coffee.

Serge turned around when he smelt the coffee.

"That's my mug. Only I drink from it," he said with a hostile look when he saw the mug in Jonna's hand. It was white and had the American National Security Agency logo on both sides.

"It was the only mug where I didn't have to chip away the leftovers from the bottom," she said and took another sip.

Serge gave her a surly glare for a few seconds before turning his attention to the screen again.

"All in all, there are four hundred, fifty thousand and ninety-eight files. Including a number of system files," he said as a program window started to scroll files from the top down.

"What's the structure of the file system?" Jonna asked.

"It's a normal tree structure with a jumbled mix of OCR scanned documents, files written in Word and then converted to PDF files, et cetera. There seem to be judgments, different types of memos and other stuff. Their internal search index sucks."

"Any personnel files?" she asked.

"Nope," Serge hesitated. "More likely, there are links to a salary system that seems to be stored on the court administration servers. At least, that's where the IP addresses point to."

"Hmm …" Jonna hummed, deep in thought. "Their salaries are of course from the District Court, but the administration is completely independent from the courts themselves. Each court has to be completely autonomous."

"What do you want to do with all the files?" Serge asked impatiently. "To download them will take a few hours. As you know, we don't have much bandwidth over the GPRS connection."

"How long will it take?"

"Around eight to nine hours."

"Then you'd better get started," she said. "While that's going on, you have other work to do."

Serge gazed at her, puzzled. "Like what?"

"You have to write a program while you're waiting," Jonna said, taking yet another sip of coffee.

"What type of program?" he asked dubiously.

"A program that solves puzzles."

"Puzzles?"

"Listen carefully," she said, putting the coffee mug down on the desk. "In a court hearing, a judge presides who is also the court president, together with three lay jurors and a court secretary who takes notes. Present during the trial are the accused, defending barristers, prosecutors, witnesses and, in most cases, spectators."

"No kidding?" said Serge, moderately enthusiastic about this lesson on "what goes on in the courtroom".

"Let me finish," Jonna said. "I have the name of a district prosecutor, a lay juror and a judge. You're going to write a program that searches through all the files and lists the documents in which all of these three names are mentioned. I suggest you start with judgment and memo files."

Serge wrinkled his forehead, concerned. Then he broke into a mischievous smirk. "Has this got anything to do with that Sjöstrand or whatever her name is? The one who killed her own daughter?"

"Listen," Jonna ordered. "You will match the following three names: Lennart Ekwall, Karin Sjöstrand and Bror Lantz.

I want the documents where all three of these names are mentioned together."

Serge picked up the coffee mug with the NSA logo and grinned. "Gotcha," he said and took a gulp.

JÖRGEN SAT UP up in the bed and looked around the unfamiliar bedroom. For a short, merciful moment, he had no idea where he was.

Seconds later, panic flooded him.

He heard noises from the kitchen and grabbed his head. The alarm clock on the bedside table said quarter past eight. He lifted the cover and verified that he was, not unsurprisingly, naked. Clothes lay on the floor in a pile by the bed. Who had emerged as the victor during last night's struggle?

He stood up, but a wall of pain hit him in the head. He was forced to retire to the bed again.

Ulrika Melin gazed at Jörgen from the doorway as he lay with his hands over his face, making remorseful noises. The night had not really developed as she had hoped. But it was not too late yet.

"Good morning," she said, putting down a tray of coffee and sandwiches on the bed.

Jörgen turned towards her, squinting with his good eye. "Good morning," he croaked.

"Are we a little hung over today?" she laughed and handed over a cup of fresh coffee.

He reached out his hand, but discovered that it shook so much that the cup would probably be empty before it got to his mouth.

"A full case of the DTs as well," Ulrika laughed and bent over Jörgen. "Do you want me to feed you?"

"No, thank you. It's about time for me to think about the final curtain," he said, making a last-ditch effort to get up.

"Speaking of final curtains," she said, quickly putting the cup aside. "There wasn't much of a finale last night, if you get my meaning. You went out like a candle just as the curtain was about to go up."

He pretended not to hear, continuing to attempt his getaway.

With a swift movement, she pushed him back into bed and held his head firmly on the pillow.

"Not so fast," she smiled.

Jörgen's head flashed with pain and he tried to smother an urge to vomit.

Ulrika smiled, carefully stroking his curly hair backwards. Her fingers kept getting tangled in his snake's nest of curls. After a while, she gave up and extricated her hand, which instead made its way under the covers. Jörgen froze. Suddenly, he was wide-awake.

He half-turned to look at the clock. "I really do have to go now," he excused himself. "I have a job to go to ..."

"So do I," Ulrika cut him off. "But that doesn't stop us from staying in bed a few minutes longer."

She looked curiously at Jorgen while her hand slowly wandered up his leg.

Jörgen started to flinch. Unpleasant tingles shot through his body like bolts.

After a serpentine meander up his thigh, her hand finally covered his penis like clingfilm.

Jörgen turned to stone. Her hands felt as if they had come directly out of the fridge.

"What do we have here?" she giggled and met Jörgen's gaze.

He closed his eyes and held his breath.

When he opened his eyes, she had already lost her dressing gown and was getting ready to straddle him; she already had one leg over him.

He was trapped.

She laid herself heavily on Jörgen's rib cage. It felt like it would break and he had difficulty breathing.

Breasts hung and dangled right in front of him and became two enormous evil eyes that refused to let go of him. He was expected to touch the eyes. Take them and passionately massage them with his hands. Let his thumb gently caress the pupils until they hardened.

But Jörgen's hands would not obey him. They were paralyzed.

He had not been with someone of the opposite sex since the first-year party in college. That episode was the first and last time. Until now, to be exact. At eighteen years of age, he had finally given in and come out as gay, because of a sudden infatuation with a man eight years his senior. He came from nowhere and entered Jörgen's life like a tornado. Everything was turned back to front, in the literal sense of the word, and the false lifestyle he tried so hard to pursue collapsed like a house of cards. Jörgen had seen the light at the end of a dark tunnel.

His lover left Jörgen four months later. Despite his great feeling of loss, his time with Abbe had taught Jörgen who he really was.

JONNA LEFT SERGE at eleven o'clock. There was nothing else to do except wait for the files to be copied and run through the matchmaker program. Besides, she was hungry, as she had not eaten breakfast, as well as curious about the contents of the memory stick that she had got from Jörgen.

She plugged the memory stick into her laptop while taking a bite of the ham omelette that she had made using air-dried Jäger ham. It was really too salty for an omelette. Serrano, or possibly Parma, ham would have been more suitable.

Two folders popped up after she opened "Removable disk (E:)." One folder was called "Video" and the other "Images". She clicked on the "Video" folder and a single file with a size of 494 megabytes appeared. The file was simply named "A". She double-clicked the file. After a few seconds, the video file started to play.

She saw a corpulent man in a black leather mask wearing a pink thong with studs on the front. The man, whom she quickly identified as Jörgen Blad, turned the camera towards a bed and disappeared from the frame.

After a while, he came back in the company of a tall woman in a light-green dress and high heels. She was masculine and a full head taller than Jörgen. She wore heavy make-up and a kind of blonde wig that did not fit properly.

The woman went over to the bed and lay on her back. Then she lifted her dress and exposed an erect penis.

Folke Uddestad, Jonna thought, pushing her plate away.

The man said something Jonna could not make out, whereupon Jörgen crept onto the bed. He bent down and took the erection in his mouth through the hole in his leather mask. After a moment's rough stimulation, they changed position. Uddestad went on all fours with his face unknowingly facing the camera. It was impossible not to recognize the County Police Commissioner. He looked grotesque under the wig and heavy make-up.

Jonna shook her head. It was like a surreal nightmare.

Jörgen was now on his knees behind the doggy pose of the Commissioner. He lifted Uddestad's dress. Carefully, he began to penetrate him from behind with slow, strong movements. From the hole in the leather hood, Jonna saw how Jörgen's reptilian tongue licked the open air.

The Commissioner's bleating became a soft rumble in the laptop speakers.

She had seen enough. Her appetite was long gone.

If this video were to become public knowledge, not only would Uddestad be hung out to dry, but the whole police force as well.

Imagine if the tabloids got their hands on the video. Images from the evidence would be waltzing through the newspapers and the internet for decades after the scandal was exposed. Somebody had actually arse-fucked their highest-ranking officer. And a journalist to top it off.

Jonna could not help grinning. It was actually a bit comical – and tragic at the same time. People's sexual preferences were of no interest to her as long as they did not involve her. Personally, she preferred so-called normal men, but after last night she was beginning to wonder if there were any of those left.

One thing she could at least be sure of. Jörgen Blad was a cold-blooded, calculating and completely scruple-free scumbag. Which was roughly what she had already suspected.

"FOUR MATCHES," SERGE announced smugly and held up some sheets of paper.

It had taken over five hours to download the material, but only twenty minutes to scan through it with the search engine once it was stored on Serge's server.

Jonna eagerly read what Serge had printed out.

WITH SOME DIFFICULTY, Jörgen stood up from the sofa he had parked himself on as soon as he had arrived at Jonna's.

"You'll get to read it after we have met Walter," she told him sharply, without lifting her eyes when Jörgen approached with heavy feet. She wanted to keep a safe distance from the now even more repulsive journalist. Partly because he reeked of booze and partly to avoid sudden urges to vomit when she thought of what she had witnessed on the laptop. Even if the County Police Commssioner had consented to the sexual acts, the blackmail increased her contempt for Jörgen.

Jörgen dragged himself back to the sofa without protesting. He lay down with a heavy sigh. His earlier, constant interest in everything that Jonna did had totally evaporated. One did not have to be a rocket scientist to see that he was suffering from the excesses of yesterday's date. He had done his bit, even if he had chosen an unorthodox way of doing it. Jonna was not convinced that Jörgen's "sacrifice" had been absolutely necessary, but he had obviously managed to plant the microrouter, and that was all that mattered. All he had left to do was to get it back.

After reading through the document, Jonna logged back into the police database. In the background, she could hear anxious intakes of breath from the sofa. After going through Serge's material and retrieving information from the police database, she was done. It took her exactly fifteen minutes and it appeared to have given her something to work with.

"That's it for me. We're done with each other now," Jonna declared, heading for the door.

Jörgen heaved himself off the sofa.

"So you mean we are quits now?" Serge asked, slightly incredulously.

"We? You mean Walter?" Jonna said.

"It's the same thing."

"Since I'm unaware of the arrangement that you and Walter have with each other, I cannot promise anything. But I will ask him when we meet up."

"Do that," Serge replied. "Don't forget the return address for the microrouters. You can drop them in the postbox when it's convenient."

"Rest assured. And, by the way, don't forget to delete everything you have downloaded. You know the score," Jonna finished off from the doorway.

Serge did not answer.

"Why didn't you stay and watch him delete the content from the server?" Jörgen asked when they sat in the car. "He could cause a lot of trouble."

"It wouldn't make any difference," Jonna explained, turning onto Hornsgatan. "It's impossible to keep track of what that guy's doing."

"You could just confiscate all his computers," Jörgen suggested with a cynical smile.

"Even if the entire flat burned down and the computers were destroyed, I'm sure that he has a back-up somewhere on the internet. Like an octopus, he has tentacles everywhere."

26 THOMAS KOKK HAD difficulty seeing any link between the owner of the building, Omar Khayyam and the investigation into the Islamist terrorist group. Omar Khayyam was not registered as a known CI in any of SÄPO's databases. Kokk toyed with the notion that Omar was Ove Jernberg's personal informant, but that did not seem to be very believable despite Martin Borg's claim to the contrary. All informants were meticulously registered in SÄPO's database, so the use of unregistered informants was both forbidden and pointless. What reason could Jernberg have for keeping his own personal informants? The only connection Kokk found was Omar Khayyam's prioritized residence visa and Swedish citizenship, which SÄPO had expedited when he defected from the Syrian intelligence agency. The more Kokk dug around Khayyam, the more confused he became about his link to Jernberg.

Thomas Kokk had a profound and unbroken confidence in Martin Borg. They had worked together for almost ten years and the thirty-nine-year-old Borg, with roots in the Dalarna province, was extremely faithful and loyal to their employer, the National Security Service. What made Martin an exceptional policeman was his sharp, analytical personality. He was never afraid to extend his working hours and he had a special ability to see solutions despite the lack of tangible evidence. Martin also had a remarkable talent for getting information out of subjects detained for questioning. His success ratio was an excellent ten to one. Out of every ten interrogation subjects, he failed with only one.

But Kokk could not overlook the fact that what Martin had told them about Khayyam did not seem correct. Either Martin was lying or Jernberg had a skeleton in his closet. He did not think either of these options seemed very likely.

To discover any irregularities, SÄPO employees were forced to undergo routine lie-detector tests. Both Borg and Jernberg had passed the test without a problem. And yet there was something about the whole story that did not feel right. The deadly shootout at the warehouse was riddled with far too many question marks.

CHIEF PROSECUTOR ÅSA Julén anxiously watched Thomas Kokk after he had informed her of the changes to the investigation.

The operational leader had been replaced and he was himself appointed as the successor, which indicated a certain degree of desperation within SÄPO.

One Security Service agent was dead and another was injured and removed from active duty. A potential terrorist had been killed in a gun battle and a second suspect had died in police custody. As if that was not enough, yet another person had died, possibly a personal informant of the deceased policeman, Ove Jernberg. Furthermore, one of the perpetrators was still at large.

"I can hardly say that the investigation is going in the right direction," Julén began. "Since our last meeting, three people have died in separate circumstances. You seem to be taking one step forwards and ten steps backwards, to put it mildly."

Kokk cleared his throat, embarrassed. "So it seems," he said, looking down at his papers as if he had some new information. He did not have any, at least not of a positive nature. The atmosphere was extremely tense.

"Seems?" Julén cried. "These are established facts, unless I'm mistaken. Or is there something else that you haven't told me?"

"Of course not," he apologized. "What I meant was that from this temporary, small setback, there are new leads we can follow. We're already following up on them."

"What leads?"

"Omar Khayyam."

"The personal informant?"

Kokk nodded. "There's no direct link yet, but we are working hard to find one. According to Martin Borg, Omar had some information on the detainees and wanted to pass it on to Jernberg. We don't know what it was."

"Is that the only lead we have?" Julén asked.

Because he had read both Gröhn's and Hildebrandt's memos, Kokk thought for a moment about the leads from RSU and County CID.

"For the time being, yes. But I am hoping to get an answer from SKL regarding the compound. It may point towards the terrorist prince," he said.

"It's important that this Hisham fellow died of natural causes in the detention cell. The slightest doubt would complicate the situation considerably," Julén said.

"Of course," Kokk agreed.

"But we're still making no progress," Julén said, irritated. She stood up. "We have pinned everything on the Islamist group because of a number of assumptions, based on a few hostile statements and financial transactions with that prince of terror who might eventually have the capacity to produce Drug-X. At SÄPO, you were very quick to make that link even though there's not one single piece of evidence to support such a theory. And the interrogations have yielded poor results." Julén felt duped by the Security Service. She had believed the presentations they had made. When SÄPO had something to say, you listened. Unfortunately, she had done so uncritically.

"That's the best we have at the moment," Kokk apologized and stood up as well. "Before we have the answer from SKL, there's not much else we can do. It's not certain that the results will give us much to go on either. You have yourself questioned the Islamists, Karin Sjöstrand, Lennart Ekwall and Bror Lantz a number of times – not to mention how much time we've spent doing interviews and background checks on their relatives. Lantz is not even under arrest. The marks around the neck of the taxi driver that Forensics say originate from Lantz's belt are not sufficient evidence by themselves. We have no other lead to investigate right now, except this gang sitting in the detention cells."

Åsa Julén looked searchingly at Thomas Kokk. "Even though the anti-terrorist laws allow me to detain this group in the cells for a long time, I'm not as keen to do so anymore. I have nothing to hold them on, not even to give them a ticket."

"To release them now would be a big mistake, if you ask me," Kokk said.

Julén stopped herself from groaning. "And why do you say that?"

"I recommend that we keep them in custody for at least another month. Some of them could weaken and start to talk a little. And by then, we'll also have more information on Khayyam and the compound that SKL is investigating."

"The detainees are still refusing to accept legal aid from lawyers?" Julén said, changing the topic.

"Yes," Kokk nodded.

"This is what we'll do," she paused, as if she had not finished her train of thought. "Keep them for one more week and do what you can. Then we have to release them for lack of evidence. Because if we don't have anything concrete in one week, then I doubt we are going to find something later. I'm convinced of that. Nobody would be happier than I would if I was wrong. But that's how it's going to be."

"One week!" Kokk exclaimed. "We won't be able to dig up and analyse all the relevant information. Why won't you use the leeway that the terrorist laws give us?"

"I don't intend to be the first prosecutor blamed for stretching these laws unnecessarily. Nobody wants that reputation. That's why you have one week from today," she explained.

Kokk nodded, not liking it, but forced to accept the Chief Prosecutor's decision. It was she, and only she, who made the decision in her role as leader of the investigation. Despite his huge irritation, he politely opened the door for the Chief Prosecutor and escorted her down to the reception area where she handed in her visitor's badge.

"ONE WEEK?" ANDERS HOLMBERG, Agency Director of SÄPO, exclaimed. "What's the Chief Prosecutor's problem?"

"That's obvious," Sten Gullviksson chuckled. "She's a woman."

Both Anders Holmberg and Thomas Kokk looked at the plump chief inspector as he chuckled at his tasteless joke.

"What can we do in a week?" Holmberg asked.

"Get preliminary results from SKL and investigate that information," Kokk replied, resignedly. "With a little luck, we'll get a better picture of Omar Khayyam. That's pretty much it."

"And how in the hell do we handle the death of one of the detainees in our custody? It's a totally horrific story."

"If he died of natural causes, then it's nothing we need to worry about. But if, for some reason, we pushed him too hard, then it will be problematic, to say the least."

"When will the post-mortem be ready?" Gullviksson asked.

"Tomorrow," Kokk replied. "Preliminary cause of death was, as already reported, cardiac arrest."

"Can't we persuade the Chief Prosecutor to keep those Muslims locked up a little longer?" Holmberg coughed. He took a sip of water to clear his throat.

"That will be difficult," Kokk replied. "She's worried that the investigation's going in the wrong direction. She doubts the connection to the terrorist prince. Neither the CIA nor the FBI has given us any details at all on his research facility. As expected, they are giving us nothing."

"If we can't get Julén to change her mind, then we must make the best of the situation," Holmberg said matter-of-factly. "It's my understanding that she's a spineless general who will only play on the winning side."

Kokk nodded in agreement. Åsa Julén was not famous for taking risks.

"I'm going to the National Police Board tomorrow and will probably have the riot act read to me," Holmberg continued. "The fuss over Ove Jernberg's death could spread like ripples on the water throughout the organization. You, Thomas, are going to have a rough ride, even more so than your team leader, Martin Borg. All eyes will be on the internal investigation. Misconduct will be punished severely this time. They'll want to set an example."

"I see," Kokk replied. "If they now conclude that it was misconduct to go to Gnesta without back-up."

"And to meet with a CI who wasn't registered," Gullviksson added.

Holmberg's office phone rang and he lifted the handset, annoyed that the switchboard had forwarded the call in spite of the blinking red meeting button. A minute later, the Agency Director's expression changed and he stared blankly into space.

"I think we can release them," he said in a low voice. "David Lilja at County CID has been looking for you, Thomas."

"What do you mean, release them?"

"One Per Lindkvist killed his three-year-younger brother at a building site in Huddinge earlier this morning." Holmberg leant on his elbows over the table. "He buried a hammer in the head of his brother, who died instantly."

"And?" Gullviksson said, waiting for the rest of the explanation.

"He couldn't explain his action nor did he remember anything about the actual killing."

The room fell silent. Holmberg leaned back in his chair with his hands clasped over his flat stomach. He looked hesitantly at Gullviksson and Kokk.

"That doesn't have to mean anything," Gullviksson said, unconvinced. He casually stretched his legs.

"I don't think you need to say anything more," Kokk said. "Is it possible that he's also a lay juror at Stockholm District Court?"

Holmberg nodded without saying anything.

Gullviksson stared first at Holmberg and then at Kokk, who had sunk into his chair.

This meant that either there were more members in the Islamist group that they did not know about or that the group was not guilty – at least, not of the crimes for which they had planned to prosecute them.

"We are back to square bloody one again!" Gullviksson cried. "If there aren't more of those Islamists out there, we have nothing other than the report from SKL to go on."

"Exactly," Kokk agreed. "The interest in Khayyam of this investigation also disappears. He is still of interest in the shooting of Jernberg, but hardly as a link in the chain to the detainees anymore."

"What about the memos from RSU and County CID?" Holmberg asked.

"Sheer fantasy," Kokk said, supported by Gullviksson. "According to the FBI, the company that sold those plaster figures has no customers in Sweden. They could have been bought in the US or some other country, and tracing all their customers is not possible. We're talking about thousands of private customers all over the world."

Holmberg nodded.

"Gröhn's and RSU's joint hypothesis that it is some ex-con wanting to get revenge by attacking the district court with something as sophisticated as Drug-X sounds highly unlikely," Kokk continued. "SKL is quite simply our best hope right now."

Holmberg stood up and looked despondently out the window. "We'll have to re-instate the extra protection for all jurors, judges and prosecutors, but how we are to do that escapes me. Are we going to forbid them to eat and drink? It's absurd. Just imagine if the lunatics behind this decide to poison the drinking water."

"Not possible, according to SKL," Kokk said. "The compound cannot exist for more than a few hours without a host organism, like the human body."

"There must be another explanation," Holmberg continued, with desperation in his voice. "A foreign power that wants to undermine our society, to put the whole justice system at risk. Perhaps the Prime Minister or some other minister has infuriated North Korea's dictator or some other madman or threatened some unscrupulous pharmaceutical corporation."

Kokk felt like the floor was caving in. He did not know what to think anymore. Every new initiative resulted in a new setback. It was so bad that they were farther from the truth than when they started. That the fate of the whole investigation depended on the SKL report was an understatement.

"In any event, it's inappropriate that the Per Lindkvist incident becomes public now. We must wait as long as possible before releasing it to the media. It's bad enough as it is," Holmberg finished resignedly.

TOR HEDMAN AWOKE after having slept solidly for eleven hours. He had been woken up shortly after the operation, but he was so nauseous after the three-hour-long sedation that the anaesthetist decided to let him go back to sleep again. The room he woke up in was small and had one window with striped curtains. The blinds were drawn so that most of the daylight could not find its way into the room.

He spotted two doors. One seemed to go to the toilet. The other must be the door to freedom. He would walk out that door as soon as he had used the first one. His bladder was about to explode.

Slowly, the pieces began to fall into place. A strange emotion bubbled up inside him, something that reminded him of when his mother had passed away. He could not help but feel a sense of loss over Jerry. They had, after all, been together for eight years. They did their prison time together and, like brothers, they had shared the cash that they had come into from various jobs. Everything felt so fucking unreal.

Carefully, he lifted his right hand and examined the bundle of bandaging. It was neatly wrapped in some light-grey plastic. He did not feel any pain in his hand. But, to be honest, he could not feel anything at all. It was as if his hand did not exist. He tried to move his fingers, but could not tell if anything was moving inside the bandaging. He could neither see nor feel if the impulses from his brain were going all the way to his fingers. He wondered if it was plaster they had used to cast his hand. It didn't look like plaster. It reminded him more of hard resin.

Tor sat carefully on the edge of his bed. A drip was attached to the top of his left hand. The bag with the saline solution hung on a frame with wheels. He stood up on shaky legs and grabbed the drip trolley. Blood rushed to his head and the room spun for a few seconds. He supported himself with the drip trolley to avoid losing his balance. If he did not empty his bladder before he was forced to take a breath, he would piss himself. He stumbled into the toilet and groped after his member with his left hand. With a smile of relief, he emptied his bladder. His urine was dark yellow and the smell was so strong that it stung his nose. It probably had something to do with the shit that came through the drip into his hand.

When he came out of the toilet, two whitecoats stood by the bed. One was a man with green trousers. The other was a young girl with white trousers and a ring in her nose.

"Are we up and about?" the man began.

"Had to take a piss," Tor croaked.

The man smiled. "Dr Eldrin," he announced. "I thought I would check up on you."

"Why?" Tor croaked. His throat was dry and he could have drunk a bucket of water.

"As you know, it was not me who operated on you," Eldrin answered. "It was Dr Fernell, whom you met before the operation."

Tor nodded. "I know."

"I'm on the day shift, so that's why you are seeing me instead of Fernell."

"It's all the same to me."

The nurse quickly made his bed before Tor sat on the edge.

"How does this feel?" Eldrin asked and carefully took hold of Tor's bandage.

"Don't know."

"Does it hurt?"

"No, not really."

"Any feeling at all?"

"Nope," Tor said uncertainly after a few seconds.

Dr Eldrin looked pensively at Tor's hand. "The operation went very well," he said with a reassuring smile. "It was a complicated procedure, but Fernell did an excellent job. He's by far the best surgeon we have here at the hospital, I have to say."

"Will I get one of those prosthetic thingies?" Tor asked, looking doubtfully at Dr Eldrin.

Eldrin lit up. "You won't need anything, prosthetic or otherwise. There'll be a certain loss of movement, but your nerves and most of the tissue will be totally restored. That will, however, require a number of not uncomplicated operations. We were forced to replace some of the bone in your hand with titanium plates."

"Titanium plates?"

"Yes, but only temporarily," Eldrin explained. "You'll be given custom-made titanium bones, grafted to replace the destroyed hand bones, in later surgery. It takes a while to make them."

"Titanium? That must be bloody expensive," Tor said, lying down in the bed.

"Yes, very expensive," Eldrin answered. "But that metal is so pure that the body won't reject it."

Tor wondered how much his hand would be worth.

"Sounds good. When can I go home?" he asked.

Eldrin laughed. "Are you in a hurry?"

"No, but I have a parking ticket that expires soon."

"Then you'll have to get someone to move the car or put money in the meter for the time being. You'll have to stay here for a few days, in my opinion. But that's not up to me: Fernell will make the decision tomorrow."

"What time is it?" Tor asked.

"Two fifteen in the afternoon," the nurse answered.

"Two fifteen!" Tor repeated and got up off his bed.

The car was five hours overdue. How the hell could it be so late? He had slept enough for a fucking year.

"I have to go now," Tor said, getting up. His head started spinning, but not as badly as before.

"I don't think so," Eldrin firmly corrected him and helped Tor back into bed.

"Let go!" Tor snapped, waving his arm. "I said that I have to fucking go now. I'll be in the shit if the traffic warden gives me a ticket."

"We can fix the tickets so you don't have to pay them because you're an emergency patient. Leave the car parked in the car park and we'll take care of the tickets later," Eldrin answered, surprised by Tor's outburst.

"I don't give a shit about the tickets!" Tor croaked. "I have to get to the car."

"Yes, but …"

"It's not parked in the fucking hospital car park," Tor interrupted him. "It's parked a short distance from here. End of discussion."

"But how did you get here?"

"I walked, of course."

Eldrin exchanged a glance with the concerned nurse.

"If you choose to terminate your treatment against our advice, then you must sign some papers before you go," Eldrin explained. "We will not be held responsible."

"Do whatever the hell you want," Tor answered. "Get the papers, or I'll walk out anyway."

Eldrin shook his head and walked away.

Tor looked around the room. "Where are my clothes?" he asked, glaring at the nurse.

"In the wardrobe," she said, pointing to the cupboard by the side of the bed.

Tor stood up, but realized that the drip was still attached to his hand.

"Get rid of this," he ordered and stretched out his left hand.

The nurse shook her head, but disconnected the drip anyway and took the needle out of his hand.

Tor had just put on what remained of his clothes when Eldrin came in.

"You have to sign on the line at the bottom," he sighed and handed Tor a pen and paper with lots of text. Tor scribbled without reading it.

"You could have fucking woke me up earlier," he said and left the room.

As he went down the corridor and towards freedom, he began to feel much better. The dizziness was gone and his thoughts became as clear as a freeze frame. It was as if just the knowledge that he was free of the hospital and its suffocating environment had made him instantly better. Hospitals and prisons resembled each other more than he realized. He was now going to take care of some serious business. He had a plan and he was going to follow it to the letter. And if he started to have second thoughts, he would ask himself what Jerry would have done in his place.

Barely fifteen metres from Omar's car, Tor stopped dead in his tracks, glued to the spot. He stared at something sitting on the windscreen. A paper note was jammed between the windscreen wiper and the glass.

He discreetly looked around him. The street was full of parked cars. It was impossible to make out whether there was anyone sitting in the cars without going up to each one and pressing his nose against the glass.

A dozen or so people were passing nearby. Some teenage punks crossed the street on bicycles. An elderly couple stood and talked in a doorway. Two middle-aged men with denim jackets stood on the other side of the street, talking. They wore typical clothes for undercover cops, neutral but practical. Both had trainers with rubber soles and were a little too athletic. They had short hair and observant eyes – definitely undercover cops.

Tor looked at a young woman searching for something in a shopping bag. What was she looking for in the middle of the pavement? Had she forgotten something in the shop? Why had she realized that now?

Suddenly, it hit Tor. If the cops had staked out the car, they would have taken away the parking ticket to avoid attracting attention. If there had not been a parking ticket on the car, then Tor would not have stopped to look around. He would instead already be sitting behind the wheel – perhaps surrounded by lots of cops with weapons drawn, then handcuffed and pushed onto the floor of a police van.

On the other hand, maybe they had left the ticket to lull him into a false sense of security. Perhaps they had second-guessed Tor and not removed the ticket.

He was totally confused. What would Jerry have done?

Jerry would never have got into this situation. He would have dumped the deal with the cop and told him to go to hell. Jerry was no grass.

Tor had to make his mind up. He could not stand there like a statue any longer – his torn clothing would soon attract attention. His height already seemed to have been noticed. A teenage baboon troop went right by him and, while passing him, the street kid at the head of the gang asked Tor if he played basketball in the homeless league.

For once, Tor had a fast comeback, asking whether the cages at Skansen Zoo had been left unlocked. It was possibly not the smartest thing to say, considering that he was alone, unarmed and generally in a semi-fit condition. He had forgotten that he no longer had a Desert Eagle to back him up. The gang stopped in its tracks and turned around. After a few seconds of electric silence, the leader of the five-man gang went towards Tor, his hand firmly gripping his crotch. He had a soft swagger that reminded Tor of an old, bowlegged fisherman.

"So you think you're hard, or what?" the baboon leader challenged him from under his cap. He took a firmer grip of his baggy jeans. It was as if he was afraid something was going to drop off.

The rest of the gang flanked him on either side, each and every one of them had narrowed eyes. Not one could stand still. They were rocking their upper torsos back and forth like boxers, jabbing.

Tor judged their ages to be between fifteen and eighteen. Height varied from five three to five nine for the tallest at the back. The street-kid leader was the shortest.

"You're goin' down, *comprende*?" the ringleader continued the challenge, thrusting his chin forwards. He raised one hand and extended his fingers in a street gesture. He continued to gesticulate with jerky arm movements as he described various threats. This was obviously some form of street sign language, but Tor had no idea what all his flapping was about.

He thought that the silly, little ringleader reminded him a lot of Benno, a neighbour with cerebral palsy that Tor knew when he was a kid. Except for the crotch holding, which, in Benno's case, would have resulted in self-castration.

And instead of Benno's slurred speech, the gang leader got his words out in batches and in some strange form of Swedish, as if he were singing and talking at the same time.

Tor did not know what the midget wannabe idol was saying and knew even less how to answer him. Instead, he checked out both of the men in anoraks on the other side of the street.

They had slowly started to move towards Tor. Maybe they were undercover cops after all. He had nothing to fear from the cops, since he had not done anything wrong. He had not been anywhere close to Omar's car yet.

"*Yo jefe*, give the crackhead a beating!" someone in the group shouted. The leader danced towards Tor, measuring him up for something that looked like a head kick. But then he stopped the kick halfway. Another in the gang whistled and pointed at the men coming towards them. The gang forgot about Tor and quickly moved on. The men in denim jackets followed after them.

Tor had been rescued by the police.

After getting into Omar's car, he did not know what to believe any more. In his hand was a flyer the size of a parking ticket. Someone had tagged his car with a discounted lunch at a newly opened bistro on Swedenborgsgatan. And he had been saved by the cops from a gang of baby gang members. Everything was getting more and more bizarre, and the madness did not stop there. He took his mobile phone from his pocket and called his psycho partner.

27 MARTIN BORG WAS released from the hospital at three in the afternoon. The bandage on his arm had been replaced with a new one and he had been given a prescription for painkillers in case he had difficulty sleeping. He did not anticipate sleep problems, but took the prescription anyway.

He thought he had handled the psychologists and Internal Affairs in an exemplary fashion. There would be a few waves for a little while, but he would get through this. All that remained was Thomas Kokk, who was very keen to talk to him. And so he would, but first, Martin had to fetch the hard drive down in Gnesta. Martin took a taxi to the Statoil petrol station in Solna, where he hired a Ford Focus.

The area surrounding the burnt-out warehouse had been closed off by his colleagues, and they had also put up a tent in the centre of the yard. He observed five police officers in the area at most – two uniforms and three from SÄPO. Some curious bystanders stood outside the police tape on the gravelled road.

Flashbacks from the shootout surfaced and he sat in the car for a few minutes, unable to move. It was only now that he realized how close he had come to dying. If Headcase had aimed his gun less than a centimetre to the right, the bullet would have hit Martin in the throat. He had been ten millimeters from certain death. Martin squeezed hard the charm in his hand. Perhaps there was a reason he had been so lucky. He dismissed that thought instantly. He had no religion. He hated religion, and everything their lies stood for, and he despised all the religious fanatics that spread their manure over the world while waiting for their rewards in the next life.

The place where Martin had hidden the hard drive was fortunately outside the police cordon. He went on foot through the forest to avoid being seen and, after thirty minutes searching, he was able to pinpoint the spot.

He pulled out a bag to put the hard drive and Omar's mobile phone in and then stashed them in the inside pocket of his jacket.

For a while, he held the gun that Jerry had used to kill Jernberg in his hand. Then he took that with him too. He left Tor's pistol.

Then he walked back to the car the same way he had come. A powerful feeling came over him when he sat behind the wheel. He felt as if he had a treasure chest in his jacket, a power wrapped in a metal casing that would aid his cause and protect him from harm for the rest of his life. His pulse raced. With a little luck, defeat could now be turned into victory.

He turned the ignition key and drove away from the place where Jernberg had lost his life. In the mirror, he saw the burnt-out warehouse become increasingly smaller and gradually disappear into the golden autumn trees.

Five minutes later, Martin's personal mobile phone rang. Tor announced that he was out of the hospital and was in Omar's car, waiting for instructions. Martin was just about to answer when it hit him. Martin had called Omar several times from his personal mobile phone on the day of the shooting. The base station used by Omar's mobile phone would have registered all calls to and from the phone, even the unanswered calls, and SÄPO would request the base-station lists from the phone company. Even though Martin used a top-up card, they could take the phone number from the list and subsequently map the position of the phone to within a ten-metre radius. They could reconstruct all the locations from which the calls were made. This realization sent a chill through Martin Borg. If they were successful in retrieving data that could prove calls were made from the police station and Martin's home in Gärdet, the story he had fabricated would slowly unravel like a ball of string.

WALTER SILENTLY EXAMINED the material Jonna and Jörgen had brought with them. No matter how hard he tried, he could not help being impressed. Not just with the documentation and its contents, but also by how they had managed to pull it off.

Despite being young and having the experience of a newly hatched chick, Jonna had succeeded where an almost sixty-year-old detective with three decades of experience had failed – and without being detected. In addition, she had broken a few minor laws in order to prevent serious crimes, even though she had just recently graduated from the police academy, indoctrinated with the ideology that the world was divided into black and white, right and wrong. She would be an excellent organiser and was definitely a potential leader.

Jörgen Blad was merely an instrument that she had used in a masterly fashion. Finally, Walter put down the documents.

"So, our three names are mentioned in all of these four trials," he began, pushing his glasses onto the tip of his nose. He looked inquiringly at Jonna.

"Yes," she confirmed. "In all four district court trials, Ekwall has been the prosecutor, while Sjöstrand was lay juror and Lantz was the judge and court president. If we had the name of another lay juror, we would know exactly which one of these four is the key. If our theory is correct, that is."

Walter hummed while thinking and lay back in his bed. He neatly folded the blanket over his chest and put his hands together. His glasses were still on the tip of his nose. Jonna guessed from his gaze that he was working something out.

"It could just as well be random chance that dictated which ones the perpetrator attacked with that hi-tech drug," Jörgen suggested. "Then the names don't mean a thing." He was desperate to read the document.

"Possible but not probable," Jonna replied. "What goes against that theory is that they all work for Stockholm District Court, except Ekwall who is employed by the District Prosecutor's Office."

"Exactly," Walter said. "If it was a straightforward attack by terrorists against the Swedish court system, in the way the Security Service are ranting about, then even personnel from other courts would be attacked. That didn't happen. On the contrary, we have yet another name to add to the list." Walter took off his glasses.

"Really?" Jörgen cried. "Who's that?"

Walter held up his finger. "Have you seen the evidence on Uddestad?" he asked, looking at Jonna.

Jonna nodded. "Unfortunately," she said abruptly.

"Why unfortunately?" Walter asked.

"You can find out for yourself," she said and handed over the memory stick.

"I see," Walter said, throwing a dirty look at Jörgen. "I just wanted to be sure that the material is authentic."

"It's definitely authentic," Jonna said.

"Good, because it seems that madame Chief Prosecutor has got cold feet over SÄPO and has finally responded to my voicemails," Walter said. "She called me and asked if I could contribute to the investigation. That Martin Borg at SÄPO has apparently really messed up and has been suspended, which seems to be a trend at police headquarters nowadays. He was involved in the Gnesta drama that is now under investigation.

Also, the head of the Counter-Terrorism Unit, a certain Thomas Kokk, has taken his place."

"So Julén has changed her mind about our memos?" Jonna asked.

"Something like that."

"What did you tell her?" Jonna asked.

"That I was suspended and couldn't contribute anything."

"That's all?" Jonna said, surprised.

"Yes, that's all," Walter replied. "Well, I did suggest that she talk to Lilja, the Drug Squad and Internal Affairs to lift my suspension."

"And?"

"She said she would do what she could, which leads me to believe that she will really try all her tricks. Some pressure from above maybe. What do I know? Together with the complaints from the owl at the police union, it may change things."

"In what way has SÄPO failed?" Jonna was keen to know.

"She didn't say much about that, except that they have switched investigators and that the Islamists will be released. The way she put it, she was back to square one," Walter replied, shrugging his shoulders.

"Did she say anything else?"

"Yes, that a former lay juror had recently killed his brother on a building site in Huddinge."

"I don't believe it!" Jonna exclaimed, feeling a sudden shiver.

"Apparently he buried a hammer in the skull of his little brother."

"What's his name?" both Jörgen and Jonna said in unison. Jonna flashed an irritated glance at Jörgen.

"Per Lindkvist," Walter said. "He was a Social Democrat lay juror and participated in one of the four trials."

Jonna flicked quickly through the document. She had seen Per Lindkvist's name, but could not remember in which trial.

"Drunk driving," Walter helped her out.

"Precisely," she said. "That man, Sonny Magnusson, who, for the eighth or ninth time, was arrested for drunk driving and got off without a prison sentence as many times. Which sounds quite unlikely."

"Why did he get off so easily?" Jörgen asked.

"Apparently, he was a director of an insurance company," Jonna said. "If the file is correct."

"Just so," Walter exclaimed. "A fat cat with good contacts and millions in tax payments to the state. A true pillar of society, who got good value for his taxes, by in staying out of prison. Expensive lawyers and contacts in the right circles certainly paid off too."

"That's a rotten scandal," Jörgen commented.

"The swine is also named in another case," Walter continued.

"A vehicular homicide in which he killed a mother and daughter," Jonna said, shaking her head. "He died himself from his injuries. What a tragedy."

Walter nodded contentedly. "What goes around comes around. Unfortunately, two innocents lost their lives because the justice system failed to put that drunkard behind bars."

"Then we have a fifth factor. Something we had not considered," Jonna stated.

"What do you mean?" Jörgen asked impatiently.

"That we see a pattern and you don't," Walter snapped.

"What pattern? I haven't even read the document," Jörgen snapped back. His headache had subsided a little, but his eye was hurting instead. Also, he was still tired and felt uninspired despite the fact that they were on the brink of a breakthrough. He did not even have the energy to take out his notebook today.

"Ekwall, Sjöstrand and Lantz were part of the trial in which Sonny Magnusson was charged with manslaughter," Jonna explained.

"If I remember correctly, the deceased mother and child had the last name Brageler," Walter said.

"Quite right," Jonna confirmed. "One Leo Brageler became a widower after the deaths of his wife and daughter. Sonny Magnusson died as a result of his injuries from the car crash, on the same day that sentence was passed on him. He would have spent six months in an open prison for the manslaughter of Anna and Cecilia Brageler."

"But that's a softer sentence than for withholding a few million in taxes!" Jörgen exclaimed.

"If you only knew how right you are," Walter muttered, sitting up in bed. He suddenly became very red in the face. "A sick system with even sicker values created by the idiots appointed to protect our society," he continued, wildly gesticulating. "In the eyes of the law-makers and politicians, the biggest moral imperative is that people comply with the tax laws and pay their taxes on time. It's so important because otherwise society wouldn't be able to function. Most people would accept that. Therefore, being responsible for the death of two human beings is not considered to be as undermining and as damaging to society as cheating on your taxes. Therefore, the penalty is not as high. And if you're drunk, which is considered a mitigating circumstance, it will normally reduce the sentence further. And if you, on top of that, are a fat cat with lots of high-up contacts in society, the sentence will be six months at an open prison. By scratching a few backs, you can get an ankle tag so that you can sit at home in your armchair with a *Chesterfield* in your mouth and a fine Cognac in your hand. Bloody hell, what kind of punishment is that?"

Walter caught his breath. He was shaking with rage.

After calming down, he took a mouthful of rosehip soup from a bowl on the bedside table.

Jonna gazed at Walter, shocked. Obviously, this business had touched a sore spot.

"I still don't see what the connection is," Jörgen said after Walter calmed down. "More importantly, I don't see who the connection is."

Walter nodded at Jonna. "I'm betting that Einstein over there has already figured it out," he said.

"Per Lindkvist made all the pieces of the puzzle fall into place," Jonna replied.

"Keep going."

"We can start by excluding two cases that the trio was involved in, because Per Lindkvist didn't take part in them."

"Three," Jörgen interrupted. "He took part in only one case. One minus four is three, the last time I checked."

"Take it easy, I'll get to that," Jonna said.

"In the trial that acquitted Magnusson, Per Lindkvist was one of the lay jurors," she continued. "All the members of the jury acquitted Magnusson. One month later, he kills Anna and Cecilia Brageler in a car crash."

"So?"

"The evidence against Magnusson was so strong that a conviction should have been a sure thing. One of the traffic patrolmen, a Hans Jonasson from the Uppsala County Traffic Police, tried to persuade District Prosecutor Ekwall to send the district court's decision to the Court of Appeal. The patrolman was very familiar with Magnusson's drunk driving because he had pulled him over a number of times and didn't live that far from the director's estate outside Uppsala. He drove under the influence more often than he was sober; everybody in the village knew that, according to Jonasson. Ekwall refused to allow the appeal despite the hard evidence of the blood test. He thought that there were more important cases to prosecute. It's all noted in the memo that's attached to the decision, which, as I understand it, is not standard procedure."

Walter nodded in confirmation. "Special statements can be attached to the court decision; however, they don't affect it in any way."

"So, is the policeman the one behind the druggings?" Jörgen thought aloud. He sat down in one of the visitor's chairs with a confused expression.

"Hardly," Jonna said. "Think who it was who suffered the most from Magnusson's drunk driving."

"Himself, since he's dead," Jörgen said, stating the obvious.

"Let's stick to the living, shall we?"

"His family?"

"Yes, indeed," Jonna said. "But still not quite right."

"Well then, that would leave the family of the dead mother and daughter," Jörgen said.

"You saw the connection even before you knew about Per Lindkvist," Walter said, looking at Jonna with a wry smile.

"Yes, but Lindkvist confirmed the connection," she said without smiling back. "In fact, I checked out Anna Brageler's husband, Leo Brageler. He lives outside Sala, a few miles from Magnusson's estate. He has worked in Uppsala for the last fourteen years with the company Biodynamics & Genetic Research, or BGR, where he's head of research."

"Bingo!" Walter said. "And BGR is in the pharmaceuticals industry, I presume."

"Even better," Jonna said. "According to their home page, they do research in advanced genetic medicine and are suppliers to larger pharmaceutical companies around the world. They have about three hundred employees and are owned by a venture capital company and the company directors."

"That's our man," Walter declared.

Jörgen picked up a notepad and began to take notes. His

fatigue was gone. Things were starting to fall into place like dominoes and he was the only member of the press who knew about this story. The finishing line was approaching fast and he was way out in front.

"What happens now?" Jonna asked. "Will you contact Åsa Julén?"

Walter laughed. "What should I say, do you think? That we have been undertaking our own private investigation, as well as hacking into the criminal records and district court databases? She would have a heart attack."

"I understand that, but there's a pressing problem which must be tackled," Jonna pointed out.

"I know," Walter said. "Tuva Sahlin."

"Who's that?" Jörgen asked and grabbed Serge's printout from Jonna's hand. Now it was his turn to read it.

"The last lay juror from case 145432-3," Jonna said. "Her life is in great danger. Or, at least, someone in her immediate family is. We have to do something."

"Like what?" Walter said sarcastically. "Call her and say, 'Excuse us, but we think that you will kill someone soon. Could you please lock yourself in and throw away the key until the Security Service figure out what the problem is?'"

"As police, it's our obligation always to prevent crime. Even when we're not on duty," Jonna solemnly stated.

Jörgen flew from his chair as if he had received an electric shock. Now it was his turn.

"I'll get the telephone number for that Tuva Sahlin," he said and started to key frantically on his mobile phone.

A fantastic opportunity had presented itself. Jörgen Blad had the chance to save a life. This would look insanely good in the journalistic masterpiece he was composing in his head.

"Well, there was another thing," Walter finished. "I asked madame Chief Prosecutor to examine the carpenter's effects, to see if he had had a bag or something like that with him at the building site. And, not surprisingly, his lunch box contained a familiar object."

"The angel of death," Jonna guessed and saw confirmation in Walter's eyes.

THOMAS KOKK READ the report from SKL a second time. He was not sure how to interpret the contents. The laboratory in England that SKL used was very keen to determine the origin of the compound. The substance had shown itself to be so sophisticated that they had obviously informed both MI6 and MI5, the British intelligence agencies for foreign and domestic operations.

According to the British laboratory and SKL, there were only a handful of companies and nations that could have developed something like this. It would have required huge resources and extensive knowledge of the latest research into progressive genes. This was the future technology for production of pharmaceuticals. One recurring word in the report was "genetic programming". In other words, coding the compound so that it quickly started cell changes in the body according to a predesigned template. And with a precision that would turn the Creator himself green with envy.

In practical terms, you could create cancer in a human body overnight. You could even choose which type of cancer and where it would grow in the body, as well as how much and how fast the cancer should spread. You could decide if it should go into remission after a year and totally disappear or if it should consume the body until death finally ended it.

You could influence the brain and the organs in the body with ease, according to your own wishes, make someone suddenly start growing by controlling their hypothalamus gland or even change a person's personality. Anything was possible when you could influence all the areas of the brain.

The compound could make a person constantly happy or persistently angry. In the same way, it could cure naturally occurring diseases. Theoretically, it could prevent the process of aging too. Perhaps even reverse it. This was as close to playing God as science could go.

However, there was no universal compound that could manage all of the body's functions. Each marker, or unique control mechanism, that you wanted to be able to programme required a huge amount of research. Different companies specialized in different areas. The traces of the compound that were found in mother and daughter Sjöstrand, Lennart Ekwall and Lisbeth Ekwall had no less than sixty-three markers. Presumably, they would have found identical samples in Bror Lantz and his wife if they had been allowed to take tests. The compound was considered the most advanced to date. You could control sixty-three different functions, which gave over three thousand unique combinations. That was a small sea of possibilities.

The samples of the food from the homes of Karin Sjöstrand and Lennart Ekwall showed traces of the compound. Their food had been poisoned.

Kokk had ordered his best investigators to investigate the companies that were on the shortlist and had also asked the National Military Intelligence Agency, or MUST, to assist if they concluded that a foreign power was providing the technology for the drug.

MUST had given him nothing. Ever since SÄPO let the spy Stig Bergling escape through the basement to Moscow during a parole visit to his girlfriend, the relationship between the two intelligence agencies was strained, to say the least.

One of the pharmaceutical companies that SÄPO's investigators succeeded in identifying was a German company called Dysencomp AG. Dysencomp claimed to be on the brink of a breakthrough and would be the first company to release an intelligence medicine. They used a Swedish supplier for research on adaptive compounds for medicines. The Swedes contributing to Dysencomp's anticipated successes worked for a company in Uppsala that specialized in research into brain markers.

Kokk did not get any farther in his reflections before Agency Director Anders Holmberg came in the door. He sat in the chair facing Kokk and unbuttoned his jacket. His pupils were enlarged, like an animal in danger.

"Listen," he said, looking Kokk in the eye. "You and I have problems. And not just any old problems. We may very soon be out of a job and, in the worst case, be forced to find a good lawyer."

Kokk looked up, surprised. "I'm not sure I understand you," he said, his mind starting to work overtime.

"Don't understand me? What kind of answer is that? The politicians in the government will want somebody's head to roll for this failure. You, in your role as head of the Counter-Terrorism Unit, are first in line, you might say. I, as Agency Director, am a strong number two. Your team leader, Martin Borg, is more or less swinging from the gallows already."

"Yes, but ..."

"Unless we do something proactively in this matter," Holmberg interrupted, "we will be on unemployment benefit for the rest of our professional lives. Do you understand what I'm saying? We have to fix this together, now."

Holmberg's face was flushed. He knew without a doubt that he would never need to avail himself of unemployment benefits because, as an agency director, he had a comprehensive golden handshake for life, regardless of the terms of his dismissal. He could even be arrested for espionage and sentenced for treason without being concerned about losing the index-linked seventy-eight thousand crowns per month that his handshake would guarantee, if he had to use it. But this was not just a question of the money, but also about saving his reputation and the social network that he had built up over so many years.

"Can you define the term proactive?" Kokk said. The conversation was turning quite unpleasant.

"Absolutely," Holmberg said, determinedly. "Someone else must take the fall for your and Martin Borg's failure. It's the same method that politicians and greedy executives use when they get caught red-handed. We have to find a scapegoat."

"A scapegoat," Kokk said, curious. "Who would that be?"

"The Prosecutor or someone in our own organization," Holmberg suggested.

"I don't know ..." Kokk hesitated, but was interrupted again by Holmberg.

"There must be someone we can sacrifice."

Kokk could not fully take in what he was hearing. It was all too surreal. His world was crashing down around him and he had a ringside seat. Thoughts swirled around in his head – nightmares. He was not even sure that it was not illegal to have this conversation.

"Who are we talking about?" Kokk finally asked.

"How about the operations leader Martin Borg?" Holmberg smiled. "That Ove Jernberg was a low-ranking officer, although he'll also have to take some of the blame as well."

Kokk sat as if paralyzed and could not utter a word. The fellow must be losing his mind.

"Borg is one of those who have had little respect for me and the new, modern organization I'm trying to build," Holmberg said. "I know that he intensely dislikes the reforms within SÄPO. He and many others have criticized the formation of RSU in the organization."

Kokk looked at Holmberg, speechless.

"We, or to be more exact, you shall make sure that Borg takes the blame for our failure," Holmberg went on, with no remorse in his voice. "With a bit of luck, Internal Affairs will do that anyway, but we must reinforce the perception that it was his information that we followed when we agreed to drag that collection of Muslims off to the prison cells."

"How do I do that?" Kokk asked. His mouth was dry.

"You will fabricate some pre-dated memos addressed to Borg, in which you strongly question the detainment of the Islamists. You don't believe they have anything to do with Drug-X. Complain about lack of communication too. You will also backdate some memos to me in which you, with some reluctance, back up your team leader and his suspicions towards the Islamists. You could also mention that you suspect that Gullviksson was on Borg's side and that you feared they were working against you."

Kokk considered lifting the phone and calling the chairman of the constitutional court committee. These infringements were so serious that they lacked precedent.

But where should his loyalty lie? Should he save himself and Holmberg from certain defeat by letting Borg take all the heat? To be sure, he had suspicions about what had happened in Gnesta, but to fabricate accusations against Borg, and posthumously against Jernberg, without a fair investigation was something else indeed. It was a miscarriage of justice.

Right now, Kokk wanted most of all to be in his mountain cabin, frying Swedish meatballs in total seclusion. If he made the wrong decision and lost his job, he would be forced to sell the cabin – his sanctuary and nest egg. And even if he could avoid ending up in one of the penal institutions, what possibilities were there for a former SÄPO chief who had been implicated in a scandal of this magnitude? Damn Borg, Kokk swore to himself. Why had he listened to him and the analyst team's waffle about terrorist princes? And where was the man? He had left the hospital and was now incommunicado.

28 *The very day that he saw them for the last time, Cecilia had asked him to go with them and see how nicely she got Lucas to trot. The pony had begun to trot "at the passage" with a beautifully bent neck and tail held up like an Arab stallion.*

He had hugged her and said what he always used to say, that he was forced to work. But this time, he had, for a brief moment, been close to changing his mind. A fleeting premonition came to him, but it disappeared just as quickly as it had come. He discarded it as a whimsical feeling.

She answered that she understood, but, in her eyes, he saw her disappointment. Next time, he had thought. Next time, I will go with her.

From the kitchen window, he saw her little hand waving through the car window for the last time. He remembered how quiet the house was when they left him. As if death had already taken them from him. Then the ominous feeling returned.

Visitors were standing outside the door. The doorbell was muffled and metallic. An echo.

He was at first greeted with silence. Then a woman with a tense voice asked for his name.

Seconds turned into infinity.

The words would not come to him. He was unable to speak, trying to find the meaning in what she had said. What was she telling him?

Passed away as a result …

The words sounded unfamiliar and somehow not. It was about death. Just as he, day after day, looked for an antidote in his work. Suddenly Death stood in front of him, wearing civilian clothes. A male colleague stood beside her. He explained that even Anna, his wife, was deceased.

A new word. Deceased. Passed away. They were deceased and had passed away.

The ground beneath him gave way and he fell into darkness.

He had been ambivalent over the fourth one. There were no more feelings of guilt. The last one remained. He looked at the angel of death for a brief moment before he stuffed it in his pocket and closed the front door. It would spread its wings one more time.

The hunt for him would soon start. It was inevitable. He was surprised that it had taken them such a long time, how wrong they had been. The answers were staring them in the face.

IN A DESERTED part of the forest to the south of Stockholm, Martin Borg and Tor Hedman torched Omar's Mercedes. All traces of DNA had to be destroyed. After a few minutes, Omar's car was in flames and the evidence of Tor's involvement in Gnesta went up in smoke.

With the bonfire, at least the tracks leading to Tor were wiped away. Naturally, they would identify Jerry Salminen using dental records and therefore link Tor to the incident. These two were connected like Siamese twins in the police database. But there would be no evidence that Tor was at the crime scene. Not so much as a strand of hair was left from which to obtain DNA. So far, so good.

Right now, Martin himself was the weakest link. With good reason, he suspected that it was going be a rough ride for him.

The internal investigation proved to be a little more complicated than he had first thought. He could feel that something was not quite right. Thomas Kokk and others had been calling his mobile phone constantly ever since he had left the hospital. The wankers at Internal Affairs tried to contact him eight times; two of the calls left angry text messages that more or less ordered him to return to Kungsholmen immediately. They had already given him a time for his personal interview in the investigation, which was tomorrow morning at nine-thirty. Even the shrinks would be present. Fuck it, I'm not an escaped criminal, he thought.

It probably had something to do with the latest story that was circulating in the press. Martin's entire investigation into the Islamists was in all the papers. If that was not bad enough, the deceased towelhead was innocent, according to the media. They were claiming that his death in custody was payback for the fatal shooting in Gnesta. How could they come up with that story when the towelhead was dead before their visit to Gnesta? Martin felt his frustration building. All of the Muslims were now released, and on the radio they were babbling on about how the Security Service were at a dead end in the investigation into the judiciary murders.

Why had they released the towelheads? Martin did not know yet and it made him furious. He could hardly ring in and ask. If he did, he would be forced to present himself immediately, which was unthinkable under the circumstances. The situation did look rather black at the moment. Traces of the truth drug would be found during the post-mortem on the towelhead. Perhaps the scalpel slicers had already found it. It would be tricky to talk his way out of that, even if he blamed it on Jernberg. But what could they really prove?

Both Omar and Jernberg were dead. He could blame Jernberg for all the irregularities with Omar and claim ignorance. That

Jernberg must have injected the Muslim with Diaxpropyl-3S while Martin was in the toilet, or something like that. The reason Jernberg would do that sort of thing would be difficult to sell. Even for Martin. But there were no other options.

Hopefully, the material on the hard drive would significantly improve Martin's chances of riding out the storm – if the hard drive contained what Tor promised. And, as the icing on the cake, it would lead Martin to the journalist sitting on the Folke Uddestad evidence.

That man has more good luck than he deserves, Martin thought and studied the heap of tatters sitting next to him in the car. Together with that Jerry character, Tor had battled with hardcore gangs of Albanians, Yugos, Somalians and other piles of shit.

It was a bloody miracle Tor was still breathing. What surprised Martin the most was that he was in cahoots with this thug. He had assessed the risks. They were manageable. There was a bigger purpose and nothing could be allowed to stop him now.

"All right," Martin said, after they got out of the car and were standing in front of a broken-down allotment cabin with white-painted window frames. "So this is where you live." He looked disdainfully at the small, red wooden hut.

Tor nodded. "Yes, it's not really my cabin, but I can use it as much as I want and as long as I please." He reached for a key in the drainpipe.

"Who owns this dump then?" Martin asked, kicking the wooden cladding.

Tor glared at Martin. "Someone I know," he said curtly and stepped over the threshold into the cabin.

JÖRGEN HAD MANAGED to trace the telephone number for Tuva Sahlin through directory enquiries. He requested the number as a text message and as a direct connection. Before Jörgen could speak, Jonna grabbed the mobile phone from his hand.

"Hello? Is this Tuva Sahlin?" Jonna asked politely when she heard a voice at the other end.

"No," a young woman's voice answered. "She's not at home – nor is my Dad."

"Do you know where I can reach her?"

The line was quiet for a few seconds.

"To whom am I speaking?" the young woman questioned suspiciously.

"I'm sorry," Jonna replied, sounding as if she meant it. "My name is Jonna de Brugge and I am calling from the Stockholm police. We need to get hold of Tuva Sahlin."

"I see," the young woman said, now with a hint of anxiety in her voice.

"Do you know where I can get hold of her?" Jonna continued.

"Yes and no," she answered. "But why do want to talk to her?"

Jonna got the impression of a daughter in her upper teens who, with mounting uneasiness, was letting her thoughts run riot. What business would the police have with her mother?

"To whom am I speaking?" It was Jonna's turn to question.

"Elina," the voice said. "Tuva is my mother."

"I see. How can we get hold of your mother?"

"You can't," the daughter said. "She's, like, on her way to Finland, or maybe it's Åland. Don't remember. It was one of those, like, ferry cruises, and she'll be coming home, like, tomorrow."

"Like, tomorrow," Jonna repeated. "Does she have a mobile phone that we can reach her on?"

"Yes, or no actually," she said. "She has one, but she has, like, forgotten it at home. She does that a lot."

"Forgets her mobile?"

"She's, like, forgetful, you know. Like, sometimes, she re-members the mobile, but forgets to charge it. She's not really into mobiles, she says."

"I see," Jonna said. "Do you know when the ship leaves and which one it is?"

"I think she said the ship would leave at, like, six or some-thing like that."

"And the ship?" Jonna continued. "Do you know the name of the ship?"

The girl was silent.

THEY WERE AMONG the first passengers to board the vessel. Tuva Sahlin lived according to the motto "one hour early is better than one minute late." Over the years, those around her had adjusted to this quirk and her fellow travellers were there-fore among the first to arrive. The cabins were not yet cleaned and the party was asked to wait in the huge, deserted bar. Tuva looked around and wondered what it would look like at mid-night. How many of the passengers would be screeching into the karaoke microphone or lying half-asleep over the tables, overdosed on refreshments and the lavish dinner buffet.

This was the high point of the year. This was the day when everyone in the small Beekeepers' Society left their inhibi-tions at the quay and adventured out to sea, far away from husbands, home and children. The cruise with her girlfriends made them feel at least twenty years younger. Even Gittan, with her one-hundred-kilo body, would be boogieing on the dance floor after a sufficient number of drinks.

The bar quickly filled with expectant guests, and her party was just about to order their first drinks of the trip when a man in a lumberjack shirt and black leather waistcoat approached. He belonged to a four-man group from Värmland province that had drunk a little too much booze even before they came on board. The women around the table watched with amusement as the man introduced himself and his companions, all of them wearing leather waistcoats and lumberjack shirts. The man, Björn, who seemed to be the leader of the pack and also had the biggest gut, offered to buy drinks, but when he got to the bar, he was distracted by a much younger woman.

Tuva had to organize the opening round of drinks herself. This was how it would be for the rest of the trip. The young ones always took first place with the guys. A very predictable pattern that did not bother Tuva as she had been happily married for thirty years. She pushed her way to the bar, which had quickly become crowded with thirsty travellers.

"Can I have five margaritas?" she shouted to the bartenders, who seemed more interested in juggling beer glasses than serving Tuva. After some futile attempts to get the bartender duo to listen, Tuva was beginning to lose her patience.

"Let me help you," a voice said, behind her. Tuva turned around and saw a man, a head taller than her, who waved the juggler of glasses over towards them.

"The lady will have five margaritas," he said, taking out two five-hundred-crown notes and putting them on the counter. "Actually, make it six," he added.

The bartender nodded.

"May I pay?" the man asked and moved next to Tuva with his elbow on the bar. He had a deep voice and piercing eyes that made Tuva both nervous and intrigued. There was something pleasant, yet also contrived, about this man.

"If you insist," she said and shrugged her shoulders.

"I'll bring the tray over," the man replied and smiled behind his well-trimmed beard.

Tuva smiled back.

AFTER GIVING THE question some thought, the girl's voice was back.

"I think it was, like, Birka-something," she said.

"Is she travelling with a party?"

"Yes."

"What party?"

"Beats me what they are called," Elina said. "It's, like, some friends from that beekeeper society."

"Beekeeper society?" Jonna repeated, as if she had misheard.

"Yes, she does all that beekeeping with the honey down by the boat shed. She really thinks those bugs are awesome." Elina's voice sounded a little bit envious.

"Do you have the number of anyone in the party she is travelling with?"

"No."

"Do you know their names?"

"No."

"You don't know their names?"

"No. Don't care either. Honey is, like, her thing – not mine."

"Have …"

"Why do you want to talk to Mum?" Elina interrupted.

Jonna heard fear rising in the girl's voice. "Don't worry, Elina," she said. "We just want to talk to your mother. It's about her work. She hasn't done anything. And nothing has happened to her. You don't need to worry. We just want to ask her some simple questions."

"How can you know nothing has happened if you don't know where she is?" Elina argued.

The girl actually had a point, Jonna thought. "I can't say anymore, unfortunately," she apologized with a white lie. "It concerns her work at the district court and, as you know, that's confidential."

"Is it about all that stuff on the internet?"

"No," Jonna lied instinctively. "It has nothing to do with it."

"There was someone else who called and asked about Mum a while ago. He asked why I was always at home."

"Really?" Jonna said, confused. "How did you answer?"

"With the truth; that I was sick with a chest infection. He said his name, but Mum didn't know who he was."

"Was his name Leo?" Jonna asked, feeling her pulse quicken.

"No, it was like Lars or Leif. He called one more time."

"What did he say then?"

"Mum said she's going to quit …"

"Do you think your father knows the number of any of your mum's beekeeper friends?" Jonna interrupted politely but firmly.

"Maybe," she said after a little hesitation. "But he's in Canada for some business meeting. Called him a little while ago, but just got voicemail. It's night-time over there, I guess."

"Probably is," Jonna said.

She finished the conversation with Elina by giving her telephone number in case her mother got in touch. She felt sorry for the girl. Obviously, the various doomsday stories in the newspapers had worried her. By whatever means necessary, she had to get hold of Tuva Sahlin before it was too late.

What could be better than a cruise ship full of partying people, constantly filling their plates from the buffet table and drinking large numbers of alcoholic drinks? How easy it would be to drug someone by slipping the compound into a drink or into the food. Towards the early hours of the morning when the intoxication of the guests was at its strongest.

A packed cruise ferry was perfect.

The catch was that no one from Tuva's family was on board. The aim of killing a family member would be lost, unless one of the beekeepers was dearer to her than her family, which did not seem probable. But then Jonna realized that because the daughter was home all the time, he would not be able to get into the house to poison the food. It must have been Leo Brageler who called and pretended to be someone else.

Jonna looked at the clock. Quarter to six. She could call the shipping company and ask the staff to look for Tuva before she boarded. But the shipowners would want to call her back at the police station in case it was a hoax call. Jonna's mobile-phone number would not be good enough.

"TIME BOMB!" WALTER cried, looking at Jonna, who was about to leave the room with Jörgen.

Jonna turned round. "Time bomb?" she repeated, looking at Walter.

At first, she understood nothing, and then she realized what he meant.

"The compound has a delayed effect," she said, gazing absently around the room. "What if he can control when the process starts? Like a time bomb?" She looked right through Walter, as if he was transparent.

"Exactly," he said. "Definitely a possibility. She gets poisoned on the ship and comes home after a twenty-four-hour cruise just in time to have a fit of rage. If her husband is not at home, her daughter is in real danger. Leo Brageler knows precisely when the ship arrives and how much time it takes for Tuva to get home. If that is his plan. It could also be to start a massacre on board the ship." Walter checked himself when he saw Jonna's distraught expression. "But don't get bogged down in that now. Remember to lock the woman in her cabin until you've got back. Don't let her out of your sight and don't let her eat or drink anything."

"But then what?" Jörgen said, agitated. Things were starting to speed up now. He felt the adrenaline pumping round his body. "What happens when we've got hold of her? We can't call the real police?"

"The real police?" Walter snorted. "Mind your language. Madame Chief Prosecutor, who owns the investigation, is my next task," he said, smiling mischieviously. "In the next few hours, I'll be using a great quantity of brain cells to create a happy ending to this story. Or, at least, a less unhappy one."

Jonna did not hear the last comment. She had already rushed out of the room, with Jörgen close behind her.

THOMAS KOKK AND Agency Director Anders Holmberg had – together with Chief Prosecutor Åsa Julén, the Prosecutor-General, and the National Chief of Police – met a bunch of ministers from the government.

All the ministers, including the Prime Minister, insisted that SÄPO continued with the investigation into Drug-X. Apparently, SÄPO had had a pep talk with some of them before the meeting. Hardly unexpected, Julén thought to herself, and started thinking about a counter move.

Holmberg and Kokk raised the question of whether it was still the best solution to allow the investigation into Drug-X remain with SÄPO, even though it seemed to be highly unlikely that the Swedish Islamist group was behind it. That a foreign power was the brain behind such an advanced compound was, however, more plausible. Therefore, it would set a dangerous precedent to allow the local police to investigate something that concerned national security. What would be the next step? To allow patrolmen to handle counter-espionage? Or let the Traffic Police to plan bugging operations?

The ministers unanimously decided that it was most appropriate to let SÄPO continue the investigation, and they made this "recommendation" to the Prosecutor-General and the Chief Prosecutor. One was forced, under current circumstances, to consider the best interests of the nation, as the Minister for Justice put it.

For a moment, the Prosecutor-General was about to fold. Julén saw the doubt in his eyes. He fidgeted and was obviously uncomfortable with the situation. Without the Prosecutor-General's support, she would be out in the cold before she could blink. She needed to act straightaway. What she feared the most was the media, not the politicians on the other side of the table. The media had the real power, and sharp teeth too; she was not going to end up as the idiot prosecutor with no future.

Julén took command, making the Prosecutor-General very relieved.

She diplomatically pointed out that the general public would not accept more scandals in the current situation, and definitely not ministerial interference. Nor would abuse of power by any authority be tolerated – definitely not by SÄPO, who were already up to their necks in problems, the biggest being an internal investigation.

Furthermore, she could not guarantee that "details" would stay in the Prosecutor's Office if they were forced to do something "unconstitutional". The word "unconstitutional" was open to interpretation by the gathering in the room.

Julén's colleagues at the Prosecutor's Office suffered from an incurable sense of justice and would, in the event of coercion from outside sources, be difficult adversaries. An open conflict between law agencies could hardly be of benefit to anyone. Least of all to the politicians responsible for those agencies. They were normally the first casualties in such situations. She finished and closed her file with its Prosecutor's Office logo. The Prosecutor-General also got ready to leave the meeting.

By distancing herself from SÄPO, Julén could save herself. She did not trust politicians. They changed opinions as often as she brushed her teeth, and SÄPO was so contaminated that everything they touched literally was fatal. If she was successful with the investigation using another approach, she could turn personal defeat into success. Turning her back on SÄPO now would give her problems in the future; she knew that. They would not forget a defiant prosecutor and losing her good name with them was a heavy loss. But the way things looked now, she had no future if SÄPO were still involved in the investigation. If nothing else, the media would see to that. So she had simply to choose the lesser of two evils: to get rid of SÄPO.

Before Julén left the meeting, the Minister for Defence, with a sheepish smile, took her to one side. He explained in a low voice that she was welcome to come and give a lecture to his generals, at a suitable occasion. She seemed to understand the art of warfare as well as did the military leaders. Perhaps, even better than most.

Julén left the meeting with a sense of victory. She had shown the nation's foremost leadership how a true democracy should be run, as well as saved herself from a career disaster.

Now she just had to arrange for that lucky mascot Walter Gröhn to start working for her in the new investigation. To succeed, she would have to undertake a few "unconstitutional" errands that were, however, worth the risk. She started to go through the list of numbers she had written down.

IT APPEARED THAT things would, for once, be a little easier than Walter had believed. With eerie timing, Åsa Julén called Walter's mobile phone just as Jonna and Jörgen were hastening through the door. Walter was not the type who believed in miracles. After Julén's call, it was perhaps time to reconsider.

"I've been meeting with the Prosecutor-General, the National Chief of Police, ministers for Justice and Defence and even the Prime Minister," Julén began, sounding upset, "as well as the Agency Director of SÄPO, and they all ..."

"You seem to have your hands full," Walter interrupted, finding it hard not to laugh. He was imagining Julén's skinny body hanging on a cross.

"I'm starting a new investigation based on the memos from you and RSU. The Prosecutor-General is backing me up. What do you say to that?"

"Say … who me?" Walter played dumb. He knew very well what she was about to suggest, but feigned ignorance.

"If Lilja gives his approval, I want you, as soon as you're able, to be my Chief of Operations in a new investigation."

"I see," Walter said, playing hard to get. "But what if Lilja says no, for whatever reason? I'm suspended because of misconduct. Internal Affairs and a bunch of bureaucrats have to change their minds before I can go back on active duty. That's not going to happen with a simple press of the Enter key."

"In this case, it's an advantage when the police investigate the police," Julén answered. "I've begun to investigate the possibility of commuting some of the charges."

"Good luck with that," Walter said. "And I really mean it."

"I'm fully aware of what needs to be done to reinstate you to the force again. Furthermore, I've been around too long not to know how to make my way in the corridors of power, even if it's against my nature to exploit that despicable system. But the situation demands that we use the most experienced investigators. And, unfortunately, you are one of them – even though I hate to admit it," Julén explained in a serious voice. "We're talking about confidence in the Swedish justice system. In particular, the agencies of law and order," she concluded, with some irony.

"It's up to you to decide what level of experience is necessary," Walter added, without any sarcasm. "Why don't you just let SÄPO investigate our theory?"

"Let's just say that their credibility is exhausted," Julén said. Walter was silent.

"SÄPO is also fully occupied with sorting out their own problems," she continued and tried again. "Of course, there's a certain prestige involved too. I'm not naive. SÄPO will do all they can to prevent the investigation moving to the CID. They have already made this clear. I'm certain that the National Crime Squad will also try to get in on the game, especially if the investigation is thrown back to the local police. But it's we at the Prosecutor's Office who decide who runs the operational side of our investigation. If the subject of the investigation is important to national security, then we are forced to include SÄPO. If a crime crosses over county borders, then usually the National Police are involved. In this case, however, everything has occurred in Stockholm and therefore it should be in the hands of the County CID. I have the support of the Prosecutor-General in this matter. That is sufficient to move the investigation legally, now that the Swedish Islamist group is no longer suspected and it isn't a national security concern. David Lilja and Internal Affairs just have to be convinced of your worthiness. But, as I said, I know which buttons to press," Julén finished her long monologue.

Walter sank onto his bed and looked at the ceiling, deep in thought. Should he share what he and Jonna were doing? How would she react? And what would Lilja and Internal Affairs say about his discreet private investigation involving computer hacking?

It would probably not make his re-entry into the police stratosphere any easier, but he thought that Åsa Julén's sudden humility made it worth taking a risk. At least, this time. When he did the maths, he realized that it was his only chance at a comeback.

29

"WE, OR RATHER I, am pretty certain who's responsible," Walter said and opened the floodgates.

The phone line was silent. Walter could almost hear the cogs turning in Julén's brain.

"How can you know that?" she said, after a short pause. "There was nothing in the memo about that."

"Because I've started my own private investigation," he said, as if it was a normal way of doing things. That was partly accurate. It was his normal way of doing things. Following the rules was not high on Walter's list of priorities.

"Private investigation?" Julén echoed.

"Due to a lack of anything to do while being laid up in hospital – where I'm doing fine, in case you wanted to know – I started my own investigation, since the idiots at SÄPO jumped in and messed it up and you turned a blind eye to our memos."

"Started it yourself?" Julén cried out, astonished.

"No, I have two field operatives assisting me."

"Field operatives?" Julén repeated, as if she did not understand the words.

"Well, I can't get out of this bloody bed and I'm suspended. How am I supposed to run an investigation?"

"You just told me," Julén answered sarcastically. "Who are your field operatives? Do they, by any chance, have names?"

Walter did not know if he should name Jonna de Brugge or Jörgen Blad or if he should cover up that part. He decided to put all his cards on the table, a gamble that not only exposed him to harm, but also Jonna. Her career could be over if the wrong people found out what she had been doing. He did not give a shit about Jörgen.

"One police officer and one journalist from *Kvällspressen*," he finally said.

It took thirty seconds of background static on the phone before Julén came down from hitting the roof.

"I don't know where to start," she began carefully. "One police officer and *Kvällspressen*." She lingered over the words as if she were trying to taste them. "I have to know the names of the field operatives who have knowledge of this. It's important to me and the new investigation. I hope you understand."

"First, I want to know if we have a deal or not," Walter said. "No repercussions for what we have done. You will need to put that in writing."

Once again, silence on the phone line.

"This was not quite what I had expected," she finally replied. "A police officer, even from another department, I can agree to. But a journalist?"

She sounded doubtful.

"What did you expect? A fortune teller with a crystal ball?" Walter muttered.

"Is the intention that this will be published in *Kvällspressen*? Or what is the plan?"

"Part of it," Walter said. "The journalist gets exclusive rights to the story and the opportunity to release his exclusive at the appropriate time. And I decide when the time is appropriate," Walter explained.

"For what reason did you drag a reporter into this?"

"I made a deal," Walter said. "He has information on a high-ranking police commissioner who apparently has dealings with some criminal elements. And we don't want those on the force. Therefore, I agreed to an exchange of information."

"How do you know he's telling the truth?" Julén asked in disbelief.

"I also have some juicy evidence of the officer being buggered by said journalist. The police officer has been blackmailed by the journalist: confidential information in exchange for not publishing the photographs and video of their intimacy. According to the journalist, the police officer has leaked classified information as well as hired two villains to murder him."

Åsa Julén thought for a while.

"What's the name of the officer?" she asked.

"No names without a deal," Walter insisted.

Once again, nothing but white noise.

"I must have all the details of what you and your field operatives have been doing. I need to see the whole picture to have a chance of saving you."

"Let's see," Walter began. "I'll start with the computer hacking into various authorities. We needed evidence to substantiate our theory."

"Evidence obtained illegally is inadmissible in court. If you were thinking of using that for a conviction, think again. Just so we are clear on that," Julén said harshly. "And computer hacking doesn't sound very attractive or lawful to me. This is not something I wish to be drawn into. If you can't produce your evidence in any other form, you should destroy it. You have more to lose than to gain."

"You can get the evidence yourself," Walter answered. "Completely legally."

"Explain."

"As a prosecutor, you can request all documents from Stockholm District Court regarding our Mr X and, with a few background checks on the criminal records database, you'll have almost everything you need."

Julén paused for a long moment.

After a while, Walter had to ask if she was still there.

"I haven't heard anything about hacking or any other irregularities," she said finally. "You have a deal. And you must destroy anything you have illegally obtained."

"I want it in writing that you will not go after my field operatives. And that you will get me fully reinstated so I can get back to work," Walter said. "I'm not ready for my pension yet."

"I can guarantee the first condition. I'll do what I can to achieve the second. It's in my interest to get you back and into the new investigation. I don't think you should overestimate the legal status of this private and confidential agreement. It will never stand up in a court of law."

"I know. It's mainly so that I can drag you down into the shit with me if you change your mind."

WALTER EXPLAINED IN detail to Chief Prosecutor Åsa Julén what he, Jonna and Jörgen had discovered. How Leo Brageler was probably the person responsible for drugging the jurors and District Prosecutor Ekwall and how he had access to the compound. The motive was also known: apparently, revenge. They were still not clear on why he had used such a roundabout method. Julén had a theory that it would be very hard to prosecute him, since he had not directly participated in the killings. In the worst case, it might not even be possible to obtain a conviction for anything except grievous bodily harm for the drug. The compound was not classified as an illegal substance, so it was unlikely that he would be convicted for the murder of Malin Sjöstrand. The others had not suffered any injury, apart from mental suffering. Julén judged the legal position to be very complicated.

Walter also revealed the name of Folke Uddestad, which rendered Julén speechless. That such a high-ranking officer, the County Police Commissioner, had leaked information to a journalist under duress and, on top of that, was involved with criminals, she found very distressing. It would also be difficult because Uddestad had considerable influence within the police force and would not be easy to get to. If he was guilty, which Julén was still having a hard time swallowing. Sometimes, the long arm of the law did not reach all the way to the top, and it was not completely without risk to go after a county police commissioner. One single mistake and she would be finished as a prosecutor.

Using a function of his mobile phone, Walter recorded their conversation, and he made Julén repeat their agreement in formal terms. That was sufficient insurance, in case the woman changed her mind. If she decided to gossip about it, she would be in as much trouble as he would.

"I want you to send an MMS message with photographs of Leo Brageler and Tuva Sahlin from the passport database to Jonna de Brugge," Walter said before they ended the conversation. "It would help if Jonna knew what they looked like. She should be on the cruise ferry by now."

"I'll see what I can do," Julén said. "But you have to understand that it won't happen overnight. To get you reinstated will take some time and effort, if it's at all possible. I'll start by requesting the information on Brageler from the District Court records."

"Do as you wish. Just do it now, not later," Walter said, hanging up.

JONNA LOOKED AT her watch. According to Birka Lines' telephone service, she had barely fifteen minutes before the cruise ferry would depart.

Jörgen was in the process of fastening his seat belt when she made a racing start from the hospital car park. The acceleration of the Porsche pinned down Jörgen, who did not have his seat belt on, and he was wedged between the dashboard and the passenger door as Jonna took the curves with tyres screaming. His lips pressed firmly together in a line as he gritted his teeth and tried to steady himself with his right leg, while she zigzagged at high speed between the cars on the Centralbron bridge.

Behind them, the Boxer engine roared and then died to a whisper as the powerful brakes gripped the car like a gigantic hand. After five minutes of this, Jörgen was ready to throw up.

Jonna saw Jörgen's white face and opened his side window. In the middle of a sharp left-hand curve towards the Slussen intersection, the vomiting began. Food debris of various colours sprayed through the air as Jörgen, convulsing, held onto the door. As they approached the traffic lights on Söder Mälarstrand, the traffic came to a standstill. Jonna looked at the time. They had eight minutes until departure. Two lines of traffic stood waiting for the green light. The space between the right-hand lane and the tunnel wall should be enough, Jonna thought. She spun the wheel and drove onto the pavement. The Porsche wing mirrors were bent backwards, with two bangs, as she scraped by the tunnel wall and the car at the front of the queue. Farther ahead, there was a van that was wider than the other cars. They heard a heart-rending, metallic screech as the outer railing scraped the paintwork along the side of the Porsche.

"Sorry, Grandfather," Jonna said to herself once they had driven past the queuing cars, which were angrily sounding their horns. She catapulted out onto Söder Mälarstrand and glanced anxiously at the buckled side door. As long as it was still there, she was content. She moved into the bus lane and pressed the accelerator to the floor. The Porsche flew like a rocket. There was now a clear lane all the way to the terminal.

As Jonna swung into the Birka Line terminal forecourt, Jörgen was ready for yet another round of vomiting. She braked right outside the entrance and pushed Jörgen out of the car before he started retching again. He got only a few metres before throwing up.

Jonna could not wait and sprang into the terminal and towards the ramp that led onto the cruise ferry. She flashed her police badge to the guards and explained that she had important business to take care of on the ship and that she did not need their assistance. Both security guards looked at her sceptically at first, but then nodded and let her pass.

But then she remembered that she was babysitting and that she alone was responsible for Jörgen's safety. She reluctantly turned around and saw Jörgen half-running, half-walking through the departure hall while wiping his mouth.

Jonna told the guards that Jörgen was a colleague. Unconvinced, they nodded, and one of them took out his walkie-talkie. She ran once again up the ramp, this time with Jörgen behind her, gasping for breath.

Seconds after they boarded the cruise ferry, the doors of the *Birka Paradise* slammed shut behind them.

LEO BRAGELER SAT down beside Tuva and served them drinks from the tray. He gave the last drink to Tuva as if it was something special, just for her. Gittan cleared her throat and winked at Tuva, who blushed at her behaviour. Tuva accepted the drink and was just about to make a toast with the others when the man in the leather waistcoat appeared. He wanted to dance – even though there was no dance music – and Tuva was closest. The leather waistcoat clumsily took the drink from Tuva's hand and tried to pull her up from her chair. She resisted and Leo Brageler moved between them. The leather waistcoat muttered something and then grabbed Tuva's drink and downed it as a consolation. Leo frantically tried to stop him, but he was too late. The cocktail glass was emptied in one swallow. It was as if Leo had seen a treasure chest sink into the sea. He was completely dumbfounded and did not move until Tuva asked him what was wrong.

The man in the leather waistcoat belched and continued his hunt for a dance partner.

WITH HER BADGE in her hand, Jonna pushed past the queue to the cruise hostess. The surprised hostess showed Jonna to the information desk.

"I need to know which cabin Tuva Sahlin has," Jonna said, leaning over the counter to look at one of the screens.

The woman behind the counter quickly keyed in the name, but found no match.

"Is Tuva Sahlin spelled as it sounds?" she inquired.

"Probably," Jonna answered and cursed that she had forgotten to check Walter's printout. They had been in such a rush.

After a while, the woman behind the counter shook her head. "No, there is no match for anything resembling that name," she said.

"Could the cabin be booked in another name?" Jonna asked.

"We have the names of all the passengers, even the ones travelling without a cabin," the woman said.

Jonna took out her mobile phone and called Elina. After three rings, she answered.

"Mum has not been in touch," the girl began.

"Are you certain that she was travelling with Birka?" Jonna said.

Silence.

"Or maybe it was, like, Viking Line," she said, unsure.

"Maybe? What do you mean, maybe?" Jonna sighed. She felt time running like sand through her fingers.

Once again, silence.

"Now that I think about it, I think, like, they were going with Birka first, but then they, like, changed to Viking. I think Birka was like, full up or something."

"Are you sure?" Jonna asked.

"Now that I think about it," she said, emphasizing the word "think", "yeah, I am kind of sure."

Jonna turned to the cruise hostess who, being curious, had stayed by the information desk.

"Do you know when the Viking Line cruise ferry departs?" Jonna asked.

"*Cinderella*, you mean?"

"Is that what it's called?"

"Yes, it sails ten minutes after us," the hostess replied.

THE BEARDED MAN, who had introduced himself as Carl, bought a fresh drink for Tuva after the incident. He apologized for having been unable to stop the intoxicated dance partner. The Beekeepers' Society toasted him and thanked him for the drinks. In the next round, it would be their turn to buy him a drink. In the spirit of equality, he could not refuse and had no less than five drinks to look forward to. Tuva thought the bartender was doing a lousy job. The margarita didn't taste the way it should. But since nobody else was complaining, she kept quiet and decided to let the good times roll.

The man with the leather waistcoat stumbled out onto the dance floor, holding a newly acquired dance partner by the hand.

"DAMN IT!" JONNA SWORE. Jörgen raised his eyebrow at Jonna's outburst.

"We have to get off the ship," Jonna said to the hostess. "Now," she added.

The hostess shook her head. "We have already left the quay. It's too late."

"I don't care," Jonna said. "You will have to go back to the harbour."

"The only one who can decide that is the captain," she answered.

"Take me to the captain right now," she ordered the hostess.

"I have to talk to …"

"Take me to the captain now!" Jonna cut her off, raising her voice.

"Do it," Jörgen added. "If you argue, we will consider it obstruction of a police inquiry. And that's a crime."

Jonna glared angrily at Jörgen, who was staring at the hostess with his healthy eye. The woman hesitated at first, but then signalled for them to follow and they went to the bridge. While they were making their way through the ship, she spoke into a walkie-talkie. As they arrived at the control tower, one of the crew, probably the navigation officer, welcomed them. He took them onto the bridge and to the captain.

A man in a dark blue uniform turned around to meet them.

"Now, what's this all about?" he began in a grumpy Finnish accent.

"We are from the police," Jonna answered, showing him her police ID. "We have to disembark immediately."

"You have to what?"

"Please be so kind as to go back to the harbour," Jonna repeated. "We have to get off this ship."

The captain looked carefully at the young woman and then at the one-eyed man in the pastel-coloured jacket standing beside her with his hands resolutely on his hips.

The captain was in his fifties and had broad shoulders and a distinct jaw line that was immaculately clean-shaven.

"The police," he said, thinking, and narrowed his eyes. "When the police want to come on board, which is not uncommon given the amount of alcohol that is consumed on board, they usually inform us of their business in advance and as soon as they come on the ship. Mostly, it is we who call the police to take care of unruly passengers who have had too much to drink. You do not storm the ship in this way and dictate how I am to run this vessel. That has never happened to me before. As captain of this ship, it is I, and only I, who makes the decisions once we are at sea."

"I think we all understand you're the captain and that you're in charge," Jörgen said sarcastically.

The captain remained unconvinced by Jonna and the one-eyed man in the garishly coloured tuxedo.

Jonna took one step closer to the broad-shouldered commander. Given her stress about the whole situation, her patience was dwindling.

"Listen to me, captain," she said, making her voice as hard as possible. "We have only just boarded and practically jumped from the gangway. You were immediately informed that there were police on board. But we have been told that we are on the wrong ship and so we need to get off fast. Therefore, I want you, or rather I'm ordering you, to return to harbour. I also want you to contact the *Cinderella* and tell them that they must not depart until we, the police, have boarded them. Is that clear, or do we still have a problem?"

It was so quiet, you could hear a pin drop on the bridge. A young woman claiming to be from the police had torn a stripe off the commander himself, by the rulebook. And while he was a few metres from his leather command chair, the place where he, with authority and an even greater sense of duty, controlled the thirty-five-thousand tonne, steel structure and its crew. In earlier times, it was an offence that would have been punished with keelhauling.

At first, the captain looked at Jonna with a blank expression. Then he had what appeared to be a coughing fit mingled with laughter. He cleared his throat. "You can order me as much as you like. But I don't have to follow your orders if I consider your order to dock the ship a risk. The harbour crew is not ready for the ship to dock again. As captain, I'm responsible for the lives of hundreds of passengers on board and that's my first priority, Miss …"

"De Brugge," Jonna reminded him. "Officer Jonna de Brugge."

"As in the de Brugge family of shipowners?"

Of course, the old seadog knows the de Brugge family, Jonna thought.

"Yes," she answered. "But the shipping business is not for me," she added, to avoid the inevitable next question.

The captain's expression became more grave.

"I understand completely your authority over this ship," Jonna began diplomatically, changing her approach. What was previously an ocean of difference between them had become a canal of commonality. They were now two people in the shipping trade, not a captain and a landlubber.

Jonna explained the situation to the now more receptive captain. Methodically, and without wasting time on details, she repeated her mission to the red-eared captain. She explained that they had boarded the wrong cruise ferry and that she needed to get onto the *Cinderella* quickly in order to prevent the loss of a life.

The captain listened with mounting interest. After a while, he folded his hands behind his back and walked around his command chair. Finally, he picked up what looked like a handset and hailed the *Cinderella*, while ordering his own crew to take the ship back to port.

Jonna felt the weight lift off her shoulders. She thanked the captain for his honourable course of action and promised to mention him in her report. She would also mention his name and his good deed at her next family gathering. The captain glowed. So much so that a few eyebrows were raised among the others on the bridge. He adjusted his captain's cap, as if he was going to be photographed, escorted Jonna and Jörgen to the door, and wished them good luck with a firm handshake.

When they came out of the terminal, Jonna and Jörgen threw themselves into her dented Porsche and drove the few kilometres to the city quay, where *Cinderella* stood, waiting. She should have sailed five minutes ago.

Once again, Jonna parked directly outside the terminal entrance and ran up the gangway with Jörgen trudging behind her. There would not be any more emergency calls with Jonna behind the wheel, as far as he was concerned.

This time, the captain and a few of the crew were waiting for them.

"Police," Jonna said, holding up her police ID.

"So I gather," the captain answered with a worried frown.

"I must find a Tuva Sahlin," Jonna said, out of breath. "And you cannot leave until I have located her."

The captain nodded. "You have fifteen minutes. Then we'll have to depart unless it's dangerous to do so," he said, looking at his watch.

"If I can locate Tuva Sahlin, then you can sail," Jonna said.

Jörgen nodded in agreement. He stood a little taller. He was actually beginning to feel like an undercover police officer. There was nothing like the power of a police badge. Maybe he should have a fake one made.

"Yes, we have a Tuva Sahlin booked on board," a uniformed woman said, looking at a list.

"Does she have a cabin?" Jonna asked.

"Yes, number 101," the woman confirmed. "Follow me and I'll show you where the cabin is. The key cards to the cabins have been handed out, so they should be there now."

They hurried down flights of stairs and into a corridor. After a dozen metres, they were outside cabin 101. True to form, Jörgen followed up behind, gasping for breath.

Jonna knocked on the door. No one opened up.

She knocked again, shouting this time that it was the police.

Not a sound could be heard inside the cabin. All they could hear was Jörgen catching his breath.

"Could you open the door?" Jonna asked, looking at the woman's key card, which was hanging around her neck. She nodded and opened the door.

Jonna pushed by, but found the cabin empty.

"They've not been here yet," the woman said. "Nothing has been touched."

"You must call her name over the Tannoy and ask her to come to reception," Jonna said.

The uniformed woman took up her walkie-talkie and asked the information-desk staff to broadcast the message for Tuva Sahlin. Meanwhile, they rushed back to the main deck and over to the information desk. Just as they arrived, Jonna's mobile phone beeped twice. Waiting were two MMS images from an anonymous sender.

The first message was a photograph of a woman with the message heading "Tuva Sahlin". The image showed a woman with short hair, large eyes and full lips. She had a slight smile. Jonna studied the image. Merely the fact that she had received the image meant that Walter had succeeded in persuading Åsa Julén. Maybe he was even back on the force, despite being in hospital. But that also meant that he, or someone else, had managed to get Internal Affairs and David Lilja to withdraw their complaints, which was quite exceptional.

Or perhaps it was not so exceptional. When the police investigate the police, there is a high ceiling. Sometimes as high as a cathedral. She wanted to call Walter and catch up on the situation, but she did not have time right now.

Jonna selected the second MMS. She shivered when the name "Leo Brageler" appeared on her display. The image showed a late-middle-aged man. Nordic, but with short, dark hair and innocent, bluish-grey eyes. The passport photo did not reveal any more than that.

Jonna could not easily reconcile herself to the knowledge that the man in the photograph had caused so much suffering for so many individuals. He looked completely normal. Not like a crackpot with a psychotic stare.

If it was really him who was behind everything.

A glimmer of doubt suddenly swept over Jonna. What if she and Walter were wrong?

30 MARTIN BORG SCANNED the room as he entered. Despite his mere one-eighty-metre height, he had to bend not to touch the ceiling with his head. Tor was at least twenty centimetres taller, but had still chosen to live in a hut built for a dwarf.

Martin constantly kept his hand on the butt of the gun in his pocket. He had, of course, checked that Tor did not have any weapons on him when they met in the car. Even though he was not an immediate risk, you could never be too careful.

Martin sat on an old kitchen sofa covered with moss-green fabric. The sofa stood beneath one of the room's two windows. He did not like sitting with his back exposed. That the Albanians were after Tor, he knew already, and he had promised to help Tor with that afterwards. But there could be other jokers hidden in the deck that could suddenly turn up on the card table. Perhaps an old score to be settled by some trigger-happy thugs. It wouldn't be the first time that the wrong person had been gunned down.

Around them lay heaps of old junk. Probably stolen goods and other stuff that the lanky git had acquired. Martin could not understand how he could live surrounded by rubbish or even why he would choose to live a life such as his. He himself had once been close to sliding into a life of drugs and crime. But he had chosen another path. He had his brother to thank for that.

Martin heard Tor searching in a wardrobe. The open door partly obscured him. In theory, he could have a weapon hidden among the clothes.

Martin took out his gun and let it rest on his knee, cocked and ready to unleash its deadly force, in case the clown behind the wardrobe door tried a repeat performance of the Gnesta drama. This one was dumb enough to start playing with fire even after he had already been burnt.

Martin was forced to have a certain degree of patience with Headcase. The most important thing was that he did not make trouble for himself or Martin. Especially now that Martin's future did not look that good. Martin had perhaps misjudged the situation and underestimated the significance of the internal investigation. Perhaps he had not been thinking with a clear head when he made that decision, but now he needed all the help he could get.

He was hoping that Omar's hard drive would, to a certain degree, help solve his predicament. If he could get hold of the journalist who was holding the evidence on Uddestad, then his problems would be over. No internal investigation could stop him. He would become a puppet master at Kungsholmen. Say a few careful words in Uddestad's ear – or the ear of any other name that was on Omar's hard drive – then, abracadabra, and they would be rolling out the red carpet for him.

Tor had changed to clothes that were, if not identical, very similar to the ones he had previously been wearing, except that they were in one piece and clean. Brown corduroys and a mustard-yellow shirt with a *Saturday Night Fever* collar.

No weapon appeared from the wardrobe. Probably because he did not have one stashed there. Instead, Tor took out a laptop from one of the kitchen drawers.

"Will this do?" he asked, showing the laptop to Martin.

"I suppose," Martin answered and examined the presumably stolen computer. It was not the latest model, and the battery was probably dead. Luckily enough, Tor had the power adaptor in the same drawer. There was, after all, some sense of order in this scrap yard.

"Why don't you use your own computer?" Tor asked.

"I told you earlier," Martin answered, irritated. "I can't leave any traces that might lead to this hard drive, nor to anything else for that matter."

Tor nodded. Computers were not his strong suit. He could, at the most, surf the internet.

After twenty minutes, Martin had installed Omar's hard drive and logged in with the password that Jerry Salminen had managed to discover. That idiot Omar had even put all his encryption keys on his mobile phone. How could he be so fucking stupid? And he had called himself the "godfather of secret information", or something to that effect.

Two woodentops had managed to decipher Omar's entire net of contacts in less time than it took for Martin to switch on the hard drive on his computer. It was just as well that Omar had gone to meet his maker ahead of time. Who knows? It could have been someone else instead of Martin sifting after information that could be used for different purposes. Then they would have had Martin's name. And God knows what he would have been forced to do.

With mounting astonishment, Martin opened file after file, email exchanges and other documents that made his pulse race.

An hour later, he pushed the laptop away. He looked curiously at Tor, who had been sitting quietly on a chair facing him the whole time. What Tor had said really was the truth.

Omar had been more than just a former intelligence officer. He had been unusually active for a has-been in the intelligence world. He hadn't been just a semi-criminal go-between or contract broker, as he had called himself. He had had money too. A considerable amount. The smarty-pants had also saved statements from various bank accounts on the hard drive, as well as lists with account numbers and their passwords. Just give the password and withdraw the cash. Data viruses seemed not to exist in his world. He didn't even seem to have updated his antivirus software. It was almost too good to be true. Or maybe it was. What if this was fake? What if it was the same as carrying two wallets? One that the mugger gets and one that is the real one? Imagine if everything on the hard drive was a trap. If Martin tried to contact someone on the list, then it would trigger an alarm, an alarm that would have counter-measures against whoever triggered it ...

"What did you find?" Tor interrupted Martin's meditation. "Is there anything we can use? Jerry thought so."

"Some of this we can use," Martin lied. "But right now, we need to focus on the journalist queer and the evidence on Folke Uddestad. Omar wrote in one of the documents that Uddestad probably had a relationship with that Jörgen Blad, and that Omar hired you and Jerry on Uddestad's behalf to retrieve some multimedia evidence."

"Yes," Tor said and felt mounting anger when he began to think about the fat journalist and the events outside his home. How the sneaky Albanians set an ambush and how fucking difficult it was to hit anything with his Desert Eagle when it was set to automatic mode. It was that ball of lard who was the cause of all Tor's problems. He was the root of all the evil that had happened to him recently. It was his fault that Tor was now forced to sit at home with a psychopath in his kitchen so that the psycho could poke around in Omar's hard drive.

Fuck that Omar! It was his fault too. He sold him and Jerry out to Haxhi. Probably for pennies, as well.

And then there was that Uddenstad, or whatever his name was. The bloke who really kicked off this shit. That was how it was. Uggelstad was the pig who had had the biggest part in

Jerry's death and Tor's tricky situation, to put it mildly. The maniac on the other side of the table had indeed promised Tor greener grass, but he could just as easily end up on a rubbish tip. Dirty cops had dumped people on the tip with a bullet in the head before. They faked gang killings and then investigated the hits themselves. It was a possibility. The guy in front of him was not all there. He could do anything.

Tor felt ambivalent. Well, that was what you called it when you were not sure about what you thought or what you wanted. Your thoughts were splintered. One half of your brain wanted to go right and the other left. Why could there not be just one complete brain?

His head was starting to hurt from all his pondering.

As long as he did not have a weapon, he was stuck. He could try to grab one of the knives he had stashed. He could surprise the cop. But there was a risk that he knew karate or some martial art. Some cops were trained in that kung fu and could kill you with their bare hands. Not like the regular cops or the riot police, who pumped iron at the cop gym and moved like rusty robots.

Tor needed money, enough money to buy another Desert Eagle or, at worst, some other shooter, just as long as it worked. Then he could take down the psycho cop and get out from under him.

He scratched his neck with his intact hand.

But then he thought of Haxhi. Before punching the cop's lights out, he needed to watch his back by sending Haxhi home to Albania in a wooden box. And he could not do that by himself. The cop had promised to put Haxhi on the to-do list as soon as they grabbed the faggot and shook him down for the evidence on Uggenstag. That was the agreement.

But what were his plans for the future after that? What would he live off, now that both Omar and Jerry were gone? If he snuffed out the cop, then even that source of income went up in smoke. Or would it be him who was smoked if he continued to work for the cop?

Tough questions. To start housebreaking again did not seem exciting. A lot of work for little money. He would, once again, be back at the bottom of the criminal ladder. To claw his way back a second time would be a fucking pain, almost impossible to do.

How close they had been with of the Original Fuckers. One filthy hair's breadth from success. To go from top to rock bottom in a few days sucked like crazy. So fucking crazy.

He would play the game despite everything. If he could not borrow one from the weekend-soldier who sold him the Desert Eagle. He would take out the cop once Haxhi was out of the way. Then he would use the information on Omar's hard drive. For what, he had no idea, but it would sort itself out later. There must have something good on it because the cop had sat for a long time staring at the screen. Everything can be sold as long as the price is right. That was what Jerry used to say.

THREE MINUTES AFTER the first name call, Jonna saw a slightly tense woman approach the information desk.

"Tuva Sahlin?" Jonna asked and walked up to the woman.

"Ye-es," the woman hesitated.

"Jonna de Brugge, police," Jonna introduced herself.

"I see," the woman said, uncertainly. "What's this about?"

"First of all, nothing has happened to your family. I'm here to fetch you."

"Fetch me?"

"Yes, I want you to leave the ship together with us," Jonna said, pointing to Jörgen, as if that would reassure her more.

"Why?" the woman asked suspiciously. "Am I being arrested?"

"No, absolutely not," Jonna reassured her.

"We're here to protect your family from you actually," Jörgen added, finding the situation a little comical. She did not look the least bit dangerous.

"Protect? I don't understand," she said, confused.

Jonna warned Jörgen with a sharp look.

"Does it concern my work with the district court?" A trace of fear appeared in her eyes.

"You could say that," Jonna began. "And I'll tell you more in the car. But first, I'd like to know if you have eaten or drunk anything on the ship since you boarded."

Tuva stared at Jonna with surprise. "Why do you want to know that?"

"Have you?" Jonna repeated.

"Yes, a welcome drink at the bar over there," she said, pointing to one of the bars.

"I was bought a drink by an insistent man as soon as we arrived. Actually, he bought us all drinks. I'm travelling with some girlfriends."

"Was it, by any chance, this man?" Jonna asked, showing the photograph of Leo Brageler that she had on her mobile phone.

"I'm not sure," she hesitated at first. "The man at the bar had a beard and intense eyes. But, yes, that's him. Take away the beard and add some intensity to the eyes, and that's him," she answered decisively.

Jörgen felt his pulse race. Now they were close. The killer, or whatever he was to be called, was here on board the ship. It could only have been him who had bought drinks for five women. Normally, you only bought a drink for one at a time. Not even the men from the women-free town of Haparanda would be that desperate if they had just got on board the Baltic Sea's number-one singles booze cruise.

"Show me the man who bought your drinks," Jonna said, taking Tuva with her. "But from a distance. I want you to point him out to me."

"He was sitting at our table when you called me, so it shouldn't be a problem," she said, as they walked towards the bar.

They pushed past the row of passengers that had formed around the bar. The chair where the man had been sitting was empty. Instead, one of Tuva's friends was using the chair as a place to rest some shopping bags.

"What's going on?" one of her girlfriends asked.

"Where did that man go?" Tuva asked, pointing at the chair.

"He disappeared just after you were called to the information desk," one of the women around the table answered.

"Did you see where he went?" Jonna asked the woman.

"Who are you?" she asked, examining Jonna from head to toe with critical eyes.

"She's a police officer," Tuva explained. "Did you see where he went?"

"No," one of the friends replied. "I didn't watch him. He wasn't that good-looking, to be honest." Her friends agreed with her.

"But he was nice. He bought drinks for all of us," an overweight woman added.

"What did he buy?" Jonna asked.

"Margaritas," Tuva said. "He brought a whole tray-full."

"Everybody got a drink. Tuva even got two," another woman in the party pointed out.

"Two drinks?" Jonna said.

"Yes, a drunk pinched the first drink out of Tuva's hand and drank it when she wouldn't dance with him. The guy who was buying looked very unhappy about it, to say the least."

"What did the drunk look like?" Jonna asked.

"Well," Tuva said, trying to remember, "he had the body of a long-distance lorry driver and was wearing a lumberjack shirt and a leather waistcoat. He was ordinary looking. He was also drunk and apparently very keen to dance."

"You have to point him out for me," Jonna instructed her and took hold of Tuva. In five minutes, the ship would depart, regardless of whether Jonna was done.

"Do you see him?" Jonna asked, her eyes scanning the disco restaurant.

"There!" Tuva cried and pointed to one of the tables. "He's sitting there."

Jonna rushed through the restaurant towards the man, where she pulled out her police badge and ordered him to follow her off the ship. The woman accompanying the man stood up, terrified, as the man began to shout once he saw Tuva. If he was being arrested because of the drink, he would buy a new one. He stood up, but Jonna stood in his way. She did not have time for any discussions.

The man obviously had no plans to leave the ship and was going to push Jonna to one side, so she quickly moved backwards so that he lost his balance and tripped forwards. After a few staggering steps, he steadied himself with the back of a chair, whereupon Jonna quickly grabbed his arms and tied them with restraints behind his back. The man yelled and shouted as Jonna pushed him from behind towards the exit.

Jörgen was fascinated by Jonna's fearlessness; the man was twice her size.

As they came out of the disco restaurant, the man's intoxicated buddies saw the two of them and rushed to his rescue, but the cruise ferry's security guards quickly intervened and, after a short scuffle, the rowdy gang was herded down the gangway and into the terminal, where they were to be refused passage. Jonna had asked the guards to detain the drunken leather waistcoats long enough for her to load their companion into her car and avoid any further rescue attempts. One of the guards – a blond, muscular guy who was the same age as Jonna – had laughed and asked how much time she needed.

Two minutes, she had answered, making a 'V' sign. He nodded and gave her a thumbs-up.

Before Jonna left the ship, she asked the captain if there were any CCTV cameras that covered the bar and the gangway into the ship. He nodded and confirmed that there were three cameras that probably covered those areas. Jonna asked to have the tapes or DVDs with footage from the time they had allowed the passengers on board.

The captain looked doubtful at first. "Don't you need permission for that?" he asked.

"Not necessarily," she lied, even though she was well aware that she needed permission from the ferry company to confiscate CCTV records. Any evidence on Leo Brageler was welcome and urgently needed. Furthermore, there was a chance that the sympathetic security guard would be on the film.

After a few seconds' deliberation, the captain asked a woman crew member to get the DVDs quickly. As they entered the terminal, Jonna asked the staff if they had seen a man with a beard leave the ship. A ticket vendor confirmed that a bearded man had just passed by, fifteen minutes earlier.

TUVA SAHLIN HAD voluntarily gone ashore, unlike the man in the leather waistcoat. She felt that she had to trust the two police officers. They had not told her anything more, except that it had something to do with Tuva's work and, when they got to the car, she demanded some answers to her questions.

"You'll have to explain yourselves now," she said, after Jörgen and Jonna had forced the leather waistcoat into the miniscule back seat of the Porsche.

"I'll explain from the beginning," Jonna said. "And you'll get the full story as we are driving. But first I have to make a call and also handcuff you."

"Whatever for?" Tuva asked, looking at the restraints that Jonna held in her hand.

"It's for your own, and our, safety."

"Safety?"

"It's part of the explanation that I'll give you shortly. Until then, you will have to trust me."

Tuva watched Jonna carefully as she punched in the number to Walter's mobile phone. For the first time in her life, she was in police custody. The thin plastic band cut into her sensitive skin.

"I have Tuva Sahlin in my car," Jonna reported.

"Excellent," Walter answered and seemed to be in high spirits. "And Leo Brageler?"

"He left the ship when we called Tuva on the tannoy."

"I see, but that's not so important right now."

"We have one more who has been drugged," Jonna said before Walter could continue.

"How did that happen?" Walter replied, as if he had misheard.

"Some guy swiped a spiked drink that was intended for Tuva."

Walter sighed. "Take Sahlin and that man to the Södermalm detention centre. Hunting the mad professor is of less importance now."

"To the Södermalm detention centre?" Jonna repeated. "Why?"

"She has to go into protective custody," Walter said triumphantly. "Julén is apparently there on some business and wants her there instead of Kungsholmen. She was very keen to meet her."

"What shall I say to the custody officer, and on whose orders, by the way?"

"By order of the Chief Prosecutor," Walter said. "Tell the custody officer that. That scarecrow has started a new investigation based on what we have discovered. Before the day is out, I'll be back on the force. Not only that, I'm also in charge of the investigation. If the gods and the Internal Affairs nutters allow me to, that is."

"It's almost too good to be true!" Jonna said, barely containing her enthusiasm.

"Yes, although in practical terms, it will not happen until Darth Vader releases me from the hospital."

Jonna wondered for a minute what that meant for her situation.

"Then I can come off sick leave and return to RSU, in other words," she concluded, after her initial euphoria had died down.

It was a little disappointing that she would not be working as a private investigator any longer, despite the risks it entailed. But all things considered, it would be a pleasure to work within the boundaries of the law again – even as an analyst at RSU.

Her work description stipulated ten per cent operational fieldwork and ninety per cent analytical deskwork. Jonna wished it were the other way round.

"Oh, there was one more thing," Walter confessed, a little too repentantly for him. A guilty conscience was not usually one of Walter's weaknesses and Jonna felt a knot in her gut when Walter's tone changed.

"I had to put all my cards on the table," Walter began. "And I mean all of them. Even the ones I had up my sleeve."

For a fraction of a second, Jonna's world rocked. It was as if someone had quickly flipped a light switch on and off in a dark room.

"What do you mean by 'all my cards'?"

"I described the parts involving your and Jörgen's activities, with names and everything. For once, it seems I have left nothing out."

Jonna didn't know how she felt about that. He, Walter Gröhn, had apparently sold her like a second-hand bookshelf on eBay. He had also offered up Jörgen Blad and, even though she did not care much about his fate, it was the principle that mattered. You just do not betray people's confidences as you please. Least of all, if they are working for a good cause. He had said that himself. How you could be forced to commit a lesser crime to prevent other, more serious ones. They had agreed on a principle of justice, to which Jonna had fully committed.

Now she was going to pay for her actions. She had expected this day to come. In a way, she had already practised her defence for the surly Internal Affairs inspectors. But that it should happen so soon and so suddenly because of Walter, she had not anticipated. It was a knife in the back.

"But you and the fairy queen can sit easy and relax," Walter blurted out. It sounded as if he was having a hard time not laughing.

"What?"

"Well, I made an arrangement with the scarecrow," Walter continued, his tone lighter now. "You have never been involved in a private investigation for the simple reason that there has never been one. The new investigation was started on the basis of an anonymous tip received by Chief Prosecutor Åsa Julén. That will be the wording in the formal report."

"And how will you make this happen, may I ask?" Jonna asked with a mixture of irritation and disbelief. She should have realized that the mischievous detective would amuse himself with something so important. No matter what the situation was, he was compelled to torment his closest associates with sarcasm, as well as various, convoluted witticisms.

"I have a written agreement – which, for now, is an audio telephone recording – with Julén," Walter said. "If she talks, she goes down with us."

"Doesn't sound completely legal?" Jonna said.

"She went from cast iron to crème brûlée in the space of five minutes," Walter painted the picture.

"Perhaps you should whisper a few words in Lilja's ear too," Jonna pointed out.

"As I said, there's just some red tape that Julén has to unravel," he continued. "In a few hours, the knot should be untangled, according to her. The movers and shakers are dancing and then the earth moves. Pity the fool standing in their way."

"She knows everything?" Jonna asked.

"Yes; it was a precondition to get the pike to bite. Even if she was just as desperate as yours truly to get back control of the investigation and get back on track again. Presumably, the woman has a lower limit with regards to sharing information. At first, I was going to play with a few cards tucked up my sleeve and keep you out of it, but thanks to my fasting stomach, I changed my game this time. Julén pushed so hard for information on the persons I was working with. I gave my tongue free reins for once and she swallowed it, hook, line and sinker. Basically, she jumped up on the table like a Christmas ham and accepted all of my terms. I just had to serve myself. She was as pliable as ..."

"Spare me the analogies, please," Jonna interrupted. "What exactly does this mean for me?" she continued, more composed.

"It means that you are on loan from RSU to the County CID under my supervision," Walter said. "The investigation is led by the scarecrow. I haven't figured out what to do with Jörgen Blad now that the investigation is official. Anyway,

Julén is very interested in Jörgen's blackmail of Uddestad and the video of the scantily dressed gentlemen. Whether it's for weekend viewing on her TV couch or something work-related was never really explained to me.

"She was, however, worried about having a journalist embedded in the investigation. I explained how the deal with the fairy queen was constructed. She bought that as well, after the usual bickering, but she didn't want to hear about any journalists running around in the police station or in any of the meetings that she attended, unless it pertained to Uddestad's activities – in which case, a separate investigation would be started up for that. Otherwise, I make the decisions based on my own common sense. That could be a bit challenging, however."

"You took the words right out of my mouth," Jonna replied.

31 "HE LIVES UP there," Tor said, pointing at Jörgen Blad's flat. Martin had parked the car so that they could see the entrance to Jörgen's block of flats from across the street. The flat was dark.

"The question is, where is he?" Martin said, thinking aloud. "He's not at his office and doesn't answer the number the newspaper gave me. We don't know if he has contacted the police either. He might be in protective custody somewhere. In other words, we know nothing."

Martin would need to do some background research into Jörgen Blad. As it looked now, he knew no more than what the dunce had been able to tell him and that was not much. He needed to use the computers at work and to do a little honest surveillance work. Sooner or later, he would get his man.

Currently, his situation was quite complicated. Early tomorrow morning, he would be sitting in the internal investigation interview room and would not have access to any police databases, since he was suspended until the investigation was completed. And that could take anything from one day to one month, even though he had prepared himself carefully and stuck to his story.

Perhaps the problem was Thomas Kokk. Maybe he had sensed that something was wrong. Was that why he and the idiots at Internal Affairs have been looking so hard for him?

He needed to come up with an excuse as to why he had not returned their calls or been at home in his flat, in case they had looked for him there.

In addition, there was the towelhead that he and Jernberg had pumped full of the truth serum. It was a sure thing that he was at Forensics for an extended investigation. They would, without doubt, find traces of Martin's innovative interrogation techniques.

Martin was just about to turn on the ignition when Tor cried out.

"There!" he said, pointing in the direction of the entrance. "There he is."

"Who? Jörgen?"

"Yes," Tor confirmed, agitated. "I'm dead certain."

"Did you see where he came from?"

"From the entrance, I think," Tor said.

They saw Jörgen get into the back seat of a sports car that was parked a dozen metres from the entrance. A woman left the driving seat to make room for the journalist to creep into the back seat.

"What in the world is that RSU diva doing here?" Martin said, talking to himself.

"What diva?"

"The one who got out of the Porsche."

"What about her? Do you know who she is?"

"Yes," Martin said.

"Is it an old flame?" Tor smirked.

"I don't see the connection between the Special Investigations Unit and Jörgen, unless he has spilled the beans on Folke Uddestad. And that's what he must have done."

"Why would he do that?"

"RSU is a unit for special investigations and analysis. It was formed by the National Police Board. It answers directly to the NPB and is populated with lots of super-intelligent weirdos who solve crimes using unconventional methods and subject profiling. But what I don't understand is why a clear-cut

Internal Affairs case ends up with them instead of the usual internal investigators."

"I thought you knew everything that goes on in the police force," Tor said.

"Apparently not," Martin said.

He made a U-turn and followed the Porsche. He let a few cars get in-between them and then stuck to the Porsche like a shadow. The Porsche did an illegal left turn and then drove south on Sveavägen. It continued down into the Söder tunnel and it eventually surfaced on Hornsgatan. After about one hundred metres, the Porsche turned into Torkel Knutssonsgatan and parked a dozen metres from the Södermalm police station.

Martin stopped the car fifty metres behind the Porsche, so that was obscured behind some parked cars. He saw Jonna de Brugge and another woman in high heels get out of the car. The woman walked as if she were cuffed. Jonna also prised a man out of the car; even he was cuffed. Unlike the woman prisoner, he did not seem as eager to follow along and Jonna had to push him forwards as they hurried towards the detention centre cell-block entrance. The journalist was obviously still sitting in the car.

Martin watched, confused, as the trio disappeared through the detention-cell-block entrance. He could not piece the puzzle together. It was as if the pieces belonged to an entirely different puzzle.

"We have to move fast," he said, after thinking for a few intense seconds.

"Move where?" Tor asked.

"Jörgen won't recognize me," he said. "I'll walk past the Porsche and up to the cell-block entrance. I'll keep watch from there in case they come out again. If they come out before you are done, then I'll improvise and delay them. As soon as I'm in position, you go up to the car, drag Jörgen out and stuff him in the boot."

"In the boot of which car?"

"The one we're sitting in, of course," Martin answered, in a despairing voice.

"But the whole area is crawling with cops. Both uniformed and plain-clothes. It's the Eagle's Nest for the South Stockholm Metropolitan Police."

"Thank you; I'm fully aware of that fact," Martin said sarcastically. "But we may not get any more chances. And I don't see many police officers in our immediate vicinity right now. Not a single one, to be exact."

Martin wondered why they had left Jörgen in the car and why he had come out of the flat by himself. Under normal circumstances, a protected witness would never be allowed to stay by themselves like this. Unless he was not in protective custody. If that was the case, then what was he doing with RSU?

It was all strangely illogical. And the only way to find out was to ask the journalist. Perhaps the journalist was withholding information from RSU. Had he not told them that he was being threatened?

It was time to move from theory and questions to action and answers.

Martin had a hire car with number plates that were fully visible. It was far from perfect, but there was little movement on the street and it was beginning to get dark. If they handled this correctly, then nobody would notice that anything had happened.

"Are you ready?" Martin asked, looking at Tor.

Tor nodded.

"I'll go on ahead," Martin said. "Wait for thirty seconds."

"If the door is locked?" Tor asked.

"Look in the boot and see if there are any tools you can use to smash the window."

"Remember, I only have one hand," Tor said and held up his plastic-cased right hand.

"Use your left hand then," Martin said. "Just get him out of the car and I'll help you."

Martin thought one last time before he opened the car door. He could still change his mind.

But then he felt the charm around his neck and he knew. It was now or never.

Tor tapped the window. He had found a tyre lever. Martin got out of the car, nodded to Tor, and walked over to the detention centre cell-block doorway. As he passed the Porsche, he saw a figure in the passenger seat. He had moved from the back seat to the front. He signaled to Headcase, who nodded back.

Martin kept on walking and positioned himself by the doorway of the detention-cell-block. From the corner of his eye, he saw Tor walking towards the Porsche, but from the wrong side.

Tor ripped open the driver's door and leaned in. A second later, the passenger door opened, and Martin could see the journalist halfway out of the car, trying to free himself from Tor's grip. The idiot was trying to drag the journalist through the driver's door.

Martin could feel his racing pulse race even faster. After some wrestling, Jörgen managed to wriggle his way out of his jacket and Tor's grip. The terrified journalist ran off in a panic towards the cell-block entrance.

Martin turned and pretended to be talking on his mobile phone. When Jörgen was just metres away from the door and safety, Martin punched him hard in the solar plexus. The journalist folded like a pocket knife and fell hard onto his back.

Martin quickly looked around. There was no sign of any people around, except for the idiot moose coming towards him.

"The bastard ran!" Tor panted.

"We have to get him in the car fast," Martin hissed.

Martin and Tor took hold of Jörgen's shoulders and dragged him, running to Martin's car. Jörgen could not make a sound. The blow to his belly had pushed all the air out of him and he was fully occupied with filling his lungs with air again.

After tossing Jörgen into the boot, Martin drove off at high speed. As they passed the doorway of the detention centre cellblock, he saw from the corner of his eye Jonna de Brugge coming out. There had been a margin of only ten seconds.

JONNA SWORE LOUDLY for the second time in only two days. Not only had she allowed Jörgen to stop by his flat on the way to the detention centre, but he had also been refused entry to the cell block because it was inappropriate to have a journalist roaming free among the staff and detainees. They had not known about their special arrangement, so that was the way it had to be.

It was Jonna's decision to let Jörgen change clothes at his flat, even though she knew the risks. But it was bloody well Walter's fault that she had to go to the detention centre, where Jörgen was not allowed inside and so was forced to stay in the car by himself while Jonna placed Tuva Sahlin in protective custody.

When she had handed over Sahlin and the leather waistcoat to the surprised custody officer at the detention cells, she had received a call from Walter, who confirmed in an exultant voice that they had been given the green light. Jonna was officially part of Julén's investigation and, once again, on loan from RSU to the County CID. As a trainee of course, he clarified.

Against all the rules and regulations, Walter was leading the investigation operations from his hospital bed. He would be forced to do that for a few weeks at least, according to an agitated Dr Täljkvist. Walter would also have access to a computer, which, although not connected to the police network, did have internet access. And he had his mobile, of course. Therefore, he would be able to lead the operations competently, and that had been sufficient for Julén, who had used her full range of contacts to staff the somewhat controversial investigation team.

"Where has the baby disappeared to now?" Jonna muttered as she saw the empty car. "Has he wandered off?"

She took out her mobile phone and called his number, noticing that the passenger door was not properly shut. After five rings, he answered.

"Jörgen?" she asked, as she heard something rasping on the other end.

"Iss ... kid ... nah ..." someone gasped.

"Where are you?" she asked.

Just breathless gasps in reply. It sounded as if someone was speaking in the middle of a storm. Then she heard faint, unfamiliar voices in the background. A second later, the call was cut off. When she redialled, she got his voicemail.

"HOW THE HELL could we miss the mobile?" Martin swore loudly and shook his head. This was the second time he had messed up a body search. The stress was making him forget elementary skills. To forget to frisk a subject for a mobile phone was as negligent as not taking a weapon from a bank robber. Luckily, Jörgen had not been able to say much after the body punch from Martin. And even if he had managed to communicate anything on the phone, he did not have a clue where he was or in what car he was lying.

Martin closed the boot of the car. Jörgen was lying in the foetal position with his back to the boot lid, presumably trying to conceal his mobile, so he had not seen Martin's face.

He now had to minimize every conceivable risk while still obtaining maximum benefit from every opportunity. The weak link in Martin's strategy was the lanky git sitting next to him. The question was whether he should continue to do business with him. Immediately after the shooting in Gnesta, it all seemed very clear. He had imagined a scenario with an obedient moron who did everything that Martin told him without thinking. Tor was now looking unreliable. He was always brooding. Perhaps the shock had worn off. Perhaps he was no longer an obedient moron, but a vengeful one instead. Late shall the sinner awaken, as the saying went.

Martin took a right turn into Långholmsgatan and then on over the Västerbron bridge. He sank deeper into thought. The situation would be coming to a head within the next hour, and his thoughts went over many possible scenarios.

At Brommaplan, he turned left and continued towards Ekerö island. After passing the Sånga-Säby sign, he drove down a gravelled road with thick forest on either side. After a few hundred metres, the road ran out and he stopped the car next to a ditch.

The light from the star-bright night sky lit up a small field in front of them.

"What are we doing here?" Tor asked.

He had been sitting quietly during the whole journey, contemplating his situation. He was an accomplice in a cop murder and would be a corpse as soon as the real cops got hold of him. Shot dead in some rigged shootout with a gun put in his hand and holes in his skull like a Swiss cheese. If the psycho sitting beside him didn't already have plans for him. Why did he need Tor now that he had the journalist in the boot? Was he going to kill two birds with one stone and finish off Tor here in the middle of nowhere? If Tor was going to make his move, he had better do it here and now. Even if he did not have a weapon. Just a switchblade. The place was perfect, and both Omar's hard drive and the ball of lard were in the car. Two possible sources of income. Jerry could always be trusted. This bloke was looking more like a loser's ticket or even a bullet with his name on it.

"We're going to get some information out of our friend in the boot," Martin answered and got out of the car.

"Why?" Tor asked. "He has the evidence in some fucking safety deposit box."

"I want to make an assessment of the situation myself," he said dryly.

Suddenly everything fell into place. The loose ends that Tor had tried to figure out suddenly connected with ominous precision, and he now knew why the cop had taken Jerry's gun. It was linked to the cop murder and as contaminated as a crackhead tart. Jerry had been holding the gun, but Tor would be the fall guy. The psycho was arranging a set-up here. First, he would shoot the bloke in the boot with Jerry's gun after he had made him talk, and then he would put it in Tor's hands so that he …

Death was slowly creeping up on him.

32

"GONE?" WALTER CRIED and knew that he was going to have a migraine shortly.

"Yes," Jonna said. "He wasn't in the car when I came out of the detention-cell block."

"Did you call his mobile?"

"Of course," Jonna answered, irritated. "And all I heard was someone gasping for breath and some strangers talking."

"Why would he want to leave?" Walter said. "He's been hanging around you like a back pack. Why would he leave?"

"We stopped off at his flat before I dropped off Tuva Sahlin," Jonna said, with a guilty conscience.

The phone went quiet. Probably the calm before the storm, she thought, and moved the phone a little farther from her ear.

"And why did you do that?" Walter finally asked, now in a stern voice.

"He needed to change clothes. He nagged me constantly about it and there was the lorry driver in the back seat complaining as well. In a moment of weakness, I let him persuade me."

"To give in to him was perhaps not such a good idea," Walter declared.

"You mean that somebody tailed us to the police station and took him by force?"

"Why not? The Finn and Headcase are both looking for our fairy queen."

"I saw no sign that we were being followed."

"No, but you can't always be sure. Good hunters are never seen. Were you never taught surveillance techniques at RSU?"

"Do you think that Headcase and Salminen would be any good at surveillance?"

"Probably not," Walter agreed. "But there might be others who are."

"Who could that be?" Jonna asked doubtfully. "The ones that shot at Jörgen on the street? The Albanians?"

"Hardly," Walter said.

"Who do you mean then?" Jonna asked, irritated. "Folke Uddestad, maybe?"

"No, not him either. But he may have hired someone more professional, some ex-KGB or GRU people. There are quite a few of them for hire nowadays."

"If that's the case, then we have quite a problem on our hands," Jonna said resignedly.

"That's one way to put it."

"To leave him in the car by himself wasn't my decision," Jonna said bitterly. "Since there were no explicit orders from Julén and yourself to allow him to enter the detention centre cell-block, there was no other option than to leave him in the car. And we were outside a police station."

Walter chuckled. "Let's write one-one in the fuck-ups score sheet then."

Jonna knew she had made a mistake letting Jörgen go back to his flat. She was getting overconfident, perhaps? Negligent? Hardly, but extremely unlucky if they had been shadowed by some retired Russian agents who then had the nerve to grab him outside a police station.

Commissioner Folke Uddestad was apparently quite innovative.

"We should send out a description of Jörgen," Jonna said, becoming overwhelmed by her sense of guilt.

Even though she did not care much for Jörgen, she felt ashamed of her naivety.

"Yours truly will take care of that," Walter said. "Now let's concentrate on bringing Leo Brageler in for questioning; he's on the wanted list now. I'm waiting for a search warrant from Julén. In the meantime, you have to go to Uppsala where you'll meet some local talent from their CID."

"I see, and who will lead the interrogation?" Jonna asked. "Should we bring him to the hospital, perhaps?"

"Lilja will lead the interrogation, with you assisting," Walter answered. "Inspector Lilja is about as proficient at interrogations as I am at cooking."

"How should I interpret that?"

"When I get out of Täljkvist's claws, I will treat you to some of my home cooking. Lilja's technique will give you a flavour of how that will taste."

So they had finally found the pattern. The fifth had been a failure, just as the first. But that meant nothing any more. He found less and less comfort in what he had done. She had stopped talking to him. He prayed for Cecilia to show herself, but she remained silent. To whom was he praying anyway? There is no God. Perhaps he was praying to his subconscious, so that it would speak to him in Cecilia's voice.

He was sitting in a park with no compass, no direction. He had no idea why he was sitting there. Perhaps he was looking for an answer; he just wanted to look Bror Lantz in the eyes.

The flat he lived in had become increasingly bleak. The house with his memories was occupied by the police. The end was getting closer and he knew what that meant. He and the others were experts on death. The soul was a chemical composition that together with electrical impulses constituted a sense of ego in the brain, nothing else. Like a memory card in a camera. The body was the camera. Empty and without content.

He knew he would never see her again. There was no life after death, but the scientific certainty of the end still comforted him. That, in the infinite darkness, he would be rid of his pain.

He was ready.

JUST AS THOMAS KOKK was about to switch off his desk lamp for the evening and make his way home to his sleeping family, he received an urgent email. It was from Forensics and concerned Hisham ibn Abd al-Malik. After a moment's hesitation, he sat back down in his chair and started to read the attached post-mortem report.

Thirty seconds later, he picked up the phone and dialled the number of his newly discovered blood brother, Agency Director Anders Holmberg. Thomas Kokk would not be with his family for many hours.

MARTIN BORG WALKED to the boot of the car and was about to open the boot lid when he heard a sound in the forest. At first, Martin thought it was a frightened animal. When he looked into the empty car, he realized that it was Tor who had run off into the woods. Martin stared thoughtfully at the thick forest.

Why had he run off now? Was that journalist story just a bluff?

There was no point in starting to hunt for Tor. Visibility was negligible and the forest was big enough to hide in. Tor did not present an immediate threat; he could not talk without implicating himself. If the idiot wanted to break their agreement here and now, there was nothing Martin could do to stop him.

In fifteen minutes, Martin would himself be gone, but first he would have a little talk with the guy in the boot.

EVERYTHING HAD HAPPENED so quickly. From out of nowhere, that Headcase had appeared and torn open the door to the Porsche. He had tried to pull out a terrified Jörgen, who instead had managed to open the passenger door on his side, throw himself out of it and run towards the detention-cell-block doorway. Just as safety had come within reach, everything had gone black.

When he came to his senses, he was lying in the boot of a car. He had difficulty breathing and a terrible pain in his back and head. Somewhere through the fog, he heard a familiar sound. At first, he could not place the familiar snatch of music, the schnapps song with little Santas clinking glasses, but after a while he remembered that it was the ringtone of his mobile phone. After fumbling in the dark, he managed to get the mobile phone from his trouser pocket and luckily find the right button. But all he could get out were cracked whispers.

Suddenly, the boot opened, and someone brutally tore the mobile phone from his hand.

His last chance of salvation was gone.

Jörgen was left in the dark and cold for some time until the boot opened again.

This time, a voice told him to pull his shirt over his head and to turn his face away. The voice was disguised, almost in a comical way. It was dark and deep, like a trailer voiceover for some Hollywood action film.

Jörgen shook with cold and the fear of death. He was still having problems breathing and it was not helped by the ice-cold air. Through a crack between his shirt buttons, he could distinguish a figure in the dark. He had something wrapped around his head to hide his face. Judging by his height, it was not Headcase.

"Where is the evidence on Folke Uddestad?" the voice muttered impatiently.

So the purpose of the kidnapping was now clear. These characters were not keen on small talk.

Jörgen did not know what to answer or even how to make himself heard. All his concentration was on keeping his breathing somewhat under control, while pain flashed between his lower back and his head. He tried to signal his inability to answer by waving a hand.

"Uddestad!" the voice boomed, even more impatiently.

Jörgen waved once again. This time, he managed to make a small sound. It sounded like a gasp.

"Let's try this one last time," the voice said, more composed.

Through the thin shirt fabric, Jörgen felt something cold and hard against his head. Shortly afterwards, he heard a familiar metallic sound.

Jörgen closed his eyes and prayed. He prayed to a god he had never believed in.

Suddenly, he created a sound. A sound left his lips between his tortured breaths.

"I can't hear you," the voice hissed. "Speak louder."

"I don't have anything anymore," Jörgen blurted out. Slowly, he was beginning to regain control of his breathing and his voice.

"Anything what?"

"The police have everything on Uddestad," Jörgen answered carefully. He had to struggle for each word.

"You mean RSU and that little cunt Jonna de Brugge who drives around with you in a Porsche?"

Jörgen nodded. How did he know that?

"What was the evidence?"

"A video and some photographs," Jörgen answered truthfully.

"What type of video?"

"A sex video," Jörgen explained.

The voice pressed the gun harder. Obviously, not the right answer.

"I secretly filmed myself and Folke during a sexual act. Then I used the video for blackmail."

"Is Uddestad really gay?" the voice asked in disbelief. The depth had disappeared and Jörgen could hear certain characteristics of what was probably his real voice.

"Yes, he is," Jörgen answered. "And he's also a transvestite. If that makes it any better."

It was quiet for a few seconds. Apparently, the voice was digesting Jörgen's answer.

Jörgen was shaking so much from the cold that his teeth began to chatter. If he did not die from a bullet in the head, he would soon die of pneumonia.

"Then it's time to wrap this up," the voice said and gestured with the pistol. "You are of no use to me any longer."

And that was the truth. If the journalist had given RSU the evidence on Uddestad, there was no more for Martin to gain. His knowledge of Uddestad's homosexuality and preference for women's clothing would not give him any advantages, not without solid proof.

"One last question," the voice said. "Not that it makes any difference. Out of curiosity, how is it that RSU knows about your, shall we say, secrets?"

Jörgen hesitated at first. Should he tell it like it was? What was to be gained by keeping quiet? Anything that would delay a bullet in the head was a blessing.

"I made a deal with them," Jörgen said.

"A deal?"

"Yes, they got all the evidence with myself and Uddestad in exchange for the full picture on the investigation into Drug-X."

"Drug-X?" the voice said, astonished.

"If you don't pull the trigger, I'll give you an exclusive on it."

"Do I look like a journalist?" the voice snapped.

"No, not exactly. We don't use force to get information," Jörgen said.

"No, but blackmail is apparently quite acceptable."

"Can we come to an agreement?" Jörgen continued. "My life for some information you can use?"

It was silent.

"Tell me, and I will decide afterwards," the voice said.

"Not until I'm safe," Jörgen said, beginning to feel that he had something with which to negotiate. The voice might possibly be interested in what he knew about the investigation into the drug and Leo Brageler.

Something else occurred to Jörgen. The masquerade. Why was he forced to pull his shirt over his head and why had the voice covered his face? Possibly because they were empty threats. Perhaps it was not his intention to liquidate Jörgen after all.

"You're lucky I'm in a good mood," the voice said. "So say what you have to say now, or don't say anything and we can end this now. I don't have all the time in the world."

"No, but I repeat my previous request to first have a measure of safety," Jörgen insisted and kept going through his chattering teeth. "You must understand by now that I can't trust someone who points a gun at my head and threatens to finish me off as if I were a temporary project."

"A classic dilemma," the voice laughed ironically. "In actual fact, I hadn't intended to kill you – hence the masked face and disguised voice. But to let you go free now without saying a word is clearly not acceptable. Either you start singing a pretty tune, and I'll keep the jacket around my head, or you don't and I'll reveal my face. In the latter case, I will be forced to liquidate you, as I'm sure you realize."

"How can I be sure you're not lying?"

"You're still alive," the voice said. "Isn't that proof enough?"

Jörgen thought hard for a few intense seconds. The voice was right.

But if Jörgen refused to talk, would he still survive? Perhaps it was worth testing the voice anyway.

"I'm not saying anything more now," Jörgen answered defiantly.

"I see," the voice said calmly, as if he had expected such an answer. "Let's meet each other halfway, then."

"How do we do that?"

"Well," the voice said, "the car you're lying in is stolen. It can't be traced to me or anyone else. You can stay locked in the boot."

"I'll freeze to death," Jörgen said anxiously.

"That is, you might say, the whole point. If you're lucky, then you'll make it. If you're unlucky, then you'll freeze to death. Your fate will be in somebody else's hands. Not in mine."

This was quite a different twist to the one Jörgen had expected. It was clear that the voice was not stupid. Jörgen became more confused.

"All right," Jörgen said. "I'll tell you everything I know. But first, answer me one question honestly."

The voice laughed. "Be my guest."

"Are you police or military?" Jörgen asked.

The voice hesitated for a few seconds. Jörgen observed that he had guessed correctly.

"What I am is of no concern," the voice replied tersely.

Better to trust a corrupt cop than Headcase and his Finnish bodybuilder, Jörgen thought. He had interviewed many police officers as a journalist and he recognized the jargon. This was definitely a policeman who also knew that Jonna worked for RSU.

"Say what you have to say or I'll lock the boot," the voice said.

Jörgen told him how he came to meet Walter Gröhn and Jonna de Brugge. How they started up a private investigation and where their subsequent findings had taken them. He also described how the idiots at SÄPO had derailed the investigation by linking it to a Swedish Islamist movement.

Jörgen took the opportunity to emphasize his role as a first-class investigative reporter. He described the traffic accident and the drunken director, the motive, and the apparent purpose of the crimes. That it was a research scientist at a biodynamics company who was responsible for the singularly advanced drug.

The voice listened patiently without saying a word. Jörgen could see, through the crack in his shirt, clouds of condensation from warm steady breathing making their way out from under the jacket. Obviously, this was a topic that he found very interesting.

When Jörgen had finally said everything that could be said, the man took his hand from the boot lid. He could almost hear the voice thinking.

Jörgen was now freezing so much that he was having speech problems again. His teeth shook like castanets and his speech was increasingly slurred.

"Do you know the name of the man behind the drug?" the voice said, turning towards Jörgen again.

"Of course," Jörgen stuttered. "If you let me get into ... the warm car, then I ... will even write it down ... for you."

"First the name," the voice said and put his hand on the boot lid again.

"All right ... take it ... easy," Jörgen stammered. "His name ... is Leo ... Brageler .... He lives ... near Uppsala."

"And is there a writ?"

Only police officers used the term "writ" instead of "arrest warrant". Jörgen was now sure that he was not in the military. Had Uddestad sent a colleague?

"Yes ... because when ... Tuva Sahlin was in protective custody ... Bror Lantz was also being picked up," Jörgen blurted.

"Picked up?"

"Yes ... he was not there ... when you ... kidnapped me. The new investigation ... not official yet. ... We were freelancing."

Jörgen tensed every muscle in his body as much as he could. Relaxed them for a few seconds, and tensed again. In that way, the brain could be tricked into thinking that the body was working and stayed warm. He had learnt the trick from one of his best friends, his father, who was a wildlife enthusiast. Jörgen did not know if it would work, but he could not think of a better idea.

Right now, he wished he were back in his childhood. Sitting next to his best friend, his dad, in front of a campfire deep in the Nacka Park national park. Like they used to do when they had made camp and pitched the tent. He wanted to hear the stories again. About the crazy squirrels that had molested a stray cat or the scabby fox that was attacked by a huge crow. He wanted to hear all the yarns and gossip again. He wanted to taste the sooty-black hot dogs speared on a freshly broken beech twig. He wanted to listen to his dad snoring so loudly that he kept the birds awake at night. He wanted to be in the woods again, not in the boot of a car, waiting to die. Tears welled up when he realized that all hope was finally gone.

33 MARTIN FOUND IT difficult to believe what the journalist was telling him, but there were far too many details that were not public knowledge to make his story anything but credible.

Whoever got their hands on Drug-X could, without doubt, become very powerful and very rich. If you could get hold of the brain behind the drug. Any morally bankrupt, corrupt state or shady organization would pay a fantastical price to have access to the architect and technology behind Drug-X. What a weapon the drug would be. Its use was limited only by the imagination. The drug would serve him and his comrades well; there was no doubt about that. It would speed up their progress by years.

He drummed his finger on the small pistol that once was Jerry Salminen's. Its connection to Ove Jernberg's death made it dangerous but also very useful. For Martin, the gun represented power and choice. The power to frame someone for a cop killing and the choice to frame whoever he wanted.

"Describe Leo Brageler's appearance," he ordered.

Jörgen stuttered out what he had heard about Brageler's looks from Tuva and her friends.

"And you're sure about this?" Martin checked.

Jörgen tried to answer, but did not have the strength.

Martin pulled Jörgen out of the boot and put him up against a tree, facing away from the car. Then he tied Jörgen's hands with a towrope from the car and looped it around the tree trunk a few times.

"If you shout long and hard enough, someone will probably hear you," he said. Then he walked away and sat in the car.

Jörgen heard the engine start and the car skid away on the muddy road.

When Jörgen could no longer hear the car, he started to yell. At first, he could only manage hoarse whispers, but after a while, he managed to muster enough strength to hear his own voice echo in the treetops. The shirt was still drawn over his head and, even though it was pitch black, it would have been easier if his eye was not blindfolded by the shirt fabric.

The cold penetrated into his bone marrow, and fatigue drew him farther from consciousness. After a while, his eyelid wanted to close, but he knew that he could not let that happen. He would never wake up again, and the last thing he would see would be the inside of his shirt.

He thought about Sebastian. What he was doing in South America and how far they were from each other. How much he missed him and the first thing he would do when they met again. His thoughts strayed to the news desk. What were they doing at the moment? Did they have any leads about what had happened? He strongly doubted it.

He thought for a while about the story, which now had a really nice added bonus if he survived this. There had been a risk that he would not be believed.

Slowly, Jörgen moved into a more pleasant state. Without moving a single muscle, the coldness became heat. Everything around him lost significance. Not even Sebastian or the exclusive story mattered anymore. He let go of all the things he thought were important. Of life itself. Of all the things he wanted and could not have. He had finally come home, to the warm campfire and, by his side, his best friend, Dad.

TO MARTIN'S GREAT satisfaction, Bror Lantz did not have an ex-directory number. Thirty seconds later, the operator had already found his address and home number.

Martin parked the car on a hill, a few hundred metres from Lantz's address. He had a full view of the house without being seen himself. He now had to think like Leo Brageler: hunted, on the run, and with a last chance to destroy judge Bror Lantz.

Had Martin's colleagues put the house under surveillance and were they, like Martin, waiting for Brageler to show up? Perhaps they had set a trap. There was a light in the window, but nobody answered the phone. To go to Brageler's house would be pointless. The police were certainly already there, perhaps waiting to ambush him. If he was smart, which Martin assumed he was, he would stay away from his house.

Martin got out of the car and walked towards Lantz's house. He pulled up the collar of his jacket and put his hands in his pockets. After about fifty metres, he passed a blue Volvo V70 that was illegally parked. From habit, he routinely looked through the tinted windscreen and glimpsed something red blinking at the bottom of the car's central dashboard. The red and green lights were a familiar sight. The CID or RSU were already here.

After another dozen metres or so, a new car appeared. A white Saab 9-5. This time, there were two people in the car. One was a blonde woman in her thirties with a ponytail. The other was a man with a short haircut and a leather jacket with shoulder epaulettes. Typical surveillance police. As predictably dressed as Santa on Christmas Eve.

Martin quickly passed by the car and felt their eyes burning into his back, even though he knew he didn't have to worry. He looked nothing like the description of Brageler. And no one outside SÄPO knew what he looked like. That was the advantage of working with SÄPO. He was anonymous. Now that the investigation had been taken away from SÄPO, the surveillance on Lantz was being carried out by officers from the local police.

There was obviously nothing for Martin to do here. He had arrived too late for the party. It was just a matter of time before the officers pulled in Brageler.

Two setbacks in less than one hour. The Uddestad train had left the station, and now Brageler's. All he had to be happy about was Omar's hard drive. Perhaps he should not be greedy and just make the best of what was on the hard drive. He took a side road, planning to circle back to the car so that he would avoid the two surveillance vehicles. After a few hundred metres, he arrived at a park.

Martin turned onto a dimly lit gravel path that snaked its way through different types of thick bush. After passing some pines and shrubs scattered on either side of the gravel path, he arrived at a poorly lit sandpit with wooden benches near the longer sides, where watchful mothers sat during the day and guarded their little treasures at play. One of the benches was in the shadow of a pine tree.

After he had passed the last bench, he saw the silhouette of a man. Martin started at the sudden encounter. Without making a sound, the figure sat on the bench in the shadows, immobile.

His right hand instinctively went under his jacket and gripped his gun. He carried on, but stopped after a few metres. Who sits in the middle of a park late in the evening and stares into the dark in silence?

Surveillance?

Hardly. They are never that discreet.

Martin continued walking. Moonlight suddenly lit up the park bench. In a fraction of a second, his luck had changed. Sitting on the bench was the perfect match to the journalist's description of Leo Brageler.

KENT ANDERSSON AND Robban Roth of the Uppsala Police Violent Crimes Unit welcomed Jonna outside the reception desk of the main entrance to the Uppsala police headquarters. Both of the middle-aged policemen looked at the once-immaculate Porsche in awkward silence. The doubt in their eyes was enough to guess at what they were thinking. Jonna explained that it was on loan from the Surveillance Unit and that it had suffered some minor parking damage. Neither of the policemen seemed to accept that explanation. After completing the formalities, they sat in Inspector Anderson's service vehicle, an Audi A6. It wasn't a Porsche, but if she found it acceptable, then Jonna was welcome to ride along. After some comments on sports cars in general, RSU and people from Stockholm specifically, they had arrived at Leo Brageler's house. Two chequered police cars had already arrived and the mandatory blue-and-white police tape was neatly set up around the house.

Jonna got out of the car and looked at the mustard-yellow house, which dated from the turn of the century. It had two stories and two small towers on either side. The window frames were painted white and, in the style of the period, ornamental carvings sat below the roof fascia boards, indicative of a love of carpentry. In some places, the paint was peeling; in others, it was bare to the wood. The large garden that surrounded the house was neglected and overgrown. The stone tiles up to the main door were covered in grass. It was as if the house had been abandoned for years and no one was maintaining it.

Roth waved Jonna through the door. A stench of decay hit her as she walked into the hallway.

"Not exactly Café Opera, eh?" Roth joked, waiting for Jonna's first reaction to the acrid odour. He was obviously expecting to see a nauseated rookie who turned back at the door. She would not give him that pleasure. No more sudden exits and vomiting for her. What could be worse than Mrs Ekwall's brain tissue on the floor?

"I once had a meal at one of Uppsala's finest restaurants," Jonna said, looking around the big hall. She really had to steel herself against the bad smell of the house. "You know the one: not so far from the main square, Stortorget." She breathed with short breaths, which deadened the stench a little. "The smell in here reminds me a little of that place."

Roth then dropped the subject of restaurants and smells. Instead, he continued into the house towards one of its many rooms.

After visiting the source of the stench, the kitchen and piles of rotting rubbish bags under the sink, Inspector Anderson called Jonna to a big room with a swivel armchair in the centre of the room. As Jonna entered the room, she got goose bumps. She saw a room that was straight out of an Hollywood film. Every millimetre of the walls was covered with pictures and photographs depicting a woman and a little girl. A light-haired woman with lively eyes and her smiling daughter. The walls were decorated with hundreds of pictures of the girl and the mother at different ages. Some of the photographs had been enlarged to almost poster size; others were as small as passport photographs. Many of the photographs were taken with horses.

Jonna went up to one of the photographs. The image was a close-up. She saw the girl, whose name was Cecilia and who would never be older than ten, holding an ice-cream. It was summer and her face was beaming. Her eyes sparkled with the light, and around her smile were traces of ice-cream. In the background, a light-blue ocean stretched endlessly and, on the horizon, there were white sailing boats. She stood on the beach. Perhaps she had been swimming. Her long hair looked wet, a little messed up and half-dried by the sun. Her bare shoulders were red and were testament to the fact that she had been wearing a swimsuit or a bikini. Perhaps she was sunburned, perhaps they were abroad.

Jonna would never know. The girl in the picture was dead. All that was left of her was the photographs and the memories of those who loved her.

34 THE FIRST THING that Walter did once he was discharged by the cantankerous Dr Täljkvist was to visit Jörgen Blad, who had been admitted to Danderyd Hospital. The journalist had miraculously escaped death.

For almost two days, he had been tied to a tree and badly frozen in the Färingö forest outside Stockholm. He had been falling in and out of consciousness. Jörgen's prayers had finally been answered by an orienteering enthusiast, who had got lost and almost stumbled over the lifeless journalist while looking for the final checkpoint. He had been three kilometres off course, which had saved Jörgen's life.

Jörgen made his statement to Walter about the kidnapping the day after he had been admitted into the hospital. He described how he had been forced to tell everything he knew about Leo Brageler to the inquisitive kidnapper to avoid execution by a bullet in the head. He explained why he suspected that his kidnapper was a policeman and that he had wanted the evidence on Folke Uddestad, but instead got all the information that Jörgen had on Drug-X. The kidnapper was satisfied with that and, to thank Jörgen, he had tied him to a tree and left him to die.

They now knew that Tor "Headcase" Hedman was involved, as it was he who had jumped Jörgen in the car. But Walter did not have a clue as to who the so-called "policeman" could be. He knew that there were members of the police who crossed the line into criminal activity. But Walter had already ruled out

Uddestad himself having kidnapped Jörgen. A county police commissioner did not get involved in that type of activity, even though he had some doubts after seeing the video in which Jörgen Blad had been drilling Uddestad in all the different ways that type of sexuality had to offer.

Walter also knew that Hedman's handpicked partner, Jerry Salminen, was dead. The investigation into the police murder at Gnesta had confirmed that one of the charcoaled corpses' adornments had belonged to the Finnish citizen Jerry Ola Salminen. The other corpse was Omar Khayyam, owner of the warehouse facility.

If they could only get their hands on Headcase, then they would solve the "policeman" riddle, which was considered to be quite a high priority. There were too many civil servants losing their morals. The only problem was that Hedman had evaporated into thin air. Not a trace of him could be found. It was as if he had never existed.

"WELCOME BACK, WALTER," Chief Inspector David Lilja greeted him and stretched out his hand. "How's the brain?"

Walter studied Lilja's outstretched hand. Not so long ago, he had wanted to see Walter in front of an investigative tribunal, and now he was greeting him like a conquering hero. His hypocrisy was setting a new record.

Finally, Walter took Lilja's hand and squeezed it until the knuckles turned white. "Thank you," he answered and put on a smile as false as Lilja's warm concern. "My brain is just fine and has been given a complete overhaul. I have a new way of looking at things now."

"Really?" Lilja said, raising an eyebrow. "What could that be?"

"That I like my job," Walter replied.

"Someone with influence obviously has taken you under their wing," Lilja said and stroked his right hand gingerly.

"Even the police union has opposed the charges against you. It has been rather stormy around here lately."

"I can imagine," Walter said.

CHIEF PROSECUTOR ÅSA Julén closed the door to her office and politely showed Walter and Jonna to the visitors' chairs.

"One always has to seek the middle ground," she began and did not sound too disillusioned about it. "SÄPO and SKL will investigate the origin of Drug-X and we will proceed with the search for Leo Brageler. As soon as we are done with Brageler, SÄPO will take him. I have made a promise to the Agency Director himself."

"SÄPO?" Walter said, with a little scepticism. "I wonder how well they'll succeed this time."

"In any case, that's how it is going to be," Julén brusquely declared. "We have other problems."

"Such as?" Jonna asked.

"It's not certain that I can get a conviction for manslaughter since he's only indirectly involved in the murders. In fact, I don't believe he can even be convicted for the charge of grievous bodily harm. It's a matter of principle. This is a legal no man's land. How am I to prove that he has drugged someone with a compound that doesn't exist and that supposedly makes the drugged person commit evil acts? Even if I could prove that case, it's not Brageler who is committing the murders himself. At the most, he is a tenuous accomplice, in the eyes of the law."

"So you're saying that the only ones being prosecuted are the ones who are not responsible for the murders?" Jonna said. "That's Sjöstrand, Ekwall, Lindkvist and Lantz?"

Julén nodded.

"But the one responsible for the murders is, in fact, Leo Brageler," Jonna said, answering her own question.

"Yes," Julén sighed. "No one can guarantee the legal outcome of this case. Neither Sjöstrand, Ekwall, Lindkvist nor Lantz have suffered any injury from the drug. They're physically healthy, even if their mental state is in poor shape as a result of their actions. Possibly, we can establish the existence of what SKL and their forensic scientists say is the scar tissue caused by the drug. In other words, a physical injury. But how much damage that injury causes the victim, we just don't know. It could go as far as having to drop all charges against Brageler. We have no evidence that it was he who poisoned the food. Just some witness statements from the youngsters who socialized with Malin Sjöstrand that describe Brageler's appearance."

"But that's outrageous!" Jonna cried. "The CCTV from the ferry, then? You can see Brageler go on board and then leave the ship."

She failed to mention that the reason she had studied the CCTV evidence so carefully was a certain Alexander Westfeldt who moonlighted as a security guard. According to the personnel manager, he was studying to be an archaeologist. Jonna was planning an interview with him later, for background information on Brageler's visit.

"It's possible that Sjöstrand, Ekwall, Lindkvist and Lantz can file civil lawsuits against Brageler and get a few hundred thousand each in damages, but that's by no means a certain outcome."

Silence fell in the office of Åsa Julén.

"Remember that we were able to prevent two incidents at least," Walter said, breaking the silence. "If Jonna had not lifted Sahlin and the lorry driver off the love boat, more than just one muscle-bound cell guard would have been slapped about. Several people would probably have lost their lives."

"Yes. Brageler was almost successful with the fifth attempt," Jonna said. "Sahlin went berserk and attacked one of the cell guards exactly one day after she was put into protective custody. A dispute over a toothbrush triggered an uncontrollable rage. One of the guards thought she had rabies. The same thing happened to the lorry driver."

Walter smiled and agreed. "She knocked out no fewer than two of the guard's teeth. That's not bad for a woman of one and a half metres in height with a match weight of forty-eight kilos."

"Brageler's intention was that she would come home and become psychotic. Apparently, it's possible to delay the effect of the drug," Jonna said.

"But why Sahlin and not Bror Lantz?" Julén asked. "He failed twice. Lantz was a failure. The taxi incident was not according to his plan, was it?"

"No, it was definitely not what he planned," Walter said. "The train was a few hours late, and the rage attack should have happened once he arrived at home. The wife was probably the intended victim."

"So why didn't he finish off Lantz first?"

"No one knows that for certain yet," Walter said. "It might have been coincidence or some other factor. It must have been difficult to observe these people and their daily routines. A full-time job that would have required infinite patience."

"And we're sure about Brageler's motive?" Julén asked.

Jonna nodded. "As you can see from the photos in one of Brageler's rooms, he was completely obsessed with his family and their deaths. He must have had an implacable hate for society and the court that acquitted Sonny Magnusson."

Julén nodded, meditating. "But who is Brageler, really? That he worked with …" She put her reading glasses on and read something from a notepad, "Biodynamics & Genetic Research, that we know. But why didn't he just kill the members of the jury from the District Court as revenge? Why all the bother of drugging them?"

Julén paused.

"Try to get under his skin," she continued. "I want to know more about the man named Leo Brageler. Not that it helps me directly in the investigation. At best, there may be some character traits that could be used against him in a trial. I just want to know with whom we are dealing. Furthermore, you people at RSU are supposed to be good at that sort of thing, profiling people, I mean."

Jonna put a pile of papers on Julén's desk. "It's already been done," she said, a touch of triumph in her voice. "No less than five RSU analysts and profilers have worked on Brageler for the past week. I think we know him just as well as he knows himself."

"I thought as much," Julén chuckled and started to leaf through the pile of documents.

"And?"

Jonna did not need to read from the file. She knew every word in the pile that Julén was casually browsing through. After living with Brageler and his family twenty-four hours of every day for the past week, she was as familiar with his life as she was the gears of her Porsche. She had spent her time, sleeping and waking, thinking of Brageler, eating dinner with him, and almost becoming obsessed with his life and his family. Dreaming of his daughter with ice-cream in her hand and the sun shining in those lively eyes.

"Leo Brageler was considered to be a very gifted child," Jonna began. "He jumped a few classes in secondary school and had, by the age of sixteen, almost attained medical-school proficiency. He was never interested in the medical profession, however, and focused exclusively on research, where the challenges were greater. At the age of twenty, he had written a number of papers on DNA and stem-cell research. He was published in some journals, but was notoriously uninterested about showing himself in public. He was, plain and simply, shy. When he was twenty-two, he was employed by BGR, which was then a small, unknown research laboratory with about thirty employees. After only two years, he was responsible for the company's research department, which had grown after a number of acquisitions."

Julén listened, doodling in a notepad.

"At the age of thirty-five, he married lab assistant Anna Davidsson. One year later, they had Cecilia. After that, Brageler became very extroverted and socialized a lot, which is unusual for people with extremely high intellects."

"That's not information that I and the Chief Prosecutor are interested in," Walter interrupted.

Julén looked up from her notepad and the doodle that had become a sunflower. After a few seconds, she returned to her sunflower and waved at Jonna to continue.

"Brageler worshipped his daughter and became increasingly overprotective. Finally, she couldn't do anything without his permission. He would sometimes ring the nursery staff five or six times a day to check that they were taking care of Cecilia. At one point, Anna apparently was going to leave him. According to friends, she could not stand his need to control his daughter's life. He loved her so intensely that it became a problem for both her and his daughter."

"I knew it," Walter laughed.

"Knew what?" Jonna asked.

"That he had a behavioural problem. As you yourself said, superintelligent people have at least one psychosocial problem."

"I've never said that," Jonna objected.

"There are those who with normal, or even lower than average, intelligence who have the same problem," Julén said. "There's nothing unusual about that. My mother was very overprotective with me when I was a child. And she never stopped being overprotective. It just manifested itself in different ways as I got older."

Walter sank back in his chair and folded his arms.

"In any case," Jonna continued, "it seems that it was his driving force and his hate grew out of it."

"From his love of the daughter?"

"The overprotection," Walter corrected her.

"Exactly," Jonna replied. "His control mania developed into a new obsession: his anger towards those who, in his eyes, had taken his daughter from him. The death of his daughter also took away his control – not just over his daughter, but control over himself. His obsession moved into a new, more intense phase after Cecilia's death."

"He shifted into anger mode," Walter said, standing up. "I would have done the same. But instead of messing around with drugs, I would have beaten the shit out of the jury in a more honourable way." The room went quiet. Images of Martine suddenly burned into Walter's retinas. He had to sit down.

"That's also puzzling," Jonna said. "The way that he seeks revenge is also unusual. He wants to achieve satisfaction by making others suffer the same way that he does."

"An eye for an eye, a tooth for a tooth," Walter said, leaning against Julén's desk.

"You could say that," Jonna said. "Old Testament justice. To simply kill them would be too merciful."

"Is he religious?" Julén wondered, looking up from her notepad. "All we need is some crazy sect attacking us too."

"No," Jonna replied. "There's nothing to suggest that. On the contrary, he left the Swedish Church when he was eighteen."

"As I did," Walter added. "You save a few hundred every month and avoid the good fathers, who can't help you book your ticket to heaven anyway."

"Are you sure of that?" Julén asked.

"If you can prove the contrary, I'll go back to church," Walter countered.

Julén shook her head. "On the subject of church," she said, "what's the significance of the plaster angels that he leaves behind? What do they symbolize? What was the point?"

Jonna shrugged. "I really don't know. Perhaps he wanted to announce that Death would soon come to visit or something like that."

"Sounds a bit theatrical," Walter said.

Åsa Julén put her pen down. The sunflower was perfected. "A warrant for Brageler has been sent to Interpol and it will be hard to make a solid case before we find him. I must also verify my reasoning concerning the legal aspects of the case with the Justice Department. As I said earlier, all efforts are focused on this case right now. But there's one issue I need to take up with you before we go our separate ways."

"Dinner for three?" Walter suggested, but was met with the evil eye from the other side of the desk.

"Before we're finished with each other," Julén said, emphasizing the words, which made it sound ominous, "I want to know what underworld connections Folke Uddestad has. Your so-called agreement with the journalist Jörgen Blad was to bring some light on that question in exchange for information on the investigation."

"That was fantasy from beginning to end," Walter stated. "There's nothing to suggest that Uddestad was involved with criminals. Other than hiring the thugs who almost wasted the journalist and leaking information so that he wouldn't publish the photos. Which, of course, is a crime."

"I don't think the Swedish police force can afford any more scandals right now. If you see what I mean," Julén said, leaning forwards.

"No, I don't see," Walter pretended. "Please explain it to me."

"The video and photographs will be confiscated as 'forgeries' used to libel of a high-ranking official in a sensitive position. There will be no repercussions for Uddestad and no information will circulate outside of this room. Is that clear enough?"

Walter laughed. "Nothing surprises me anymore. As they say in the States, 'same shits, different taste'," he said, walking towards the door. He couldn't actually afford to object more than that. He himself had just been saved by the same type of backroom negotiations.

Jonna smiled at Walter's attempt at English humour.

AGENCY DIRECTOR ANDERS HOLMBERG was more than satisfied. He had succeeded in getting Åsa Julén to be sensible and to return the investigation of Drug-X to SÄPO. However, the honour of arresting Leo Brageler would fall to the local police. The only thing that disturbed Holmberg was that it was the County CID who had found the crucial piece of the puzzle.

In time, the media would calm down, and the outcome had been mostly positive, if not for the suspect who had died in police custody. To his chagrin, that story would be buzzing around the media like the proverbial fly in the soup. Forensics had found a well-known American interrogation barbiturate in the body of the deceased, which, under no circumstances, was to become public knowledge.

Martin Borg had blamed his colleague Ove Jernberg, who supposedly had obtained the drug from the owner of the Gnesta property. Holmberg had also been pressured from higher-ups to exonerate Borg for the SÄPO mishaps. Thomas Kokk was surprised over certain individuals' interest in Borg's well-being. Holmberg had been forced to make some changes to both the official and unofficial versions in order to accommodate the individuals pressuring him. It would be Jernberg who took all the blame.

Kokk looked at Holmberg on the other side of the desk. The last week had been the toughest test that he had faced during his entire career as a policeman. To blame someone who could not defend himself, someone who had been killed in the line of duty, must be one of his most dishonourable acts. He was just as surprised over the degree of favouritism within the authority. That it existed, he knew; he was a beneficiary from it. The esprit de corps within the police force was strong and those who had different opinions were quickly frozen out. But the fact that Borg suddenly had so many supporters high up took him by surprise. He had an uncomfortable feeling that he was being denied some crucial information.

"I don't think Martin Borg has told us everything," Kokk began.

"It makes no difference anymore," Holmberg said abruptly. "Jernberg will take the fall. We have to throw the media a bone and he's it. Before we release the dead Muslim's body, the post-mortem report must be modified and all traces of that American truth serum must be removed from the body."

"His story is quite far-fetched ..."

"Once again, Thomas," Holmberg said in a stern voice, "if this gets out, there'll be a bloodbath in the media. The journalists will mow us down like the paper targets on the shooting range. The Muslim died of a heart attack. Jernberg was shot during a police operation. Period."

"County CID has given us the name of a man who could be the one who shot Jernberg in Gnesta," Kokk said. "The partner of the deceased Jerry Salminen. His name is Tor Hedman. But Borg's description doesn't fit him. According to Borg, he was a short, thin foreigner. Hedman is a tall Swede. I think Borg ..."

"Thomas!" Holmberg cut him off and looked him straight in the eye. "Don't lift any more rocks now. We're riding out the worst media storm since Olof Palme. Let the storm blow itself out and you'll see day-to-day operations get back to normal very soon. Some things are just not meant to see the light of day."

Holmberg was presumably right. The problem was that Kokk had lost his moral compass. And he did not know in which direction he was heading.

"Now we must focus on getting hold of Drug-X," Holmberg continued. "How it is manufactured and how that Leo Brageler was able to disperse it. It could be a dangerous weapon in the wrong hands."

Kokk nodded. Then he stood up and went back to his office. He sat down heavily behind his desk and gazed at the photograph of his family by his computer screen. Within a minute, he was going to make one of the most difficult decisions of his life.

A LONG CHAIN of events had taken Martin Borg to his current position. A drunk on the wrong side of the road for a fraction of a second and Martin's life was thrust into unknown territory. A new chapter in the book of his life.

He had followed Leo Brageler from the park bench to a flat in Södermalm. According to the list of names in the building entrance, it seemed to be a sub-let flat. He had used the unimaginative name of "Eriksson".

Martin's plan was evolving. When he had got the information from the chatty journalist, the plan was simple. To save his own skin and ensure that he could continue to work on the strategy that his comrades had adopted. But the situation had changed. New opportunities had surfaced and he had been given one chance in a million. If he did not take it, then he was no better than the fools that he despised.

He was playing a high-stakes game now. First, he was going to use the names on Omar's hard drive to get reinstated. Beginning tonight, he would start making calls and see how useful the names were. Afterwards, he would be making a house call at Mr Eriksson's.

A sense of invincibility rushed through Martin. The power the drug had been proven to have could change the balance of power in the world.

Martin was puzzled that Brageler did not seem to understand that he could make money on something so advanced. Instead, he went around hunting court employees just because a drunk had killed his family. Presumably, the brilliant scientist had cracked and become irrational. There was a thin line between genius and insanity.

The question now was: who else was involved in the research for Drug-X? Leo Brageler could hardly have developed something so sophisticated by himself. Martin needed to get back into the investigation. He needed to be able to search the databases and keep informed. There was little time to waste, and he would get only one chance.

35 WALTER LOOKED OUT of the window of his office. It was Christmas Eve and, from the darkened sky, large white snowflakes were sailing slowly towards the ground. Lately, he had been afflicted by a melancholy bordering on depression. Despite help from the National Crime Squad, and an arrest warrant issued by Interpol, Leo Brageler had disappeared as if the earth had swallowed him up. After two months of intense searching, they did not have an inkling as to the whereabouts of Leo Brageler or Drug-X.

His only comfort in the situation was that SÄPO was doing just as badly. Neither the German corporation nor the Uppsala company knew about anything that had to do with Drug-X and instead attributed it to research that had been carried out without the company's knowledge. Brageler was the head of research at Uppsala and had the means to undertake research outside management control. There were no co-workers to question. None of Brageler's colleagues had the faintest idea what SÄPO was talking about.

SÄPO was strangely passive when it came to tracking down Drug-X. It was as if their investigation was running in first gear, which reminded him of when he joined the Palme investigation team which had a mediocre level of enthusiasm and dedication. True to form, Walter had also managed to create a new enemy. This time at SÄPO. A certain Martin Borg had taken a dislike to Walter and the feeling was mutual.

Lilja was, however, under his thumb. He had closed ranks and was even more manageable than before the big role reversal. That Lilja licked boots was no surprise, but that he kept so many pairs polished was a big surprise to Walter. But as long as he backed Walter up, there was no sense in getting wound up. He would soon need Lilja's support, given the developments at SÄPO and the upcoming struggle with Borg.

Walter looked at the clock. It was six-thirty and he was beginning to feel hungry. He gazed at his desk, which was piled with heaps of paper. Murder and beatings by the hour. It never ended. Not even on Christmas Eve, the biggest family holiday of the year.

He walked down the empty corridor towards the lifts. There were not many people still in the office, or even in the police station. Some were at home on call. But the majority were off and gorging themselves on the Christmas ham and schnapps and staring at the bald announcer from Gothenburg as he lit candles on national TV. Thirty minutes later, Walter opened his fridge and opened a tin of pea soup and put the soup in the microwave. He turned on the stereo, and from the speakers flowed the music of Chuck Berry. After warming the pea soup, he parked himself on the sofa with the plate on his knee. He dropped a large dollop of mustard onto the plate and ceremoniously consumed his meal. It was, after all, Christmas Eve and then, you should eat with dignity. Even if it was just tinned pea soup.

In many ways, it was the same as last Christmas. But then he had also eaten the traditional pork *Prince* sausages and ready-made meatballs. He had fallen asleep by ten, after two beers and a bad film that he could not remember. As a Christmas present, he had given himself an iPhone, a small miracle of technology that you could even make phone calls with.

This year, it was a completely different Christmas present. Santa had been to Walter's house with a trip. On New Year's

Eve, he was off to the Azores, of all places on the planet. A minute group of islands in the middle of the Atlantic where it was cold even in the summertime. After seeing a wildlife programme about the Azores, he had, for some reason, booked a trip. Why, he did not know. Perhaps because there would not be any package-holiday tourists there. Or because it was an exotic place with a lot of pensioners.

Walter had just taken his fifth spoonful of the pea soup when the doorbell rang. He froze with the spoon in his mouth. It was Christmas Eve. Santa had already been and gone. But he could have heard wrong. One of those phantom ringing sounds in his head. It had happened before. And after Darth Vader's butchery in his head, it was only going to get worse.

He waited, listening to the silence. But then there was another ring. This time, it was for real.

Walter opened the door and was greeted by two plastic carrier bags. He recognized the hands holding the bags, as well as the knitted hat that stuck up behind it.

"I heard that you normally celebrate Christmas Eve with yourself and a telephone call," the voice began. "Is that really true?"

"What are you doing here?" Walter asked, surprised.

"Are you alone?" Jonna asked, putting down the bags.

Walter coughed a dry cough. "Yes. Who else would be here on Christmas Eve?"

"Have you eaten yet?"

"Not really," Walter lied.

"What do you say to some homemade Christmas food?"

"Well, there's always room for that," he said and made a mental note to put the pea soup in the bin. "Don't you have a family to celebrate Christmas with?"

"Yes, but to call it celebrating is a bit of an overstatement. Besides, I've just come from them. And the way my family celebrates Christmas, I can only take about one hour at the most. I can explain another time."

"I see," Walter said.

"Good, now can I come in or shall we stand here and small-talk a little longer?"

Two hours later, Walter was vegging out on the sofa in front of the bald announcer from Gothenburg, whose candles had burned all the way down to the candlesticks. He looked at Jonna who was holding a wine glass filled with a divine red liquid. He himself was finishing off his fourth glass of wine, an absolutely delicious red wine from Portugal that she had brought with her. Together with the extremely well-made Christmas food, Walter had gorged himself.

"So what are you up to at RSU nowadays?" he asked, turning the wine glass casually.

"Nothing that has to do with Leo Brageler," Jonna said regretfully. "Organized crime. It has moved onto the internet big time."

"Sounds exciting," Walter said, smothering a yawn. The food and the wine had made him a bit drowsy.

Jonna twirled her wine glass. "He must have repressed a lot of emotions," she said.

"If you're talking about Brageler, then I can't really blame him."

"No, perhaps not. I wonder where he is now."

"He has probably fled the country," Walter said without sounding convinced.

"According to SÄPO's investigation into the company he worked for, he must have done his research outside the company premises. At least, that is the term they used. Apparently, he had modified a substance that was intended for a completely different purpose but that already had the basic properties that he needed."

"I'm not convinced he acted all by himself," Walter said.

"You think that others in the company were involved?"

"Not necessarily," Walter said. "Why not over the internet? Just look at how that slippery eel Serge Wolinsky works with his hacker buddies."

"Do you think the compound has spread that far already?" Jonna asked, with a worried look in her eyes.

"You can never rule that out. We should hope that it isn't the case. It would be a drag to have to do prison time for murder at my age," Walter said with a wry grin. "What's invented can't be uninvented."

"No, I suppose that's true," Jonna agreed and sank down in the sofa. "At least, Jörgen Blad finally got his exclusive."

"He certainly did. And then some," Walter said. "He made it out alive and became a celebrity within a few weeks."

"He's apparently publishing a book about the incident as well."

"That doesn't surprise me in the least," Walter said. "Nowadays, every soap actor and politician is writing a book."

They sat in silence for a while. Then Walter remembered a telephone conversation that he happened to overhear.

"Why do you call your father 'Jockum' and not 'Daddy'?" he asked, immediately regretting the question.

She was silent. The only sound was the TV announcer from Gothenburg blowing out the candles.

"Every family has its problems," she said, without taking her eyes off the TV. "It's just the degree of magnitude that separates them."

"So true, so true," Walter said in a soft voice, trying to mitigate his clumsiness.

"To answer your question, Jockum is not my biological father. And my family is anxious not to advertise that fact."

Walter smiled self-consciously. "No?"

"I am adopted," Jonna said.

Walter nodded without saying a word. The timer on the TV indicated that the show would soon be over.

WALTER CAREFULLY ADJUSTED the blanket over his unexpected guest and turned off the light in the living room. The night had turned into morning and she had fallen asleep on Walter's sofa. He could hear faint breathing and he could see how her eyelids twitched as she dreamed. For as long as he could remember, and that was a long time, he had not had such a pleasant Christmas Eve. They had talked like father and daughter. Agreed on most things, but not all. There was, after all, three decades between them. They had talked about everything, from work issues to political ones. After an hour, he gave up trying to make her into a political leftie, as he was himself. She had opinions that were just as strong as Walter's. She was not a supporter of any party; instead, she wandered in a liberated no man's land, taking the best ideas from many parties. He had to take his hat off to her open and broad-minded way of thinking. He understood why RSU was so interested in this new generation of talented recruits. They were as unbiased and curious as Walter was old and narrow-minded.

Time had flown by, just as it always did in the company of good friends.

He crept into his unmade bed and put his hands behind his head. The shadows from the window danced on the ceiling, and he wondered if they would return tonight. The faces that never disappeared. The faces of the dead.

He closed his eyes and felt the wine permeate his body. The bed rocked gently as if he was anchored in a bay and gently swayed in a soft breeze. He felt content. Jonna was like him in many ways, the way he had been thirty years ago. Just as ambitious and full of life. Just as naive and innocent.

But, most of all, she resembled Martine a lot.

Sometimes life does not turn out the way you expect and he had to find happiness here and now. For the first time, he felt that he could reconcile himself to the loss of Martine. If it was the wine, it mattered not. Tomorrow morning, he would wake her with a nice breakfast on the sofa. Omelette and toast with marmalade. And coffee, brewed from freshly ground beans.

Walter turned over and switched the radio on. From the speakers, barely audible, U2's "Magnificent" poured out. He closed his eyes and let himself be swept away by the long, soft chord changes. Now. Now he could finally sleep.

EPILOGUE

WITH NO WINDOWS, the room was in permanent darkness and was cold. Damp ran down the uneven, stone walls and onto the floor. The mattress he laid on was never completely dry. He did not know how long he had been here. Two, perhaps three months. Time had lost all significance. The interrogations and beatings were becoming increasingly vicious. Sometimes electric shocks, sometimes drugs. Most of them were old, close to the end of their lives but driven by an implacable hatred. He did not know who they were, where they came from, or why they were so determined to discover what he had created. He understood that his only way out of here was as a corpse. They had not hidden their faces.

But he was already prepared and feared nothing. He would have ended it himself if they had not found him first. He cursed his mistake. Leo Brageler observed his wounds in the dim light that found its way under the door crack. The end would be a liberation. Not a day passed by that he did not dream himself away from the torture. To simply disappear into the infinite darkness. He prayed to be dead. Just like Anna and his beloved Cecilia.

Don't miss the action-packed sequel to *Anger Mode*. Here are some excerpts from *Project Nirvana*, the second book in the Walter Gröhn trilogy.

ONCE AGAIN, HE had taken a life. First, a deep stab in the kidneys to silence the victim. The extraordinary pain put the victim into a state of paralysis. Then a short pause before the final strike that drove the knife blade through the throat. The strike that separated the soul from the body. He was a true artist. An artist of assassination, who helped others to remove their problems. He could have used more modern methods, such as a gun with a silencer, but that was too easy. It was like drinking watered-down vodka. He wanted to feel the death spasms in the victim's muscles.

The white surgical gloves he wore were now coloured red. He inspected them for a while and then closed his eyes. He was known in Russia as *Mjasník* – the Butcher. Always terrifying to his victims and equally as respected by those who hired him.

WALTER PARKED A short distance from the main gate, so that the car was hidden by some trees. The SWAT team got out quickly from their vehicles and silently positioned themselves in front of the gate. The security guard unlocked two huge padlocks. The black-suited policemen fanned out in groups of three. Jonna unholstered her Sig Sauer and removed the safety catch. Walter did the same. Together with one of the SWAT team, they made their way along the fence. With torches set to dim, they began inspecting the caravan locks. The mist reduced visibility almost to zero. Like ghosts crouched against the rows of caravans, they examined lock after lock. It was time-consuming and, despite the cold and the damp air, Jonna was sweating. Clear beads formed on her forehead and ran down her temples. She felt the adrenaline rushing through her veins. The condensation from her breath mixed with the mist to form a milky white cloud. She watched Walter's silhouette, slightly to her right. Like a mirage, he floated in and out of the mist. Surprisingly, he moved nimbly for someone with a damaged spine. She held her weapon in both hands, pointed at the ground in front of her. Jonna whispered to Walter, but he did not hear her. Instead, he disappeared into the fog. She looked up so she would not lose track of the SWAT officer. She just had time to see the fog swallow him up as well. As she moved rapidly to catch up with the officer, whose name she did not even know, she heard something break under her shoe.

"I CAN SEE that you do not fear death," the old man began, folding his hands.

Leo Brageler squinted in the direction of the brittle voice.

"Don't you want to know who we are and what we want?"

The man took out a packet of cigarettes from his inside pocket and lit a cigarette with shaking hands.

Leo Brageler had asked himself that question. The man behind the voice, a voice he had not heard before, seemed to be reading his thoughts. Could he be the leader of these lunatics?